I0747627

A Gift of Words
Fiona Van Housen

The Emerald Diaries – Secrets of an Irish Clan
4th Edition, published September 2023

Copyright © 2023 by Mary Murphy. All rights reserved.
www.marymurphy.ca

A Dove Creek Studios Book

First published in 2009. This edition is a substantial edit from the original book, though the story remains intact.

Though this novel would be considered a work of fiction, its purpose is to acknowledge that which is reality: genealogical ancestry. Though this novel surrenders to impish flights of fancy, its intention is to communicate the deep-rooted power of family, particularly the women therein. There are historical references and facts included that serve to embellish the storyline and place the reader in time and culture.

Foreword copyright Will Millar, willmillar.ca

Frontispiece illustration *A Gift of Words* © 2009 Fiona Van Housen

Design, editing, and pre-press by Kera McHugh, time4somethingelse.com
Cover and other interior illustrations created with the support of MidJourney AI image generation, midjourney.com.
Back cover photo of Newgrange, Ireland © 2019 Andrew Kearns, licensed under the Creative Commons Attribution 2.0 Generic license.
https://creativecommons.org/licenses/by/2.0/deed.en

"When Parents Ask Their Children To Be Noisy" is used by permission by Blue Panther, Keeper of Stories, the Manataka American Indian Council.

No part of this book may be reproduced or transmitted in any form or by any means, electronic or mechanical, including photocopying, recording, or by any information storage and retrieval system, without permission in writing from the publisher, except by a reviewer, who may quote brief passages in a review.

ISBN: 978-1-7387936-2-4

The Emerald Diaries
Secrets of an Irish Clan

by Mary Murphy

Foreword by Will Millar

Dedication

*To my clan, especially my own parents,
Bridget and Michael Murphy,
who brought me here.*

FOREWORD

A word or two about Mary Murphy

"This race and the country and this life produced me. I shall express myself as I am."
James Joyce

Ireland has always been a country where the bards and seannachí (storytellers) were well-respected. Mary Murphy has inherited that old art. She sings the old ballads with the soul that only a woman of the land can do. She weaves a tale with the same love and magic that generations of seannachí used to cast spells over their hushed listeners.

As you journey into Mary Murphy's tale, you may just catch an emerald breeze from the western sea across the ancient rocky headland and hear a faint cry of a fiddle on the sea wind. You will move closer to the fire's heat and travel far and wide across distant hills as the magic catches 'ahold of ye'. Like the listeners in the cottages of long ago, you won't want the story to end.

So, as the old dreamweaver said, "Let us go forth, the tellers of tales and seize whatever prey the heart longs for, and have no fear, for everything is real and all things are possible, and the earth is just a little taste on the tip of the seannachís gifted tongue."

Sláinte!

Will Millar – Irish Rover

PRONUNCIATION GUIDE

Irish word	Pronunciation	Meaning
Aidan	Aye-din	Male name
An Claiomh Solais	On clay-iv sulis	Sword of light
An Clann Teach	On clon chok	The family home
An lucht siúil	On luckt shewil	Irish travellers
Beannact leat	Ban-ocht lat	Blessings on you
Brachabhí	Brak-a-vee	Name created by author for caves of the north and the birthplace of the Mobhrí
Brídín	Breeg-een	Female name
Bríghid	Bree-id	Female name
Caitlín	Cat-lean	Female name
Céilí	Kay-lee	Musical gathering or party
Chroí	Cree	Heart
Ciara	Keer-ah	Female name
Claddagh	Clad-dah	Name of ring and area in galway
Coir na dagda	Core nah dagda	High druid in irish mythology
Cruinniú na clan	Cree-oo na clan	Meeting of the clan
Currach	Kur-ach	Traditional fishing boat
Danú	Dan-ooo	Goddess
Daoine Sidhe	Deena-she	Faery folk
Dermuid	Dermid	Male name
Dónal	Doe-nal	Male name
Donncha	Don-khah	Male name
Ealga	Ale-ga	Female name
Earrach	Air-ock	Spring
Eimear	Eemer	Female name
Éirú	Ay-roo	Goddess
Fáilte Abhaile	Fawl-cha ah-wall-ya	Welcome home
Falias	Fail-ee-is	Mythological northern city
Findias	Finn-dee-is	Mythological northern city
Fir bolg	Fair-bullug	First inhabitants of ireland
Fómhar	Fow-her	Autumn
Geimhreadh	G-eev-rah	Winter
Gorias	Gurr-ee-is	Mythological northern city
Gráinne	Graw-nyahh	Female name

Irish word	Pronunciation	Meaning
Inis Oirr	Inish ear	Smallest of the Aran Islands off west coast of Ireland
Iora rúa	I-raa roo-ah	Red squirrel
Lia fáil	Leah fawl	Stone of destiny
Lú	Loo	Member of tuatha de danaan
Luain	Loo-in	Monday
Milis	Mill-ish	Sweet
Mobhrí	Mah-vree	Name created by author
Murias	Muire-ee-is	Mythological northern city
Niall	Nile	Male name
Niamh	Knee-iv	Female name
Nuada	New-ada	Irish god
Odhrán	Awrawn	Male name
Ogham	OH -um	first written irish language using cut marks
Oonagh	Una	Female name
Orlaith	Or-lah	Female name
Pádrig	Paw-drig	Male name
Ríonach	Ree-on-ochk	Female name
Róisín	Ro-sheen	Female name
Samhradh	Sow-rah	Summer
Séamus	Shaymus	Male name
Saoirse	Sayer-sha	Female name
Seannachí	Shan-a-key	Storyteller
Searlait	Share-lat	Female name
Sin-seanmháithair	Sin–shan-waaher	Great-grandmother
Siobhán	Shiv-awn	Female name
Sláinte	Slawn-cha	Cheers
Sleá luin	Shlaw luhin	Spear of lúgh
Tadhg	Tie-g	Male name
Tomás	Toe-maw-s	Male name
Tuatha de Danaan	Too-aha day dannan	Second wave of irish inhabitants
Uirsea	Yerss-ya	Name created by daughter of author
Úla	Oola	Female name

PART I

When the moon creeps over the night petals—
when the sun breaks open the blackened sky
into a scarlet and golden light
when the very breath you take
becomes a frosty vapor before your eyes

When the frozen earth—
begins to thaw into the colour of wild plum
feel feel
your wealth of hope and promise
Descended seeds
burgeoning
to verdant spring

~ Mary Murphy

Gorey, County Wexford, Ireland
2014

*T*hree crowing cockerels, vying for ascendancy at the rupture of dawn, did their utmost to rouse Norah from night's deep slumber. She foiled them, however, and hugging her pillow, she curled into a fetal position under the white duvet and groaned, unwilling to emerge from its pleasurable warmth. Here she remained, drifting in and out of consciousness until the insistent alarm clock finally nudged her to full wakefulness.

Sighing deeply, Norah rose, slid two naked feet into well-worn slippers, wrapped herself inside the faded red fleece dressing gown that lay in a heap at the bottom of the bed, and shuffled down the hallway to the kitchen. She filled the kettle with water, dropped a black tea bag into a slender porcelain cup, and leaned wearily against the counter to wait.

A grin flashed upon Norah's face as she eyed the piles of neatly stacked post on the kitchen table. She was indeed grateful to her mother for having collected it in her absence, but it was so typical that her mother had organized it with such attention to detail. Magazines in one stack, business-looking envelopes in another, personal in yet another, and the all-pervasive and inevitable rubbish in the last. Norah was not yet in the mood to rifle through it all and gently closed her still sleepy eyes.

The gusting wind smacked a blossoming tree branch hard against the kitchen windowpane. Norah flinched, and shuffled once again, this time to the sitting room to start a fire in the wood stove.

It felt good to be home. The ten days in Canada at the International Writers Conference had been a whirlwind; and a trial of patience. True enough, there had been some positive aspects to the trip, but mostly, it was the usual politics of who knows whom in the foreground and petty nitpicking in the background.

Norah just wanted to write. Having never been one to join in the peculiarities of the writer's world, she was seen as talented but shy, and to some, aloof. Norah would be the first to agree with this assessment. She knew her leanings were that of an introverted extrovert. Once behind a podium, or when interacting with customers, her genuinely bubbly nature bloomed brightly, but her day-to-day preferences aimed toward solitude and privacy.

Writing for newspapers, magazines, and alternative publications had been a superlative way to launch her career, and she would be forever grateful for all those opportunities. Norah's dreams had been substantially bigger than that, though. She had, after all, completed a full-length novel the previous year entitled *Dreaming in Lilac.* It was a fantasy, in which the main protagonist viewed life in shades of black and white, as though looking through an old monochrome camera viewfinder—but whose dream world was teeming with gloriously vibrant colourscapes. This champion becomes preoccupied with finding ways to enter, and stay in, REM sleep; to stay in living colour. As the story unfolds, the dichotomies of the two worlds collide, producing a cascade of extraordinary experiences.

Having thrown that debut novel into the publishing wind, it had been whisked away on a swift current. Norah's book won two literary awards and could be found in most bookstores in English-speaking countries. Her new contract was due to go to press in late summer and consisted of twelve short stories, each pertaining to a month of the year.

Norah sat on the floor in front of the roaring fire with her tea, and let her eyes wander about the room. Her great-grandmother, Caitlín Norah Sinnott, had purchased the house in 1915. There were times when Norah felt she could hear the voices and see the shadows of not only her long past relatives, but the shadows and voices of all those that had lived there before. It was not so much that the rooms were housing ghosts; it was more an acute sense of the strong and energetic lives that had occupied and loved the place, a perceptible presence of those who had left their indelible mark in the very air she breathed.

Úla, Norah's mother, had never been interested in ownership of the property, even though it was she who was next in line to inherit it. Úla had her own home not far away and was only too happy to see Norah become the new owner of the family home.

It was a two-bedroom, one bath home, with a large airy sitting room and small front parlour. It had been well looked-after and had received many upgrades over the years, one of which was a fully enclosed, double-glazed glass conservatory that extended out from the sitting room. This was the location Norah elected to furnish as her office. There was ample room for her mahogany desk (another item that had been handed down), and all the accoutrements of being a writer.

Standing high above the glass, the day-lighted, bare deciduous trees allowed the scant sun to enter in the dark and dreary winter months. In the foliaged seasons, the trees created a sweet, scented canopy; a bursting green umbrella that Norah found to be extraordinarily inspiring.

The privacy of the home is what pleased her the most, however. It was only ten minutes into town by car, but the acreage on which the house sat felt secluded and remote. One had to exit from the main road onto a narrowly paved one. This road wound its way up for a few kilometers and rose abruptly to the crest of a hill.

Here the view was spectacular, overlooking a verdant valley and the distant Irish Sea. Immediately over the crest of the hill, on the west side of the road, stood a barely visible postbox and a dirt and gravel drive. The twisting driveway was not much more than a path really, lined on either side with tall trees that joined their branches in the centre as they stretched themselves toward the sky. The drive ended at a clearing, where the single-storey house proudly stood. Off to the left was the original barn. It too had been amended over the years and kept in admirable condition, though as the repository of all things, it was in definite need of sorting.

Norah prized the two voluminous oak trees that framed the barn. As a child, she spent countless hours with her nana, burrowed up in the tree house reading books, playing cards, and fabricating stories. Now, the branches of the taller tree stubbornly cradled the well-loved, and long-abandoned, semi-dilapidated structure.

There was a good acre of land at the front of the house boasting fruit trees, flower beds, lines of rose bushes, and a variety of herbs and plants that Norah did not know the names of. All these features had been planted, more likely strewn, in a wildly whimsical fashion by her previous relations.

Over the front door hung a wooden sign with the words 'Fáilte Abhaile' (Welcome Home) in scripted lettering. The rear of the house opened up to several acres of wild grasses and wildflowers.

Raspberry and blackcurrant bushes surrounded the property. There was an abundance of white clover and knapweed, as well as bell and ling heather. The rich black soil kept all the shrubs, trees and flowers strong; thus providing a paradise for the local wild birds. Robins, jackdaws, blackbirds, and finches—along with Norah's favourite song thrushes—thrived and relished the delectable banquets provided. The land itself was mostly level but sloped gently downward to the rear and ended at a deep tree line and hedgerow. Beyond that was farmland that belonged to her neighbours John and Mary Dogherty.

Norah's nana, Bríghid, always kept the bird feeders full throughout the winter and the two would often 'top them up to the brim' together. Her nana dearly loved the song thrushes, which is why Norah loved them best. She never became cross with these thrushes, even when they pilfered her apples.

Sitting quietly on the grass while watching the antics of all the birds brought them both immense joy and when the song thrushes landed, Nana would light up.

"Would ya look at that handsome fella. Greedily gobblin' up my seeds. Now he'll fly up to those branches and chatter away like nobody's business. Yes, we hear you loud and clear, you."

Norah would oftentimes nestle her head beneath her nana's arm; she felt secure there. Not to mention the fact that Bríghid always smelled of fresh lavender from the soap she made and used. Norah, to this day, could not smell lavender without falling backward in time to those significant moments.

2

Norah had just swallowed the last sip of tea when the telephone chimed. It was Dónal.

She and Dónal had met six months earlier and were now on the verge of making major life changes. Norah, now thirty-four, had ventured into a few serious relationships but none seemed to sate her appetite for a deeper connection. The consequences of her choices were not always easy, and there were times when loneliness would pull her into a murky, dark emotional abyss. She was convinced that committing herself to someone who was mis-aligned with her general life direction could and would only lead to ultimate failure. And failure in this area was not something she was willing to risk.

Mostly, she enjoyed her single life, untethered from anyone else's needs, and with responsibilities only to herself and her work. Meeting Dónal was what some might call a simple twist of fate. Norah had only just moved into the house. She had walked down the drive to the postbox unusually early one morning and as she neared the end, she heard the ringing of a mobile phone, followed by a deep male voice.

"Hello, Dónal here. Hello, Dónal here."

Norah wondered why he repeated himself like that, and also wondered what someone was doing wandering such a remote road at such an hour. Since trees obscured her drive, the man walking along the road was startled when she stepped out, and he stopped in his tracks.

"Ehh, morning," he said.

The equally startled, and startling, grey parrot on his shoulder spoke with the same voice.

"Hello, Dónal here."

Norah and Dónal both laughed.

Dónal's car had overheated near the top of the hill, and he had decided to explore the area while the engine cooled.

"Do you need water for the radiator?"

"That'd be much appreciated. I've a water bottle in the car, but I doubt it'll be enough to feed the thirsty beast."

"Come along then, I'm sure I have a watering can or something. I can drive you back to your car if you like."

"That's most kind of you . . . ehh . . . ,"

"Norah."

"Norah. My name is Dónal in case you've not guessed by now."

Again, they both laughed. "Beautiful parrot," Norah said.

"Thanks. Her name's Luain and she's an African Grey. They're remarkable birds, acquiring not just vocabulary, but sounds as well. Once they reach the age of two, they really begin to increase their lexicon. Luain here is picking up more and more words as she ages.

"Yes, well, I was sure I heard a phone ringing. It's uncanny how real it sounded."

Coming to the top of the drive and into the clearing was always Norah's favourite part of returning home, and as they did so, Dónal said, "This is quite the place you have here, Norah. Is it yours?"

"Yes, it is, I'm happy to say."

"Absolutely brilliant. Look at this land. I was going to comment on the number of trees as we were walking, but I was too wrapped up in talking about Luain. That barn, all these roses and flowers. Look at all that lavender and calendula. Foxglove, yarrow, comfrey and so much more."

"You certainly know your plants, Dónal."

"That I do. I'm charmed by plants and their healing properties, and I love my very meager herb garden."

"Really? So did my nana, who lived here before me. Actually, my family has a history of gardeners and herbalists. Is that what you do for a living?"

"Yes and no. My name is Dónal, but people teasingly call me Jack, as in Jack-of-all-trades. I've always had several passions and was never able to settle on just one career. I like it though; it makes my life full and interesting. I work part time at Carring Park, keeping the gardens tended in the spring and summer. They allow me to run with ideas and experiment with varietals, etcetera so that's fulfilling. I also do carpentry work, assist a local taxidermist, and have been working with a beekeeper."

The two settled into an easy and jovial patter. Dónal's eyes sparkled as they walked around the property, and Norah eventually invited him in for tea.

Sitting at the table, Dónal asked, "And you Norah? What are your passions?"

Leaning back in her chair, Norah stared out the window for several seconds, formulating her answer. Dónal sat patiently awaiting her response.

Norah liked the question. In fact, she liked him. As she began to speak about her writing career, Dónal leaned forward, his eyes laser-focused and intent on listening. This surprising body language inspired Norah to expound on her process. Men often seemed put off by her career as a self-employed writer, as though it was not a legitimate way for a woman to earn a living. Mostly, when she told a man (whether a potential mate or not) about her work they would cross their arms, take a step backward, and condescendingly say, 'Oh really?' Humans could be so amusing . . . when they were not irritating.

"I love how words make us feel. If the words I write succeed in evoking emotions, then I have done my job. Whether speaking or writing, I think our words affect those around us. Words can make us laugh, think, wonder. The bottom line in my writing is that I enjoy the alchemy of conjuring precise words to allow my readers to form emotional relationships with scenes and characters."

"Do you think about that intentionally when you write? I mean, do you pick a direction and move toward it?"

"Sometimes. Mostly I endeavor to jump into the currents of the muse and fly with them. That's not to say I don't think about where I might go with a thought or character. It's just that despite that initial idea, I may be suddenly swung in a totally new direction. I've learned that characters take on a life of their own when you let them. Sometimes they're my sanctuary when I no longer wish to participate in my own daily realities. They're alive to me, living breathing mortals. Often, I find I have to scoot out of my characters' way so that they can narrate their own story. I'm really their secretary taking notes."

They both laughed.

"There have been oodles of times when I've been shocked by the choices they make, or the circumstances into which they willingly submerge themselves. Sometimes, as their secretary, I'm tapping away at the keys, and thinking, 'No! Don't do that; think about the consequences,' or, 'clever, clever, I never would have thought of doing that.'"

Dónal nodded approvingly. "Sounds rather magical really. The alchemy of words as you say."

"Yes, Dónal. It is exactly that."

"I venture you become attached to some characters more than others?"

"Absolutely. Yet, I have to say, even the characters who I would find distasteful, should I meet them in real life, still feel connected to me in a peculiar way. I have a responsibility to objectively enter the psyche of the characters in order to write with an understanding of their choices. They have to trust me to listen and write with neutrality, though I dare say, it's not always easy, and I've had to contain and edit some of the dictation."

Three hours passed before Norah drove Dónal back to his car, and in the end, she had agreed to go out for a bite the following evening. Neither was interested in anything too formal when it came to dining, and they agreed that O'Leary's pub would be just the ticket.

Dónal collected Norah at eight sharp. O'Leary's had a relaxed atmosphere, a decent menu, and it also boasted an ample dance floor. The owner, Pat O'Leary, was a reasonable musician himself, and took great pride in providing diverse nightly music for his customers.

Time flew by as swiftly as a swallow on the wing. Before they knew it, the large, antique grandfather clock in the corner of the pub chimed ten. Five musicians arrived and began to play at a quarter past the hour. Within minutes, some of the locals were up dancing to lively reels.

"Do you enjoy shaking a leg, Norah?"

Chapter 3

"Indeed, I do. But I'm no match for the pair already on the floor."

"They won't even notice us. Come on."

Norah gulped the last of her wine and took Dónal's hand. Dónal was extremely light on his feet and although Norah was laughing with glee, she was also feeling rather clumsy by comparison. When the tune concluded, the fiddler stood and began to sing an *a cappella* song, sending everyone back to their seats.

"Much as I'm truly enjoying myself, I really must think about getting home. I've some deadlines that I have been avoiding."

"Right then. Let us retreat from this establishment and deliver you to your secretarial duties."

3

*T*he week that followed was a busy one for both Norah and Dónal alike. Consequently, they barely spoke and did not see one another.

Norah and her mother, Úla, had decided to arrange a party for the transfer of land ownership to Norah. The surrounding neighbours had been living in the area for innumerable years and although they all knew Norah, they did not relate to her as the owner. It was agreed that a céilí would undoubtedly set the record straight; and put it in motion for the following Saturday night.

The day of the party dawned brightly. Norah was anxious to see Dónal again. She was unsure how to negotiate the depth of emotions that ran through her since their first meeting. Her fingers drummed against the countertop and her foot tapped upon the floor as her mother filled two large stainless teakettles.

"What are you like, Norah? You're darting about like a chicken with your head cut off. You're making me bothered. The apple tarts are cooling, and the biscuits are just out of the oven. All that's left is the tea. Why don't you go keep an eye out for the neighbours? I can finish up in here."

Norah cocked her head at her mother and acknowledged the rising emotion within her was irrational. Her mother had, in fact, been extremely helpful in organizing the evening and had taken on many of the tasks that Norah was not fond of doing. A niggling part of her, however, wondered why her mother felt the need to sporadically deride her. Deciding to not 'poke the bear' she simply nodded and flitted to the parlour window.

Gazing out, Norah watched as a chickadee scratched at the earth near the outside flower pots. "What *am* I like?" she asked softly aloud. Butterflies merrily danced inside her as she stood looking out the window, thinking of Dónal. *Just breathe, Norah. Calm yourself.* The chickadee took no notice.

She had never primped and preened for any man to the extent she had this evening. Never in all her dating days had a man extracted such queer behaviour from her. Norah had donned countless clothing combinations, nixing and throwing most of them on her bedroom floor before settling on a blue cotton skirt, a purple V-neck and a golden headscarf. To her own surprise, she applied gardenia oil behind her ears and rose lipstick to her mouth. When she had finally emerged from the bedroom her mother had said she looked simultaneously comfortable, casual, and striking. This comment caused Norah to sigh with relief.

As Norah stared out the parlour window, her mind returned to O'Leary's Pub and the exhilaration she felt when Dónal's hands gently landed around her waist.

"Mother, here come the Callaghans!"

The Whelans came up five minutes later, followed by the Murphys from up the hill and the Dohertys. John and Mary Doherty were known and loved for their home brewed ale and Norah could see them unloading jugs of it from their green 1964 Morris Minor.

Norah played welcoming hostess but kept a keen eye out the front window. Sure enough, right behind Aideen and Brendan Sheil, strode Dónal. Úla came up behind Norah.

"Well, he is a prize if I ever saw one."

"Yes. Isn't he splendid?"

It was not long before glasses were filled and the sounds of music and dancing feet thundered off the walls and floors.

Norah's heart pounded as Dónal took her hand and said, "Can I swing you round like I did before?"

The evening overflowed with laughter and joviality, and solidified Norah's ownership of the land in the eyes of the neighbours. More importantly, it solidified the reality of herself and Dónal.

Dónal had experienced a rough few years. Not long after his five-year marriage collapsed, his father had died of heart failure. As his mother had passed when he was only fifteen and there were no siblings, he was now adrift, alone. He sold his parents' home, and rented a cottage out in the country; invested most of the money from the sale of the home and drew a small monthly allowance from the interest. Two years had gone by since that sale, and he was still residing in the cottage.

Both Norah and Dónal had been reluctant to jump into the deep end of the relationship pool and for a long time they felt it best to leave their housing status unchanged. Lately though, the sorrow of being separated from each other greatly outweighed the fear of commitment and perhaps loss. There was a deep understanding between the two; they both craved truth, they were both passionate about their work (and each other), and they each saw great value in the others' passions.

Neither wanted to analyze the powerful mystery of their first meeting; and were pleased that they could each safely take refuge and escape into one another when the world became ferocious.

One evening, as the fire embers burned low, Dónal asked, "What have we got to lose that we both haven't already lost?"

Norah could not deny the truth in that simple but poignant statement. She had to be honest with herself and concede that she had become withdrawn in an effort to prove her self-sufficiency. Her independence had become a badge of honour and she had worn it proudly, but Dónal was, to her, like coming home. It was some of the simplest things that made her love for him deepen—the delicate way his strong hands tended the flowers, or the way in which he could so effortlessly generate laughter from her, or the tender words he would whisper in her ear as they lay together. She had difficulty believing that someone could love her as unconditionally as he so obviously did. When had her protective shell fallen away? Why had she not noticed? Did it matter?

They decided to convert a section of the barn to create an office/private space for Dónal. This would satisfy their need for closer proximity to each other yet still allow them their own required private areas. Not conventional by any means, but neither of them would be considered conventional by most standards.

Norah collected her laundry basket and began loading the washing machine. Her phone rang, flashing Dónal's name on the call display. She smiled. Dónal had driven out to County Offaly, to Tullamore, to attend lectures facilitated by the FIBKA (Federation of Irish Beekeepers' Associations) several days before Norah's return home from Canada. She eagerly pressed the answer button.

"Hiya, Dónal. Yes, I'm home safe and sound. Really? Early? Tomorrow?" Norah listens intently, "I miss you too . . . something terrible. No, I haven't gone to collect Luain yet, but I will this evening or in the morning. I think I may go out to the barn and begin sorting through the boxes that my nana left stored in the loft. How is the bee loud glade?"

They spoke for a few more minutes and signed off. Norah picked up the gift she had bought for Dónal while in Montreal. She had spent a fair amount of time looking for something distinctive to bring back to him, and in the end, had ironically bought him an Irish poem, that was surrounded by a stunning watercolour painting.

Dónal's love of bees was verging on obsessiveness and he often commented on how perfect Norah's property would be for bee boxes. His unsubtle remarks regarding possessing these boxes had been a bit of a concern as Norah had apprehensions about bees, but she had promised to give serious thought to yielding to a few boxes at the back of the property, provided that she would not be asked to tend them.

In Montreal, she had happened upon an outdoor art show as she strolled the city streets and had been taken with an artist who had set up his easel at the far end of the exhibit. His technique and the grace with which his right hand flowed across his canvas transfixed her. While most sellers were trying to engage the throngs of people that wandered down the long walkway, he simply sat, fully engrossed in his art. He did not notice her standing behind him until two young boys whipped by on their scooters and hollered, jarring him out of his concentration. He smiled at her and scratched his cheek, leaving a blue streak from the passing bristles of his brush.

There were several large paintings on easels, and a fair quantity of smaller canvases stacked one behind the other, leaning against a low-lying stone wall.

Norah bent and rifled through his work, appreciating the diversity of not only the content, but also the intensity and the delicacy of colours and contrasts. The second from the last was the one she now held in her hands.

The background was a subtle wash of lavender, yellow and blue; while in the foreground, surrounding the hand-written poem, was a world of flowers and honeybees. The yellow background colours were fashioned to give the impression of hives. The painting translated a peaceful, thriving world of tiny wings and dripping nectar. It was not only a perfect gift for Dónal; it also completed the thought process that Norah needed to permit the addition of hives to the land. The poem was one of Dónal's favorites, written by W.B. Yeats.

The Lake Isle of Innisfree (1890)

I will arise and go now, and go to Innisfree,
And a small cabin built there, of clay
and wattles made:
Nine bean-rows will I have there, a hive
for the honeybee,
And live alone in the bee-loud glade.
And I shall have some peace there, for peace
comes dropping slow,
Dropping from the veils of morning to where
the cricket sings;
There midnight's all a glimmer, and noon a purple glow,
And evening full of the linnet's wings.
I will arise and go now, for always night and day
I hear lake water lapping with low sounds by the shore;
While I stand on the roadway, or on the pavements grey,
I hear it in the deep heart's core.

~W.B. Yeats

5

Norah stretched and yawned, then gave herself a vigorous shake, hoping that might dispel her mental inertia. Sitting at her desk was often the best way to propel herself into a creative writing frame of mind and so made her way, wearily, to her chair, collapsing into it. Phone calls could wait 'til a decent hour to be returned.

She swiveled her chair in slow circles, all the while glancing at the photographs taped along the shelves of her desk. Norah knew she should be immersing herself in her writing but was finding it hard to concentrate. Her first few stories had materialized relatively easily, but recently, writer's block had set in and that, combined with travelling, was creating mental strain and pressure, which is never a good thing for a writer to feel.

Writer's block was not an overly rare occurrence for Norah, but she could usually resolve it in an odd but effective manner. It was not something she talked to people about, but when writing desperation struck or, frankly, when any part of her world became thorny, Norah would call on her inner voice. She knew full well that it was a peculiar quirk, but this inner voice had been with her since she could first remember. Her inner voice had a name. Genevieve.

Some of Norah's earliest recollections included Genevieve. She would sit and chat away to her imaginary playmate on a daily basis. When she went to her nana's house, this very house, Nana would encourage her to talk to Genevieve and would set up extra teacups and plates for Genevieve at the table. Her nana was a great one for storytelling and would include both Norah and Genevieve in many of her fanciful tales. Caves would be built out of sheets, boats out of chairs, faeries appeared, and other unearthly magic abounded.

A spherical crystal had hung suspended from a window casing in Nana's sitting room, scattering rainbows when the sun shone. Norah and Nana would purport to have captured the light in bottles, and days later, when it was gloomy, would open the bottles of light into the darkened room, pretending to step into the released rainbows. Her nana would take her on make-believe journeys to visit long past relatives. The two would sit on pillows as though they were straddling horses and ride to faraway lands, always with Genevieve in tow.

Displayed atop a little chest of drawers in the main bedroom were two purple stuffed sock toys, which her nana had received when she was just a young a girl. Norah would occasionally be allowed to place them on the bed and play with them carefully. This was always a great treat that Norah never took for granted.

One day, when Norah and her mother had come to Nana's for tea, she was given permission to 'visit' the toys, who were named Larry and Kitty. Norah was talking and laughing with the two (and Genevieve of course), when Úla burst into the bedroom and admonished her daughter for continuing to play with her imaginary friend, Genevieve. Úla insisted that Norah stop such foolishness and make some 'real' friends.

Tears instantly overflowed onto the child's flushing cheeks. Norah quietly whispered that Genevieve *was* a real friend, and one that both she and her nana loved and cared for. But Úla simply spat out, "Don't be ridiculous, you're far too old to believe in such nonsense," as she abruptly turned on her heels, and stomped away.

Norah sat on the bed feeling hurt yet determined. Wiping her face with her sleeve, she wondered what she had done so wrong for her mother to hurt her so deeply. She could hear her mother and Nana loudly talking about Genevieve. At that moment, Norah decided to keep Genevieve as her secret friend. Norah did make a few local friends but always included Genevieve in her mind. She would whisper to Genevieve when she was alone or when she was lying in bed waiting for sleep to come. Her nana still included Genevieve when Norah and she were alone. Nana's house was the one place that Norah could feel free to speak out loud to her friend.

Though Genevieve was still part of Norah's life, these days she did not often speak out loud to her. Genevieve had become more like her conscience, her voice of reason, and a name to call upon when feeling perplexed. As Norah sat at her desk, she wondered if part of her drive to write fantasy-driven books was a deep desire to retreat to a world of childhood imagination; retreat to the magical time she had spent with her nana and Genevieve.

Norah missed her nana, Bríghid, tremendously. It had been a year since the accident and Norah still had days when she would think she must tell her nana this or that, only to realize she was gone. Bríghid, though elderly, was very independent, lived alone on her farm, still drove, and kept herself fit by walking and gardening. A few months before the accident, they had been sitting together, and had talked about aging and loneliness. Bríghid also spoke of her own mother, Caitlín, Norah's great-grandmother—and relayed the many ways in which Norah was like her; not just in looks, but also in disposition.

There were times when Norah thought her nana was trying to prepare her for the inevitability of her passing. One particular conversation was still fresh in Norah's mind.

"Norah, your mother seems to lack the 'what if' gene. You, on the other hand, have always had the ability to see things not only as they are, but also as they could be. Never forget that life is as deep and mysterious as we allow it to be. We don't all have to follow the rules of science. I, for one, know that if we look through the veil of this life, there is a realm of possibilities beyond most people's imaginations. There is so much I wish I could relay to you, but your mother, well, she is a rather scientific woman. Working in that medical laboratory is, for the most part, a good place for her. She can prove cause and effect. She can deduce through evidence. Ever since she was knee high, she needed proof of everything. Still does I suppose. I have made her promises that I must keep. But, Norah, when I have passed, do not be surprised if life brings you unexpected gifts."

"Nana," Norah had replied, "I hope you're not planning on going anywhere. Your words are making my heart ache. Is there something you're not telling me about your health? You look strong enough to plow the back field with a fork."

Her nana had thrown her head back and laughed heartily.

"Never forget the stories I have told you, nor the games we played when you were a child. By keeping those memories alive, you keep me alive, whether I'm with you or not. Life is like an onion, my dear; more layers than can be easily counted."

One autumn afternoon, Bríghid decided to drive south to a friend's home. When she did not arrive, her friend had contacted Úla. Eventually, Bríghid's empty car was found near Enniscorthy, parked near a bridge that crossed the river. The officials deduced that she had stopped to look at the swiftly flowing river and had fallen in, or had suffered an attack of some sort and had fallen in. Her body was never recovered.

6

*P*erhaps it was nostalgic recollections combined with the adjustment of Canadian versus Irish time that was causing Norah to feel woeful, but either way, it was of no matter. Work was out of the question.

Thinking about Dónal, on the other hand, gave Norah an instant emotional uplift. This prompted her decision to focus her energies on wandering out to the barn to begin the no doubt laborious task of sorting through her nana's stored belongings. The sooner she addressed the clutter, the sooner she and Dónal could engage the contractor they had selected for the renovation.

Norah threw on her coat, grabbed a torch, her phone, several large empty rubbish bags, and sloshed her way through deep puddles, out to the barn. The blackened space became dimly lit as she opened the hulking timber door and pulled on the flimsy dangling light cord. The bare bulb above her head swayed, buzzed and flickered, causing numerous shadows in the barn to dance. Norah eyed the three lonely horse stalls as she made her way to the back of the barn, contemplating future possibilities of housing creatures for which they were intended.

Feeling suddenly inspired, Norah ran up the narrow steps to the loft. The squeaking of the wooden floorboards, mingled with the pungent odour of musty hay, brought pleasant memories to mind. Two scruffy doves flew from atop the rafters, fluttering about the place before coming to rest on a woodpile down below. The irritated couple's beady black eyes glared at the brazen intruder, and they commenced to fluff their feathers, and coo their annoyances.

Norah proceeded to wander the loft, steering clear of the edge, running her fingers along old furniture, cardboard boxes, and bookshelves. It was hard to know where to begin.

"Let there be light," she said aloud.

Throwing wide the sets of thick bedraggled curtains that hung askew on their rods, Norah exposed two neighbouring windows. Though this action did make a smattering of difference, the filth of the panes, along with the layered cobwebs, did little to alter the loft's muted light. Moving to the bookshelves, Norah spread and scrutinized the numerous magazines and papers.

"Nothing worth keeping here." Into the bag they went. Many of the empty glass jam jars were chipped and they joined the papers in the bottom of the bag. Several boxes, stacked on top of and next to each other, caught Norah's attention and she began to open and examine the contents of each. The top three boxes held winter clothes, summer clothes, tablecloths, and shoes. These boxes she brought down the steps and placed near the barn door. Her mother could rifle through them and take what she wanted. The rest would go to the Charity Shoppe. The next stack of boxes held more jars, old pots, pans and glassware. These, too, were placed by the barn door. There were two boxes of books on herbs and native plants, which Norah knew Dónal would be pleased with. The last box was crammed into a space behind and under an old card table. Norah knelt down and tugged hard until the box dislodged.

It was a peculiar looking green box, covered in dust. Norah leaned closer and wiped away the grey particles with her right hand, causing a puff of the delicate trespassers to swirl outward. Two words were written across the top. The name 'Caitlín' was clearly visible. The other word was barely legible, and Norah could not make out what it said.

Placing the box on the open card table, Norah excitedly realised the box must have belonged to her great-grandmother. The green box was held together by brown twine that broke easily apart under Norah's strong fingers. The first thing to greet her eyes was a bulky object wrapped in tissue paper. Removing the tissue revealed a lacy item, wrapped in plastic. What emerged from the plastic was a floor length, cotton and lace dress, with a high collar and long lace sleeves. Though the fabric had yellowed with age, it was still breathtaking. Yellow-white pearls encircled the neckline and on down the front of the garment to the narrow waistline. Norah held the dress up to her body in a deep hug.

"Oh my," whispered Norah. "This is glorious."

7

Norah's great-grandmother, **Caitlín,** had been what some would call eccentric. She was a woman who, through individual preferences and life circumstances, lived life along the opposite grain whenever possible. She had arrived at the village in a cart pulled by a white and a black horse. A young baby girl, Bríghid, barely out of wraps, lay alongside her contented and unchallenged by their mode of travel. Caitlín claimed to be a widow from a distant county in search of a better life for herself and her daughter. It was a scandal to be sure. An outspoken young woman, travelling alone with a child, plenty of coin in her pockets and a determination to be reckoned with; most villagers found these characteristics to be unnerving at best.

Caitlín's overall unconventional sense of style and grace unfailingly left its imprint on those with whom she came in contact. Her petite, straight backed, spirited gait caused many a head to turn as she circulated among the villagers, portraying a beautiful, yet mighty storm, unwilling to abide by the laws of platitudes.

She had bought the Malloy's property immediately upon seeing it and had worked the land with the sweat and passion of any able-bodied man. Unless working the land, her untamed, wavy, nut-brown mane tumbled loosely to the small of her slender back.

Those who dared venture a sustained pause to survey her cocoa-coloured eyes would no doubt have been privy to a fervent and deeply mysterious soul. Caitlín was quite cognizant of the effect she had on others, especially women. This undeniable truth perturbed her greatly, for a time. Then one day, as she shopped for supplies, she overheard three little girls whispering about her.

The eldest spoke with the confidence of one who desires to project their superior understanding and insight. "My ma says people think she must have been bewitched by the Daoine Sidhe ("people of the mounds" aka faery folk), and that her little one is a faery herself; that the two of them might be faeries just the same!"

The second child took a sharp intake of breath. "Don't be tellin' me Alma. Ye know we don't live far away from the pair o' them."

"Ma says she has a voice as pure as a rare blue sky, which is a sure sign of faery people. She says even the little one hums to herself—another sign."

The third and youngest child ventured into the muffled conversation. "My mammy said that she might steal some other children if we're not behavin' ourselves. I daren't be bold."

The eldest continued to pontificate. "Go away with you. Suren' you've no need for to worry, Anne. There's naught a faery who'd be wantin' the likes o' you!"

"But what if the faeries are lookin' for a child? Or worse, what if they're changelings? Oh dearie me, they may be lookin' for a child to steal away."

Haughtily, Anne added, "And what's wrong with me anyhow? Why wouldn't the faeries want me?"

Caitlín could only chuckle as the three girls argued over whether Anne's body and soul were worthy of stealing by the immortal faeries or changelings. So, the village people thought she and Bríghid were 'gone away' with the faeries. This information certainly answered many questions for Caitlín, especially with respect to the furtive, hushed tones that ensued when they visited the village. What had once perturbed her now amused her. Truth be told she rather enjoyed the mystique, proving yet again her unique sense of self.

Furthermore, the two were odd ducks out. Caitlín and Bríghid would think nothing of walking barefoot down the winding lanes singing to the trees, and Caitlín was often seen balancing on the edges of the footbridge, exposing her delicate snow-white legs. She never seemed to care that the hems of her dresses tended to be threadbare or shabby, or that their clothes in general were overall in dire need of repair. She and her daughter Bríghid would spend hours sitting by streams looking through what had been described by folk as a scope of some kind. Caitlín's idiosyncrasies made it difficult at times to live in a remote and insular community, especially when one was not a member of the local church.

Still, she had the best cabbages, potatoes, and berries in the area; and the eggs she sold had shockingly orange-yellow yolks. Her apple trees produced abundant, unblemished fruit, and were as sweet as any apple could ever hope to be. And, she had a gift for finding and growing healing herbs to make just the right tinctures for relieving most any ailment.

Caitlín never married, nor had any interest in courting, which was probably just as well. Given her life circumstances, it was also understandable. Men found her beguiling, but far too independent, and therefore avoided approach. This suited Caitlín fine.

Bríghid, grew to be as independent and as unusual as her mother. The two women worked the farm and herb business for many years together and it must be said that they did gain well-deserved respect from the majority of villagers.

Laying the dress to the side, Norah peered once again into the green box. A pair of cream-coloured shoes with a similar pearl design were wrapped in soft white paper. She thought the dress and the shoes were about her size and was pleased that she and her great-grandmother were so physically alike. Norah even had the cocoa-coloured eyes and wavy nut-brown hair of her elder relative.

A large dark leather book peeked through the next layer of aged tissue paper. Gingerly, Norah removed the book and slowly unwound the fine brown ribbon that held it closed at a centre clasp. The front and back covers were so decayed that they were well in the process of pulling away from the spine.

What met Norah's eyes, when she opened the book, was elegant handwriting in blue-black ink. An azure ribbon on the inside cover held a small skeleton key. The key was only about an inch and a half in length, and the solid crown was etched with a swirling design. The pattern looked familiar to Norah, but she couldn't put her finger on where she had seen it before.

Norah read the first few sentences.

> *I am hoping this diary survives through all life's unexpected movements and uncertainties. I am also hoping that a future female family member is reading it, for a female alone will understand its importance and implications. I am known as Caitlín Norah Sinnott. This, however, is not the name given to me by my parents, Grace and Liam Furlong. At the time of my birth, they lovingly named me Genevieve Norah Furlong.*

Norah let out a yelp and dropped the diary onto the table. "Genevieve? Are ya joking?"

The instant roaring of Norah's pumping heart permeated her ears, along with a sweeping heat, as blood surged through her veins. Feeling lightheaded, Norah picked up the diary and sat cross-legged on the dusty loft floor. As she re-opened the diary, a black and white photograph fell to her lap. It was a photograph of a woman that anyone would mistake for herself, except for the fact that the photograph was vintage.

The woman in the photograph had to be Caitlín, rather Genevieve, wearing the very dress that was now draped on the table alongside Norah. The shoes in the photo, were undeniably the same as the ones Norah had just removed from the box. Caitlín . . . Genevieve . . . was small boned and finely featured. Her smile was full and genuine, and Norah could see how she would be viewed as both elusive and beguiling. There was a slight mischievousness about the way the corners of her mouth arched as she smiled and the intensity with which she eyed the lens of the camera.

In her right hand, Genevieve held what looked like a kaleidoscope, about a foot in length. From one end, silver threads of light glimmered, as though a blast of light was escaping. On closer inspection, peeking from around the corner of the barn, just behind Genevieve, was the impish face of a little girl of about ten years of age. It was obvious that the child knew she was being a little cheeky by imposing herself into the photo, as proved by her hand semi-covering a broad grin. Of course, the child had to be Norah's nana, Bríghid.

Genevieve, Genevieve. Her great-grandmother's birth name had really been Genevieve Norah Furlong. Where did the name Caitlín Norah Sinnott come from then? Still feeling lost and bewildered, Norah placed the photograph back in-between the two pages and returned to the diary.

Caitlín/Genevieve

I **am known as** Caitlín Norah Sinnott. This, however, is not the name given to me by my parents, Grace and Liam Furlong. At the time of my birth, they lovingly named me Genevieve Norah Furlong.

My parents were the gentlest of people—good-natured, hard-working and honest. Liam was a horse trainer by trade and was especially proud of his accomplishments at the O'Reilly Stud Farm, which was not far from where we lived. Mr O'Reilly was a generous man who thought very highly of Liam's obvious gift, and therefore kept him intermittently busy with the care of his prized horses. While Liam was not a veterinarian, he was versed in alternative medicines and—on more than one occasion—had saved the life of a horse with herbal treatments, poultices, and remedies. Horses invariably relaxed under his gentle touch and soothing vocal timbre. Being a musical sort of fellow, frequent evenings would be spent with himself playing the concertina and singing, while my mother, Grace, worked on her loom weaving beautifully-coloured wool into salable clothing.

Grace was even-tempered and reflective. Nothing seemed to ruffle her feathers and she took life, in general, in stride; rarely letting her emotions get the better of her. That is not to say she was not compassionate and loving; she was assuredly both these things.

She would be more likely to ask questions rather than make assumptions and owned an inner wisdom that confounded me, as I was more like my father, who could be quite wide-eyed and susceptible to outside influences.

My father often complimented her, commenting she would make a wonderful diplomat; assuring me that she could, if given the chance, settle world-wide political squabbles. She would laugh off these endorsements, but the sparkle in her eyes gave away her inner delight.

If life presented challenges, her immediate response was to become very quiet. She would rock in her chair with a cup of hot tea and remain there for an unspecified amount of time. Then, rising, would say something along the lines of, "I have three possible solutions."

My mother told me that the moon was full and bright on the night I was born. It had been a dazzling sunset and my parents had thoroughly enjoyed their Sunday dinner of salmon and potato cakes. The moon had risen honey gold over the far hills as they sat listening to the crickets merrily singing in the long twilight. My father rose and went to the shed to collect turf, for although it was a clear evening, there was a bit of a nip in the air; and my mother had requested a fire so she could sit and drink her evening tea in front of its crackling warmth.

Mother had ambled out to their small barn where Jenny, the white mare, was waiting to foal. It was strange that Jenny was still carrying, as according to my mother's calculations, the mare should have given birth a good two weeks earlier. A sharp pain exploded inside my mother's body as she neared the barn door. At the same moment, Jenny neighed and snorted. My mother gripped the barn's horizontal wood handle and called for my father, Liam.

By the time Father raced to the barn, Mother, well-laden with child (me), had staggered inside and was standing at Jenny's stall door. The equally laden horse was grunting and whinnying. Even though she was sweating from the intensity of the electric contractions, she tried to comfort Jenny, to reassure her that everything was going to be fine. My mother could barely move with the constant waves of pounding quakes running through her. When father asked if she could make it back to the house, she answered with a sound so deep and unearthly that he opened the empty stall door next to Jenny, to the fresh straw, and laid my mother down. My father held her hands, words of encouragement and love falling freely, all the while wishing he could share the burden of pain and effort. Jenny let out an ear-piercing whinny. Father turned and called her name as her foal began to emerge. A few seconds later, still in my caul, I was born into the loving hands of my father and mother.

Many's a time I would ask my mother to tell me 'The Story' again, while sitting quietly on the hearthrug, playing with her discarded wool. I loved knowing that I was born at the same moment, in the same place and in the very same straw as Luna, our new, pitch-black horse. My parents had named her Luna, since she was born in the late evening of a full moon. Given that my birth was so highly unusual in its place and time, and the fact that I was born in the evening, next to Jenny, our mare, as she birthed Luna, they named me Genevieve. The first syllable matched Jenny; the last matched the time of day. This was one of the many real-life stories that my mother would tell me—stories about me as a baby or about our little farm.

She was also a great one for spinning tales, especially on long winter evenings, when darkness enfolded the earth like a cloak, and we were confined to the indoors for extra hours. I had a vivid imagination and would close my eyes and drift into semi-slumber, where I could picture all the people and places of which she spoke. I especially loved the story of the 'Enchanted Dancer,' which my mother said was a true account by a distant relative, named Teddy Quinn.

Teddy had been out gathering kindling in the woods on a chilly autumn day. He looked up to see a young woman standing by a Hawthorne tree. She was a startling sight and though he could see her clearly, she was quite transparent. She wore a long-sleeved red shirt and black waistcoat with a brown scarf tied around her head. Her hair was in plaits tied at the bottom with red ribbons. A flared, brown, calf-length skirt showed legs in brown wool stockings, and upon her feet were soft black dance shoes, laced up to above her ankles. She was standing in a dancer's position—straight backed, hands at her side and up on her toes.

She stood like this for a minute or so and then slowly lowered her feet to the ground. Bringing her hand to the brim of her head, she looked left, right and behind her. She bent forward to peer around the tree, as though she were searching for someone. She resumed her position on her tiptoes and again waited patiently. After another minute or so she lowered herself once again, and sat on a nearby tree stump, pouting. Her image slowly faded into the colours of the wood until she was altogether gone.

Teddy had a gift for seeing these kinds of things and was not at all alarmed. Knowing that Hawthorne was a sacred tree symbolizing fertility and marriage, he assumed she was looking for her beloved. He finished gathering his kindling for the evening and walked back toward his cabin. As he came out through the clearing another curious sight beheld him. This time it was a young lad. He, too, was translucent and was playing a fiddle. He paced back and forth, back and forth. Every now and again he would stop playing his fiddle and call out, but Teddy could not hear what he called. Neither could he hear the music emanating from the instrument, but he could see the passion with which it was being played. Teddy watched him for a few minutes until the fiddler walked, with apparent agitation, into the woods and faded from view.

Teddy returned to the same spot the following night and the night after that. Both nights he came upon the dancer, up on tiptoes, waiting. He spoke to her.

"If it's the fiddler yer lookin' fer, he's back this way." He began walking toward his cabin, but she just looked at him in a quizzical manner. It was as though she could see and hear him but could not understand him. To her, perhaps, he was the ghost.

The fiddler was back at the cabin again when Teddy returned.

"This'll never do," said Teddy aloud. The fiddler faded into the dimming light and Teddy set his mind on a solution.

The next evening, Teddy returned to the woods with his basket for kindling and set it on the ground. Within ten minutes the dancer returned and took up her position. Teddy removed his own fiddle from the basket and walked slowly back toward his cabin. Once he was out of sight of the dancer, he began to play a lively reel. The dancer heard the music and leapt with joy. She danced, one foot crossing over the next in a straight line toward him. He had to keep up quite a steady pace to keep ahead of her, which was not an easy task while trying to fiddle.

When Teddy got within fifty paces of his cabin, he ducked behind a tree and ceased his playing. He could see the fiddler pacing, playing his own fiddle tune. The dancer stopped a moment and then smiled. She heard him and danced her way out of the woods and up towards his restless figure. They stood before each other, he fiddling, she dancing. Then they both stopped and leaned into each other . . . a long-awaited embrace. The young man gently raised the girl's chin toward the sky and kissed her. He whispered something to the girl that Teddy could not hear. The young man began to play once again and the dancer to dance. Soon after, they made their way into the woods and disappeared.

I loved this story because it had a happy ending. I could imagine the pair of them continuing their life beyond ours.

One evening when I was ailing with a high temperature, my mother came to my little bed and lay beside me. She told me that we would be leaving our home and would be going on a travelling adventure. I did not want to leave our cozy life in the cottage, as it was the only life I had ever known. I loved falling asleep in summers' long twilight and waking to the chirr of the wren, gleefully announcing the birth of all things new. I began to weep, and my mother gently cooed.

"Hush my dearie, this will be a beautiful journey that we will all take together. Hush now and I will show you something special."

My mother slid her hand inside her apron pocket and removed from it a long glass and wood object.

"Genevieve, hold this up to the candlelight and look through."

I took the cylinder in my six-year-old hands and did as she bade. I held it up to the candlelight and peered through, tears still pooling in my rich brown eyes. I remember this moment so clearly, for it was a moment in time when I knew my life was to be redefined. A time when I knew my life would never be the same.

I whispered, "Mother…oh Mother…it's so beautiful."

*N*orah's phone interrupted her solitude. She laid the diary on the table and scurried down the stairs, still reeling from her discovery. Distracted and out of breath, Norah answered the phone.

"Norah? It's Patricia."

Patricia, Norah's publisher, had not wasted any time in calling to torment her about her writing deadline.

"Yes, yes I'm fine, and just home." Norah hesitated. "Well, no, actually I'm not fine. This is a most amazing thing I

. . . the most amazing . . ." Norah's voice trailed off as she held the phone to her ear.

"Norah, are you there? Norah, look here . . ."

Patricia was not one for small talk and did not even ask what the amazing thing was, just jabbered about deadlines and editors climbing all over her for work to review.

Norah spoke confidently about the book's progress to placate Patricia, but the reality was that Norah was quite far behind schedule and knew her editor was rightfully anxious. Raising her eyes to the ceiling, Norah lied and indicated to Patricia that she was working on the book at present and that she, Patricia, could tell her editor, Clive, that she would deliver him a segment of work in a day or so. This news precipitated relief in Patricia's tense tone and within a few minutes, much to Norah's relief, she signed off.

Slipping the phone into her coat pocket, she climbed the loft steps again, anxious to get back to the diary. Norah thought about Genevieve, causing an eerie strangeness to shiver through her. Once again, the mobile rang, and this time Norah could see from the call display that it was her mother. After some brief chitchat, her mother suggested that they meet in the park for a morning walk, since the rain had ceased. Norah immediately agreed, as she wanted to talk about the green box and knew there would be no point in her trying to write. Norah took the box from the loft and brought it to her office. She wound two large elastic bands around the front and back covers of the journal, to keep them intact, and placed it back in the box.

Her mother was standing by a bench feeding bits of bread to eager jackdaws and pigeons when Norah arrived. The women walked along the tidy path, past bare tree limbs and dormant wild rose bushes. A few jackdaws noisily followed them in hopeful anticipation that more bread would be thrown for their hungry stomachs. Eventually though hope was lost, and they joyfully became distracted in dive-bombing a stray cat.

Norah's mother was leaving in a few days, to go to Vermont with a handful of colleagues. Úla was the lead researcher/writer for a medical research laboratory, and the end results of their current study were to be published in a science journal. Norah knew she would be receiving a list of things to keep organized in her mother's absence. Not surprisingly, Úla removed a note pad from her coat pocket.

"Here is a small list of 'if you wouldn't mind seeing to's', while I'm away. I have to tell you Norah, that I do feel somewhat reticent about going to Vermont. What if I run into Phillip?"

Phillip, Norah's father, had deserted them when Norah was only three years old. He and Úla had met as field researchers and had married within a month of meeting. Five years later, just before Norah's third birthday, he announced that he had fallen in love with an American fieldworker (visiting from Vermont), and that he was leaving; to make his life 'a little less complicated.' Norah had always felt that it was she who made his life complicated.

Initially, he sent cards and parcels at Christmas and on her birthdays, but gradually the letters and parcels dwindled, until they disappeared altogether. The only things Norah inherited from her father were a blue Swiss army knife and an appalling sense of direction. (She sometimes felt she could get lost going from her kitchen to her car.)

Norah said, with a slight tone of apprehension, "Mother, I've begun to clean out the barn for the renovations. I've been up in the loft sorting through boxes and such."

"Oh, yes? We never did get to the barn when we cleaned out the house after…well…after the accident. I can't imagine there would be much of any importance there though."

"Well, actually Mother, on the contrary. I've come across something that seems incredibly valuable."

"Valuable? Really? Interesting. Well, the place is yours now, Norah, so finders keepers as they say. What did you find?"

"I found a box with items belonging to Caitlín, I mean, Genevieve, oh it's all so confusing."

Norah's mother stopped walking and stared nervously at her daughter.

"What?" she said, her voice low and trembling.

"Why the worried look? What a strange reaction to something that I thought would bring you pleasure? I thought you'd be excited to learn of the existence of the box and its contents. I haven't gone through it all yet, but so far there is a beautiful long dress, a pair of shoes, and a diary with a key attached to the inside cover."

"Give me the box Norah," said her mother in a bossy tone.

"Give you the … okay, what's this all about? Why do you want the box … and no … you can't have it. It's mine now. Remember, finders keepers and all? It was never yours to begin with so why would I hand it over to you now? Is there some family secret I should be protected from?" Norah asked sarcastically.

Úla put her hands up to her face and rubbed her temples. "A dress, shoes, a diary, and a key. Is there anything else in there?"

"As I said, I don't know what else might be in there, as I haven't had time to look, but I doubt there's much else. Oh, yes, there's a photograph of a woman who must be Caitlín—Genevieve—wearing the dress and shoes that are in the box. She looks shockingly like me; or I guess, I look like her. There's also a rascally little girl in the background who I assume must be Nana. She does look like a rascal I must say."

"Norah, I don't really want to get into this. I am so mad at myself. Why didn't I think? Oh, why didn't I look? You must not have that box, Norah. Trust me, you must give it to me at once."

"Mother, I do trust you. However, I'm very much like you in that if I'm forbidden against something, I naturally gravitate to that thing like a magnet. I'm more curious than ever now."

Norah and her mother continued to row for half an hour, Norah refusing to forfeit the box, Úla giving no acceptable explanation for doing so. Finally, believing the matter settled, Norah climbed into her car, exhausted. Before even getting her keys to the ignition, the sound of Úla tapping her short but well-manicured nails on the passenger window, pleading for Norah to give up the box, caused Norah to groan vociferously. While it was true that Norah and Úla were not always aligned in their approach to life, and that Úla did have a tendency to verbalize her opinions in a not-so-subtle way, this level of animosity was uncommon and did not sit well in Norah's stomach. Norah ignored her mother's plea, started her car, and left Úla standing on the footpath, utterly flabbergasted.

11

The storm had broken, and filtered sun peeked through scattered bilious clouds, throwing shafts of light through the window and onto Norah's chilled legs as she lay on the couch. A sparrow pecked at the smattering of seeds left in the bird feeder but was quickly chased away by a larger rival. Droplets of rain slid down the windowpane. Norah watched them fall. Soon, she fell into fitful sleep, dreaming of squawking parrots, noisy cars, and neighbours quarrelling over property lines. In the dream, the neighbours were buzzing her doorbell.

Norah woke to the realization that her door chime was indeed sounding. Looking at her watch as she rose from the couch, she quickly noted that two hours had passed. Pushing back the curtain that covered the small glass panel on the front door, Norah could see her mother's apologetic face. Norah made a pot of tea and the two sat on the sitting room couch.

"We have much to discuss Norah," said her mother, "and I have absolutely no clue as to where to begin. Have you finished looking through the box?"

"No, I haven't. I got home, lay on the couch, and fell asleep. I woke to you buzzing the bell."

"Is the box handy? I mean if you'd agree to let me see it with you it might make explanations easier."

Norah nodded, fetched the box from her office and laid it on the floor between them.

"It says 'Caitlín' on the top as you can see, but it also says something else, and I'm not sure what it means." said Norah.

Norah's mother had to squint and move up close to the box in order to see the faded words. "Humph. You don't have much Irish language in your vocabulary, more's the pity. 'sin-seanmháthair' is what is written here, which means 'great-grandmother' in Irish."

"Ahhh, I see," replied Norah. "That certainly has a lovely ring to it, and I do wish I could've met her. After reading just a few pages of her diary, I feel strangely close to her in a way that's difficult to describe. It's as though I've known her all my life." (Norah was specifically thinking of her inner voice when she said this.)

Looking down at her folded hands, Úla quietly replied, "Yes, I believe you have."

Norah felt another chill run under her skin but decided to let the comment pass as she opened the box. Standing, she unfolded the floor length dress and held it up to her own body. Her mother stood as well and gently took hold of one of the lacy sleeves.

"This is a marvelous dress, Norah. I'd love to see it on you someday." Norah could hear that wistful, undercurrent of curiosity about her unmarriedness.

"Come 'ere, let me show you the shoes that match."

She lifted out the shoes and laid them on the couch. Norah handed the diary to her mother.

"Don't mind the elastic bands. The front and back covers are so old that they're beginning to fall away. I added the elastics to keep them tight. Just read to the page where the ribbon lays," coached Norah, "that's as far as I have read."

Norah's mother began to read, all the while shaking her head and making clicking noises with her mouth. After a few minutes she looked up, met Norah's gaze, and heaved a heavy sigh.

"It's true then. It's really true. She tried to make me believe, she really did, and I just didn't…I couldn't believe…no…I wouldn't believe. I suppose I was too frightened. I am frightened still. Let us look at the rest of the box's contents."

Norah too, was beginning to feel alarmed, as she peered back into the green box. The next item from the top was a small box. Norah removed the lid and picked out a brown and gold leather hair clasp. "She must've worn this while working the farm."

She handed this to her mother and returned to the box. Wrapped in tissue paper was black and white coarse horsehair, joined together to form a long plait. Two hand-made envelopes lay at the bottom of the box. Norah's mother opened the first one and read the words on the delicate yellowed paper.

> *If you have found the leathered book*
> *And find the secret of which I speak,*
> *Possession grants the power to reach*
> *The haven of your wildest dreams;*
> *I marvel; let the newness come*
> *I hunger; to meet the ancient ones*
> *I desire; with optimistic glee*
> *That you will come at last*
> *To me*

The two glanced at each other.
Norah opened the second envelope.

I hope you are reading this Norah, my dear grand-daughter. For if you are I have no doubt in my mind that you will figure out the mystery of our family. You are a writer, a conduit, and a seeker. Go treasure hunting. Follow the trails, read the diary, and for pity's sake, convince that mother of yours that life can be an unscientific mystery. I have written as much of the oral history as I know. I tried to pass it all to your mother, but it was not to be.

My choices, for reasons that I cannot reveal at present, are to let this box and its contents get lost into the abyss of life, or to believe that this box will find you, and that you will seek its treasure. Your mother told me long ago that you would be the next in line for this house, and I have full faith that you will uncover my green box.

I feel absolutely certain that we shall meet again on the other side. Remember the stories, Norah my dear. Remember our play adventures. Remember it all. Norah, you are so like my mother, Genevieve.

This diary is not only my story but also the stories of so many that went before me. I spent many months writing not only my memories but also stories handed down from previous generations. There are also detailed diary pages from some of the many members that have gone before. There is another diary, that you will find when you find the treasure. We come from a long line of seannachí which I hope will prove to be in your favour.

Your loving Nana

Norah looked at her mother inquisitively. "Do you know what this means?"

Úla nodded and rested her head back on the couch pillows.

"When I was a little girl, Norah, your nana would tell me stories about all sorts of things. She never tired of creating whimsical tales of beautiful lands with interesting characters. Her stories could go on for many nights running, like chapters in a book. They were in-depth enough to include the detailed conversations among the people of which she spoke. I didn't devour them as most little children might, however. I was notorious for interrupting her with comments such as, 'but that couldn't really happen,' or, 'there is no such thing as a multi-coloured sky!' Nana would quietly argue that there are many things that have no explanation and therefore there could indeed be other realities if we only opened our minds and hearts to them. Your nana's openness to otherworldly things and my need for absolutes was a constant battle for both of us.

"I suppose I was what one would have to call a five-year-old skeptic and a family anomaly, as science always won over imagination. Every story she told, resulted in a barrage of questions from me, producing tension between us. You may not like this Norah but even now, as I sit here reading this, I can't help but wonder if my mother simply wrote all of this, herself."

A pained look swept across Norah's face and her mother added, "I'm trying to wrap my head around all of this Norah. Don't look at me so judgmentally."

Norah shifted uncomfortably. "If there is one thing I can say about Nana, is that she was filled with integrity and was never prone to deceit. Besides, flip through the pages. You can see the difference in handwriting all the way through. I'm just surprised that you are basically calling Nana a liar."

"I'm simply trying to convey how I feel and felt Norah. I never said she was a liar *per se*, I just don't trust things that seem, shall we say, enigmatic. There was no one for me to confide in regarding this aspect of my life. Think about that for a minute before you judge *me* too harshly."

Norah nodded. "I remember Nana being disappointed that you never showed interest in her stories. As we sit here talking about it, though, I admit, I can also see how frustrating that was for you, too, given your personality."

Úla raised her eyebrows in surprise. "Thanks for that comment, Norah. Your nana's ways of thinking did not always align with my way of seeing the world. Growing up, I thought she was more than a bit mad. Her flights of fancy and delusional episodes were so embarrassing to me.

"When I was little, my friends and I loved to play in the fields along the tree lines and by some of the local streams. Hours were spent investigating; keeping a keen eye out for signs of faeries and faery forts, messages from forest creatures, like leprechauns or brownies; sprites and pookas. I went along with it all so as not to be the 'odd one out', but while they were all immersed in their quest, I would be looking for worms, tadpoles, scat, algae, or other science-oriented things.

"When I was a pre-teen, one of my friends had a cousin visit from Canada, and the cousin brought with them a Ouija board. My friends and I sat taking turns calling those who were departed. They all called forth dead musicians, family members, or actors. When it was my turn, I asked for a connection to Charles Darwin. When they all looked at me as though I had ten heads, I backtracked and, thinking quickly, called upon an actor we all loved who had died the year previously. I said something like, "O wait, I've changed my mind. I want to contact Humphrey Bogart."

Norah and Úla both laughed so heartily that Norah leaned forward, snorting. "Oh my god Ma, that sounds so much like you!"

Úla wiped an amused tear from the corner of her eye saying, "Okay well back to my earlier years and my mother. When I was almost six my mother told me of a far-off land where the water from the central well tasted like sweet apples. Two long lost relatives had come to the central well to meet for the first time in many years. As usual, I had to interrupt and explain to her that there was no such thing as well water that tasted like apples. I was more insistent than I'd ever been in the past and after a few minutes of listening to my determined discourse my mother slapped her knees with her hands and stood up, proclaiming, 'That's it. I think it is time.' 'Time for what?' I asked, and she said, 'Time for you to see the truth with your own eyes.'"

Norah looked across the sofa quizzically, wondering if Úla was about to get uncharacteristically fanciful.

"My mother walked over to her desk, the very one you work at Norah, opened one of the small drawers on the left and removed from it a ribbon with a little key attached to the end; a skeleton key with a solid crown."

"The key in the diary!" exclaimed Norah.

"Yes, Norah. I would say it must be the very one." Úla took a deep breath, and slowly exhaled.

"Mother told me to wait patiently where I was, and she went outside. She returned a few minutes later with something wrapped in brown paper. The object inside was a sturdy wooden box. The box was a little larger than a shoebox and had etchings and a little lock. The key, of course, slid easily inside and I could hear the lock tumble. She looked at me with her loving eyes, grinned, and opened it. Something lay wrapped in plush burgundy cloth. My mother lifted it out gingerly, placed it on the kitchen table and unrolled the material. What lay inside was a kind of glass and wood scope about a foot in length. It was the most beautiful and unusual looking thing that I had ever seen.

"The glass was black and white, and the wood was deep brown, almost black. There were copper bands encircling the top and bottom. And the other thing I remember is the etchings in the wood. They were cut marks in a very peculiar pattern.

"As I said," Úla continued, her eyes looking upward, remembering, "I thought it was very beautiful but at the time couldn't figure out why it was so hidden away. I immediately began bombarding my mother with a litany of questions. My mother had put her finger to her mouth and said, 'Sssshhhh…come and look with your questioning eyes.' She twisted the object in her hands and turned it toward me. I rose from my chair and looked through. I assumed this was all just some silly game that my mother dreamed up for my amusement, or hers more like—just another one of her fanciful ideas. I looked through the eyepiece for a few moments and jumped back in fright. 'Be not afraid, Úla,' said my mother. 'There's no need to be afraid.'

"I took a step forward and looked through again. Then, I ran out of the house and down the lane. I could hear my mother calling, 'Úla come back…Úla.'

"I didn't stop running, Norah. I ran for what seemed like an eternity, but it was really only as far as the footbridge that ran over a little stream. The same one that's just down the road here. I sat underneath the arched sanctuary on a large rock and watched the water flow downstream. I remember picking up a tiny stick and writing arithmetic equations in the sandy soil for a time. This was logical. Ask a question—find a true answer. Facts. That is what I desired. Facts: not some illusionary tale about impossible places. I didn't return home until dusk.

"A familiar yeasty aroma of freshly baked bread wafted through the breeze as I approached home. As I came through our front door I could hear the sound of something bubbling on the stove. My mother turned to me and held out her arms. I flew into them without hesitation, pleading. 'Please mother, I don't want to talk about it. I don't want to see. I don't want to. Ever.'"

Norah leaned forward and stroked the dress. "Did you ever look in this scope again? Did you ask for an explanation? Do you know where it is now?"

Her mother frowned. "No. Your nana tried innumerable times over the years to re-visit the event, but I refused to discuss what had transpired or what I had witnessed."

"What did you witness?"

"It was many years ago, Norah, and I know my memory has fogged a little, but what I saw was a beautiful field. In the field was a woman with two horses. She turned to me and waved. It was incredibly real, Norah. It was as though I was in the field with her. The light was golden, and a breeze gently blew through her hair. It was so real and at the same time completely inconceivable. It just didn't make sense. I therefore ran away and wouldn't talk about it again.

"Several months before Nana disappeared, she tried one more time while we were weeding her front garden. True to form, I stubbornly refused to engage in the conversation. In exasperation, she gathered a large pile of discards and flung them into her wheelbarrow. Tilting her head in that way that she had, she said something to the effect of, 'I will find a way, I will find a way.'

"Thinking she meant that she'd find a way to discuss it with me, I just let it go, but now I know she meant she'd find a way to you."

Norah smiled gently, unable to hide the twinkle growing in her eyes, as Úla continued.

"I remember my father clearly. I remember his deep-set blue eyes. I remember him bouncing me on his knee. I also remember the utter torment that my mother went through when his young heart gave out unexpectedly as he worked in the back field. He lies in the one grave that we know about in our family. Whenever I asked my mother about our family history, I was told that our family had been swept into a beautiful and unusual home, not of this world."

Norah looked at her mother sideways, "Not of this world?"

"Norah, I've told you that we're the last of our line. That's somewhat dishonest, I know, but you must understand the extent to which I thought she was mad.

"How would you react as a logically minded person?" Úla implored. "I pressed her once about where the graves of our relatives were, and she told me there were no bodies to bury. She did show me trees she had planted in honour of the past relatives at the back of the property. She said planting the trees was her way of erecting head stones for everyone. I didn't know what to think, frankly.

"Then you came along and began talking to this Genevieve character and flying off to imaginary places with your nana. I became terrified that you might have the same delusions and or mental instabilities. I was in a quandary as to what to do. So, I did what I've always done, which is to run, to ignore and to lull myself into a false sense of belief and security that nothing unusual revolved around any of us. That's why I have always told you we were the last of our line. That's why I have always told you we were not sure where our families were originally from: to keep you from asking questions. To keep your vivid imagination at bay."

Norah sat in stunned silence while Úla picked at a loose thread on her skirt.

"You know, I remember so well the time I gave out to you for playing with your make-believe friend, Genevieve. I am sorry, Norah. So sorry."

Norah frowned. "Believe me, you don't have to remind me. The reality is, Genevieve retreated to my inner world and for the large part became my reliable conscience. I still go to her in times of need."

Swallowing hard, Úla replied, "Genevieve was such a precious part of your world, and I crushed that . . . or tried to. I won't claim to have acceptable excuses but I can tell you that my mother's stories were still lingering, and she was forever trying to find ways to talk about that experience with the scope. She often spoke about her mother, who, as you now know, was given the name Genevieve at birth. I suppose hearing that name spoken by you so many times pushed me to my brink and caused me to panic. Your nana and I argued something fierce that day and she was exasperated with me, I know."

Norah stopped for a moment and took a quiet breath, trying to decide if now was when she could let her mother off the hook for that hurt.

"Let's put that away for now, shall we?" suggested Norah. "I think we should read this diary together. That is, provided you can listen with an open mind and heart. I have no intention of sharing this with you if you're going to be questioning every sentence and everything that may seem illogical to you. My guess is that we're in for a very illogical ride."

"I promise to sit here and keep all scientific comments at bay. It will be a challenge, but I know I need to hear what my mother has been trying to convey for so long."

Chapter 12

"Right then. I shall read from where we both left off."

Norah took the book from her mother's hands and flipped to the page where the ribbon lay.

12

Genevieve/Caitlín

My mother, Grace, slid her hand inside her apron pocket and pulled out a long glass object. "Genevieve, hold this up to the candlelight and look through."

I took the glass-and-wood object in my six-year-old hands and did as she bade. I held it up to the candlelight and peered through, tears still pooled in my cocoa-coloured eyes. I remember this moment so clearly, for it was a moment in time when I knew my life was to be re-defined. A time when I knew my life would never be the same. I whispered, "Mother . . . oh Mother . . . it's so beautiful."

"Yes, Genevieve, it is."

I could not stop looking through the scope. "It is surely the most beautiful place I have ever seen. It is even more beautiful than our own farm and I thought we lived in the loveliest place on earth. Who is that woman by the stream, and why is she bowing? And who is that man bending down to the stream? He is looking this way now and tipping his hat toward me."

My mother took the scope, looked through and smiled. "That woman is my mother, your nana. Her name is Orlaith. That man is my father, your granddad. Granddad Donncha. They are meeting you for the first time and are trying to communicate with you."

"My nana and granddad? Why are they in there? How do they fit?"

Laughing, my mother said, "Ahh, now it is time for a story, my darling one. This is a special story though and one that you must keep secret. At least, secret to all but those in our immediate family, including your eventual husband. Do you understand that, Genevieve? It is very important that you understand this, as there are people who would not believe this story and there are people who would do most anything to get their hands on such an object as this."

"Yes, Mother, I understand and give you my word not to tell anyone or talk to anyone unless it is our close family . . . or my eventual husband."

My mother laughed and said. "Then I will tell you, my little one." She looked through the scope, then returned it to her apron pocket.

Úla interrupted Norah reading aloud. "You know Norah, if you'd been a boy, we were going to name you Donncha."

Norah's eyebrows raised in delight. "Really? I never knew that, and coincidentally, it's a name I have thought of over the years, in terms of, if I ever had a son. It is one of my top three names."

"What're the other two?"

"Hugh and Vincent."

"Those are nice, I guess," Úla said, unenthusiastically.

"So, you don't like them," replied Norah, unsurprised by her mother's judgment. "This is why parents should keep their baby name ideas to themselves until after the fact."

Úla bristled. "No, those names are fine. It's just that Donncha is better to my mind."

Norah sniffed. "For the love of . . . let's just get back to the diary, shall we?"

Orlaith and Donncha as told by Grace

Your nana and granddad, my mother and father, Orlaith and Donncha, met during an unexpected and unseasonably wicked storm. My mother, Orlaith, was an only child, like me, like you, and she lived with her mother on this very farm. It was April 16th, Orlaith's 19th birthday, and it was her birthday wish to go hunting for wild mushrooms. It had been a fine-looking early morning with only a few scattered clouds, but by midday black storm clouds had gathered in close and there were distant rumblings of thunder. Orlaith had taken her usual path through a shelter of trees that led up to the hills. She knew these paths like the back of her hand, and therefore felt quite safe and protected from the elements.

She had it in her mind to gather a basket of wild mushrooms to fix mushroom stew for their supper. Wandering through the little forest and nearby hills had been Orlaith's favourite activity since she was a child. Growing up on an isolated farm with few friends, she had come to enjoy her solitude and quiet wanderings. It never ceased to amaze her how easily nature created its own beauty in every season. *The Four Seasons* was a song her mother had taught her about each of the seasons and she sang it as she walked.

Geimhreadh…Earrach…Samhradh…Fómhar
Winter…Spring…Summer…Autumn
Buds brood far below the surface
In the glen white with snow
Ruffled wings on naked branches
Slanted light so swiftly goes
Iron kettle, leaves brewing
In the cottage on the hob
Silhouettes gaily dancing
From the mantle up above

Geimhreadh…Earrach…Samhradh…Fómhar
Winter…Spring…Summer…Autumn
Bend down, sow narrow furrows
Tawney seeds drop with care
Obsidian clay take them under
Lie beneath Earth's great lair
Yonder wakes dormant orchard
Yonder neighs a foaling mare
Apple trees blossoms stirring
Ancient gifts so soon to bear

Geimhreadh…Earrach…Samhradh…Fómhar
Winter…Spring…Summer…Autumn
Four a.m. cock is crowing
Hush not 'til midnight chime
Heat descends penetrating
Incense of petals rise
Tranquil be mind and spirit
Resting by the river bed
Sinking to quiet slumber
Dreams so quickly wed

Geimhreadh…Earrach…Samhradh…Fómhar
Winter…Spring…Summer…Autumn
Mend the thatch where light is seeping
Reap the grain before the frost

Glory flames red and golden
Shaken from trembling boughs
A haon do tri ceathair séasúir
One two three four seasons all
Waxing waning rising setting
Days of life propelling all

As an early teen, Orlaith had begun to follow Sika deer paths along the stream beds and had discovered some remarkable areas with rock croppings and deep swimming holes. She had always been enamored by the native red deer. Due to the continual deforestation of Ireland, red deer numbers had declined dramatically, but Orlaith always kept a sharp ear out for the low-pitched mating calls of the males. Their rich red coat complimented the lush green of the land and contrastingly, in winter their darkened grey-brown, blended flawlessly with the naked trees.

Once, in peak season, she spied two mature stags. They were a fair distance from where she hid but it was a splendid show of nature in progress nonetheless.

The larger of the two sported a sixteen-point rack of antlers, while the smaller boasted fourteen. The two stags threshed the surrounding vegetation in a mighty effort to prove their superiority, until, at last, the larger of the two roared, lowered his head and advanced to clash antlers with his rival. Though the prolonged show had been indeed dazzling, the four females (who were the subjects of the ruckus) were seemingly unimpressed. They nibbled delicately on the grasses, occasionally looking up at the two stags as though they were bored by the trials and disturbed by their garish behaviour.

Orlaith had tried to move closer but stepped on a pile of decaying leaves and dry twigs causing a loud crackling noise to bounce through the trees. All the deer stood to attention for a moment and then sped off, the rival on his own once again.

On this day, however, the only sign of animals was badger scat that lay in heaps on the dirt.

By the time Orlaith's basket was three-quarters full, the cloudy day had turned wicked. Rain began to fall in torrents. Wind, thunder, and lightning reared themselves like a wild runaway horse charging at full force, and it seemed that every living creature was scurrying underground or to some sheltered cover.

In the distance, Orlaith saw a cluster of mushrooms standing tall and white. Though the thunder and lightning were increasingly close, she decided to gather these last few mushrooms before making her own swift retreat. Orlaith squatted and picked the near perfect specimens. 'A fine end to a fine afternoon,' she said aloud.

The din of a barking dog caused her to look up. Might there be someone else out in this desolate place? Perhaps a dog had escaped from a farm and gotten lost?

Suddenly, there was movement in the brush. A large wolfhound was approaching at great speed. Not knowing what to do, Orlaith stepped behind the large tree and held her breath, hoping the hound would run past. The hound did run past her in fact but turned soon after. Seeing her there, he bounded toward her with curiosity. His husky yapping had ceased, and his tail was high, so Orlaith felt it was safe to crouch down to him. He ran straight up to her, panting, and nuzzled underneath her arm. She spoke to him as anyone might speak to a dog.

"Hello boy, what a fine boy you are."

A moment later, she heard the voice of a man calling, "Tadhg…Tadhg…come Tadhg."

The young man could now see the two and made his way to them.

"Sorry," he said. "He looks to be a bit of a brute, but he's harmless just the same. I hope he didn't scare you."

Orlaith looked up at the stranger. He carried a large rucksack on his back and from his belt there hung a leather water bag. He was a good six feet in height, with curly jet-black hair pulled back in a short makeshift ponytail. His beard was thick, his eyes green and she guessed him to be about her age. As far as Orlaith was concerned, he had a smile that could have melted butter.

Being at a loss for words, Orlaith said, "A Northern storm to be sure. The wind pushes that icy rain past the skin and straight to the bone."

The stranger nodded in agreement, removed his rucksack and pulled from it a long piece of rope. This he put around the neck of his dog.

A clap of thunder above their heads made Orlaith recoil as a bolt of lightning struck a tree not far from them. Another thunderclap came directly, as did another bolt of lightning. Orlaith got such a fright that she jumped and pushed her body up against the tree she had been squatting by. The next strike flew from the sky and struck the very tree she stood beneath. As the tree began to quake, Orlaith screamed. Limbs tumbled to the ground, with a strong odour of burning wood. The stranger pushed her so hard that she flew crossways and ended up on her back in the middle of low underbrush.

It took a moment for Orlaith to struggle to her feet as ear-piercing thunder ranted and raged above her. She did not see the stranger when she recovered her feet, and at first assumed he had made for the shelter of another tree. Tadhg was barking by the fallen limbs of the stricken tree. It was then that she saw him lying face down in the dirt, with a tree limb across his leg and several large branches covering his head and shoulders. She ran to him and knelt down, removing the branches from his face and calling to him. When he did not respond, she lifted a smaller limb up and away from his leg. She called to him a second time and rolled him over onto his back. Still not responding, she removed his water pouch and undid its spout. Orlaith's heart pounded as she raised his head to her lap and poured water into his mouth. Tadhg whined and lay at the man's side, licking his hand. The stranger blinked and then opened his eyes.

"Thank goodness," cried Orlaith. "Are you…can you move…are you all right?"

The stranger looked up. "In the sense that a tree has just fallen on me and that rain is falling from the sky in buckets, then I would have to answer no, I am not all right. In the sense that I have just woken up in your arms and am looking into your blue eyes, then I am indeed quite fine."

Orlaith flushed crimson and turned her gaze away from him. The stranger realized how forward his comment had been.

"I'm sorry," he said. "I did not mean to embarrass you, dear lady. Here, let me try to rise to my feet and we shall see how the legs feel."

The man rolled to his side with a look of panic in his eyes. "My pack! Where is my pack?"

"It's right here," Orlaith reassured him. "Remember, you removed it to get a lead for your dog?"

As he stood, the man could see where the pack lay and he limped to it. After inspecting the contents, he sat back down on the ground with a look of relief.

"I think I have slightly twisted my ankle but if I just sit here a minute or two all should be well."

Orlaith looked at the stranger. "You pushed me out of the way and took the blows that I would surely have received. I may not have fared as well as you. I am grateful to you, sir."

"The name is Donncha," said the young man. "I apologize again for embarrassing you with my forward words."

Orlaith grinned. "I was a little flustered by what you said. I don't see many people and I surely don't get many compliments, but no matter, no harm done. I am just glad that you are not badly hurt for I don't know what I would have done if you had been injured."

Orlaith looked to the weeping sky and returned her gaze to Donncha. "My name is Orlaith."

Donncha's heart skipped a beat, as he was searching for two people, one of whom was named Orlaith, and who's surname was Murphy, but directly after noting her first name, she added, "Smith. Orlaith Smith."

"The pleasure is all mine," he said, slightly disappointed she was not the Orlaith Murphy he was looking for. The thunder now moved in the distance and the rain, while still streaming down, was less intense.

Orlaith kicked the soupy dirt with her boot. "I should be getting back home, if you think you can manage on your own that is. Are you just passing through? I've not seen you in these parts, though as I said, I don't venture out much."

Donncha looked intently at Orlaith. His mouth curled toward his nose and his eyebrows danced up and down as if trying to decide whether to answer her.

"Believe it or not, I live very close to here."

"Really?" Orlaith asked eagerly. She knew her voice had sounded high pitched and tried to recover from her unintentional excitement by slowly continuing. "Are you visiting the Richardsons then?"

"No, I am not. I have a place not far from here. You might very well find it a strange place, but it is unoccupied land that I have come to temporarily call home. You see, I have travelled extensively for the past several years and have not been able…or rather…have not stayed anywhere long enough to grow roots."

Orlaith could see a pained look cross Donncha's face as he spoke.

"I must say, however, that this area is indeed beautiful, and I have set myself up in a way I have not done for a long time. Perhaps I can think of stopping for a while." He looked at Orlaith and smiled. "Yes, maybe I could stop awhile."

"I must go. The light is beginning to fade, and I have a long way to walk yet. I think my mushroom hunting shall have to continue another day."

Orlaith hesitated and then boldly blurted. "Donncha, let me thank you for being so gallant. Today is my birthday you see, and I came out to pick mushrooms to make stew. Would you care to join me, us, my mother and me, for supper this evening? If you can walk all that way that is…and if you would like to…you may not want to which of course is fine but if…"

"Orlaith, I would like nothing better," interrupted Donncha. "I will find myself a stout stick to lean on, and if you and your mother do not mind a hobbling, soaked stranger tagging along for supper then I would be delighted."

They made their way along the winding narrow paths talking of simple things such as weather and the signs of spring. Tadhg stayed close now and eyed Donncha and his walking stick as though he were a nursemaid minding a child. They arrived at a small but finely kept cottage just as darkness fell. The front of the barn was lit by lamplight where Orlaith's mother stood looking toward the path from which they came.

"Orlaith!" called her mother. "I was getting worried. Where were you all this time?"

Orlaith's mother was relieved to see her daughter, but unsure of what to make of the young man she had beside her. There was something unnervingly familiar about him. Orlaith relayed the events of the day while they all made their way into the house.

14

Orlaith's mother, Teresa, was not only accepting of Donncha, but also genuinely seemed to enjoy him. She had birthed Orlaith at a fairly late age and was now getting along in years, thus getting concerned about her daughter's future. There was a familiarity about his manner and enthusiastic nature that Teresa found comforting.

The evening passed easily and quickly, and Orlaith was more than a little chuffed when her stew turned out to be pleasing to Donncha. It was far too late to hike back up to the hills, so Donncha took Tadhg and a wool blanket and went off to the hayloft in the barn to sleep.

"Orlaith," her mother had said after Donncha had retired to the barn, "you two seem to get on very well. I have a good sense about him. I don't think you should be at all concerned about our family history. I can see a look of concern on your face, my dear one, but at some point it will be necessary to trust someone enough to be honest."

Donncha and his dog, Tadhg, came frequently to the cottage over the course of the next few weeks. He was eager to help with the tilling and planting of the garden, and the mending of the fence that surrounded it. He was strong, able-bodied, and hardworking, yet he was also a sensitive type of man who would not only bring bundles of wildflowers and herbs but would contribute rabbits or other wild game to their table.

One day, when they were walking in a meadow, collecting dandelion greens, Donncha asked if Orlaith would be interested in seeing where he lived. She was both keen and curious, as he was quite secretive about his home. In previous conversations, he would deftly steer dialogue about his living and family situation in opposite directions. Orlaith and her mother had decided that it would be best to leave that point alone.

He was obviously the kind of person who was private about certain aspects of his life. He always turned up at the cottage clean and energetic, so what did it matter that he did not desire to share parts of his life? There were certainly parts of their lives that they had not yet shared with him. Sometimes, while they all sat to a midday meal, Donncha would expound on some of his travels over the past few years. He had a habit of closing his eyes when he told stories, which Orlaith found to be quite charming. She and her mother would listen to the hypnotic drone of his voice and drift to the places and people of which he spoke.

Orlaith quickly agreed to accompany Donncha to his home. Early the next morning, the two took off with Tadhg in tow.

Donncha had fallen in love with Orlaith the instant he had set eyes on her but had known that the repercussions of this could mean an end to his travels—and an end to a long and important search. He was weary of travelling and found himself daydreaming of a life with her. Daydreaming of a life that could be. He had come to trust her as he had trusted no other, save his father, and had begun to feel lost when he was not in her presence.

They walked in silence through fields and meadows; zigzagging across familiar streams (where Orlaith had so many times bathed), and up to the rise, to the very place where they had first happened upon each other. Here they made a sharp turn to the north, and wandered along a narrow, barely trodden path. Trees were thick and gnarled, entwining into each other, straining and competing for the infrequent coveted light from above. A delicate, pleasant musical sound reverberated through the trees that was most alluring, yet strangely out of place. Donncha pointed to one particularly thick cluster of branches that rested upon each other in layers. He carefully pulled the centre apart.

"Welcome to my humble home," he said.

Orlaith expected to walk through the brambles and branches and see perhaps a minuscule cottage or shack. She had readied herself with several positive comments she might make to help him feel at ease, but upon entering the unusual enclave, she found she had no words to speak.

Donncha took a deep breath and followed in behind. The first display to meet Orlaith's eyes was a magnificent archway about seven feet off the ground, made from tree branches and greenery, anchored to oak trees on either side. Rope wound around the base of the trees and interwove with the branches to make the archway both sturdy and taut. Tied along the arch were strips of brightly coloured fabric and long thin pieces of tin and copper. The tin and copper dangled, swaying and tipping against each other, in the blustery breeze, creating the musical sound that Orlaith had heard.

Donncha clasped Orlaith's hand and passed under the arch. "Not what you expected, I'm sure but come, and let me show you my kingdom."

The little path on which they walked was lined on either side with earth-toned river rocks in a spectrum of browns to rusty reds. A smile swept across Orlaith's face with each step into Donncha's world. He had ornamentally crafted many of the surrounding trees in a wildly playful fashion. The first tree she approached held a wooden box with a carved bench underneath it. Orlaith touched the top of the box and looked at Donncha. Donncha nodded his permission for her to open it. Inside were four books wrapped in thick cloth:

Poetry To Live By, Oliver Tate

A Walk in the Deep Shadow of Day, F. O'Maonlai

The Ghost Tree, Finbar Adams

The Woman From Heather Hill, Máire ní Murchú

"This looks like interesting reading. May I ask what is in the box attached to the next tree?"

"Feel free to explore anything you like."

The slender box held paper, charcoal, a green pen, and a bottle of black ink. Some of the sketches were of the surrounding landscape and some were filled with what had to be his writings. Orlaith crossed to the other side of the path. These trees had a vast array of items hammered onto them: a rusted old teapot here, a broken wheel of a cart there, a piece of carved wood resembling the shape of a woodpecker just to the left, a ladle hanging akimbo . . . it went on. On one tree, with a big burl in its trunk, Donncha had arranged bits of natty sheep wool surrounding it to make it look like a person's head, with hammered buttons for eyes.

Several carved out tree stumps housed damp black earth with wildflowers. Various trees held wooden plaques, with words burned into them. 'Tranquility,' 'Truth,' 'Nature,' 'Life,' and some had quotes: 'To thine own self be true,'

'Necessity is the mother of invention,' and 'Listen not with your ears but with your heart.'

Orlaith was enchanted by this endless gallery. She passed two large tree stumps without detecting anything out of the ordinary, but Donncha drew her back to them. The stumps were about waist high, and upon closer inspection, Orlaith could see that either side of the stumps had notches cut away. Donncha leaned over and tugged up on the notches.

The secret lid, once removed, revealed a hollowed-out centre, which held supplies wrapped in heavy, rough cloth. He raised another lid. More supplies as well as a few sacks of potatoes. Donncha tenderly clasped Orlaith's elbow as they ambled toward a tall rock face, draped in old hessian from about ten feet up. Large rocks kept the fabric in place on the ground, and rope ran from the top to what Orlaith assumed was the back of the rock face.

Bending down, Donncha shoved the anchoring rocks aside, setting a corner free.

"Wait here a tic." He proceeded to enter under the flap and within a few moments, Orlaith could hear Donncha calling her name.

Initially, all she could see was the glow of a single candle, but as her eyes adjusted to the new light, and as Donncha continued to put a match to wicks, the most astonishing and magical place came into view. Once fully illuminated, Orlaith could see it was a one-room rock cave, about eight feet in height, fourteen feet wide and twenty feet long. The rock ceiling varied in height, so parts of the room were a bit taller than others. There was a small wooden table to Orlaith's left side that held a small collection of dishes, tea, and an open book.

Two tree stumps served as chairs by the low-lying table. All along the rock walls were crevices, where a plethora of candles were nestled. The dripping wax cascaded down the walls in multi-coloured layers. The walls also held hanging beads and feathers, and provisions like onions, garlic, and bunches of dried herbs. One larger crevice held two cook pots and three large jugs. The other side of the room housed a taut rope across a small alcove, where clothing hung. Underneath the draped clothes were two sets of boots, a shovel, an axe, rolled rope, a fishing rod, and a shotgun. The very back of the room was home to a stack of turf.

All of this circled around an odd sort of metal stove with a pipe running up and out of the top of the cave. Two woven rugs ran parallel along the length of the dirt floor, on either side of the stove; and directly behind the stove, also on the floor, was a neatly made bed covered with wool blankets. Tadhg nosed his way through the front entry and immediately retreated to a reclined position next to the bed. Heaving a great sigh, he closed his eyes.

"This is unbelievable. You live here, Donncha? That is to say, it is an amazing work of art in every shape and form. How long did all this take to construct?"

"Yes, I do indeed call this home. I found this cave several years ago when my father and I were travelling together. The stove and tree stumps were already here when we found it. I can only speculate on who created this place. I had wanted to rest a time from my travelling, and this seemed like a perfect hide-away. The rest of the decor is of my own fashioning. I have been here a few months now and quite like my surroundings, but I can tell you that I was most grateful for the comparatively mild winter temperatures this year.

"Once there is a fire going in here it is quite cozy. I have an outside cooking area and a lean-to where I keep my turf. I keep an assortment of supplies in the tree stumps, and if you listen carefully, you can hear the nearby stream. There is a place for cleaning my fish and game, and an outhouse of sorts downstream. I have found special spots for bathing and for water collecting upstream. I have everything a man could want. At least, everything a man needs. Almost.

"I can see you have a multitude of questions, Orlaith, and I mean to answer them all, but let me first make us some tea and light a fire to warm the place. Sit yourself where you please and I will get some water. That book on the table has some lovely poetry, should you be interested."

Donncha took a jug and left Orlaith to her devices while he headed out to the stream.

15

Orlaith sat on one of the stumps by the table and let her eyes wander. While the room was most assuredly odd, it was also homey, and Orlaith could see how a man like Donncha could be happy enough in such a place. Tadhg was busy dreaming. He whimpered, twitching his legs, no doubt in a dreamy pursuit. Orlaith picked up the open poetry book and read.

The Thrush's Nest
John Clare

Within a thick and spreading hawthorn bush
That overhung a molehill large and round
I heard from morn to morn a merry thrush
Sing hymns to sunrise, and I drank the sound
With joy, and, often an intruding guest
I watched her secret toils from day to day
How true she warped the moss, to form a nest

And modeled it within the wood and clay
And by and by, like bells gilt with dew
There lay her shining eggs, as bright as flowers
Ink-spotted over shells of greeny-blue
And there I witnessed in the sunny hours
A brood of nature's minstrels chirp and fly
Glad as that sunshine and the laughing sky

Thoreau

Live in each season as it passes; breathe the air, drink
the drink, taste the fruit, and resign yourself to the
influence of each. Let them be your only diet, drink
and botanical medicines. Be blown on by all the winds.
Open all your pores and bathe in all the tides of nature,
in all her streams and oceans, at all seasons.

To affect the quality of the day, that is the highest
of the arts.

I would fain improve every opportunity to wonder and
worship, as a sunflower welcomes the light. The more
thrilling, wonderful, divine objects I behold in a day,
the more expanded and immortal I become. If a stone
appeals to me and elevates me, tells me how many
miles I have come, how many remain to travel – and
the more, the better – reveals the future to me in some
measure, it is a matter of private rejoicing.

I am grateful for what I am and have. My thanksgiving
is perpetual. It is surprising how contented one can be
with nothing definite – only a sense of existence. My
breath is sweet to me. O how I laugh when I think of
my vague indefinite riches. No run on my bank can
drain it, for my wealth is not possession but enjoyment.

Orlaith thought that a man who was enamoured of poetry as beautiful as this must be made for her.

Donncha returned with a full jug of water and a tin box. These he placed upon the table. It did not take long to get the fire blazing and the tea brewing. The tin held buttery tea biscuits, which he scattered on the upturned lid.

"Help yourself to sugar if you like, and to biscuits."

After re-securing the door, Donncha sidled up to the table, cleared his throat, and nervously pulled on his right ear lobe. "Orlaith, I must confess that my reasons for being in this place are long and involved. I have been alone and wandering for so long. I was beginning to fear that I would never have even a single root to plant. My story is so bizarre that I fear you will think me a lunatic and run out of here in a fit. It is, however, a chance I must take, for the honest truth is that I am over the moon in love with you. There, I may have just said the hardest part, and I will understand if your feelings for me are of a non-romantic inclination."

Reaching across the table, Orlaith gently laid her hand on top of his. "I have a hard time believing that your story could be any more out of the ordinary than the one I planned on confessing to you today, Donncha. As I mentioned once before, I have not been raised in a manner of most females of this time and therefore do not know what is proper versus improper in the ways of professing love. I must rely on instinct to guide my utter lack of experience. I must respond to your words in the only way I know how, which is directly.

"I have felt a deep love for you since the day we met. Even my overprotective mother cannot deny the obvious and has assured me that if this love is as real as it seems, you will understand my history and not think that I'm the lunatic!"

Along with the ensuing laughter came their first kiss.

Donncha reached for his book of poetry. "Would you like to read something? I wrote it a few days ago. It is about you. Perhaps my written words will…well…here."

From the back of the book, Donncha freed a folded piece of paper and shyly handed it to Orlaith. He then turned and tended the fire, while Orlaith read the black inked words.

Her love is a thresher her love is a plow
Turns my heart over right over somehow
It's firmly planted so deep and so pure
Orlaith my lady my fancy
By the heat of the sun by the light of the moon
Together we bask we're flowers in bloom
Wind it may blow rain it may lash
But nothing can topple our loving
It's floating I am on the air I dare say
Up here in the loft up here where I lay
I wish on her shoulders my kisses could land
T'would be heaven on earth in the morning
Is there a bright glimmer perhaps maybe more
Orlaith one day would see fit to be sure
To wear on her finger a circle of gold
So lovingly placed by my own hand
Her love is the wind I'm carried somehow
Away from this earth straight up to the clouds
To fly like the bird on careless flight
I no longer know the days hour
But what do I care if it's day or it's night
What do I care if it's wrong or it's right
For when I'm with Orlaith my world's in a skid
So gladly I roll and I tumble
I see in the future a life oh so grand
We'll dander on down to the surf and the strand
Or wander the boreen to be quite alone
Or stop for a chinwag at Ruari's
After a time our dotes will be born
The pram will come out its wheels they will turn
He will have dimples she will have curls
And the cradle will rock on the ocean

Orlaith lowered the paper to her lap. "Donncha, I don't know what to say."

"Do you like it?"

"Oh yes, I love it!"

Donncha returned to the table and took Orlaith's hands in his.

"Good. I was eager and nervous to show it to you. I have been travelling, Orlaith, for five years—give or take—and have combed this country in search of a specific person. Though I am keen to find this person, this mission is really for my aging father, who can no longer travel. He and I have travelled countless miles on this quest, and to be honest, it feels as though we are searching for some Holy Grail. In my father's eyes, it is a Holy Grail. Three Holy Grails in fact, but I will come to that. I go back to visit my father and update him on my travels every so often."

A sudden clap of thunder startled them both. They noticed the hessian straining against increasing wind, and rain began to fall. "The weather has been so peculiar of late," said Orlaith, distracted.

Neither wanted to get caught in another savage storm, nor did they want to cause undue concern to Orlaith's mother. They quickly tidied the dishes with the remaining water from the jug, stirred the coals and made their way from the enclave. The two moved at a brisk pace back along the paths without speaking.

Turf smoke rose from the chimney of the little cottage as they crested the top of Corcra Hill. Donncha took hold of Orlaith's hand as they hastened down the soggy grasses with Tadhg running along their side.

Teresa was in the barn brushing Milis, their black mare. Peeking her head into the barn, Orlaith announced their arrival and the commencement of a soon-to-be pot of tea. Once inside, they hung their damp coats on the wooden pegs behind the door and began stoking the cook stove. When the tea was made, the young couple sat at the table. Donncha ran his fingers through his beard, and chuckled.

"I promise you Orlaith, I am not a madman, though when I tell you my story, I fear you might hand me my hat and show me the door. I wouldn't blame you, so I wouldn't, but I do ask that you give me a chance to get through some of this before showing me the underside of your shoe."

Orlaith too, chortled. "Sure, c'mere to me Donncha. Your story could be no more, shall we say, out of the ordinary, than mine."

Donncha leaned back in his chair, nodded slightly and closed his eyes.

16

Donncha

My parents had been married just five years when I made my way into this world. As fate would have it, I was never to know my mother, for she died within a few days of my birth. My father is forever telling me that I am the image of her, save for my height and thickness of hair, which I inherited from him.

When I was born, our country was still festering from the open wounds of the Great Hunger—or famine, as some would call it. My Da, like many people, called it the Great Starvation. He said I should always remember those wretched events; I'd be stronger—and better—for it. My parents had barely survived those years and my mother, once a robust woman, had become weak with illness. There were so many maladies rampaging the country, they never knew which one she actually contracted, but it weakened her sorely, and this, without doubt, is why she did not survive my birth.

Da spoke about those days vividly and often. During my growing up years he would drum facts into me over and over, lest I forget important details. I think I can quote him close to verbatim:

"The starvation was the result not only of successive crop failures but the insufficient and ineffective relief for stopping the outbreak of disease and hunger. Your mother might have survived if medicine and food had been distributed among the Irish population.

"Potato crops had failed before, but the consecutive years of failure are what crushed us. We Irish were utterly dependent on the potato for our survival, so its failure in 1845 and beyond, was death itself. No one had any food reserves or money for rent. It was human misery of the highest degree. Streets swarming with beggars, villages ruined or totally deserted, and unsympathetic landlords.

"People were dying of starvation in their homes, in fields and on the sides of roads. Cholera, typhus, dysentery; these diseases took more lives than the lack of food. When you think of the thousands of people being buried in shallow roadside graves, as families wandered the country in search of food, it is not surprising that disease played such a huge role in the overall death toll."

My father would go red in the face with anger when he spoke of those days.

Ireland, at that time, was part of the United Kingdom, which was the wealthiest country in the world, but when the crisis hit, they ignored the Irish people. The UK was afraid that their social structure would collapse if they began giving people food they did not pay for.

England sent scientists to study the cause of the potato failure, instead of sending food to the starving people. The abundance of food leaving Ireland during those years was criminal. British landlords continued to make cash through the exportation of grain, wool and flax, while thousands were dying in the streets. Thousands were dying of hunger and Irish grain was being exported to England. The responsibility of feeding the poor fell on charity groups. Many soup kitchens served soup made with unsanitary water, which made people even sicker than they already were.

Then came the Amendment Act of 1847. No peasant with a holding of one-quarter of an acre or more was eligible for relief. Tens of thousands of farmers had to part with their land. Nearly two million of us died of starvation or disease in just five years. Another million left the country, many dying on wretched ships before reaching their destinations.

I did not have a usual childhood. My mother was gone and my father was left with an infant. There was no way on this earth for him to care and provide for a newborn, so he packed our few possessions and brought us to his mother's home. His mother, Fiona, was an exceptional woman who lived alone in a wild and untamed area in the west. She was quite overjoyed to have my father, whose name is Odhrán by the way, come to her for assistance.

Acquiring provisions was a challenge at that time and in that place, but thankfully, my nana possessed a sheep, chickens, and a root vegetable garden. My father was an excellent fisherman and would often be gone for two or three weeks at a go if there was any work to be had on the coast.

One of my earliest memories is my Nana Fiona swinging me in fabric tied between two trees. I can still feel that rocking motion and hear the rush of the river as it passed alongside us. There was one very old song she loved to sing called 'Odhrán a Chroí.' She named my father Odhrán because of that lullaby. It is quite lovely really. While I am speaking of names…well…the thing is…my father has called me Donncha since I was little lad of about two, but that is not the name I was called when I was born. For reasons I shall later explain, he decided to change my original name, which was Rónán, but I will get back to that.

One particular day, when I was about a year old, Nana said she had me rocking in my cloth world, a young woman in the early stages of pregnancy happened along the path. My nana thought she recognized her from the village, but since she herself so rarely ventured there, she was unsure. The woman was weeping. Startled she was, as we came into view and she wiped her hands across her face to clear her tears. The young woman noticed me in the rocking cloth and moved closer. The two women fell to talking and the young woman asked about me. When my nana told her the story of my father and me, she began to weep again.

"'Whatever could be wrong with you, child, to be weeping so? Are you not joyed at the thought of having a wee one of your own before too long?"

"I am over the moon with it", replied the woman, "but I have just had word that my husband's fishing boat is gone missing. Séamus, my husband, went fishing off the coast yesterday and the currach did not return last night. There is a search on in case their boat has been knocked up on the rocks somewhere. I am sick with worry."

"Dear oh dear, that is hard to bear. My son Odhrán is out fishing. I hope he is all right as well."

"I am sure he must be Mrs, the other man on the boat is named Tómas. Only two of them went out in that currach yesterday. The fellow who came to tell me the news said the day had started beautifully. His exact words were, 'Sure wasn't the mornin' as clear, bright and glistening as a new-honed knife.'

"Séamus dislikes venturing out on the ocean on a perfectly clear, calm day. He always says that the purity of a clear blue sky is downright deceiving."

'Give me a few clouds and an old bit of breeze so I can see the face of the day and be prepared for any and all possibilities. A clear, blue sky lulls one into complacency and lures men out far beyond their safe limits. If men drop their nets, become complacent, and a harnessed storm rears out of the blue, well, there is nothing to be done for it.'

"The day had done just that. Gone from tranquil to turbulent, and within an hour turned into an out and out gale along the coast. Several currachs and boats had been severely damaged, some upturned or thrown on their sides, but the currach with Séamus and Tómas did not return.

"The sea town is too far away for me to walk to so I must rely on one of the dockworkers to get to me in his buggy for news." The woman looked off in the distance for several seconds as if searching in her mind for the little boat before continuing.

"I should be making my way back as it is a bit of a walk. I felt I needed to breathe off some of my anxiety and try to sort myself. There is nothing I can do but wait. It was lovely to come across the two of you, though. I must admit to feeling the better for it."

"What is your name?" asked my nana.

"Siobhán Murphy. And yours, Mrs?"

"You can call me Fiona. This is Rónán. I do wish you all the best Siobhán. If you are ever inclined to visit, we are usually here or at my house just up that other path there. The welcome mat is out for you, but I do like to keep private."

"Thank you, Fiona, Indeed, I think you will see me sooner than later,' declared Siobhán, smiling broadly."

Fiona did see Siobhán again, the very next day, in fact. There was a rap at the door at midday. Siobhán was distraught, as the fishing boat had still not been found, narrowing the chances of the men's survival.

"What ever shall I do? I am four months along with child. My husband may be dead, and I have no one. No family. My husband's family is in the far south and we have not had contact with them for two years."

"Only two days have passed, so there is hope yet, Siobhán. However, given the circumstances would your husband's family not take you under their wing?"

"I wouldn't even venture to try, Fiona. You see, my husband, Séamus, had been a priest since a very early age. He had never been called to the cloth, but as the second eldest boy, well, you know how it is. His elder brother would inherit the farm. Being the second son, the word 'priest' was stamped on his forehead since birth. He and I met when I stopped to help him retrieve papers that had scattered around the road just outside the rectory. He thanked me and went inside.

"As I continued down the road, I saw a paper wedged in a gorse bush. It was a list of names with duties beside each one, so I knew it was belonging to him. Naturally, I walked back to the rectory and knocked the door. Séamus, who was known as Father Murphy, was pleased as punch to have the list returned and invited me in for tea. The rest of the story is complicated and exceedingly long but suffice to say that his leaving the church was devastating. Leaving the church for a woman was unforgivable in his family's eyes, and when we left, ties were severed. It has never been resolved."

Siobhán came to see my Nana Fiona and me every day. After the second week, she brought news that sections of the currach had been found washed up on the seafront, but no bodies had been recovered.

What Siobhán missed most about Séamus was their conversations. They did love each other, yes, but what they prized most of all was the ease with which they conversed.

Siobhán temporarily moved in with Ciara, her midwife, who was in need of help with an array of things. As Siobhán was skilled in the healing arts, it made for an easy transition. My Nana Fiona, amazingly enough, gave Siobhán permission to tell the midwife where she lived, given the circumstances. Siobhán was adjusting slowly and comforted with the knowledge that Séamus would live on through their child. Visiting us on a regular basis made her stronger by the day.

*D*onncha had been so engrossed in the telling of the story that he failed to notice Orlaith's mother appear at the front door. He also failed to hear Orlaith rise and walk toward her mother. When he opened his eyes, he was taken aback to see them staring at him, looking visibly shaken. Mother and daughter had their hands wrapped around each other, as if holding onto something for dear life.

Donncha jolted out of the chair in alarm and whispered. "Orlaith, Mrs Smith, what is it? What have I said to distress you?"

The three stood staring at each other.

Orlaith's mother finally broke the silence.

"Donncha? Rónán? You look nothing like…well, maybe your height, but you….oh dear…I am surely going to faint."

Orlaith led her mother to a chair at the table. All three sat.

"Mrs Smith, how have I upset you so? I've not even got to the strange part of my story yet."

"You have not upset me in the way you might think, Donncha. Aw, dear me, life is so peculiar." She paused for a moment to collect herself. "Donncha, we also have a secret. I, too, am not using my true name. My name is not Teresa Smith. It is Siobhán. Siobhán Murphy.'

Donncha's eyes saucered, his hands dropped to his sides, and his mouth gaped wide. *Did he hear that correctly? After all these years, could the door to freedom have opened? Could they be on the verge of walking upon the euphoric path of reunion?* Regaining himself, Donncha leaned forward and looked into the eyes of his beloved. "Orlaith, when we met, I held a very brief glimmer of hope that you might be the Orlaith I was searching for, but then you gave the name Smith, so I quickly let it go. I've searched so long and so far, I couldn't invest in that false hope."

Siobhán tsked. "How can this be happening? What are the chances of you two meeting and ending up here at this table?" Siobhán wiped the steady trail of tears from her ruddy cheeks with a sweep of her hand, and a long silence hung in the small cottage, as all three shook their heads in disbelief.

Orlaith was the first to speak after what felt like an eternity. "Something mystifying has occurred. That is assuredly so," she whispered, staring at the rising steam from her cup.

Siobhán gently touched the back of Donncha's hand. "Tell us the rest of the story as you know and remember it, Donncha, and please, try not to think about us sitting here. Just tell it with your eyes closed and head back, the way you always do.'

Donncha leaned back in his usual manner and closed his eyes. After a deep inhalation, he continued.

Siobhán, I mean…you? . . . came often. One day, my father, Odhrán, returned just before you…Siobhán, arrived. His arm was splinted and in a sling. He was hobbling, using a walking stick.

He had slipped and fallen on a fish of all things. There was not much he could do with a broken arm and badly bruised hip, so he returned home to heal. He was not altogether unhappy, as he could now spend time with his mother and son, and he had earned enough money to see them through for a while. My nana spoke about you, Siobhán, and my father said that he did indeed know Séamus and wasn't it a shame to have been taken by the sea like that, especially with a child on the way. A terrible pity.

Norah closed the diary and looked over to Úla.

Úla shrugged her shoulders in quiet response.

"Is this truly the first you've heard of all this, Mother? There's so much to take in here. It's staggering."

"Basically yes. There is, at times, a nagging familiarity, but I believe this to be mere memories of what I have always dismissed as your nana's imagination."

Norah shook her head. "It boggles my mind to think about how offhand you so often were toward Nana. The more I read the more you confound me."

This comment irked Úla. She pursed her lips and crossed her arms tightly. Deep down, she knew her daughter had every right to say what she did.

A few agitated moments passed. Finally, Úla let out a small sigh and unwound herself into her chair.

Norah re-opened the diary, then looked once again to her mother, as though searching for signs of betrayal.

"Mam?"

"Yes, Norah."

"Is…is Norah my real name?"

Úla chortled, then laughed. "Yes, Norah is your only name. Úla has always been mine, at least, as far as I know."

Norah relaxed back into the deep, comforting cushions of the couch, briefly glancing at the crackling fire in the wood stove and began to read once again.

Donncha, Odhrán, and Siobhán as told by Donncha

I think I shall stick with referring to you as Siobhán for I am confusing myself otherwise. My mind is still racing, trying to put all these pieces back together.

Siobhán arrived not an hour later. As I said, she had taken to visiting every day. My father and Siobhán had an instant rapport, and they and Nana Fiona had many a fine day playing with me. Da got into the habit of walking Siobhán back to the midwife's house as he said it was good for his hip to get the exercise.

Not wanting to disturb the woman in the house and not wanting to set tongues wagging more than they already were, he would leave her at the top of the road not far from the house and watch until she was safely inside. Weeks went whirling, and by and by Siobhán became heavy with child. Siobhán did visit once in a state of unrest. When we asked why she was so nervous, she relayed that a few minutes before her arrival to Fiona's there had been a rustling behind her. She got an awful fright when she turned to see a person dressed all in black swiftly move behind a stand of trees. Unsure what else to do, she simply hastened to Fiona's. Da ran immediately outside, rushing down the path but returned fifteen minutes later with nothing to report. Siobhán chalked it up to nerves and hormones playing tricks on her, but Father was extra cautious after that.

One afternoon, my father was walking Siobhán home. As they neared the riverside, she stopped abruptly and clutched her belly, taking in a deep breath through her teeth. My father knew all too well what it meant.

Flashes of my birth, and the death of my mother shortly thereafter, came rushing at him like the gushing river they stood beside. They were much closer to my nana's house than to the midwife's so he made the decision to return there. Siobhán knew she would not be able for the long walk back to the midwife's, so she quickly agreed. My father was justifiably anxious. Nana took Siobhán to her bedroom, made her as comfortable as she could, and set Father to work with gathering herbs, making tea and cutting cloth into strips. By the time the sun had begun to dip, Siobhán was in the throes of hard labour. All Da could do was to amuse me in the sitting room while listening to the eerily familiar animal sounds.

There was a knock at the front door just after midnight. No one ever came to the door, especially at that hour; my father slowly, suspiciously opened it. To his great relief, it was Ciara, the midwife. He did not even get the chance to greet her before a deep moan rose from the bedroom. The midwife pushed past him and into the back room.

Five hours later, my bedraggled nana emerged announcing the birth of a healthy baby girl. The midwife determined that Siobhán needed extended bed rest, and if Nana agreed, should stay put until she was stronger. The name Siobhán chose for the child was Orlaith.'

"One day led to the next and the house became a home. My father and Siobhán slowly but most assuredly fell in love. When my father asked Siobhán to marry him she said yes immediately, but Nana Fiona knew that before they wed, Siobhán must be told about the scope that belonged to the family."

Donncha opened his eyes and leaned forward in his chair, looking from one woman to the other.

Orlaith raised the teapot saying, "I think we all need a hot drop," and proceeded to top up all three cups with tea, as Donncha rubbed his hands together.

"After all these years, how could I have happened upon you two in such a remarkable way? I always expected that I would recognize you, Siobhán, from the description my father constantly relayed. This might seem naïve, but I did not recognize you at all."

Siobhán stood from her chair, saying, "I'm not surprised in the least that you did not recognize me Donncha, for you were just a babe the last time you saw me. I certainly did not recognize you, as you look so unlike Odhrán. Perhaps something would have sparked if you had used your original name, Rónán. There was something familiar about you, as though I had known you somehow, when Orlaith first brought you here.

"I so well remember passionate conversations with your father about Ireland's devastation. Our deepest sadness was, of course, the unnecessary loss of life, but we often spoke of the ravaging that our language took. So many of the families that died, or left, spoke only Irish, while the political leaders and the rich were English-speaking. After over two thousand years of a dominantly Irish speaking country, a five-year catastrophe all but destroyed it.

"I have kept my eyes and ears out for your father for years but had given up all hope of ever seeing him again. I thought about travelling in search of the two of you, but instead, did as your father had asked, which was to flee, try to settle in a safe place and wait for him to find us. We have had a good and safe life here and I am grateful for that. I really had given up all hope, but here you are. It feels like only yesterday that Fiona and your father sat me down to tell me about your family's scope.

"Your nana said that it had been passed down through the female bloodline on your mother's side. It had come to your great-grandmother, Róisín, by chance."

*D*onncha **stood and** stretched a few moments before re-taking his seat.

"Yes, indeed," Donncha asserted "Pure happenstance it was. Róisín had been hanging wash on the line when an old woman of the road approached asking for food and shelter for the night."

The Old Woman of the Road as told by Róisín

The old woman was striking in her looks, as she had one green eye and one blue. She was obviously unwell, consequently I invited her in, fed her and let her sleep on a cot by the fire. There was no improvement in her health the following morning and, in fact, her watery eyes and hot forehead confirmed her suffering. Laying cool compresses on her face and wrists did little to reduce her rising temperature.

The ancient woman was deeply touched by my attention and care. Her eyes followed me moving around the house, cooking and seeing to chores. After a second night passed, the woman asked for the small cloth bag she had brought with her and I tucked it gently under her arm. The woman said she was now ready to leave this world and enter the next. She had searched, in vain for her long-lost sister, but could neither search nor delay any longer.

I assumed the old woman was delirious, as her fragile hands dipped inside that cloth bag and removed an object wrapped in purple velvet, saying, 'I have been the caretaker of a sacred scope that is magic—pure and simple.' If used correctly, she'd said, one could be transported to a place called 'An Clann Teach'; roughly translated, that would be 'The Family Home.' Her family was all there now, waiting for her and her sister. The scope had been handed down from mother to daughter until that family had no more daughters, at which point the last living female of the line would hand it to an appropriate, trustworthy, and deserving female who was wise in the ways of the earth.

I suggested the woman take a rest and get a little sleep, but she was having none of that, and insisted I listen to her tale.

"You see child, I cannot find my sister and I am the last daughter in my mother's line. My sister was born a few minutes after me, so she is the youngest and rightful minder. I must hand this power, the magic scope, to a female or dispose of it. If I do not pass it down, this scope will turn to dust in five years. No other families will ever enter An Clann Teach. Now, there may be a few who know of its existence, who would use it for ill, but this must never happen. Do you understand? This cannot happen or all will be lost to the families who live there."

I still believed the old woman was raging, but I was so drawn into the story and wished that perhaps such a place existed. I asked where the scope originated.

The old womans eyes glowed with pride and emotion and she heaved a deep-rooted sigh. It was evident, as she began to speak, that a long-held responsibility was being lifted off her shoulders, shed like the skin of a snake.

"I believe that you, my dear, if you chose to accept this gift, will be the new minder. What are its origins you ask? It comes from the second-wave of inhabitants of this sacred island. The Tuatha dé Danaan."

From her bag, she withdrew a small, well-worn leather book. As she handed it to me, she shared its story, the yellowed pages crinkling beneath our fingertips as we both felt its ancient energy. "This has been passed down many, many times and I am unsure who first penned it. It tells the origin story of this magical object. Here, please, read the words from those that have gone before."

19

The Tuatha dé Danaan

A race known as Tuatha dé Danaan or People of the Goddess Danú reigned over ancient Ireland after they conquered the Firbolg. The Danaan were a powerful people, gifted in many ways, including arts, science, poetry and music; though they are best known for their powers of druidry.

The Danaan's acquired and brought skills from four northern cities of Findias, Murias, Falias and Gorias. When they departed the four northern islands to seize Ireland, they were gifted four treasures, or talismans, one from each city. From Findias, they brought *Lai Fail*, the Stone of Destiny, which roared when touched by the foot of Ireland's rightful King. From Murias, they brought Dagda's cauldron, known as *Coir na Dagda*. It is said that no one ever walked away hungry. Gorias sent them Lú's spear, *Sleá Luin*. Whoever fought with this spear would be victorious in battle. Lastly, from Findias they brought Nuada's Sword of Light, *An Claiomh Solais*. There was no escape from this once it had been unsheathed.

These treasures represented the four elements. The cauldron—water; the spear—fire; the stone—earth; and the sword—air. The people erected a sacred site; a magnificent stone structure constructed to align with the night sky and the heavens. On the morning of the winter solstice, the first rays of the sun would strike the front of the structure. Light would flood the pitch-black inner chamber through a roof box, which was specifically designed to capture a thin beam of light. The stretching light beam passed into the passage and onto the rear stone. This sacred chamber was, and still is, a place of great power.

What is generally not known, is that there was a fifth treasure given to the Danaan. It was given by a druid priestess named Uirsea to Éirú, one of the Danaan high women. The treasure has come to be known over the years as 'the scope,' because it resembles what we now call a telescope, but its proper name is *Mobhrí*. It does not represent an element—it represents family; specifically the mother. Roughly translated it would mean, 'my reason'. My reason for being that is.

While it is undeniable that males play a vital and important role in the proliferation of life, it is the females who guarantee the survival of our species. It is the mother who carries the child from conception, who nurtures it within her own body and, after the perilousness of childbirth, nurtures it with her own milk. It tends to the mother, who is called upon in life the one thing we all desire, that being, unconditional love. It is the mother who weaves the invisible thread that binds us all.

Uirsea created this Mobhrí especially for Éirú to pass on through the female lines, to keep the Druidic Goddesses alive. Éirú was given instruction by Uirsea on its use. I want to stay focused on the Mobhrí and not meander down the path of elaborate details concerning the use of the monument. Éirú was instructed to enter the chamber on the third year of the winter solstice with the Mobhrí, in order to activate its power.

The Tuatha dé Danaan began preparing for the third-year solstice thirteen days before the event. The celebratory site they chose was atop a hill, where a massive oak tree stood. The tallest of the Danaan men walked in a circle, one hundred and fifty paces, to create an outside wall circumference. Large stones were piled thirteen high. The thirteen-stone-high wall was constructed by the men as a sign of respect for women's thirteen monthly cycles.

Five openings were incorporated as part of the wall for the representations of the gifts bestowed upon the Danaan's by the northern cities. Once that outer wall was completed, the eldest woman, Oonagh walked into the centre of the circle. From there, she began to wend a spiral path, while the Danaan people followed, laying stones behind her wide enough apart for two people to walk. Oonagh finally exited through the opening nearest the oak. In the centre, where Oonagh had begun her spiral walk, the Danaan people dug a deep firepit, over which they placed a hand-chiseled stone slab.

Eating, singing, and dancing commenced. The festivities and fire continued into the wee hours of the morning, until the high priestess deemed it time for chanting. The stone circle was surrounded inside and out by the Tuatha dé Danaan as Oonagh began a low melodic chant. When several seconds had passed, she touched the arm of the woman on her left and she too began to chant. This routine was repeated until everyone present was chanting in low rhythmic tones. Inside the stone circle four female attendants: one child, one adolescent, one new mother and one grandmother, waited by the fire.

At the direction of Oonagh, the chanting ceased and there remained only silence, save for the hushed breeze blowing through the long grasses. Éiru was carried inside the circle by four men, through the fifth opening in the wall. She sat cross-legged on a small wooden dais; her dark robe and thick hair decorated with leaves, roots, and sweet scented herbs; her large eyes accentuated by purple dye smeared in upward strokes along her cheekbones.

Also on the dais were four bowls and an object wrapped in purple cloth. The men gently lowered the dais to the ground in front of the four waiting females and returned to the outer circle. The four then surrounded Éiru. The robed woman stood, black hair cascading down her back to near her knees. The attendants removed the flora from her robe and hair, and dropped them into the water of the hand-carved stone tub.

Subsequently, each of the females lifted from the dirt a wooden bowl. Éiru untied the sash of her robe and let it slide down her shoulders to the ground, revealing all of her moon-coloured skin. The youngest female approached and rubbed a dark green paste made of grass and clay from the first bowl to the tops of Éiru's feet.

The girl said, "This represents the gift of earth. The place where we walk through our days as well as the place to where we will return at our journey's end."

The second bowl, picked up by the new mother, consisted of black ash, taken from the young mother's dwelling. She rubbed the dusty powder in and around Éiru's navel.

"This I place at the core of motherhood; the place from which we cut the new child away from our inner fire and into its own breath."

The adolescent picked up the third bowl. This smaller bowl was empty, but bore a cover. There were two holes through the lower rim, opposite each other. Holding the bowl to Éiru's throat, the girl blew through one end so that her breath exited out the other, and onto Éiru's throat.

"May our breath live on through our stories and through our song."

Finally, the grandmother picked up the fourth, larger bowl, which was filled with a mixture of sea, river, and rainwater. From the centre, she removed a luminescent crown made of seashells, river trout scales, and salmon bones. This she placed on Éiru's head.

"Water is the sustainer of all life. It slakes our thirst and nourishes us with abundant gifts. For this we are truly grateful."

The grandmother dipped her fingers into the water and touched the temples of Éiru. She then poured the remaining liquid atop Éiru's head. The salty fluid trickled down her forehead, her mouth and chin, and dripped to her bare feet.

Éiru was handed the purple cloth. This she unrolled. The Mobhrí was nestled in its centre and Éiru lifted it up above her head.

"May wisdom and truth be shown to us by the power about to be granted to me by Uirsea of the North."

Éiru handed the Mobhrí to the grandmother and stepped up to the tub. The chanting commenced, as Éiru slowly immersed herself into the sweet and spicy scented water. Two High Priests approached. One sat at her left side, one at her head. The one at her side lifted her arm from the water and began tattooing her wrist with a spiraling blue and green snake. The other tattooed her forehead with a purple and gold one.

The process was concentrated and extreme. First, the pointed sticks were dipped into hot flames, then into a dye mixture, and then into Éiru's skin. The priests executed this task with precise, swift, staccato rhythm, hands flying back and forth with their sharp tools. The chanting aided Éiru in her resolve to withstand the process, as did the constantly warmed water from the immersion of hot stones and the encouraging words of her attendants.

The chanting continued for just over an hour, as Éiru reclined in the water and received the undulating symbols of power and mystery. These symbols formalized a new status for Éiru—that of High Priestess. Éiru was helped from the water and dried with animal hide. A new deep purple robe was placed around her shoulders, and she was ushered back to the wooden dais. The Mobhrí, protected in its purple cloth, lay nestled in her lap.

The same four men carried Éiru down the hill as the Danaan people followed behind, until once again, Éiru was gently placed on the ground, this time at the entrance. The Tuatha dé Danaan joined hands for a second time and chanted as Éiru entered and made her way back into the deep chamber. Éiru removed the Mobhrí from its cloth and held it in her cupped hands.

It had the look of glass, wood, and metal, but it was actually made from white and black crystals from deep within the northern lands and the caves of Brachabhí, where Uirsea lived. The crystal was hollowed out through the centre, much like the sacred place where Éiru stood. A metal element, which to this day has not been discovered by mortals, allows the crystal tube to be twisted, like a modern-day telescope. The section of the Mobhrí that was made of wood was ornamentally scribed with letters of the first Irish language, known as Ogham.

Éiru could hear the chanting of her people as the sunlight made its way over the distant hills. Holding the Mobhrí in her left hand, she slowly twisted it with her right. As the narrow ray of solstice light entered the sacred chamber, Éiru pointed one end of the Mobhrí up toward the roof box, welcoming it. As the light made its way to the back of the chamber, so did she, until her back rested against the farthest wall. The crystal began to emit an ethereal humming sound, matching the exact note that the Danaans sang outside the monument. She held the scope to her heart. She could feel the warm light pass through her and onto the wall behind her. The chamber was fully illuminated now.

The crystal sang, the Danaan sang, and Éiru sang. The Druid Uirsea appeared before Éiru. She was back lit by the whitest light Éiru had ever seen. Its radiant glow gave Uirsea's short curls a luminous chestnut halo. Éiru had never felt so full of absolute joy and love. Tears flowed freely at the realization that she had been the chosen one. How could she be so worthy of this honour?

As if Uirsea could read her thoughts, she smiled, and the light around them grew brighter still.

'You are my chosen one, Éiru of the Danaan.'

Speaking in a clear and melodious voice, Uirsea instructed Éiru in the ways of the Mobhrí. When she had finished, she raised her hand in farewell, and slowly faded.

As quickly as the light had come, it vanished—gone for another year. Éiru emerged from the dark and out into the morning sun. The people gathered round to hear what Éiru had experienced. First, she described the encounter in the chamber, and then gave an account of what had transpired with Uirsea.

"Uirsea has revealed to me certain truths and future events. There will come a time when the Tuatha dé Danaan will be forced to leave this place. Our memories and monuments will remain for thousands of years, and future people of this land will know our names and speak of us with great respect and awe. Where we go will remain to be seen and it may very well be that we are forced underground. But through this Mobhrí, our earth goddess will survive. It is to be handed down from female to female, preferably mother to daughter, or sister-to-sister, beginning with me.

"At the time of my choosing I shall set free the light from this crystal and enter 'An Clann Teach', the family home. Here my family members and I can be reunited and live in an abundant other land forever. My daughter or sister in turn may do the same. If the female is the last in line on the mother's side, then she must bequeath the Mobhrí to another; this woman must be trustworthy and wise to the ways of the earth goddess, for if this Mobhrí winds up in unscrupulous hands, negative forces could easily destroy An Clann Teach. Should this Mobhrí be lost, or should there be a time when it lays with no minder, it will crumble to dust after five years.

"I will teach my daughter how to unleash the Mobhrí's power and she, in turn, will teach her daughter. As a reward for her service, she may, at the time of her own choosing, retreat to An Clann Teach. She will know when the time is correct. She may be twenty, she may be ninety. Her age does not matter; she will know when it is her time. She must, however, transfer ownership of the Mobhrí to a female who knows its magic and the responsibility that its ownership bears. Our descendants will live on the earth long after the Danaan have retreated to their New World. The Tuatha dé Danaan will have the pleasure and duty of passing along this Mobhrí, quietly and secretly, among the future inhabitants of this our holy land.

"We must now pray for the blessings bestowed upon us. We must give thanks for The Cauldron of Water, the Spear of Fire, the Stone of Earth, the Sword of Air, and the Mobhrí of the Mother; of family."

Norah slowly closed the diary drawing a deep breath as she did, then looked to her mother, exhaling loudly. "Are you thinking what I'm thinking?"

Cocking her head to the side, Úla replied, "If you're thinking about putting the kettle on, then the answer is yes."

The two women moved about the kitchen, silently, each deep in their own thoughts. Norah removed a new box of biscuits from the press and laid a handful on a plate.

Úla held up a hand in protest. "None for me thanks. I'm watching my weight."

Norha promptly replied, "Oh don't worry, these are gentle biscuits." Úla laughed. Norah did too, adding, "I mean they're just plain tea biscuits, nothing with coatings or loads of sugar."

"Go on then," sighed Úla, "put my name on a few. And, let's get back to the journal."

20

As they returned to the sitting room, steaming mugs in hand, Norah noted, "There's nothing quite compares to the aroma of a fresh cuppa."

"Couldn't agree more," replied Úla. "Now then, where were we? Oh yes, Róisín was about to open the treasure."

Old Woman of the Road as told by Róisín

I was so engrossed with the story, I hardly noticed the old woman opening her bag to remove an object wrapped in cloth. She placed it in my hands.

"Go on dear girl, open our treasure," the old woman invited.

Hands slightly shaking in anticipation, I unrolled the cloth to find the very Mobhrí the woman had spoken of.

How fine it was. The white and black crystal, wood, metal—more beautiful than any object I had ever seen or owned. The old woman was beaming with pleasure. Still skeptical but fascinated, I asked if she would show me how the Mobhrí is activated. The crone said yes, in a day or two, when she was feeling stronger, she would indeed not only show me how to unleash its power but would be handing me its authority and responsibility, if I chose to accept it.

Two days passed without incident. I continued giving the woman herbal tinctures and teas, and the woman became quite revitalized. The last evening we were together, we sang well into the wee hours of the morning. Both of us went to sleep feeling a strong sense of kinship.

The next morning, I arose later than usual and when I went out to start the tea, neither the old woman nor the cloth bag was to be seen. I flung wide the front door and leapt off the two front steps, tossing aside the tea towel still in my hands. The old woman was standing under a large ash tree in the bright morning sun, turning this way and that, and covering her eyes with her long slender hands. I ran to her, out of breath.

"You didn't think I had left you, did you, dear?" she asked.

"Well, I did think that perhaps you had decided to leave without saying goodbye."

"Not at all, not at all. You are my choice; you are the one. I would never have done that to you. It is a perfect spring day. The blossoms have all but burst forth, the sun is shining, and this is the perfect spot, yes, the perfect spot. At this moment in time, I shall return to my family, and you shall learn how to use the Mobhrí. At this moment in time, you will decide whether to carry on the living history of the Tuatha dé Danaan.

"Listen closely. The Mobhrí must be hidden in a safe place. It will not rust or decay but keeping it covered is wise. Do you see the marks on the wood? This is the first written language of our people, Ogham. These marks represent the Goddess Danú.

"When it is your time to depart from this earth, you must find a place that is extremely private. Once you release the light source you will have but two hours in which to enter its splendour. You can adjust the length of time the light shines with this one thin band, here, see?" The old woman turned the slender black band counter-clockwise. "You can set the shine time for half a minute if you like, or, as I said, for up to two hours. If that time expires before you are ready, the light will disappear and you will have to re-activate the Mobhrí. This is important information, for if you are entering An Clann Teach alone, you have the two hours to find a safe place to store the Mobhrí and return to the light. You are young and I feel strongly that you will have a daughter to hand this to.

"Many husbands and families live in An Clann Teach. We all pray that the man you are soon to meet and love can be trusted. I cannot imagine you falling in love with the kind of person who would not be delighted with this eventuality. It is true enough, however, that you will prob-ably have only the one child. The keeper of the Mobhrí has tended to have only one, or perhaps, as in my mother's case, two children. This is why I have been searching for my younger sister. We were separated thirty years ago, when a woman we did not know saw us open the light for our mother and father to pass into. My sister and I created a diversion. The woman chased my sister in one direction, thinking she had it, while I ran in the other with the Mobhrí wrapped in my shawl.

"If I do not depart soon, it may be too late, for I am older than you might guess. I must do what I must do. I have left a note on my pillow with information about my sister.

If in your travels, you come across her, I would ask you to send her to us.

"To activate the Mobhrí, you hold it in your hands in this manner." The woman held out her palms in a curve and let the Mobhrí cradle in them.

"Take a deep breath and repeat these words: *Goddess Danú An Clann Teach.* You must then bring the Mobhrí up to your chest, like this, and give it two turns to the right."

As the woman did this, beams of light shone out through the end of the crystal. Looking at the light pouring from the open end of the Mobhrí was very like peering at water in a stream when sunlight penetrates it; crystal clear, slightly undulating and pure. The woman gave the Mobhrí two turns to the left. The Mobhrí shone no more, but the light beam remained in front of us.

"If you wish to see inside the scope, to see An Clann Teach, then give it one turn to the left.

"I can hand this to you now my dear girl. Do you wish to be the minder of this ancient gift, or shall I bury it somewhere and let it return to dust?"

I instantly agreed to be the minder. With that, the woman handed the Mobhrí to me and spoke for the last time.

"You have been so very kind to me and I look forward to seeing you again, down the road. I am weary and will now bid you farewell. Mind yourself and do not let this get into the hands of anyone who might use it for ill."

She wrapped me in her weary, frail arms which still held me strongly for a good few moments, and then into my hands placed two pearls and a golden ring.

"These pearls belonged to my sister and me, given to us by our parents before they departed. They are yours now. If you ever come across my sister, show them to her so she will know you are my chosen female and the rightful minder of the Mobhrí.

"My mother gave the gold ring to me. You can pass this along through your female family line as well, as that is part of its tradition."

The old woman stepped into the beam of light. The expression on her face could only be described as euphoric. She raised her hand and both she and the light slowly faded.

I stood for a number of moments, marvelling at what I had just witnessed. When I returned inside I found a paper the old woman had left on her pillow.

I know the chances of you coming across my sister are slight, but I simply cannot leave here without someone knowing about her. I am sure, if she is still alive, that she is looking for me as well. She is not that notable a person. When last I saw her, her hair was quite white but still had a smattering of auburn colour, but thirty years will have changed many things. She was of average build and quite ordinary looking, like myself. She walked with a slight limp, as one leg was a little shorter than the other. Her most distinguishing marks, though, would be hard to miss. Like me, her right eye is green and her left is blue. Her name is Eimear. There is one secret I carry for her, that is known only to me, until this moment, and that is, that she was desperately in love with someone from the village where we lived. While this in itself may not sound unusual, it was, for the person she loved was the shoppe-keeper, whose name was Catherine. She never professed this to anyone but me.

Donncha looked to Siobhán, "Would you like to continue with your memories?" Siobhán did not hesitate and took up where Donncha left off.

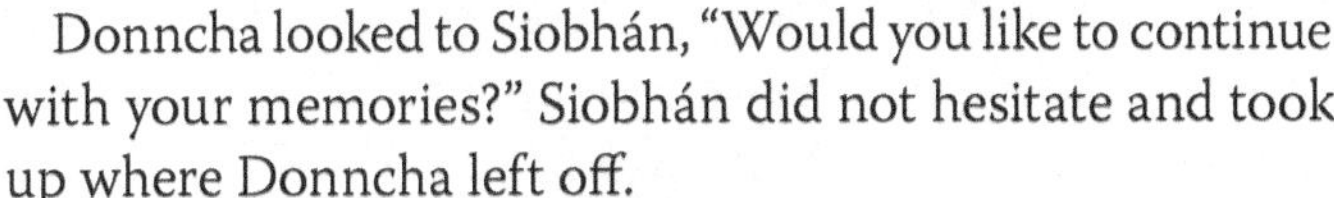

21

Siobhán

When Odhrán, asked me to marry him, I was overjoyed. Tongues, however, had already been set to wagging about us living under the same roof with no consecrated vows. The villagers were emphatic in their petition to investigate such scandalous activities. Father John, who was the local parish priest, was well aware of the fact that my husband had perished at sea. He was also aware that I had been lodging with the midwife, Ciara, but that one day I seemed to vanish. The villagers whispered to him that the local midwife had been setting off on long walks every few days. They all rightfully assumed that it was to me she went and told him such.

Orlaith was barely a month old, and I was still recuperating from her difficult birth. The midwife arrived that day and examined Orlaith and me, pronouncing us well, but urged me to remain inactive until my body regained its lost strength. At her departure, elevenses tea was set at the table. A beautiful morning it was, thus Fiona opened the two windows by the dining table to allow fresh air to circulate throughout.

Involved in our hearty chat, we were. So much so, that none of us heard the approaching Father John. Life is ironic, is it not? If we had held our conversation on any other day, if we had heard him approaching, or even if our windows had been closed, life would have turned out very differently. As it happens, not only were we deciding how to go about our marriage, but this was also the day Odhrán and your nana chose to tell me about the Mobhrí.

We decided it would be for the best to wait a few weeks to wed, until I was stronger. Odhrán would go to the local Father (the very one under the window) in the morning and make arrangements. If the conversation had ended there, Father John could easily have been pacified and would likely have left things alone, without incident.

However, Odhrán and Fiona indicated that before I agreed to marry Odhrán, I must be told of their family history and responsibilities with regard to a secret treasure that they possessed. This, we were sure, piqued Father John's curiosity and he thus continued his motionless eavesdropping.

Odhrán and Fiona recounted the story of the Mobhrí and the importance of its existence and safekeeping. I, being the kind of person that I am, was captured by the implications of such a gift. Fiona even brought out the scope, to demonstrate. She turned it once to the left and I eagerly gazed through the eyepiece. We spoke at length about An Clann Teach, and the Tuatha dé Danaan. I am sure Father John was mortified by what he heard.

The following morning, Ciara banged emphatically upon the door. Out of breath and shaken, she was. According to what she had just overheard while passing the Saint Frances Chapel, the clergy, some of the townspeople, and two constables were making their way to Fiona's, to deal with the unspeakable evil alive and well within the place. Some pagan icon was needing to be destroyed, according to Father John. What scared the midwife most were their plans to remove the children and place them in Catholic homes.

Of course, Ciara knew there was no evil within Fiona's home, and the four of us quickly deduced that Father John had come for a poke-around. It confirmed our suspicion that it had been Father John who startled me on the path some weeks earlier. We realized finding an open window would have been too great a temptation for the man who no doubt passionately preached about the woeful nature of temptation. He must have slunk beneath the widow in order to listen to our conversation, as there is no other way for him to have known the intimate details of our lives and history. Odhrán was panicked and angrily paced the floor. Fiona, being a calm, collected and logically-minded woman, removed herself to her bedroom, and returned a minute later, carrying a bag.

The bag, she said, held not only the Mobhrí, but a tin with the little money she had saved, a watch, two pearls and a golden ring. The ring was handed to Odhrán, who quickly put it in his pocket. Odhrán and I were very confused as to what Fiona was up to, but she quickly laid out the reality of the situation.

There would be no stopping the onslaught, therefore the logical solution for their predicament was for her to retreat to An Clann Teach, as she would not be able to outrun those who were headed our way.

Of course, Odhrán and I spoke up directly and were adamant that she should join us in flight. Fiona was resolute in her thinking, however, as she emphasized that the children's lives were now at stake. That should be the focus and priority. Going to An Clann Teach was not a burden and in fact, the thought of seeing her mother again was a beautiful thing.

Poor Odhrán, his face went ashen with the thought of losing his mother, but he knew it was the logical choice if they were to save their two children. In the last moments, before Fiona stepped into the light, she stood before Odhrán and touched his flushed, wet cheeks. She softly said, "Odhrán my cuisleán (dear one) we shall meet again down the road. There is no need or time for sorrowful good-byes. You must do as I say and move forward in life."

Our bags were not very big—we did not have very much. It took only minutes to assemble ourselves. Ciara walked with us down the path and along the river, to where the main dirt road led to the village. We had decided to cross and make our way over the headlands, to avoid the village. The midwife was in the lead and crossed the narrow road first. Odhrán, the children, and I had only just begun to cross when we heard voices. A rabble of villagers was in full view, running toward us, shouting. We crossed to the opposite side, alarmed and distressed that we had been seen.

Thinking quickly, and probably saving us all from a fate unimaginable, Ciara said, "They are looking for a man, a woman and two children". Her instructions were clear-headed. She had us switch cloaks and I was to take Orlaith and go over the headlands, since I was still too weak to move very quickly. Taking Odhrán's bag, she cradled it, as one would hold a baby. She, Odhrán and Rónán would move back across the road, making sure the advancing mob saw them. The three would make their way back from whence they came, drawing them away from Orlaith and me.

Your father and I knew it was the only thing to be done. I had the Mobhrí in my bag as well as half the money, the watch, and the pearls. The throng was getting closer, and we did not even have time to say a proper goodbye. All he said was, and I have remembered this as though it were yesterday, "Go. I will find you. If it takes my entire life, I will find you and Orlaith. Go somewhere and stay put until that day. I love you Siobhán. Never forget that."

He removed the golden ring from his pocket and slipped it upon my uncontrollably shaking finger.

We were all distraught but there was no time to devise another plan. All I could do was quickly affirm my love for him and turn away. I had to protect Orlaith and myself. They would have separated us if we had been caught. I also had the Mobhrí, and it was I who had accepted that responsibility.

Siobhán

I moved **quickly through** the trees and made my way to the headlands. It was rough going, as the underbrush was thick, and my clothing kept getting caught in brambles and gorse. Once I reached the headlands, I stopped to rest for an hour. All I had in the way of food was a loaf of bread. I ate half of it to keep my strength up and continued along the ridge for some three hours. I eventually came upon an old, indistinct path. This I followed down to a wider road. Though the day was drizzly, I was in a sweat from the exertion.

I must have looked a sight, as a farmer making his way down the road in his cart stopped to ask if I was needing a lift. I gratefully accepted and when he asked where I was headed, I simply said, 'away.' I sat next to him, trying not to think of what had just transpired. I knew my only hope was to focus on staying as emotionally detached as possible. I knew if I thought too long and hard about Odhrán and you, Donncha, I would collapse into interminable tears.

The farmer was content with silence, and we pushed on for a good two hours, until we came to a small harbour town. I thanked the man for the lift, and he handed me a small sack.

"Not much there," he said, "but I had a big enough break-fast and I have no use for that now. Mrs Flynn always has tea waiting."

I gratefully accepted his offering and continued along the road next to the harbour. I was hungry, as was Orlaith, so I found a private place to rest and respond to our needs. Not resting long, I kept walking, though my arms were full sore from carrying a baby and a bag.

I spied a young couple tilling a small plot of earth and stopped to ask if they might have a room for the night. They had no room in the house but indicated that I was welcome to bed down in the barn. I gratefully accepted their kind invitation to sit with them for a meager but delicious meal. Soon after, I retreated to the barn where Orlaith and I fell into a deep sleep.

I awoke later than I had planned. The sun was close to midway in the sky. I fed Orlaith and went to say goodbye to the couple. They offered me a place to stay for a few more days, but I was anxious to get on my way. From a shelf, the woman took down a cloth sling and put it over my head. Nuzzled in the cloth, Orlaith looked like a little bird in a nest and the burden on my neck and arms was greatly reduced. A loaf of fresh bread was also given to me and, grateful for these kindnesses, we set out on the road once again.

The next several days were a bit of a blur as I was still in a state of shock and wished only to put miles under my feet. I was fearful that some might be looking for me, thus decided a change of name could be wise. I renamed myself from Siobhán Murphy to Teresa Smith. Teresa was a name I had considered for Orlaith, and Smith was a common enough name to be accepted wherever we ended up. Orlaith's name remained the same, being such a wee babe she was as yet unknown to anyone.

I eventually met up with a band of *an lucht siúil*, or Travellers, who brought me here to the far coast. I had stopped to sit on a low stone wall one morning as the sun peeked through black and white bilious clouds. I raised my face to its glow, enjoying steady penetrating heat that I knew would not last very long.

A child's high-pitched squeal roused me from my tranquility, and I looked toward its owner. A little girl was running toward us. Running in front of her was a scruffy orange cat. The long-frayed rope attached to the cat's collar dragged along behind it. The cat jumped atop the wall on which we were seated and ran along it for several yards, until it reached us. It eyed us for a moment, shook its front paw and proceeded to sit and lick its chest fur. The child was still running toward us. I gently reached down and clutched the soaking wet rope.

The child ran to us, gasping, and explained that her name was Margaret. She was seven years old and her cat, named Piper, had escaped her grasp and run away. When I asked where she lived, she looked around in dismay. She and her family had only just arrived to the area and she had been running so long that she was not sure where she was. Droplets of tears formed in her eyes. I assured her that together, we would find her family. I handed her the cat rope and took her hand in mine. Recollecting my things, and holding Orlaith close, we headed down the road, moving in the direction from which Margaret had run. Nary a minute had passed when a stout woman came hurriedly toward us. Margaret ran to her.

The Travellers were a quirky lot. The band that I met, like many of the Travellers of that time, were displaced famine survivors with no homes, no land, and little money. They survived by begging, wandering the country, and taking whatever odd jobs they could acquire, or if need be, stealing. Though some of the children from this family group were quite young, there were no infants, so Orlaith was therefore doted upon and argued over. Brídín, the eldest female, was a force to be reckoned with. Her robust figure and outspoken bossiness would have been hard to live with on an ongoing basis, but she held within her a heart of gold. She took it upon herself to strengthen me. There always seemed to be an extra portion that needed to be eaten and it fell to me to do the job.

Her husband, Lorcan, was a tiny fellow and seeing them together was quite comical. He was wiry; the number one on a hall door. He moved quickly and spoke faster than anyone I have met to this day, while Brídín moved like a tortoise and spoke as though time had nothing better to do than wait.

They had two handsome sons and Margaret. I barely saw the young men as they would be gone all day, knocking doors, begging pennies, stealing chickens, or what have you. Margaret dearly loved her mangy-looking wild cat. She did not want to let the beast out of her site, so Brídín had tied a slender rope around its neck in the hopes that Margaret could keep it captive.

Not everyone was happy with our presence. Brídín's father, Joseph, was not enthralled with either one of us. As far as he was concerned, we were interlopers, as were two other people travelling with the group. It is fair to say that he had lost trust in life itself and was not shy about expressing his aggravations or misgivings.

His prized possession was that of a half-broken chair upon which he would sit, smoking his pipe. He oftentimes glared at us and would obsessively pull his pocket watch in and out of his waistcoat pocket, dropping the very unsubtle hint that it was time for us to go.

He was a resentful man, bent and frail, yet rather commanding. His intent gaze and nearly toothless snarl would at times make me nervous and downright uncomfortable.

Mostly, I could not help but pity him and the hardships he had been forced to endure. While he and Brídín had survived the great starvation, his wife and four sons had not. The five had all died with nothing in their stomachs but bitter grass. The startling thing about Joseph was, at nightfall, when the instruments materialized, when the songs were sung, he would come alive. I think the music was what kept him from going mad with grief. It was plain to see that he would retreat to a distant place in his soul, where life was joyful and full of hope. The next morning, however, would see him back again in his chair with a scowling face on him. Brídín would give out to him for his behaviour but he would just grumble and turn his back to us all.

He mistrusted me but was downright abrasive with the two other visitors who had linked themselves into the chain of their band. Interestingly enough, the two other people were of the Choctaw Indian Nation from the Americas.

To tell you the truth, I have no clue how the Choctaw Nation discovered the sufferings and atrocities befalling the Irish, but in 1847, they called an assembly, and their people raised several hundred dollars toward famine relief.

The Choctaw knew the pain of starvation all too well. In the winter of 1831, thousands of Choctaw people were removed, by force, from their ancestral lands in Mississippi. They were sent to Oklahoma, but almost half of them perished during the relocation. While this may not seem to have any bearing on the Irish people, it possesses a compelling parallel.

The two Choctaw recounted their history and explained to me that sixteen years previously, as part of the European colonisation, their people had suffered grievously due to their oppressors. This prompted their sympathetic generosity and show of solidarity, if you will, to the Irish people.

The Choctaw sent two members of their nation over to Ireland with the funds. The woman was named Mantema, meaning 'to deliver something sacred'; the man was called Anoli, which translates as 'to convey news'.

These two were chosen because their names fit the purpose of the journey. Mantema and Anoli had decided to travel through Ireland for a time, to get a real understanding for the Irish people and our history. They had met Brídín and she, being the caretaker that she was, had taken them under her wing, just as she had Orlaith and me.

Margaret was entranced by the two Choctaw: by their skin—a beautiful shade of copper, compared to her stark alabaster—and their straight pitch-black hair, compared to her apricot curls. She loved their folkloric tales and at night we could hear her re-telling the stories to her cat, much to the amusement of us all, especially Mantema and Anoli. Margaret's favourite was *When Parents Ask Their Children To Be Noisy.*

This title caused Margaret to double over with laughter and since hearing it, she constantly looked toward the sky for signs of an eclipse.

When Parents Ask Their Children To Be Noisy

Do you know what an eclipse is? Today we know that when the moon passes in front of the sun and blocks it out, all is still safe. But our ancestors believed that an eclipse was dangerous. They thought a black squirrel was nibbling at the sun!
They knew that noise frightened squirrels. So, whenever a solar eclipse began, all of the people would make a terrible noise until the squirrel was frightened away from the sun.
Children were asked to scream, shout and yell while Grownups shot rifles into the air and banged pots and pans together. It was a frightening racket! And do you know what? It always worked.

As much as I loved that tale and others, and some were shockingly similar to Irish ones, what I remember most is a poem they would recite from a tribe called the Gabrielinos, from the western Americas. I do not know if it even has a title, but I remember it to this day, as it is every mother's prayer.

I know not if the voice of man
can reach to the sky
I know not if the mighty one
will hear as I pray
I know not if the gifts I ask
will all granted be
I know not if the world of old
we truly can hear
I know not what will come to pass

in our future days
I hope that only good will come
my children, to you

One evening as I sat in the caravan taking care of Orlaith's hunger, Anoli and Mantema wandered inside. Brídín had just handed me a strong hot cup of tea and had seated herself at the head of the table, with Margaret at the far end. The table possessed only three proper legs. The fourth consisted of chunks of wood stacked atop each other, thus the table tended to wobble precariously when in use.

Margaret kept a firm hold of her cat's lead and stroked the matted fur on its struggling body. Within a few minutes, the creature flopped to her lap, surrendering to the futile attempt of escape.

"Tell Anoli and Mantema about the selkies, Mammy."

"Selkies?" inquired Anoli.

Brídín gestured for the two Choctaw to sit. The sizable brown teapot on the table's centre was full with piping hot liquid. Brídín poured the brown-black tea into four chipped cups and passed the sugar bowl to Anoli.

"Tell them the story of Declan McNamara of Inis Oirr and his selkie," prompted Margaret.

"Indeed," replied Brídín. Selkies are half-seal half-human creatures who make a habit out of slipping from beneath their seal skins to uncover their human form, to luxuriate on the craggy rocks by the sea.

Stories of both male and female selkie seals are common among Irish and Scots and many of their stories share striking similarities. Declan McNamara, of Inis Oirr, is one such tale . . .

23

The Selkies as told by Brídín

nis Oirr is the smallest of the three Aran Islands, off the west coast of Clare.

Declan McNamara was a bachelor who lived alone in a cottage on the Eastern shore of Inis Oirr. He and his four elder brothers had been born and raised in the cottage built by their grandparents. There were not many residents on the island by the time Declan and his brothers came of age, and his brothers had long and ever ago departed for the mainland to find wives and employment. Declan had no intention of ever leaving the island, or the cottage, as he relished the detached life of an out islander. When his parents passed on, he inherited the home.

A self-sufficient bachelor by the age of twenty-eight, Declan's traditional gardening methods—which consisted of mixing layers of sand and seaweed on top of rocks to create fertile soil—kept him amply supplied with potatoes and other vegetables. Like most men on the islands, he was also a skilled fisherman. Declan and his father had built themselves a good strong currach that Declan kept in pristine working condition.

"A what?" interrupted Mantema.

"A currach," repeated Brídín. "It is a lightweight boat made from canvas, stretched over thin flat strips of wood and covered in tar. It is built to withstand the rough open seas but is still quite vulnerable to large swells and hidden rocks. It is said that the fishermen of the Aran Islands made it a point to never learn to swim, since the chances of survival in the frigid waters was so low. They felt it better to swallow the icy water and drown quickly."

Declan went out in his currach one fine morning but was having little luck in catching any sizable fish. Resigning himself to the defeat of the day, he let his little boat drift along the shore for a time, enjoying the rustic landscape of the island. Just before turning into his favourite bay, as he rounded a jetty of rocks, Declan sat bolt upright in a state of half shock, half embarrassment. Amid the assemblage of rocks lay a woman of immense beauty wearing nothing but an untroubled smile.

The oar that had been in his left hand fell to the bottom of the boat with a resounding crash, causing the woman to flinch and rise to her elbows. Try as he might, Declan could not remove his gaze from the woman's dark enchanting eyes. The woman seemed surprisingly unperturbed by his presence. In fact, as she wiped several strands of hair from her forehead, her smile grew to twice the size it had been.

She clutched in her hands what Declan thought to be a dark anorak. As she stood, her drenched ebony hair fell around her. With an impish grin, the lovely vision dove headfirst into the pounding surf. Declan cried out, as surviving in the bitterly cold January waters was near to impossible. Leaning over the side of the currach, he could see her nimble form swim beneath him. Then, she was gone.

He spent an hour scouring the coastline, calling to her, but the only returning sounds were of the frothy waves breaking upon the rocks. That night, as he ate his brown bread and seaweed broth by the light of his hearth fire, he considered a queer notion. *What if the raven-haired beauty had been a selkie?* Declan pulled from his shelf a dusty book given to him by his brother Eamon. Finding the chapter on selkies, he read about their transformation from seal to human and back again. The book recounts numerous sightings of these beautiful supposed mythological beings, shedding their seal skin, exposing their human form beneath. He read how the sea is the only home in which they are truly free, though many have been known to survive and live with human mates on land.

Though Declan longed to see his beauty again, life and work distracted him, and two months passed without incident. Then one day, as he rowed his currach toward his neighbour's bay, he heard a disheartening cry. As he edged closer to the rocks, he caught sight of her. The ends of her long hair were ensnarled in the neighbour's fishing net. The harder she struggled the more tangled she became. Her right hand flailed wildly at the net in an effort to free herself, while her left hand kept a firm grip on her sealskin.

Declan spoke softly and edged slowly toward her. He promised to free her from the net if she agreed to return with him to his cottage and become his wife. Having no alternative, she nodded her agreement. Declan gently took hold of her sealskin and placed it in a canvas bag on the bottom of the currach. Then, using his knife, he cut away the knotted black strands from the net and lifted her from the water.

"I shall call you Saoirse as it means 'freedom'. Freedom is the one thing I know you will one day reclaim. For now though, you shall be my wife and the mother of my children."

Saoirse and Declan had many fine years together and produced several healthy children, but as is the way of all selkies, the call of the wild and foaming shoreline, combined with the call of her unearthly family became too great a necessity to deny.

Declan felt a pounding in his heart as he returned home one day from fishing, only to find a letter upon their bed, along with the golden ring that Saoirse had worn on her right hand.

Now it's home I go
Under the waves I dive
Under the winds that blow
To you I've left three sons
A host of daughters
Upon the bed the ring you gave
I won't deny our love
Won't regret the years I've stayed
You can't deny you took them from me
I've traded in my locks
For my skin of leather
That I found beneath the thatch
I've traded in our love
For the surging of the sea
With her wild and foaming shoreline
I shall reclaim the fold
Of my unearthly family
They have no doubt been waiting long
Then on the rocks beyond
In the noonday sun I'll dry
Again the seal with woman under
Now it's home I go
Under the waves I dive
Under the winds that blow
Under the winds that blow[1]

---

1 "Selkie Seal Woman", song by Mary Murphy from her CD *Thirty Waves Out*

Siobhán rose from her chair and laid the now sleeping Orlaith on a cosy sheep skin rug that Margaret had placed in a wicker basket. "You are quite the seannachí, Brídín," she said, adoringly. "I could listen to you for hours."

Brídín blushed, trying to deflect the compliment. "Ahh well, a good tale tells itself."

Siobhán lovingly countered, "Without the gifted tongue of the seannachí, a story that could be bright and rapturous is merely a grey stain."

Siobhán

The Choctaw visitors and I would often wander the back lanes and roads with Orlaith, ever the happy little bunting, being passed between the three of us. On one of these wanderings, we met a man named Mr Nevin, who owned a farm in the area. His household consisted of himself, his three sons and his ailing wife. The long and the short of it was that his wife was unable to perform many of the household tasks due to her weakness. He inquired if I might be interested in a mutually agreeable solution.

He offered me an opportunity I couldn't refuse. A small cottage, food, and turf in exchange for household tasks and upkeep that his wife was no longer able to do, and that he could not keep up with while farming. As the three sons were already old enough to work on the farm, I felt sure I could manage this while Orlaith was still so young.

I became quite able bodied in the ways of mending, chopping wood, and gardening. I do not own this place. It still belongs to the Nevins, but I have, rather . . . we have, had many peaceful years residing here. It has been a wonderful place to raise Orlaith.

The first night we slept here, I sobbed for hours, finally releasing the stress and sadness of what had come to pass in my life. Though a dark cloud covered my head the next morning, I also felt grateful to all the people who had come to our aid. Many's a time I think about the kindness and care that was bestowed upon us at that time and do not know how we would have survived without it.

I spent years expecting Odhrán to knock on the front door. As time went on, I assumed it was not to be, and carried on with life as best I could. The hardest part was not knowing what had become of the two of you. Had you been caught, separated, or were you perhaps even dead? These were the questions that would cause me sleepless nights. I cannot tell you how relieved I am that life has been kind enough to show me these answers. Tell us Donncha, what happened to you and Odhrán after I ran with Orlaith up to the headlands?

Úla interrupted the reading. "Norah, speaking of the seannachí, I thought you were going to do a course in storytelling in Donegal."

"Oh, yes. I was." Norah responded flatly. "But one needed to have a fair grasp on Irish language, and I frankly hardly remember any of it from school."

Úla tsked, "Yes, you really should re-learn some of it." Then she tsked, again, which increasingly annoyed Norah. "I mean, as a writer, dear, you should be at least a little versed. It's a bit surprising you've been so apathetic about it."

Norah held her tongue. There were many ways for a person to state their opinions, but Úla was never one for thinking before speaking. Carefully considered words and judgments seemed elusive to her. Norah decided on a response both simple and absolute.

"I'm not having this conversation right now." And she returned to the book.

Donncha

Of course, I do not remember that momentous day. My father said that the midwife's quick thinking is indeed what saved us all.

We moved at lightning speed, Da told me, urged on by Ciara and her quick, strategic thinking but every so often he'd trample brush with his feet, or leave an obvious footprint. At one point, he tore a small piece of cloth from his shirt and stuck it onto a gorse bush, in order to keep our pursuers heading toward us and away from the headlands where you had fled with Orlaith.

It was at this point that my father and I parted company with the midwife; yet another goodbye that required many words with no time at all in which to speak them. Ciara removed the cloak from her back and handed it to my father. It remains his solitary keepsake of you, Siobhán. Ciara continued walking along the low-lying hills, while my father and I began a rapid descent down an entirely different path.

My father was resolute in his decision to hasten to the sea. As heartbreaking as it was going to be to leave his homeland, he concluded that taking us far away, to England, would be the best and safest course of action. He would, in a short time, return to the woman and home he loved. He knew work in England would be more plentiful, and retreating to a place where there was no chance of being found was the best thing to do for Siobhán's sake. He had expected we might return within six months or so, but as you now know, that did not come to pass.

The distracted ticket master gathered up my father's money and instructed him to write his name in the passenger logbook. Not until Da handed the book back, did he remember he had planned on signing with an alias. Alas, it was too late. The ticket man glanced at the page and then up to my father.

'And the little lad? We need his name as well,' he'd said. 'Sorry,' Da replied, and in that moment, he changed my name from Rónán to Donncha, to perhaps confuse those who might be searching for us.

As our ship pulled away from the dock, he spied four men making their way through the crowds, looking intently at people with babies. He was certain that they were looking for a man, a woman and two small children.

My father had never been off the island. Stepping from the boat into a new country made his legs quiver and his mind spin with fear and uncertainty. The first item on his agenda was to find lodging for us. Da said that finding housing was merciless. When landlords answered the door and heard my father's Irish accent, they would either verbally abuse him by flinging nasty comments like gunshot or slam the door in his face.

A night watchman found us one morning, asleep in an abandoned building. He was Irish himself, as well as a father, and took pity on us. He is the one who gave us the address of a widow, Mrs Bruce, who owned a boarding house by the docks. She did not slam the door, nor did she make nasty comments about our homeland. On the contrary, she was kind and generous. Her own children had grown and left home, and she missed having 'little sprouts about the place.' She became my surrogate mother for the thirteen years that we resided with her, and we loved her dearly. She passed away not long ago I am sorry to report, but she was our saving grace and our great fortune.

Work was extremely difficult to obtain but my father was an excellent fisherman. He charmed the wife of the owner of a fishing vessel and started work. My da spent long hours on the water, with Sunday being his one free day. Those are the times I remember best as a child. We would go for long wanderings, skip stones by the sea or perhaps read a book by the fire. As I advanced in years my father taught me to fish and shoot. He taught me carpentry and would read poetry to me before falling asleep. This is where my love of words comes from.

My father worked his fingers to the bone, saving pennies whenever he could, but it was years before he had saved enough money to bring us back here to look for the two of you. Mrs Bruce liked to think of herself a matchmaker and would introduce single women to my father. Many a Sunday evening women would happen to drop by to have a cup of coffee or drop sewing off to Mrs Bruce.

Mrs Bruce would sometimes comment, "You know Odhrán, I do believe that Sophie has a glint in her eye for you," or, "Well, dear me, wasn't she a lovely specimen of a lady? I think she might like it if you were to tip her your cap."

Once, a friend of Mrs Bruce had asked if she could take a boarder for a few days. Mrs Bruce had long and ever ago decided against boarders, but when she found out that the person in question was a single woman of the same age as Odhrán, she quickly agreed. Mrs Bruce spent the day in the kitchen, preparing a baked ham, potatoes, mushy peas, and fresh dinner biscuits.

It was a Sunday night that the woman in question was due to arrive, which was, as usual, the day my father and I spent together. Mrs Bruce was quite insistent that we be home for 'a lovely dinner with a new friend.' I think I must have been about eleven at the time, so I was on to what Mrs Bruce was up to. Throughout the day my father would groan at the thought of another introduction.

He said, "Perhaps we could serve her sheep eye soup. She wouldn't much like that now would she, Donncha my boy?"

We were a bit late getting back to the house. We could see the silhouette of Mrs Bruce by the window. She pulled back the delicate lace curtains and gestured to us as we headed up her drive.

Father wondered if this one would be as prim and proper as that last one, Miss Peregrine. If she had her nose any farther up in the air, she would have stumbled into everything.

We gave each other a sideways glance and let go hearty laughs. We two decided to walk in with smiles upon our faces, as Mrs Bruce always meant so well. Also, a Sunday ham with Mrs Bruce's no doubt trifle dessert had us salivating.

Mrs Bruce opened the front door, wearing a worried look on her face, which did not bode well for the evening. We were not at all prepared for what met our eyes though when we entered the sitting room.

The guest was very robust. She was six feet tall if she was an inch and generously round in front and behind. She pried herself from Mrs Bruce's prized blue antique chair and I swear to this day that I heard the chair groan with relief. The disheveled hair piled high atop her head easily added another four inches to her height. Her voluptuous form came bounding to where we stood like a mighty wave rolling toward a shore. And her prodigious mouth, which was heavily made up with bright red lipstick, descended over me onto the top of my head. Bending forward, she wrapped me in her mighty arms.

Her frame encapsulated me, thereby suffocating me for several seconds. When at last she eased up on her grip, I was subjected to a fierce odour of flowery perfume rising from her dress, engulfing my senses. My olfactories were instantaneously overpowered with the horrid scent and I wriggled free, audibly gasping for air. As I did, her high-pitched cackle let loose and filled the room. Panic reared in my father's eyes, as she looked toward him. Fortunately for him, he was spared my fate when Mrs Bruce announced that tea was ready to be served.

Miss Abigail Burgess was certainly the most flamboyant person I had ever come across, and one could not fault her for a lack of humour. The main trouble was that in her mind everything was cause for boisterous cackling.

Mrs Bruce began gathering the dinner dishes, but I quickly rose from my chair saying, "I'll take care of tidying, Mrs Bruce." A quick glance at my father, and he too rose, joining me. "Yes, Mrs Bruce, Donncha and I will take care of this."

We knew Mrs Bruce would have loved to be released from the overpowering personality of her visitor but alas, she was the hostess, thus was held hostage—imprisoned in a cell of vociferous discourse.

Standing at the sink, my father whispered, "I have never in all my life . . . "

The evening was predominantly spent watching and listening to Miss Burgess expound on every topic from mousetraps to Mozart. It was as though we were attending a one-woman play with front row seats. We three were captivated, it must be said, especially when she relayed the fact that she was a first cousin of James Burgess, one of the infamous conspirators of the bullion train robbery of 1855.

When I noted I was unaware of any such robbery, her eyes grew wild with delight. The story of her cousin burst forth from her with the subtlety of an overflowing volcano. We were once again caught up in the mighty flow of her exuberance.

Her cousin had been a train guard, you see. It was he, Burgess, who had informed the two organizers of the robbery that a shipment worth twelve thousand pounds would be moved from London Bridge station to Paris via the South Eastern Railway. It had been a daring and brilliant heist, according to Miss Abigail, and she was 'altogether tickled to be related to such a fellow'. The gang of thieves was subsequently caught, and her cousin had been sentenced to penal transportation for fourteen years. Her tone was downright hostile when relaying their capture, as though the criminals should have been left alone; allowed to get off scot-free.

By three days end, Mrs Bruce was beside herself with frustration, as Miss Abigail followed her around the house like a lost puppy in a constant state of chatter. Much to my father's relief, the Miss Abigail experience became the last of the match-making efforts by Mrs Bruce.

Da was never interested in any of the women Mrs Bruce invited home, Siobhán. As a matter of fact, he barely took notice of women in general. His heart was spoken for and that was that. I know he had dreamed of happening upon you as we disembarked from the ship on our return, but of course that was just an unrealized fantasy.

We spent years travelling from town to town, village to village, looking for you. We even returned to Fiona's home, hoping you might have left some kind of clue as to your whereabouts. Two years ago, my father became extremely ill. The doctor was initially discouraging about his chance for recovery, but thankfully Da is a rugged man and he pulled through. His heart had been weakened, however, and the doctor told him in no uncertain terms that his life on the road must come to an end or it would be the end of him. My da's face wilted as a flower would when plucked from the ground and left in the hot sun.

I could not bear to see him so downhearted, so I promised to continue the search alone. Initially, he declined, saying that the two of you were lost to him and that I needed to begin my own life. He had dreams of continuing life with you in An Clann Teach and of reuniting with his mother, Fiona. Surrendering the search would put an end to all that.

I convinced him that my passion for finding you was as great as his and I was passionate for a time. This last year, though, had become more difficult for me. Then I met you, Orlaith, on that stormy day, and suddenly I did not care to continue my search. I had planned on telling you my history and then, depending on your reaction, settling on my next step. I never dreamed when I awoke this morning that the day would end in this astonishing way. I must write to my father immediately and tell him this great news.

25

Genevieve, Grace and Liam

Genevieve sat upright in her little bed. "Are we allowed to look into the Mobhrí when ever we wish?"

Grace righted the collar on her daughter's nightshirt, replying, "That's a wonderful question my little one, but truth be told, none of us know how long this power may last, thus, the owners must be very careful not to overuse it."

Seeing the genuine look of disappointment cross her daughters face, Grace added. "I'll tell you what. Let's all three have one more quick glimpse of our future home. Are you ready to wave to my parents, your grandparents, Orlaith and Donncha?"

After a brief revisit, Grace returned the Mobhrí to its protective cloth and Genevieve exclaimed, "I am ready, Mother, for our adventure. Whatever it might be. Tell me, did they all see Mr Odhrán again?"

Grace laughed at the comment.

"Oh, indeed they did. Donncha, Orlaith, and Siobhán travelled to Odhrán, back to a reunion both joyful for reuniting, sorrowful for the loss of time. And, time had changed many things, as it always does. Siobhán and Odhrán became close friends. Orlaith and Donncha married and had a daughter, me, a year later. They named me Grace, as they felt that grace is what had shined down upon them all.

Liam wandered to the bed and sat on the opposite side of Genevieve. "I loved that story. Daddy, can you tell me a story too? I am not tired at all!"

"It's a story you want, is it? Let me see now. Remember the old woman who originally gave the two pearls and gold ring to Róisín?"

Genevieve nodded. Liam leaned over the bed, took Grace's hand, and laid it in his own.

"This is that very ring, Genevieve. There are several stories of how this type of ring and its symbolic nature came to be. It is called a Claddagh ring. How about I relay the three versions of this ring's origins and you can decide which version you prefer as truth?

The Claddagh

The first story is about a woman from Galway, named Margaret Joyce. She married a wealthy merchant from Spain, named Domingo de Rona, who frequented Galway to trade goods and wares. She proceeded to Spain with him, but he died, leaving her an enormous fortune. Margaret returned to Galway and eventually re-married, to a man named Oliver Óg French, who was the mayor of Galway in 1596. She was rewarded one day, for her good works and charity, by an eagle, which dropped the original Claddagh ring into her lap.

The second story revolves around a man called Richard Joyce. He was a man from the small fishing village of Claddagh, on the coast of Galway. He was aboard a ship headed to the plantations in the West Indies when Mediterranean pirates captured the ship. The crew was sold to slavery and the ship taken. Richard was engaged to be married in six months time, to a woman from his own village. Shortly after being captured, he was sold to a Moorish goldsmith, who was in need of an apprentice, and subsequently taught Richard his trade. Richard had a great gift for goldsmithing and soon became a master himself. However, his heart ached for the fiancé he had left behind and so he crafted a ring in her honour.

Many years passed and William III of England came to the throne. He negotiated an agreement with the Moors in which all captives would be allowed to return to their homelands. The Moorish goldsmith did not want Richard to depart and offered him his only daughter's hand in marriage, along with half of his fortune, if he would stay in Algiers. Richard was honoured to be held in such high regard, and he had become quite fond of the goldsmith and of the people he had come to know. But he longed to return to his homeland and to the woman he had left behind.

He was understandably quite worried that she might have married in his absence, but upon his return, he joyfully found that she had remained single in the hopes that he might one day come back to her. Much to her parents' aggravations, she had vowed to wait for him or die a spinster. Richard presented her with the ring he had made, and they were married. He set up his own goldsmithing shoppe in the town of Claddagh, and hence forth, the ring became known as the Claddagh ring.

As you know, Genevieve, this ring has two hands holding a heart with a crown on top. The third story goes far, far, far back, to the time of Ireland's beginning. Some say that the right hand of the ring represents Dagda, the father of the gods. The left hand represents Danú, who as you just heard, is the ancestral and universal mother of our people. The heart represents the hearts of all mankind and that which gives us the everlasting music of our people.

The crown represents Beathauile, who is not a person, but relates to life as a whole. These beautiful rings have become heirlooms down through time and are passed from mother to daughter, just like the Mobhrí. As you can see, the ring is on your mother's left hand and the heart is turned towards her, which indicates that her heart is spoken for. If a woman is not spoken for, then she wears it on her right hand with the heart facing out."

"I am sure that last story must be the true one, at least I think so. Mam, what ever happened to the sister of the old woman?"

"From what I understand," Grace continued, "a year after the old woman departed, Róisín met the man who would become her husband. They married and she moved to his home, not far away. He was a farmer and used to sell at the markets. She, of course, told him about the course of events before they wed and he was very pleased by it all, yet so busy that he paid only partial attention to the story.

"He used to tell her about all the people that would come to buy produce and meat from him, as so many had queer ways about them. One day he offhandedly commented that the woman with the two different-coloured eyes had not been round to buy for a few weeks. This, of course, aroused Róisín's curiosity and she asked about the woman's age and height, etc. Her husband had forgotten all about the old woman and her sister but promised to ask about her on his next selling day. After inquiring with some of the regulars, he came to find that the woman lived not far away, but she was ailing.

"Róisín ventured out immediately to find her. This was not easy, as she had to walk a long way and was six months along with child. She arrived to the woman's house and introduced herself as a friend of her sister's. The woman was uncertain about inviting her in, so she showed her the two pearls and the golden ring from her pocket. She had not carried the Mobhrí, as it was too precious a thing to wander with. Though her story sounded plausible, and the old woman did recognize the items before her, she was still reticent about asking her in. It was then that

Donncha's great-grandmother spoke of the one secret that only her sister knew.

"It was ironic that her sister had come so close to finding her, only short by a few kilometers, but that is the way of life sometimes; and the twin was indeed sent to her sister and family the very next day. This changing of ownership did have the added bonus of extending family lines that would end up in An Clann Teach.

"Perhaps the faeries helped find her," quipped Genevieve. "They can do oh so many odd and amazing things, perhaps they helped."

"Perhaps they did," replied Grace.

Genevieve eyed her father inquisitively. "Would you go away with the faeries, daddy?"

"No, Genevieve, I don't believe I would." Liam replied.

Then a prankish smirk lifted from the corners of his mouth, and he tickled Genevieve under the chin. "That is, not unless you and your mother were coming with me!"

"We'd go with you, wouldn't we mother? We'd go anywhere with you!"

Grace spoke up. "Three peas in a pod, that's us, so it is. Speaking of going places, Genevieve, you know how much your father loves working with horses, and has been both a trainer and a medical caretaker of them for many years?"

Genevieve nodded affirmatively.

"Do you remember the man, Mr Nicolas, who came to see us a week or so ago?"

Genevieve nodded a second time.

"Right, well, he is a man from America, friends with Mr O'Reilly. As you probably know, your father has trained several horses at Mr O'Reilly's stud farm. To make a long story short, the American man, Mr Nicolas, so highly admired and regarded your father's abilities and results with those horses, that he has offered your father a five-year position to train horses on his 'ranch' in America. It seems a ranch is what Americans call a large farm like the O'Reillys', where they breed and train horses, or raise livestock instead of food crops. It pays quite well, and at this point, with work being so scarce, we feel it is in our best interest to take the position."

26

Grace

Mr O'Reilly presented me this travel journal in which to write thoughts, experience and such. Such a thoughtful gesture.

We have one month in which to ready ourselves for the journey. We are allowed one travelling trunk and two suitcases. We don't have suitcases, but we do however have one trunk and two large wicker baskets. The baskets, I will fill with things we might need on board, including a few items of clothing, herbal remedies and toiletries. We will fill the trunk with the bulk of our items.

Liam and I have spent hours discussing what to do with the Mobhrí. We came to the conclusion today that it would be safer travelling with us, so I will sew it into the hem of one of my heavy woollen skirts.

We have been told that the most important items for passengers to have close at hand are exit papers, money, of course, and tickets. We will travel by horse and cart to

the bustling port of Queenstown, in Cork[2], at the south
end of this island.

17 April
Grace

*We leave tomorrow at first light. My emotions teeter
between a sense of utter panic and curious excitement.
The horses, of course, must remain but at least they
are with the O'Reillys and will be well looked after. Mr
O'Reilly will be taking us to the port to meet our ship.
We will be travelling in a horse drawn cart that has a
coverlet, which will at least keep the cold drizzle off us.
It will take us two or three days to get to the Cork docks.*

20 April
Grace

*It's been a wearisome three travel days since we joined
the scores of other ship passengers, over 200, for embar-
kation procedures and settling into this journey.
We did not expect this many people to be waiting to
board our departing steamship. There seemed to be
an endless number of queues to get through before
we were able to board our vessel, the SS Voyager. We
began this morning at the ticket queue, where they
checked to be sure that all our paperwork was in
order. Liam and I had to answer a series of questions.
Some seemed logical, like name, age, sex, marital
status, occupation, etc., but there were some we were
not expecting, such as whether we had ever been in
prison, or an almshouse, or an institution, or if we were
polygamists or anarchists!
The men were separated from the women, to be bathed,
de-loused, and briefly checked by an attending physi-
cian. There were a few unfortunates who were deemed*

---

2 Cobh (pronounced Cove) was renamed Queenstown in 1849 to
commemorate a visit by Queen Victoria, but was renamed Cobh once again
in 1922 with the foundation of the Irish Free State.

unfit for travel and, sadly, denied passage. We were given vaccinations that are routinely administered to immigrants. We then had to wait in yet another queue to be given our final stamp of approval, while our baggage was fumigated with foul smelling powder.

The ship line has special jetties along the West Beach, where outgoing passengers take tenders to the ships waiting near the harbour entrance. We were told that all 223 Irish immigrants would be boarding this day. The SS Voyager already had nine hundred some odd passengers aboard from its original departure point in Liverpool, England the day before. First and second-class passengers were brought aboard first.

We, as third-class steerage passengers, were last. The first and second-class passengers were nowhere to be seen when we boarded, so they must have been taken directly to their quarters.

Liam, Genevieve, and I have found ourselves a sheltered spot under a small archway and sit waiting for instructions that we know will eventually come. Even though it is rather wet and chilly, we are happy to be on board at long last.

21 April
Grace

I write this on my bunk with Genevieve asleep next to me and Liam on the bunk above us. I heard a seaman say that the ship is only three-quarters full. This is good for us in steerage, since this is where the bulk of the passengers are.[3] I feel rather queasy, so I am chewing on some peppermint leaves.

3　Steerage was enormously profitable for the steamship companies and many ships could hold up to 2000 immigrants. With the average cost of a ticket at $30.00 and the average cost of feeding an individual at sixty cents a day, the net profit was tremendous. This pricing was for a one-way crossing. Crossing the Atlantic at this time from Ireland was approximately eight days, depending on weather conditions and if the ship was delayed upon arrival at the landing harbour.

The rain came not long after we boarded. We were enveloped in a shroud of grey mist that was escaping through iron plates, as the hissing steam ship advanced. The ship's bells resounded incessantly, as we made our way past Roche's Point and entered the channel. We passed a Cathedral that is being built atop a steep slope. It was not until we passed that site that the captain announced instructions to the new passengers. First, we were arbitrarily filed and counted, then split into three groups, each of which were led in three opposite directions.

We were shown down a narrow set of steps, all squeezing past the ship's machinery. This was challenging, as there was scarcely enough room for one. Keeping track of family members and coordinating luggage was tricky as we made our way through the dank, tube-like passages. Next, it was down another steep stairway into the enclosed lower decks. It was rather claustrophobic, and I noticed many people looking uncomfortable.

Later
Grace

We have only been below deck for a couple of hours and already I have concerns. Most everyone here is soaked from the exposed hours in the elements. The smell of wet wool and nervous, sweating bodies is already powerfully foul. There is scarce ventilation and people are beginning to be sick from the ship's movement.

We have a small supply of food, though our appetites are all but gone, and we are as far from the toilet rooms as one can get, but they are still overwhelming. Having the two berths closer to the centre of this room and up against a wall feels fortunate. Those near the stern will have to endure the most intense motions of the ship. I am glad Liam had thought of such things beforehand. We are basically in a large room, maybe eight feet tall. Among the many berths, there is little room for passenger aisles, and it scares me to think of having to escape these confines in an emergency. There is no fresh water

*in the toilet area so we must be content to keep our-
selves clean with salt water that coughs its way out of
a rusty tap. Cleaning will be an almost impossible task
and will no doubt aggravate the already sour air.*

Later
Genevieve, via Grace

*I am glad mother is writing for me as it would take me
forever to write all this out myself. (You are welcome
Genevieve… my pleasure.)*
*I did not feel very well when I awoke; mother says I will
have to grow 'sea legs'. We had bread and butter for
our breakfast, but we will have to eat the ship's fare
for the rest of the trip. So many people from so many
countries! There are we Irish, as well as accents from
England, Scotland, and Wales. There are many accents
I do not know, but we have been told that some passengers are from as far away as Poland, Sweden and even
Russia. There is a Russian girl about my age that I have
seen a few times today. I think she is very pretty with
her big brown eyes. We smiled at each other and waved,
but I do not think she speaks English. Maybe later if
I see her, I will try and talk to her. She carries a cloth
doll that is so very colourful and I would love to touch
it. I would show her my stuffed bear if she would like
to see him.*
*I heard some men talking this morning and they said
that the thing captains fear more than anything else on
a voyage, is fire. I never really thought about that before,
but I can see why they would fear it. We are only able to
leave our quarters once a day and we are going to walk
along the deck for our hour this morning.*

Later still
Grace

*Genevieve was determined to meet the little girl with
whom she is enamored. As we walked the deck this
morning, we could see the little girl heading toward us
with her mother and baby brother. As they approached,*

Genevieve held out her bear toward the little girl and wiggled it to and fro. The girl held out her doll and the two smiled. They speak no English and obviously none of us speak Russian, but the girls giggled together and that was lovely. Perhaps they will find a way to communicate after all.

The allotted space for our deck time is in no way adequate for the amount of people in steerage. I cringe to think what it would be like if this were a full sailing. The space is limited and is in the worst part of the ship. We are exposed to the most violent motion and the smoke and dirt from the stacks blow down upon us. There are odours from the hold and the galley, too. What should be a literal breath of fresh air is not anything near to that, but it feels jolly to be out of our incommodious hole. Thank goodness the sun is shining. That cheers us all.

Bedtime
Genevieve, via Grace

The girl I like, and her family, have bunks that are not terribly far from ours and this afternoon (after waving our toys at each other earlier while up on deck) she wandered over to us with her cloth doll in one hand and her baby brother on her hip. We put her brother on our bunk and sat playing with him. I like the brown and yellow scarf she wears on her head and her unusual shoes. Her clothes are very colourful and bright compared to our grey and brown woollens. Her doll is dressed very like she is, with embroidered patterns weaving themselves into nature scenes. I wonder if her mother made her clothes like my mother makes mine. We played clapping games and I think she really likes me. I like her, even if we can't talk to each other. I hope we can play again tomorrow.

Bedtime
Grace

It is such close quarters down here in our section of the ship. There is no privacy at all, and I cannot imagine having to spend more than ten days out at sea. Two men got into a fight this evening over divergent political opinions. I don't see much sense in it, truth be told, especially out here in the middle of the Atlantic. Perhaps they have drunk all the alcohol they brought aboard and can spend the rest of the voyage at peace, or at least, not at war.
The ship's doctor was called after one man hit the other in the head with an empty bottle. Luckily, the man getting the stitches was a few sheets to the wind and will not feel the effects of the fight or stitches until tomorrow. It must be difficult being a doctor on these ships. Not even two days out and the doctor has been down here at least four times that I know of. Two children took very ill, and he had to bring them some sort of syrup to settle their stomachs. There was the fight I just mentioned and this afternoon a woman, who spoke no English, and is about five months along with child, was carried away in tears. I hope for the best but can only assume the worst. It is lights out in five minutes, so I shall put the journal away.

Norah closed the diary, marking the spot with the ribbon. Stretching lazily, she remarked, "How long have we been reading? This journey sounds like a nightmare if you ask me. I have enough trouble flying coach. How did they do it?"

"Indeed, it was quite a bit different back then," reflected Úla. "But we all do things when needs must. Speaking of needs must, those couple of biscuits aren't taking care of hunger pangs. Would you have a little something we can make? I'm suddenly famished."

"Of course, and I agree. Cheese sandwich?" offered Norah.

"Mmmm, I'm trying to stay away from dairy." answered Úla as they walked into the kitchen. "This room is so darn dark. You should get a roof window or at least another window . . . or something. I couldn't stand this."

Norah let the comment on her dark kitchen pass and focused instead on her mother's food requirements. "Right, I forgot about the dairy thing. How about a ham sandwich?" suggested Norah, as her mother opened the fridge, exclaiming, "Oh dear God, Norah. When's the last time you cleaned your fridge? I think you've things growing legs in here. Perhaps we should run out for a bite. Besides, I'm thinking of giving up meat 'cause they say it really isn't good for the gut, so ham won't do. Hope you don't mind me saying that there is also something sticky under my feet. I think your floors could use a going over as well."

Norah rolled her eyes with displeasure. "Of course, we can go out if you want, but must you criticise everything?"

Úla swung her head around the open fridge door to look to her daughter in utter surprise. "I'm not criticising Norah, just making a few helpful suggestions. How about the chipper for lunch?"

Norah chortled, "Oh yes, no dairy and no ham 'cause they are bad for you, but greasy fish and chips . . . "

Úla closed the fridge door a bit too forcefully and immediately regretted it. "Oops," she said. "Didn't mean to do that."

Norah knew it was probably simpler to let it all slide. "I have some frozen vegetable soup from a couple of days ago. How about that with this gorgeous wholegrain loaf from the village bake shoppe?"

Úla nodded in agreement. "Sure, that would be perfect, thank you."

Norah got the soup going on the cooker. "You know, Mam, I'm so tired at this point. Can we take up diary reading in the morning? I'd like to eat and then relax a bit; collect Luain and go to bed good and early. Come for brekkie in the morning?"

27

The following morning dawned bright and cheery. After a pot of Barry's tea, eggs, red beans, and toast, the two women returned to their places in the sitting room.

Norah opened the book to where the ribbon lay and looked to Úla. "So, how are you feeling at this point about the truth of it all?"

Shrugging, Úla proclaimed, "You know me, Norah. I like absolute proof. I haven't had that yet, but I am also experiencing rushes of unfamiliar empathy and solidarity with my mother, and all these past, shall we say, relations."

Norah sat open-mouthed in disbelief. "You're one hard shell to crack. Christ, no wonder you and Nana had such communication issues. Didn't you say when we started reading all this that you should have had a stronger faith in Nana's stories? What more evidence do you need! So, what? I'll have to send you to An Clann Teach in order for you to get on board?"

Úla's face flushed with aggravation. Not only did she dislike being judged, but she was not used to Norah standing up to her. "Let's just see if time changes my opinions, shall we." She then added, a bit too passive-aggressively, "You've not walked in my shoes, Norah."

Rebelliously, Norah slipped her own shoes off her feet, let them drop noisily to the floor, and opened the diary.

22 April
Genevieve, via Grace

Her name is Anechka. I know this because I pointed to myself and said my name, then she did the same. I think it is a beautiful name. It turns out that she has an older brother I had not noticed before. He came to our bunk with her today (instead of her baby brother) and pulled a handful of yellow and green marbles from his pocket. His name is Aleski, and I think he is about nine years old. He likes to draw and carries a little notebook and pencil in his trousers pocket. He drew Anechka and me sitting on our bunk and then gave me the sketch as a present. I will treasure it, even though my head looks far too big for my shoulders and there are many rubber marks on Anechka's face.

22 April
Grace

The woman the doctor took away returned today looking pale and sorrowful. She surely must have lost the child, given her disposition and tearful state. Such a shame.

24 April
Grace

What a night! I was not sure we would survive it, but thankfully all is well. We were barely finished our evening meal (if you want to call it that: hard bread and a small dollop of unbuttered potatoes), when the steamship began undulating with mighty ferocity. Passengers had been told before boarding that garlic, onions, and whiskey were great remedies for sea-sickness. There were, of course, vendors selling these

*things—briskly—on the dock. I had brought tinctures,
which I administered to us and to Anechka's family,
though they did little good in the end.*

*I can only assume the waves we were riding were
immense, as one moment we would lurch to one end
of our bunk and the next moment we were thrown to
the other. We all held as tightly as we could to our
bedsteads. Shouts, prayers, and sobs could be heard
in several languages. Everyone was ill, despite their
dockside purchases. At one point, a loud blast sounded, followed by a rattling shock. Then our ears were
stung with the shrill of the ship's siren, the pumping
exertion of revving engines and the rumble of many feet
running above us.*

*Some passengers were up and away to the steps leading
to the upper portions of the ship to try and free themselves from our confines. Some panicked when they
realized that we had been locked in from the outside.
The din was deafening. We were all thinking that we
might become one of the ill-fated vessels that would
not survive the Atlantic journey, or that we would be
perhaps blown off course by the high winds.*

*Liam had wedged himself into the lower bunk and
acted as a buffer for Genevieve and me. This I was
grateful for, as many people were thrown from their
beds and onto the hard metal floor. The storm lasted
for many hours. There was no sleep to be had, what
with the tossing of our bodies and the ever-increasing
percentage of illness.*

*The storm ceased as abruptly as it had commenced.
Seamen opened the hatches and ventured into our
quarters, only to turn quickly away for fear of becoming
ill themselves with the foul stench of the place. Women
and children were allowed three hours up on deck,
while the men and a few crew cleaned the steerage area.
When we returned, sawdust stuck to the damp floors as
well as our feet and shoes.*

*We were given to understand that we had actually hit
a small iceberg during the storm. The visibility had*

been so negligible that the captain had let the sirens sound to prevent a possible collision with other ships that might have been in the vicinity. The seamen tried to make light of the night, but anyone could see the fright in their eyes and could hear the relief in their shaky, tired voices.

25 April
Genevieve, via Grace

The last 24 hours seem like a blur. Everything mother said is true and I was very afraid that we would perish beneath the waves.
I went over to the bunks of Anechka and Aleski earlier. They had a boy from England, named Peter, with them. It was nice to speak to him, I must admit. He had a deck of unusual cards with matching pictures on them. He boxed them, laid them face down and we then had to try and find the match to the one we overturned. It was a game we could all play, as no words were necessary, and we all laughed and laughed for what seemed like hours. Then Aleski and Peter played marbles, while Anechka and I dressed and undressed her doll.
Father says we only have a few days to go before we land in New York City. I will be so happy to be on land again and off this ship, but I will miss Anechka, Aleski and Peter. Peter says his family is going to a place called Philadelphia. His Uncle Lewis will be meeting them when the ship docks. I have no idea what will happen to my Russian friends.

26 April
Grace

I was in the toilet compartment early this morning, doing my best to take care of my washing needs, when the ship gave a sudden pitch to one side. I was thrown off balance and grabbed hold of the tiny sink. I did not fall, but my skirt wheeled out to the side, causing the hemmed Mobhrí to clank harshly against the foot rail. I returned to our bunk in an upset frame of mind, fearful that I might have damaged the Mobhrí in some way. My heart leapt to my throat as I heard a noise emanating from my skirt hem. The churning of the engines and the noise of the day concealed the intermittent sound, but I hastened to unpack my sewing kit and snip the hemline apart.

Genevieve arrived back from visiting Anechka's bunk to find me hovered over the blankets, my back turned away from the aisle. I had been pressing and prodding the different segments of the Mobhrí, trying to mute its ever increasing and insistent croaking, but to no avail. I did not want to open the light for fear someone might see.

As I lie here remembering what then transpired, I feel very grateful for my daughter.

"Let me have a go," said Genevieve.

"Do be careful, won't you? Do not open the light under any circumstances," I replied.

Genevieve took the Mobhrí and scooted under the blankets to the darkness there. I could hear her whispering and within a few moments saw a faint light glowing from beneath the covers.

"Genevieve," I whispered, my face down to the bulge of her body beneath the covers. "Genevieve, do not open the light, do you hear? Genevieve?"

More whispering intermingled with giggling. Then all was quiet. All was dark.

Genevieve poked her little head out from underneath the blanket, her broad smile shining at me.

I said, "Who were you whispering to? Why did you open the light when I specifically told you not to?"

"I was whispering to some of them; I do not know who they were."

"They?"

Genevieve went on to tell me exactly what she saw and heard.

*"Yes. Since what you were doing wasn't working, I
thought I would talk to it... to them. I thought if I was
the Mobhrí being taken away from my homeland,
the place I have always dwelled, I would be terribly
frightened. I whispered, 'Have no fear, you are safe
and with us.' Then the light began to shine of its own
accord. I looked in one end and there were four people,
men, looking at me. A tall slender man said, "Cé leis an
Mobhrí seo?" (Who owns this Mobhrí?)*
"I whispered 'Mham.' (Mammy)
"Ní fhaca mé riamh cheana tú." (I never saw you before.)
*"A second man approached and pointed to me. "Chona-
ic mé go deimhin tú." (I saw you indeed.)*
*"Then I said, 'Is maith sin.' (That is good.) 'An bhfaca tú
mé féin agus Mhamai thuas ar an gcrann sa ghairdín?'
(Did you see myself and Mammy up on the tree
in the garden?)*
"Ceart." (Correct.)
*"They told me to count to sixty and to bring you to them,
so that they could see you. All they want is to know all
is well. I said 'Rachaidh mé suas chuif mo mháthair
nóiméad.' (I'll go up to my mother for a minute.)*
*"The tall man nodded and said, "Fanfaidh mise anseo
leat." (I'll wait for you here.)*
*Indeed, both Genevieve and I huddled under the blan-
kets and upon the men's return, we assured them that
they would be well looked after. I never would have
guessed that the people of An Clann Teach would feel
the loss of the homeland. Since I am the current minder,
perhaps they can feel the rent of my own heart as we
push father away from the shores I love so well.*

27 April
Grace

*There is excitement and fear aboard this ship today.
Rumours about life in America flow like streams. Stories of glory and riches, as well as stories of sorrow and
rejection, circulate. I cannot imagine having to step*

off this ship and into a new language. We are nervous enough with our accents. What can Anechka's parents be feeling? I shiver at the thought.

Physically, we all look a wreck from the voyage and the lack of hygiene, and many people are coughing. Emotionally and mentally, we are all on tenterhooks and there is an eerie silence looming now that our journey is coming to an end. One can feel the ever-increasing state of anxiety, especially among the non-English speakers. Entire lives will hang in the balance of whatever doctor and inspector we encounter on these foreign shores.

Despite the nervousness, there was a great singsong tonight. It started out with the two men who had gotten into a squabble that first night, each professing that their country had the most beautiful ballads. They each sang a song and their voices echoed through the metal room. Then a woman, perhaps from Russia or Poland, sang. As soon as one person completed a song, another would pick up after a minute or so. Liam and I sang 'The Long Road Home,' me singing harmony to his melody. Various instruments were also brought out and played. It was a spectacular night and at one point, a seaman came down and sat listening for a while. Interestingly, Liam sang the last song of the night. It was the song he had written about the sailing ships. Our quarters became quiet when he concluded, and no one ventured to continue. He calls the song 'Thirty Waves Out.

Right the main sail anchors away
Our ship it's Amerikey bound
30 waves out so far from our ground
No telling when we'll return
We're told there's a land where profits abound
Fortune is laid at ones feet
I being eldest am destined to ride
On the ship they call Alvery
Last night came a gale fierce as a quake
Swell drove us up on our side
13 were thrown 40 remain
Weary and raw to the bone
There's one man aboard with a flute and a song
But most are saddened by tales
All we desire is our home and our hearth
Not these cold and pitiful bunks
There may come a time when home I'll return
Full pockets of silver and gold
But I tell you now I'd trade them all in
In a heartbeat I'd trade them all in
So raise the main sail anchors away
Our ship it's Amerikey bound
30 waves out so far from our ground
No telling when we'll return
No telling when we'll return[4]

---

4   "Thirty Waves Out", song by Mary Murphy from her CD *Thirty Waves Out*

28 April
Grace

We are told that we will arrive in the late afternoon, ahead of schedule. Everyone was anxious this morning while walking above deck. A thick blanket of fog engulfed us. I would say we were all hoping to see a glimpse of land, but it was not to be.

Later
Grace

It is late afternoon. We have come to a halt, the engines are quiet, and the captain has sounded the horn. Does this mean we are landed at a dock? Why do they not inform us of our situation? The doors are locked so there is no hope of anyone investigating. There are three men knocking at the door, calling out for information, but if you ask me, it is a waste of time.

Later still
Grace

The three men eventually gave up and went back to their bunks. There is nothing to do but wait. A seaman finally appeared with bags of stale bread to 'tide us over'. He said we are in a holding position. At present, the first and second-class passengers are being seen to by the American doctors for their arrival examinations. "When will we be able to leave?" someone called out. "When they are ready for you," said he, "it will be a while yet."

2 hours later

It is getting very late. I am most anxious to disembark, but there is not a thing to be done but wait. Genevieve, Anechka, Aleski, and Peter sit together on the bunk below, while Liam and I lie on this top bunk, talking about the future.
It is most interesting to see how people respond to tense situations. Several people are playing music at

*the far end of the ship. There is a middle-aged couple
with rosary beads whispering to themselves in prayer.
Many people rifle through their papers for the ump-
teenth time, checking and re-checking documents and
money—rehearsing answers to the possible questions
they will be asked. There is one young woman looking
quite fearful and I do believe she may be in early labour.
Her husband is holding her hand and talking quietly to
her. I have heard them speaking up on deck and think
they may be Polish. There is no point in me going over
to reassure her, as I would not be able to communicate. I do keep an eye on her though, as I have assisted
in several births, and if need be, will offer my limited
experience. Some are writing in books, and I assume we
are not the only ones making notes of our journey.
I shall get the children back to their bunks as it looks as
though we may have to sleep another night on board.*

29 April
Grace

*A little while ago we were all informed we would have
to wait another whole day, as there was a ship that had
docked before us and we would just have to wait our
turn. The seaman told us that we were in the quarantine area at the entrance to the lower bay of New York
Harbour. We had reached that point after five p.m.[5]
and therefore would have to wait until the morning.
This was quite a blow to us all.
We were granted a brief time up on deck. As we
emerged from the ship's doors, many people sighed and
cried at the sight of the tall statue. This statue symbol-
ized a new home, a fresh beginning and hope for future
generations. We could see three large steamships. One*

---

5   Ships were only examined between the hours of seven a.m. and five
p.m. If ships arrived after five p.m. they would have to stay anchored for the
night.

*was at a far-off dock and was loading passengers for a
journey to who knows where. The other two steamships
were the S.S. Stanton and us.*

*As we watched, lines of new immigrants were lowered
onto a smaller boat and transferred to the infamous
Ellis Island; the very place we would all be brought
to. Such a time-consuming process. We witnessed two
separate instances of baskets falling into the water.
One was retrieved and handed back to its relieved
owner. The other must have been weighty as it sank like
a stone in a matter of seconds. The devastated family
had no time to react. They had to watch as the water
swallowed part of the world that they had brought. Too
soon, we were led back down below and were fed lumpy
porridge and more stale bread.*

30 April
Grace

*We were visited by a crewman this morning, who deliv-
ered the news that we'd be disembarking within the
hour. A roaring cheer rose up throughout the compartment, accompanied by surly comments from some. The
uniformed man's voice rang high above the din of the
crowd, struggling to be heard.*
*"We will be moving through the narrows leading to
Upper New York Bay and then on into the harbour. We
thank you for your continued patience."*

Later
Genevieve, via Grace

*Anechka came to our bunk, and we hugged one another
goodbye. I removed a thin green and yellow yarn
necklace from around my neck and placed it over her
doll's head. Anechka laughed and hugged me again.
Then she removed her headscarf and tied it around
my bear's neck. This brought tears to my eyes, and we
hugged for the last time, waving to each other, as she
made her way back to her family.*

28

10th May
Grace

I am currently sitting in our more than adequate bedroom suite at the Nicolas Horse Ranch. My right foot is elevated on a pillow, as I slipped on a wet floor last night and sprained my ankle. I have decided to pass a fair amount of my time writing the events of our landing and arrival to this place that we will call home for five years. Something about all this feels momentous, and I want Genevieve to be able to remember it well. Just now, Liam is out with Mr Nicolas and his horses. I can see Genevieve sitting on a wooden swing, under an enormous sugar maple that is just outside the bedroom door, leading to the back gardens. It feels as though we are in a paradise, of sorts. A strange, but possibly wonderful one.

This country is seemingly overflowing with so many kinds of trees. Our country at one time was similar in that regard. My mother used to tell me a story about iora rua (red squirrel) who was able to travel from one end of Ireland to the other without ever touching the ground. I knew it was not truly accurate, but it did help me understand just how many forests used to be on the island of Ireland.

Over time, settlers of course played a key role in defor-estation. Land was needed for livestock and farming. However, when Queen Elizabeth I came to power, things took a dramatic turn for the worse.

At this time, there was a proverb. 'The Irish will never be tamed while the leaves are on the trees'.

Queen Elizabeth ordered destruction of all woods in Ireland to deprive the Irish rebels, who were rising up in opposition of England's colonisation, of shelter and places to hide. Not to mention the fact that her navy ships were being built using Irish Oak. England's continuous and unquenchable thirst for power included destruction of wildlife and woodlands, as well as our native language.

It has taken us all several days to restore our strength after the voyage and distressing arrival. As it turns out, we were not supposed to be steerage passengers at all. Mr Nicolas had given the job of acquiring our tickets to one of his staff. The staff member had been swindled. (We now understand that this is not an uncommon occurrence with some ticket sellers.) He had been assured that we would receive second-class tickets, but the seller had taken the difference in monies between the second-class and steerage-class accommodation and pocketed a tidy profit. Mr Nicolas tried to track down the seller but to no avail. He is long gone, no doubt on to swindle other travellers.

When we did not disembark with the first- and second-class passengers, Mr Nicolas went to the main office to inquire about us. The passenger list was checked, and he was told we were in the steerage section. There was nothing he could do but wait for us to emerge from the quarantine and processing area.

First- and second-class passengers had been allowed to disembark right away, having had on-board medical evaluations. American citizens did not have to have medical checks and were ushered immediately off. The rest had been taken directly into the New York harbour. We third class passengers had to wait to be screened at Ellis Island.

After speaking with Mr Nicolas, we learned that Ellis Island can only handle about five thousand people a day for processing. It is not unusual for another ten to fifteen thousand to wait on ships for several days just as we had been forced to do.

While the tall lady holding a torch stood in the distance, we docked and were directed to a large waiting area.

Here we were given name tags with our individual manifest numbers on them. We were assembled into groups of about thirty-five, according to the manifest letters and packed aboard the top deck of a barge. Everyone's baggage was indiscriminately piled in heaps on the lower deck.

It was so strange to put our feet on solid ground. We found ourselves touching walls and railings for support to steady ourselves. We had thought our ship's compartment had been at times unbearably loud, but I can tell you that nothing could have prepared us for the clamour of this place. We were met by several interpreters from around the world, all yelling at us in shrill voices.

They must have sounded like a quenching rain in the desert to many of the passengers, who up until that moment had been unable to communicate with the rest of us. These interpreters had highly stressful jobs and we were surprised at the patience they bestowed on us all. For many non-English speakers, these people might be the only ones who kept them from being deported back from whence they came.

Our guide was extremely hard to understand. He had what we now know is a typical New York accent. We had to get used to the dropped consonants and the strange inflections. The slurring of words at lightning speed was to us, very like hearing a new language.

Upon entering the main building, we were told to leave our hand luggage to the side while we were processed. The interpreters split us into groups of about thirty and led us up a steep flight of stairs toward the registry office. Two doctors stood at the top of the stairs. One watched as the passengers ascended and looked for signs of heavy breathing, coughing, lameness etc., anything that might indicate a medical condition or symptom.

The second doctor would examine each immigrant as they reached the top. He would check eyes, ears, nose, heart, lungs, hair, neck, hands etc. White chalk lay on a little table next to him, and if the doctor deemed an immigrant suspicious, he would mark their clothing (shoulder) with a specific letter to correspond with his concern. Mr Nicolas has since told us that this medical exam was called the 'six second exam' and explained what the different letters signified.

Six Second Exam

Ct	Trachoma
N	Neck
X with a circle	Meant definite symptoms had been detected
K	Hernia
C	Conjunctivitis
P	Physical and Lungs
E	Eyes
L	Lameness
Pg	Pregnancy
Sc	Scalp
F	Face
H	Heart
Large X	Marked high on the right shoulder indicated a suspected mental defect
Ft	Feet
S	Senility
Small x	Marked on the lower part of the right shoulder indicated suspicion of disease or deformity
D	Goiter

The family members who were cleared would continue with their processing and then return to the medical inspection area to wait for their relatives, who had been delayed for further medical inspection. This waiting was sometimes brief, but at other times could take several days. They were shuffled into a large waiting area, where they would be given food and floor mats for sleeping.

Those not cleared were deported back to their departure port. This was excruciating for families. Snap decisions had to be made as to who would remain and who would return. Sometimes entire families returned so as not to be torn apart. Other times certain members would stay while others would return, in the hopes of being able to emigrate at a future date. Children who were twelve years of age or older were allowed to return alone, to hopefully be met by relatives. Children under twelve had to be accompanied by a parent or guardian. After our medical examination, we were separated into male and female areas and were made to quickly shower with disinfectant.

Liam was the first to meet the immigration official, while Genevieve and I stood back. The official was asking him a litany of questions and I hoped I would have the same answers when my time came. He stamped a card of some sort and thrust it at Liam. Not looking up from his papers, the immigration man yelled, "Next!"

I approached and sat in the chair, Genevieve standing by my side. The unfriendly official had a harsh voice and stared at us as I answered his questions, as if he wanted to catch us telling lies. He asked about our ability to read and write. He asked how much money we had brought, if we were being met by anyone, where would we be staying and for how long.

After all we had been through, it was these immigration men who had the power to decide an immigrant's fate. He could decide if we were, as the sign above him read, 'clearly and beyond a doubt entitled to land'.

Another sign to the side of him read 'Federal legislation of 1891 mandates the medical inspection of all arriving immigrants. This law allows immediate exclusion of all idiots, insane persons, paupers or persons likely to become public charges, persons suffering from a loathsome or dangerous contagious disease, and criminals'. Much to our relief, the immigration officer stamped our two cards and nodded us curtly away, yelling, "Next!"

Our landing cards in hand, we were sent to a money-changer and changed the little money we had into American dollars. Many immigrants not only exchanged their country's currency into American dollars, but also sold jewelry and heirlooms. Gold, silver, and precious stones are set at a daily value that is displayed on a chalkboard. Many people did not understand the exchange rate but gave up whatever they had to ensure they would land with as much money as possible.

29

Úla interrupted Nora's reading. "You remember Marion from my office?"

"Yes. The one with the enormous spectacles."

"They're not that enormous. She calls them…stylish."

"If you want to call wearing a snorkelling mask stylish, then yes…stylish."

Úla tsked and wagged her finger at Nora.

"A friend of hers gave her a book on the history of the eastern United States, since we are headed there. She said the book noted that the first immigrant to enter America by way of Ellis Island was a fifteen-year-old Irish girl named Annie Moore."

"Really? That's interesting. When do you think that would've been?"

"I think she said 1892, or thereabouts. Anyway, please, do continue."

12 May
Grace

We were ushered out another set of doors and onto a barge headed to the harbour. Upon landing, everyone was sent off into the New World.

We had been told that Mr Nicolas would be waiting for us. Walking through the front doors was indeed over-whelming. Scores of people were waiting for relatives; many had signs. There were families being tearfully reunited while others were relaying the harsh realities of loved ones having failed to make it through. There were screaming children, policeman blowing whistles, food vendors, and ticket sellers everywhere. We had come from the vast ocean to a vast sea of faces, none of which we knew.

Genevieve and I sat with our luggage, while Liam went walking, looking for Mr Nicolas. I was beginning to get worried as to his whereabouts. Shortly thereafter, Liam returned, alone. We had no way of knowing why Mr Nicolas was not there. The 'what if' questions popped into our minds, but we decided to wait a little longer before getting too concerned.

The crowd was dissipating as the evening neared. A vendor was selling baked potatoes and that was a comforting thing to us all. Just before sunset, a man came swiftly through the crowds. Liam jumped up and waved, a look of relief sweeping across his face.

Mr Nicolas apologized for all the confusion. He had been told that it would be well into the evening before we would be released into the city. It was at this point that we learned we had been given the wrong class of tickets.

Without any further delay, Mr Nicolas brought us by horse-drawn carriage to a famous nearby hotel.

Though we were exhausted en route, our tiredness faded quickly as we stared, open mouthed at the enormity of the city.

The Furlongs

"Here we are folks," said Frank Nicolas. "Welcome to your first night in New York. I have your room keys in hand, so I'll take you to your room and meet you back down in the lobby, in an hour, for dinner in the hotel's dining room. I'm sure you're all anxious to eat and then sleep in a real bed."

Genevieve responded excitedly, "But I am not tired at all!" Then promptly proceeded to yawn.

The three had been so weary upon entering the hotel they scarcely noticed much of anything. The room had a huge plush bed, its own toilet and even a stout tub, which they all took advantage of before heading down to the lobby. The three newcomers donned their Sunday best clothes, all of which were wrinkled and in need of airing.

Mr Nicolas could clearly read the expression on their faces as they entered the bustling lobby. High society New Yorkers were, as usual, dressed to the nines, compared to the Furlongs foreign simple clothing. Mr Nicolas approached and spoke in a friendly tone, as passers-by stared at the three people who appeared to have just been plucked from the pages of a history book.

"Have no fear, my friends," he offered. "You'll get used to this place soon enough. Let's go eat and then you can get off to bed. We need to be up early in the morning."

The room looked more like a palace than a dining hall. Crystal chandeliers hung low from tall, rounded ceilings, flower arrangements decorated the centre of each table under which lay deep-blue flowing cloths.

A tall young man ushered the four to the back of the room. (Not surprising, given the bedraggled attire.) The chairs were large with soft red plush cushions on the seats. The aroma of fresh food was enticing; and only then did the Furlongs realize exactly how hungry they were.

Genevieve viewed the setting in front of her and said, "I don't mind sharing."

Mr Nicolas cocked his head. "Sharing? Sharing what, Genevieve?"

"With whoever is going to sit with me."

"Why do you think someone would be sitting with you?"

"Well, this can't be all for me, can it?"

Mr Nicolas laughed heartily and began pointing to the items before her, offering a lesson in table service.

"Here is your serviette, or napkin, your dinner plate, soup bowl, bread and butter plate with a butter knife, water glass and two wine glasses. You don't drink wine though do you, Genevieve?" he asked, with a sly grin. "Fish fork, dinner fork, salad fork, service knife, fish knife, soup spoon, dessert spoon and cake fork. What do you think of that?"

Genevieve heaved a great sigh and replied. "I think people in New York live complicated lives."

Grace and Liam were highly relieved that they did not have to explain to Genevieve what all the settings were for, as they had no clue either.

Mr Nicolas apologized profusely and often about the ticket mix-up and Liam was assured that any future travel would be overseen by him personally. While very grateful for the news, Grace and Liam were not altogether displeased to have lived through a steerage class passage. A bump up to second-class would be all the sweeter and it had been an educational experience, especially for young Genevieve.

30

The **Furlongs had** expected a mansion of sorts, what with the wealth that obviously occupied his pockets, but instead, they pulled in front of a modest horseshoe-shaped one-storey home. The centre courtyard held an enormous man-made pond, with water lilies and a huge array of Japanese fish, called Koi; which Grace found incredibly stunning.

The main rooms were open and airy with no walls separating the kitchen from the dining and living area. The polar opposite of Irish homes which are smaller and separated by doors. The living room window held a dramatic view of numerous corrals with at least twenty grazing horses.

Quarters for the newly arrived family were at the far end of the house—one large bedroom with a separate small office. The office had a little bed for Genevieve, as well as a small wardrobe with a round mirror, and a table at which she would be able to sit to do schoolwork.

14 May
Grace

Liam and I both find Mr Nicolas to be a remarkable man. He is the kind of person who puts you instantly at ease and embraces you as family.
It did not take very long to go from the bustling city to the outskirts of the area. We passed through several towns and stopped at a little eatery on the side of the road. A square plank of wood wobbled in the wind, white paint displaying the name, 'Mrs Johnson's Eatery'. We entered through a squeaky screen door and sat ourselves at a table by the window.

Genevieve looked at her setting of a knife and fork and said, much to our amusement, "Ach, now this is more like it."

Mr Nicolas suggested we try something called a "hot dog." It was all the rage he said. It sounded rather odd to us, but Liam said he would give it a go. Genevieve and I declined and took the safe road with vegetable soup and cheese sandwiches.

We pulled in to Ellenville at dusk. Ellenville is about ninety miles north-west of New York City. The town is a modest size with buildings on either side of the narrow main street. The general shoppe ('store' they call it here) looked quite large and Mr Nicolas pointed out the new library that had just been completed. The ranch, he said, was only another twenty or so minutes from the town.

Pulling on to the ranch's winding, tree-lined road was dazzling. The freshly whitewashed picket fence that ran along either side radiated a bright welcoming glow to our temporary new home. We passed two young men, just out of adolescence I'd say, paintbrushes in hand, as we neared the house. The boys rose to get out of the way of the carriage and waved to Mr Nicolas. We slowed to a walking pace to lessen the swirling of dirt and Mr Nicolas stuck his head out the carriage window calling, "Nice job boys!" The two boys smiled and said thank you in very broken English.

"They're from Russia," Mr Nicolas said. "Their father is a brilliant and innovative building designer that I met a year ago while on business in the city. He had made his way over here two years ago and was saving to send for his wife and sons. Sadly, his wife died of pneumonia six months ago, and that's when I helped him bring the boys over. They are hard-working young men and I think they will thrive once they have acclimated and learned the language."

"How many immigrants do you have working for you Mr Nicolas, and how did you come to be such a caretaker?" I asked.

"First of all, if I am to call you by your first names,
then I would request that you call me by mine,
Frank. Agreed? Good.
"There are perhaps two dozen immigrant workers
employed here at any given time. I was born into very
fortunate circumstances, so it feels good to be able to
help them out like this. They all get room and board
and a monthly salary, but they work darn hard for it, I
can tell you, and I have rarely had to dismiss anyone."
"Your family must be so proud," said Liam.
Frank chortled. "My parents and most of my siblings
care only about themselves and we, therefore, do not
see each other very often. It might seem peculiar to
say, but I feel closer to some of my employees than to
my own family.
"I do have one brother, Julian, whom I like very well.
He was outcast from the rest of my family, you see,
he is a gifted acrobat, of all things, and travels with
a prestigious circus.
"Ah, here is the house now."

14 May
Genevieve via Grace

I got to name a baby horse today! There are a few horses
having babies and Mr Nicolas said I could name one.
The baby is mostly white, but she has three black socks,
and on her back there is a black pattern that looks like
two fountain pens pointing at each other, meeting in
the middle at the nibs. That is what I decided on, Nibs.
Mr Nicolas really likes the name and said I was very
clever to have thought of it.
Mr Nicolas is a very nice man and I think we will be
happy here. I have never had a swing before and I get to
swing outside our room with my bear, who is wearing
the scarf Anechka gave him. I wonder what became of
my friend? I wish she were here with me now.

7 October
Grace

These last five months have just flown by. So many things to write about, where does one begin?
I continue to dispense school lessons to Genevieve three days a week. One day a week she attends a local school for maths and art lessons and to meet other children. That leaves her three days a week to explore the ranch, spend time with the horses, and play. Getting her to concentrate on schoolwork can, at times, be as bad as getting a fish to cease swimming.
Frank Nicolas approached Liam about leading an instructional weekend for horse ranchers/trainers with hands-on training and problem solving. It was extremely well attended and is now to become a once every six-month endeavor. Liam suggested that the next series should allow attendees to bring problem horses with them, so he could address specific problems firsthand. Mr Nicolas, Frank, is ecstatic with the idea.
I have begun to draw. I found a sketchpad and pencil in one of the kitchen drawers and on a lark sat outside under a beech tree and began sketching. I enjoyed the process so much that I made it my morning ritual after tea.
Liam has been so busy that I did not think he was paying any heed to my activities, even though I had mentioned that it was a pleasing pastime for me. However, as I climbed into bed one night, I felt something hard under my pillow. To my utter delight and surprise, I drew out a large sketchpad with several pencils of assorted thicknesses, and a small slide rule. I squealed with delight as Liam whistled and raised his eyes to the ceiling. He was paying attention after all.
Genevieve came to say goodnight and saw me writing in the journal. We have decided to be more diligent about writing together. We shall see.

31

7 November

There is much excitement on the ranch today as Frank's brother, Julian, is coming to New York with the circus. The circus will open just outside the city in two weeks' time, but Julian will have a week before the opening to visit the ranch.

9 November

What did I expect from a circus performer: quirkiness, rawness, a person of questionable manners, possibly brash behavior, and rowdy conversation? Julian is the antithesis of all these traits. Such a charming and gentle young man he is; full of remarkable narratives and noteworthy specifics. Genevieve has become his shadow, which he does not seem to mind in the least. He is slight, lithe, and strong, which is, I am sure, quite advantageous to an acrobat. We are all looking forward to seeing him perform, as the little bits of show-manship we have already seen are stirring.
Over breakfast this morning, he spoke of how both the German and American military have dispatched observers to travel with circuses. The military officers procure meticulous notes on the intricate organiza-tion and planning of travelling circuses. We were at first surprised that any military organization would spend the time, energy, and resources to follow a

circus around, but Julian enlightened us on the reasoning, which proved to be both startling, and in the end, highly logical.

Julian

There are certainly a copious number of circus companies that are haphazard and shoddily run. Some torment their animals and treat their performers poorly. The military steers clear of such irrefutable organizations, they give circuses a bad reputation. There are several circuses, like ours, which run a tight ship and have a gleaming reputation for organization, animal treatment, and care of less fortunate people, who are in the sideshow acts. I refer to side-show performers as less fortunate people, as their physical challenges have caused them to be ostracized by their families and the public, in general. The truth of it is that we, as circus employees, are all seen as entertainment, sure, but also as people to avoid in the real world. The side-show acts draw people in droves as they are seen as novelties and aberrations, but some of my closest friends are part of the side-show acts.

The military has rightly come to acknowledge that there is much to be learned from us. Think about it. We are constantly on the move. We move vast quantities of performers, workers, animals, cages, tents, chairs, carts, games, rides, instruments, souvenirs etc. The carting of food for the animals alone is mind-boggling. Timing and organization is everything. We have to be able to erect and dismantle in the fastest yet safest time as is humanly possible. And, we must accomplish these tasks in every type of weather imaginable.

Erecting a circus is like building up a mobile city. When that ticket booth turns its sign to 'open,' we have got to be ready to meet and entertain scores of people. When that big tent flap springs apart, all must be in order.

We are living in a time when the circus is and extremely popular form of family entertainment. We are easily accessible, exciting, and most importantly, affordable to the vast populous. Even those who cannot afford the big tent shows can usually afford the slight entry fee for the other booths and sideshow acts.

What does the military do? Move large quantities of men, armaments, food, supplies, etcetera in all kinds of weather and adverse conditions, and they must move frequently and be as organized as humanly possible.

This is not something people think about when they come to the circus and indeed there is no reason for them to. We are entertainment pure and simple. No denying that.

32

Yao Jun as told by Grace

Yesterday we saw, first-hand, just how complex circus construction is. Julian's company travels with 34 rail cars, the last of which holds workhorses that pull wagon-loads of materials and animals to the site.

Erecting a circus tent and game booths is indeed like building a city within a few days. We were welcomed and treated with great respect as family and friends of Julian's, but as with most strangers, were eyed cautiously and with a good degree of mistrust. Pleasant as many of these people seem, I would not want to be on their disagreeable side. I find that they house within themselves an element of danger that I am not comfortable with.

Genevieve was enamoured with the children and the animals. Four of the older children took her with them on a tour. This was, for the most part, fine, as the children were lovely. There was, however, an incident that was both curious and disconcerting.

Genevieve returned to us pronouncing that the children had taken her to a woman named Yao Jun. She had been setting up her wagon to present tea leaf, hand, and card readings. As Genevieve went to shake her hand, the woman turned her palm up and ran her finger along its center.

"You have a secret, do you not little girl?"

Genevieve did not reply but the woman continued.

"Oh yes, it is a secret of great importance. Return to me in one hour and we shall see what we shall see in the tea leaves."

When we returned an hour later, Yao Jun welcomed us into her wagon with a great smile. She is a woman of compact stature, but in possession of a larger than life personality. She wore a red garment embroidered with gold and silver threads running along the seams, and a red swath of cloth tied loosely around her black shoulder length hair. It was hard to tell what age she was, as her body gave the impression of a young woman, but the lines around her eyes suggested she was closer to forty.

Fabric hung from the ceiling and along the sides of the walls. Spicy incense burned in a minuscule golden cup. Yao Jun invited us to sit on pillows around her small round table, close to the floor. From a side table, she removed three white porcelain cups. They were wide, shallow cups, with symbols painted on the inside. She explained that the pictures on the inside were Chinese astrological symbols.

Yao Jun removed the lid from a tea canister and placed about a teaspoon of loose tea in the bottom of each of our cups. As we drank our tea, Yao Jun told us about the characters in the cups.

"Did you know that the Chinese have the oldest astrological record in history? A complete Chinese cycle takes sixty years, and those years are divided up into five simple cycles of twelve years each. Twelve animals were assigned to each of the twelve years.

"It has been said that right before Lord Buddha departed this earth, he summoned all the animals to him, to bid him farewell. Only twelve animals presented themselves to Lord Buddha, and as a reward for their devotion and loyalty, he named a year after each one, in the order that they arrived. This is why, to this day, we have the year of the Rat, Ox, Tiger, Rabbit, Dragon, Snake, Horse, Sheep, Monkey, Rooster, Dog and Boar.

"When you are born there is an animal ruling that year. The Chinese like to say, "That animal is the one that hides in your heart and nature." These animals are combined with five elements. Wood, ruled by Jupiter; Water, ruled by Mercury; Fire, ruled by Mars; Earth, by Saturn; and Metal, by Venus.

"Do you like this information?" asked Yao Jun.

Genevieve and I felt a bit giddy about it all but said, "Assuredly." *Who were we to question anything? We were holders of the Mobhrí for goodness' sake.*

"Then I shall continue," Yao Jun said.

"There is much to know about each animal," she continued, while removing a small deck of cards from under the table. Each card had an animal drawing and a synopsis of the personality traits written by way of poems as well as explanations. She also unrolled a rice paper calendar.

"This is my new lunar calendar. It begins in January of 1800 and shows up until 2020! It is easy to find what animal and element you are."

Yao Jun leaned over the table and peered into our cups. Seeing that they were close to drained, she gave us our instructions.

She told us to leave about a teaspoon of tea in the bottom of the cups. Then we each placed our cup in our left hand and turned it three times in a quick swinging motion. Yao Jun said this motion was the equivalent of mixing a deck of cards.

Those few seconds of swirling the leaves created pictures of our past, present, and future. She instructed us to very slowly, and with the utmost of care, turn the cups upside down over our saucers. We left the cups to drain. The leaves clung to the inside of the cups for what must have been two minutes while the liquid drained away. When Yao Jun turned the cups back over, the leaves were stuck to the sides and bottom of the cup. They looked to us like scattered leaves, haphazardly clinging to the interior.

In reality though, our subconscious minds, according to Yao Jun, directed the hand in the turning of the cup to arrange the leaves in particular shapes, all symbolizing our lives.

She said, "The handle of the cup represents the client, as well as the home, or the present abode. The leaves that have clung to the rim are situations that may occur quickly. Below the handle are indications of present and immediate happenings; the further into the cup one looks, the further away the events, until the centre is read, which denotes the distant future."

Yao Jun read our leaves with great and detailed accuracy. She described the close relationship of Liam and me. She spoke of a journey over water and a house where many horses roamed. She spoke of having many years of good fortune and of remaining in our present surroundings for longer than we had initially anticipated. This was startling to hear.

Yao Jun looked curiously at the two of us and said, "I clearly see you both hold the same secret. It is a powerful one. I can see trouble surrounding this issue. Not now, but in the future. The leaves tell me it is not only a verbal secret, but also a physical one. Most interesting. I would love to know what this is.

"There is an object that holds great power. It is old, very old and must be kept safely hidden away. I cannot see what it is, for that is unclear. You have it with you though, not far from here. Most curious. So much of your past and future relies on this very object. It is beautiful, yet there is fear surrounding it and its safety. I can see a lower case e, next to this object; this indicates the initial owner's name begins with the letter 'E'.

"There is much travelling in both your cups for a time. These lines and dots, formed by the dust and smaller leaves, show journeys. I see return journeys to and from the same place. This cross upon one of the future journey lines shows vexation of some kind. There is a toad like symbol here at that same cross line indicating sorrow. At the same time, on the other side of the cross line there is a flower and a star, indicating joy and success. Most unusual.

"There is a lower case 'b' by your future cross line, Genevieve. I believe this is the first letter of your future child: a daughter. There is also a cat on the side of that line, indicating misfortune in and around that time. But wait. Once again, the opposite side of the cross line holds a crescent moon, which is very joyous and foretells illuminated time.

"Your cups have so many similarities. I have never seen anything like it. Lastly, I see countless symbols of family. From the tip of the cup to the center of the cup, this family symbology runs throughout. I must finish getting my room ready, so if you don't mind, I shall ask that you leave now."

We thanked Yao Jun and tried to tidy our places, but she was adamant that we leave everything and leave immediately. It was an abrupt departure. We had, after all, spent longer than anticipated in her workspace and we felt she must have been anxious to ready herself in time for the evening's onslaught. It was as though she was agitated by our reading and was trying to be rid of us quickly.

Some declare tea leaf reading as a hoax, but her declarations were extremely accurate, a fact that cannot be denied. As we departed, I handed her a few coins, which she graciously accepted.

A blonde-haired boy of about ten approached and asked Yao Jun for money. She tossed him a coin and he replied, "Thanks Ma Yao."

"My adopted son," Yao Jun said, with a strained chuckle.

The boy looked toward Genevieve and smiled. Then he ran off.

"A fine-looking lad," I replied.

"Yes, yes, I adopted him a few days after he was born. His mother was a young Swedish immigrant girl with no means to keep him, I think. She was in labour when she tapped on my friend's door. My friend brought her in, helped her have the boy, and then the mother left in the middle of the night. The only thing the girl left with the child was a name.

"I visited two days later. My friend already had five of her own and I had none, but wanted one, so I took him. So simple really."

We thought the adoption story was rather odd, but we thought Yao was rather odd too, so we laughed it off. As we made our way back toward the big tent, we could see Liam waving to us in the distance.

Liam approached excitedly. "Feel like taking a side trip for an hour?"

"A side trip? To where?" I asked.

"Just down the road. A cousin of Frank's has a small farm and was just given a runaway mare. I thought I would have a look at her. Just for a few minutes."

"Liam, let us not beat around the bush. Yes. We shall go with you but let us not pretend we will be gone for less than two hours. You and a wild horse for a few minutes are just not possible. It is still early, and as long as we are back in time for the opening parade, it will be fine."

Just then, Julian, accompanied by Yao Jun's boy bouncing along with him, approached and asked if Genevieve would like to wander with them for a bit.

"Please Mother, may I? I will stay close to Julian, I promise. I don't really want to go see a wild horse."

"I suppose it would do no harm but mind yourself and don't get into trouble or wander off. Your father and I shall venture over to this wild mare and meet you back here in two hours. Agreed?"

"Agreed," replied Julian. "I'll have to finish getting ready for the parade anyway, so that suits me just fine. Come along you young ones, let's wander."

As the three walked off, the slender boy ran his fingers through his wavy blonde hair, looking sideways at Genevieve with a wry grin, "My name is Jonathan."

33

*J*ulian, Genevieve, and Jonathan wandered zig-zag-gedly around the circus grounds while Julian shared stories, made introductions, and regaled the children with flamboyant re-enactments of travelling life. Jonathan pulled pastel-coloured sweets wrapped in white paper from his trouser pocket and offered them to Genevieve. Genevieve eyed the pretty treats with longing, but declined them, so as not to appear brash. Jonathan stared at her in disbelief.

"Oh, come on, I can see you'd like them. They're very delicious. Called saltwater taffy, and they melt in your mouth," he drawled, almost taunting but just kind enough to be convincing.

Genevieve looked to her shoes. "Well, perhaps if you and Julian are having one, I would join you."

With that, Jonathan stuck his hand into his opposite pocket and removed six more. "Plenty to go around!"

Jonathan was elfin for his age, but like his adopted mother, had a bountiful personality. When Julian excused himself momentarily to converse with one of his troupe members, Genevieve was stuck for words and an awkward silence ensued.

Then Jonathan boldly pronounced, "I'm adopted you know. Yao got me as a baby, but I'm adopted. That's why I don't look like her."

While it had been true that Yao Jun had described to him the foundation of his entry into the world, Genevieve found the blurting of this personal information to a complete stranger rather cheeky, and wondered if all American children were this forthright.

Julian was relieved when he saw Genevieve's parents advancing toward them. Grace had a look of relief on her face as well, as the horse incident had taken longer than Liam estimated (no surprise there) and they were almost fifteen minutes late in returning to the meeting place.

It was late afternoon when the parade commenced. Animals, jugglers, musicians, clowns, acrobats, all parading and dancing through the streets, in a pre-show extravaganza. The excitement was palpable, and the over-the-top display would no doubt have swayed any naysayers to do an about face and attend the show.

The Furlongs were seated in front row centre with Frank Nicolas, in the much sought after box seats, that offered a terrific all-around view. Concessionaires began passing through the rows of seats, selling peanuts, cotton candy, souvenirs, and programs. Grace bought a bag of peanuts, one program, and an elephant pin.

Lights were dimmed, and as the band began to play, a mighty cheer echoed through the crowd. A large flap opened from the outside centre of the tent and a parade, much like the street one, commenced.

Everyone in the audience loved the horses with their feathered caps, and the sparklingly dressed men and women who rode them. The full house cheered and clapped as the jugglers followed with their antics. Then the ringmaster made a grand entrance. He was very large man, not just in height, but also in girth. As he welcomed everyone to the first show, a clown snuck up behind him making faces and miming his movements, much to the audiences' delight. Of course, when the ringmaster turned, so did the clown and this cat and mouse game continued until a second clown emerged, to foil the first.

The individual performances were artistically executed and had everyone utterly amazed and impressed. Julian and his troupe had the audience on the edge of their seats for the acrobats featured time. Liam noted the incomprehensible faith and bravery it takes to fling oneself from a platform, twirl in midair, and trust that your fellow acrobat will be there to catch you. Frank agreed and said he would be very relieved when his brother eventually gave up the lifestyle for something less dangerous.

The second half of the show included a magician/illusionist, which left the crowd agog. The big cats were a huge hit as were the small dog acts and jugglers. All in all, it was a magical evening.

PART II

34

A soft whimpering caused Norah to raise her eyes from the diary. Úla removed a hanky from inside the sleeve of her woolly cardigan and wiped briny drizzle from her cheeks.

Norah's prior annoyances softened as she eyed the genuine sorrow in her mother's aging face.

"I can't help feeling as though I have been disloyal, Norah. All these years, Mother has been trying to tell me these stories. She must have viewed me as a rather cruel daughter. I wouldn't listen. Wouldn't indulge her. Perhaps I was a daughter she liked well enough but didn't love, because of that."

"No, I believe you to be wrong. I know Nana accepted you for who you are: a beautiful, intelligent daughter with an unfamiliar philosophy. Sure, you had some differences, but I'd say she accepted you for not only your obvious strengths but also for your human foibles. But make no mistake. Love you, she did." Norah hesitated, then added, "As do I."

Úla curled her legs beneath her and stuffed her hanky back into her sleeve. Taking in a sharp, full breath, she blurted, "Enough blubbering. I'm anxious to know what happens next."

Norah's surprised expression brought forth a new wave of emotion from Úla, and she removed her hanky once again, "Something radically shifted in me as I've learned about New York and a family connection I didn't know about before. I can't explain it. It's like a light was turned on, and I know I'll not be able to turn it off again. What is this that I am feeling, do you think?"

Norah smiled, "It's called acceptance and faith. Acceptance of our lineage and faith in your own mother's truthful story. You've stepped over the threshold of logic and into the expanse of mystical. Welcome aboard," said Norah, smiling. She patted her mother's hand in a gesture, she knew, relayed camaraderie before returning to the pages.

Letters Across the Atlantic

My Dear Grace and Genevieve,
You have only been gone for two weeks and already I
am anxious for your return. I am, of course, glad that
you are back on our home soil for a little while, but
life is just not the same without you. I look forward to
receiving word as to how you are. Give Jenny and Luna
a scratch from me!
Your loving husband and father,
Liam

My Dearest Liam,
We are fine and are recuperated from the voyage. You
would think that after all the back and forth we have
done over the last several years, I would be used to the
ocean, but alas, I am always joyous when I set my feet
on the good solid earth. Jenny has a swollen right back
leg, and the vet is with her as I write.
Your post was delivered yesterday. Genevieve loved
your card and gift. I do have a small concern, however,
regarding Genevieve and Jonathan, that I wish I could
discuss with you directly. Upon our return to the cot-
tage, Genevieve ran straight to her baskets and brought
out the notes she and Jonathan have sent each other
over the past couple of years. She even brought a letter
he gave her on his last visit to the ranch. He told her
not to read it until she arrived at the cottage. Honestly,
I know they have been good friends, but I do hope this
is not turning into a crush. What do you think?
Love to you, always,
Grace

Chapter 34

Hello Daddy,
I met one of the cooks on the ship and I told him I was
turning twelve. He knocked on our cabin door the next
day, my actual birthday, and he had in his hand a
lovely little apple tart with a candle in it.
Thank you for the beautiful butterfly pendant. It is
around my neck, and I love it!
Mother said she forgot to tell you about the letter I
found aboard the ship. I went to bed one night with my
journal and dropped my pencil down the side of the
bunk. I had to use a second pencil to get the first up
and as I did, I noticed a scrunched bit of paper. Mother
and I managed to retrieve it, and to our surprise it
was part of a letter that had obviously been written on
board by a passenger! It was written by a Scot, by the
name of Hamish Adlam. Here is what it says. (The first
page was missing.)

> *…can I say to it all. It has been six years since I*
> *stole aboard a sailing ship from Oban bay. Only*
> *a boy, barely sixteen, and I now return, six years*
> *later, a man of 22. My mind is overly full with*
> *thoughts and memories of all the work I have done*
> *in order to capture the illusive immigrant dream;*
> *blasting mines, digging for gold, and working*
> *the rails in blinding snow with countless other*
> *Irish and Scotsman.*
> *I went searching for paradise, searching for that*
> *dream, but found only dust, ice, and disappoint-*
> *ment. America was not at all the jewel I envisioned,*
> *and she did not advance me, except in years. I tell*

you, the last few months I have done nothing but dream of going home. It is as though my spirit is swept away from me at night and I fly over the miles on blackened skies. I land and sit by the warmth of a crackling fire, listening to my old friend Angus play an aire, soft and low on his grandfather's fiddle. I have tried desperately to make a go of it, Gregory, and I will miss your company and the things we would get up to. I will miss the craic, the card games, and the girls of course. But Island ties won't let me go and I look forward to rattling down the cobblestones once more. I will write when I am settled, but you can write to me at me mam's and I will gladly reply.
Marrory Adlam
Ibis House
Oban, Argyll
Scotland
Best to you Gregory,
Hamish Adlam
Isn't that amazing? Mother says she is going to post it to Hamish in care of Marrory Adlam. Isn't that brilliant? I want Mam to put our return address on it, but she says no, let it be dust in the wind, falling on a doorstep.
Love,
Gen
(I am thinking of calling myself Gen)

Dear Gen,
All is well here. Where does the time go? Nibs misses
you; she neighs and stomps her feet whenever I am in
her sight, as if asking me where you are. Tulip is doing
great and it's hard to believe that she was once a wild
runaway. Her colt should be born right around the
time of your return.
Hamish Adlam is it? That is quite a story all right
and I agree with your mother, regarding sending it
along as, what did she call it? "Dust on a doorstep"? I
love her terms.
Mind your mother.
Your loving father

35

Norah and Dónal sat together in the mid-morning sun. Norah closed the back cover of the diary.

"That's all there is, Dónal. After Mam and I read the diary, we searched the house and barn but to no avail. I've not found another diary or any clues as to where this Mobhrí might be. Probably we should just get on with life and see what turns up. I do feel strongly that something will turn up, though. There's got to be something else in that barn. My nana had faith that I'd find it and I don't want to disappoint her. Mother and I explored all the bags and boxes from the loft just before she left for Vermont, a couple of days ago, in search of something that might steer us in the direction of the Mobhrí; but . . . nothing." Norah smiled broadly, adding, "Úla, the ever-pragmatic and even-keeled scientist has become a shape-shifter. She's obsessed with finding the Mobhrí, now. I'm surprised she actually left for Vermont, she was so fervent in her digging in the barn."

Dónal shaded his eyes. "Well, I'm sure she forgot all about it once she left."

Norah released a howl. "Forgot about it? She's e-mailed me six times. 'Look here, check there, what about this?' She must be driving her colleagues mad with her frequent and unexplained interruptions of meetings and such. She's driving me mad, just the same. I told her yesterday to pull back from it all and concentrate on her work. I should probably take my own advice."

Dónal wrapped his arm gently around Norah's waist and drew her to him.

"At least it's unlikely she will talk to anyone about it, so there's that." Norah added.

"I'll be here to help. You know I will." Dónal reminded her. "And don't concern yourself. I'm keenly aware that this should be kept well under wraps. My lips are sealed. There's so much to think about in these pages. It may be a good thing to have a respite. When we begin to convert the barn, who knows what we might discover? Speaking of that, the loan has come through. We can order our materials now. I have also ordered my bee boxes, thank you very much indeed."

"I'm so sorry Dónal. I've been so distracted with this diary; I haven't even asked about your bee seminar. Tell me all."

Dónal rose from the porch and began dancing around Norah in an odd fashion.

"What on earth? Why are you acting the maggot, Dónal?"

"It's the bee dance, my Norah. I am a bee dancer, telling you that this is the perfect nesting site."

"What are you on about?"

Dónal's eyes gleamed, and his voice became childishly animated as he told Norah about scout bees looking for appropriate nesting sites, when original nests become too crowded.

"Here, let me draw you a diagram."

Dónal removed a crinkled piece of paper from his pocket and plucked a stubby pencil from behind his ear. Kneeling in front of Norah, he began a crude drawing of the internal design of a beehive.

"Honeybees are tremendously intelligent. They build their nests in an organized and city-like manner: a place for everything and everything in its place. I thought about them as you were reading about the circus in the diary; bees work as a tight team in order to survive, too. We are going to…rather I am going to…give them a pre-fabricated home, but in the wild, Oh Norah, in the wild."

"Need I ask? Okay, I'll bite. Tell me Dónal. Tell me about bees in the wild."

"Well, since you're forcing me, I shall. In a nutshell, they build their nests to function in perfect harmony. Wax combs with hexagonal cells are built to rear the wee ones, and serve as storage compartments for honey, pollen, and nectar. Some bees patrol the exterior of the hive, dancing to attract the foraging bees. 'Pass me some food' is what they're saying in the dance movements."

"So, you were just dancing around me because you're ready for tea?"

"No. A food dance only lasts about a minute or so. My dance was far more complicated, and if I was a bee, could have lasted a half hour."

"Dear me. I shall keep that in mind for the future, Dónal."

Dónal began to dance once again. His words became breathy and expressive.

"When an old colony has an excess number of workers and is overcrowded, a new site is necessary. The majority of workers will leave the nest with a queen and attach themselves to some overhanging tree limb or a thick cluster of branches. The workers have to operate quickly, as the queen's food is stored in their stomachs. Since food is relatively limited at this juncture, they must find an abandoned nest site before all their stomach-stored food is gone and before the workers die. It's complicated, as the new site must be good quality if it's going to survive for many years."

"How long will they check the real estate market?"

"Could be up to a week. Generally, though, they find something within a couple of days, especially if they choose a neighbourhood wisely.

"So, the swarm sends out scouts, or as you would like to have it, estate agents. Each scout spends extensive time finding, reviewing, and critiquing abandoned nest sites. By this I mean inspecting the interior and exterior, as well as observing the surrounding area for possible future food sources.

"Once a scout finds what she thinks is a suitable site, she returns to the swarm. The worker bees covering the top of the swarm await the scouts' return. Upon her arrival, she will, as I said, dance for fifteen, perhaps even thirty minutes. The dancing bee narrates, if you will, the location and quality of the nest site she has found. The worker bees read her movements as one might read a good novel."

Dónal sat back down next to Norah, out of breath and starry eyed.

"Whoa. That really is awe-inspiring Dónal. I had no idea. So, then they call the moving van?"

"Perhaps, perhaps not. There are many other scouts out combing neighbourhoods as well, and they too are returning to the workers to dance about the sites that they've found. Each site has different amenities, and the worker bees reject many of the dances, waiting for the right one. The scouts dance to internal tempos and gracefully move their nimble bodies to specific angles depending on and according to the amenities they've discovered. The longer the dance, the better the site."

"But how do they reach a consensus?"

"Consensus occurs when most of the scouts are dancing about the same site. When this decision has been made, a scout will take a buzzing run at the swarm, dispersing the workers, causing the cluster to break up and take to the sky. The guide bees lead the way to the new site by using chemical cues and wing rhythms, though by the time the swarm has been dispersed, most of the workers already know how to get to the site."

"Honestly Dónal, how have I lived this long and not known any of this? I can tell by the glint in your eyes that you've a lot more to tell me."

Dónal stood and danced momentarily. "Yes, indeedy. After tea."

36

*N*orah could hear the reverberations of hammering in the barn as she sat at her desk. Though it could be a bit distracting, she did enjoy the time delay from the hit of the nails to the echo of the sound pushing past her. Dónal's workspace was coming along quite nicely and would be a lovely addition to the property. Meanwhile, Dónal was busy unpacking the bee boxes and supplies. He had cleared, pruned, and readied the back acreage with great care in anticipation of the new arrivals. He was now referring to the coming bees as his 'other queen and her consorts', which Norah was chuffed with.

The two had gone to the barn before the renovations and had rummaged around the place, looking for any clues as to where the Mobhrí might be. Crawling along the dirt with two long knives, they pushed beneath the earth, in hopes that something might have been buried there. They ran their hands along the barn walls in search of a secret panel. They even pulled apart three old bales of hay that had stood atop each other for years. All they found were spider webs, stones, an old horseshoe, and a family of mice.

Dónal was pulling a splinter from his thumb with his teeth when Norah brought him out a cup of tea. Luain was sitting on the railing of the porch, copying the sound of Dónal's drill.

"Tea for you, my dear."

"Reading my mind Norah, thank you."

Luain squawked. "Yoo hoo, hello."

Norah scratched the bird's neck. "Yes, hello to you too. So, my bee man, any day now you'll become a beekeeper."

"Well, a hobbyist anyway. If it proves to be a success, then I may end up a sideliner."

"I used to be one of those at school dances."

"Funny. No, a sideliner is one who sells honey or bees as a secondary income. I don't ever see myself as a full-time apiarist."

"Those boxes look interesting."

"I bought ten of them. I built a raised wood foundation down by the trees so these boxes will be off the damp ground."

"Why do you have a roll of greaseproof paper?"

"These frames can slide in and out of the boxes. See? Each frame holds a sheet of the paper for the bees to get a head start with. They produce their own wax, but this is a starting place for them to build honeycomb on. When we, I mean . . . when I am ready to harvest the honey, we, I, can simply slide the frames out and extricate the honey."

"And I know you'll look oh so stylish in this white net hat. Makes me feel all buzzy inside."

"I prefer to look a lunatic than get stung. Bees are very attracted to the heat of breath."

"Mmmm," Norah leaned over and slowly kissed him.

"Oh yes, I definitely think you should wear that hat." She kissed him again. "Definitely."

Norah rose to her feet, and as she did, picked up a pair of smooth white gloves that lay beside the boxes.

"Can they not make these in another colour besides white? I mean, it would be much more interesting to see you in blue tweed. I can tell by the look in your eyes that you are about to impart some new knowledge into my overtaxed brain."

"La la la," he sang, and continued, "Bees' natural predators tend to be things like birds and badgers and such. In other parts of the world, skunks and bears would be their predators. Bees have naturally evolved to be wary of all things dark and furry. Smooth white clothing makes them less fretful and defensive."

"So … would you …"

Dónal's phone rang, and he answered, with Luain repeating after, "Hello, Dónal here."

He and Norah gave each other a smile, both recalling the day they met. Dónal gave Norah a 'thumbs up' signal and spoke excitedly, with many affirmative responses.

When he hung up from the call he said, "The supplies came just in time. That was James. It seems my bees are ready for delivery. Don't look concerned. Some of their bees from one hive took flight and they clustered not far away. Since bees don't fly at night, they were able to capture the lot of them, queen and all, and have them ready to bring to me."

"Will you name your new queen?"

"I hadn't thought of it."

"I have."

"Yes? And what name have you chosen?"

"How about Gráinne?"

"Ehh. Gráinne … as in the pirate queen from the fifteen-hundred's Gráinne?"

"That is who I was thinking of."

"Sure, why not? Seems appropriate."

Norah grinned.

"Norah…I hope you're not planning on naming all the bees. It would be impossible, you know…Norah… Norah?"

37

By the end of day, Norah's keyboard was clicking away in perpetual motion. The printer spat out page after page for editing. This was a relief, not only because her deadline was drawing near but also because writing helped her escape the constant mental strain of searching for that seemingly elusive treasure.

Her office, which was usually kept quite tidy, had become a shambles. Papers lay strewn five deep on her desk. The rubbish bin spilled over the brim. Story-line ideas on sticky notes, which had fallen to the floor, stuck to her feet as she drifted about the room. Dónal, finding Norah in tidy-up mode, kindly offered to assist in the daunting task of organizing and sorting.

Norah sat quietly at the table, staring into space, and barely touching her meal. Dónal rubbed his foot against hers under the table.

"What's the trouble Norah? Thinking about . . . it?"

Norah nodded and sighed.

"Thank you for helping me sort my room. Not very professional of me to let it get that discombobulated."

"You're welcome. Perhaps you're not as professional as you like to think."

"What?"

"Yes, well, I just read an interesting study about people who think they're professional but after taking a simple four question test, found out that they were not as with it as they thought."

Norah eyed Dónal skeptically.

"Yes?"

"Yes. I think you should take the test right here and now as a matter of fact."

"Okayyy…Why does this feel like I'm about to be bamboozled?"

"Don't be daft."

Dónal rose from his chair and went to his pack. He came back a few seconds later and slid two pieces of paper toward Norah, saying,

"Four questions, not very difficult. Go."

Dónal watched Norah read. He watched the corners of her mouth turn upward in a smile and into a laugh. He loved to hear her laugh.

1. How do you put a hippo in a refrigerator?

The correct answer is: Open the refrigerator, put in the hippo, and close the door. This question tests whether you tend to do things in an excessively complicated way.

2. How do you put a rhino in a refrigerator?

Did you say, "Open the refrigerator, put in the rhino and close the door?" Incorrect Answer. Correct Answer: Open the refrigerator, take out the hippo, put in the rhino and close the door. This tests your ability to comprehend and to think through the ramifications of your prior actions.

3. King Kong is holding an animal conference. All the animals attend except one. Which animal does not attend?

*Correct Answer: The rhino. The rhino is in the refrig-
erator. Do you not remember that you just put him in
there? This tells us about your memory.*

*Last question.
4. There is a one-mile stretch of land that you must
walk across which is known to be inhabited by
hungry ferocious lions. How do you manage it?*

*Correct Answer: You walk confidently across it. Have
you not been listening? Do you really not remember that all the lions are at the animal conference?
If you got this wrong, then you do not learn well
from previous mistakes.*

Norah laughed as she sighed, "How do you always manage
to make me feel better? Even though I'm obviously not a
professional, as I got them all wrong, I am laughing."

Norah went back to work after the two sorted the kitch-
en. Dónal poked his head into her office at half six. "Just a
reminder, we're going to the cinema tonight. We should
leave in about two hours."

"Thanks, Dearie-o. I will just do a few more things here
and I will get ready."

Norah scratched her head with a pencil. Sometimes,
the problem with tidying is that you put things away but
later forget where you put them. Norah wondered where
the piece of paper with her storyline notes had gotten to.

"Now where did I put that?" she queried aloud.

Norah riffled through her file cabinet folder labeled
'story ideas'. The paper was not there, and she hoped it had
not been tossed into the fire with all the other discarded
paper. In a flash, Norah remembered her three-ring-binder
with completed stories. This she withdrew from her shelf

and opened to the front page. There, tucked in the inside flap of the cover, was her paper.

"Right here in the inside flap," she said to no one.

It was as though someone had tapped her on the shoulder . . . and whispered in her ear. She suddenly recalled something that her nana had said in the letter.

"Remember, that things are not always as they appear. The answers to some of life's greatest treasures can be found in obvious places."

Norah hurriedly removed the diary from her bottom desk drawer. Not really sure what she was doing, she followed her intuition; untied the ribbon that held it closed and removed the elastic bands that held each cover together. The front cover was very frayed, and Norah replaced those bands. The back cover was in better shape. Norah slid two fingers gently down the inside of the back cover and stopped at the ripped spine. Turning the book on its side, she gently pulled apart the frail interior. A solitary, folded sheet of paper was slipped inside the cover.

Not quite able to reach it with her fingers, she placed the diary on her desk, and ran to their bedroom. Hastily, she dumped the contents of her small cosmetic bag out on the bed.

Dónal had just stepped out of the shower and asked why she was in such a frenetic state.

"My tweezers! Where are they?" Norah scrambled through the pile, as several items rolled to the floor, until at last she had the tweezers in her hand.

She looked at Dónal. "The diary . . . it has another piece of paper . . . in the cover . . . I need to get it out!"

Norah ran back to her desk. Dónal followed, still shedding water.

Norah slid the tweezers carefully inside the opening and extricated the paper. It was a missing page from when

Genevieve and her father had been corresponding. They had all noticed a missing page when they were reading the diary but assumed it just had fallen out long ago. The found page read:

Father,
Mother and I decided to bring the Mobhrí to the river
last week. We saw some people we have not seen before:
two women. I thought they must be about one hundred
years old, but mother assures me that I was looking at
them through very young eyes. They were drawing in
the sandy soil. It was a drawing of a tall tree. Inside
the tree was a carved pattern: the same one that is
on the Mobhrí. They nodded their heads as if we were
supposed to understand something, but we still have
no clue as to what they were trying to relay to us. Two
more days before we leave. We shall go say goodbye
to Jenny and Luna tomorrow. I cannot wait to see you
and am bringing you some seeds as you requested.
Love
Genevieve

Dónal looked at Norah's joyful face. "This obviously means something to you. I can see that look . . . Norah."

"Dónal . . . Yes . . . of course! Nana and I used to spend hours in the tree house reading, telling stories, and having tea parties. It's the key that tells me where I need to go. Let's get to the tree house."

Norah and Dónal stood under the tree house, looking up at the aged structure.

"Shall I have a look first Norah? I mean, to check for structural stability?"

Norah hesitated. One the one hand, she wanted to be the first up. On the other, she had, over the years, come to be more than a little uncomfortable with heights.

"Well . . . all right . . . maybe . . . if you don't mind."

The lowest rung of the wooden ladder was fairly high, given that the tree had grown over the years. Dónal stepped on the first rung, and it instantly collapsed under him. Ten minutes later, Dónal had set up the old metal ladder and was checking the rungs as he climbed, re-hammering those that were loose.

"Dónal. I have changed my mind. I think I would like to be the first one up in the tree house. If I get nervous and change my mind, I'll come straight down and let you do the honours. Right?"

Dónal checked the rungs as high as he could and came back down. He handed Norah the torch from his back pocket.

"They are looking grand up top Norah but mind yourself."

"I figure that if my nana could make it up there, then I had better be able to, fear of heights be damned."

Norah took a deep breath and began climbing. It was surprisingly exciting to be returning to a place of such positive memories, and her nervousness began to bend toward joy. Spider webs blocked the entrance. Norah wiped them aside. Entering that familiar but small space was euphoric, especially when the light from the torch illuminated the room. As a child, it had seemed that there was ample room. Funny that.

Norah crawled along the floorboards to two little wooden windows. Time and weather had glued the wood swollen shut, but Norah heaved her shoulder against them, and they flew open. Musty smelling leaf debris fell to the ground. She waved and called down to Dónal. As daylight streamed into the place, Norah sat back, hitting her head against something. She turned to find a hanging crystal.

Memories flooded in with the light and Norah let her senses fall into celebrated recollections. It was as if she were in a time capsule. Throw pillows lay side-by-side along the far wall. A long wobbly wooden shelf, held up by chipped red bricks, still supported clay pots and old teacups. Norah crawled to a spot that she had utterly forgotten about. A large poster of a black horse hung askew on a wall. The photo had decayed long and ever ago, but she was not concerned about that. After removing the picture and laying it on the floor, Norah eyed the hollow hole in the trunk of the tree. Though some unknown creature had created the hole, she and her nana had furthered its depth by gouging away at it over many visits.

It had been Norah's secret place, where she kept 'private' things. When she was little, her private things comprised a deck of old playing cards, some sweets, a few perfume bottles, and notes that she wrote to Genevieve. She and her nana were the only ones who knew of the hideaway's existence. Why she had not thought of it until now was a mystery, but life is like that, full of mysteries, just like her nana had stated in her note. Above the hole was a tiny carved symbol she now recognized. It was the same scroll pattern that was on the head of the skeleton key.

She raised the torch and shone it into the hole. The light brightened a few cobwebs and the long-forgotten, afore-mentioned articles. A small black spider scurried along its web and curled up into a ball in a far corner.

"There's something in here!" she yelled down to Dónal. "Sorry little guy," she said aloud to the curled black ball. Wiping most of the web aside with her torch, Norah plucked out the contents of the hole. The cards, the perfume bottles and childhood letters were at the forefront, while something bulky wrapped in cloth lay at the back.

She and Dónal sat on the ground at the bottom of the tree. Norah explained about her childhood hiding spot.

"My old playing cards and things were at the front of the opening, and this was behind them."

Norah held the bundle out in front of her crossed legs and untied the string that held it closed. From it, she removed a dusty wooden box with a tarnished brass lock, and a transparent plastic bag, similar to the one she'd found in the barn. From the bag came another diary.

The two hurried back to the house, to Norah's office, where she detached the skeleton key from the first diary's ribbon. The wooden box itself was beautiful. Brownish-purple and, when wiped clean, quite polished. Norah slipped the key into the lock. The two smiled at each other as the lock clicked open.

Norah's mind was swimming as she lifted out and unrolled the object wrapped in purple velvet. It was, to Norah, even more magnificent than the diary pages had described. There was a large note, in her nana's hand, taped to the top.

If you are reading this Norah, then you have succeeded in finding the Mobhrí. I have done my diligence. I do not have to worry about your mother's feelings that I have forced anything upon you, for you have pursued this moment of your own free will.

Let me quote from the first diary and a reference to your great-grandmother Genevieve (a.k.a. Caitlín). She had arrived at the village in a cart pulled by a white and a black horse. A young baby, barely out of wraps, lay alongside her, seemingly contented with their mode of travel. Caitlín claimed to be a widow from a distant county in search of a better life for herself and her daughter.

Of course, that baby in wraps was me. This is the farm my mother, Genevieve purchased. These life events will no doubt prove disturbing Norah, so I am giving you fair warning.

These are Genevieve's diary pages. . . .

Sitting together with her beloved on the couch, legs entwined, Norah blurted, "Oh, Dónal. While I'm ecstatic for having found the Mobhrí and second diary, I'm also down-right petrified to read what Nana was referring to; about this next passage being disturbing enough to warrant a warning."

Dónal pulled Norah closer. "I'm here, Norah. We'll continue on together. Whatever is in these pages, it's all in the past, so keep that at the forefront if you can. None of it can't be altered, right?"

Norah nodded her agreement and cracked open the tattered leather diary to the first page.

Genevieve

Extremely **harsh events** have brought me to this time and place, hence I must concentrate on things that are to come and not dwell too sternly on the past.

I have assuredly been deceived, but I have not been defeated. I promised my parents to stand strong through it all, and that is what I intend to do, for all our sakes, but especially for the sake of my daughter, Bríghid.

Truth be told, my youthful naiveté got the better of me and I fell in love with a confidence trickster.

My mistakes have forced me to walk a fresh path, forced me to create a new identity, and most disturbingly, forced my parents to depart before they were ready to do so. But I will come to that.

I recall reading an article pertaining to spiders on one of my last trips to New York. Most spiders are loners and keep their captured rewards for themselves. There are however, a few species of spiders that employ cooperative tactics in order to survive.

According to the article, these rarities live in mighty communities. One particular species, that lives in Ecuador, hunts in packs. Their nests house thousands of individuals. After hanging threads down from low lying leaves, they proceed to hide themselves upside down, underneath the leaves, until prey becomes ensnarled in their dangling strands. Once trapped, an assembly drops down to do what all spiders do: encase the prey and inject their venom. Working as a team, this species cooperatively returns their catch to the nest, where they share the bounty with the community.

While the web that captured me had only two hunters, the article was reminiscent of my experience, thus I think of these spiders when reflecting upon past events.

They were a clever pair, Yao and Jonathan Jun. They took their time, laid in wait, and pounced. The first couple of encounters with Yao Jun were memorably odd at best. The tea reading, while intriguing, was a little disconcerting. My mother and I both felt abruptly dismissed from her trailer in what you might call a 'here's your hat, what's your hurry?' manner.

My next interaction with Yao occurred at the end of the circus' opening night. My father and I were by the snake exhibit. He was engrossed in some uninteresting adult conversation with Frank Nicolas, about who knows what. I let go of my father's hand and bent down to re-buckle my sandal. Yao Jun squatted next to me and whispered something along the lines of, "You are like these snakes. You have skin I can see, but it is false. That too I can see. You hide something underneath."

She took my hand and abruptly turned it palm up. "Yes, yes, I look closely and I see another skin."

She tried to draw my hand closer to her face, but I pulled away and snuggled myself into my father's side. My father looked down at me and then at Yao Jun.

Yao smiled and said, "Your daughter is so pretty."

Yao was indeed correct in her readings. My mother and I did travel quite frequently, between Ireland and New York. Our family did hold a powerful secret. My father was asked to extend his contract far beyond the original proposal. Though we all longed to return to Ireland permanently, it was impossible for my father to turn down such steady, lucrative earnings when times were so hard back home. Expenses were minimal as our housing and basic expenses were covered in his contract; therefore, he was able to deposit handsome sums into their bank account, for as he would say, 'our future nest'.

Julian would unfailingly visit us when he passed through the area with the circus, and it became a habit that he would bring Jonathan with him to the ranch. Even though Jonathan was a few years older than me, we got on famously. I was not afraid to go frog hunting, or to swing from a tree rope, playfully releasing myself into the navy blue depths of the nearby lake. Jonathan would often remark that I was not like most girls. He hated most girls and would just as soon leave them be, like leaving green beans to go cold on a plate.

I liked Jonathan. He was funny and clever and a wee bit bold in my eyes when it came to talking back to grownups. As the years went by, I found myself pining over his absences, though I would be loath to tell anyone this, as I felt unsure as to what I was actually pining for. I was still a child, but the pit of my stomach twirled when I saw him, or for that matter, thought of him. I wrote a childish poem that I would recite for days after he would depart.

> *The sun has left the sky*
> *The fields are golden dry*
> *The trees by night do sigh*
> *And only I know why*

Months would pass without seeing him and I would continue to live my days, but I would think of him often. There were times when my lonely heart felt like it would burst. It was these times that I went to the barns. Though the Nicolas Ranch had dozens of horses, there were certain ones that caught my interest. Nibs, of course, was my favourite; she and I had a beautiful alliance. I was one of the first people to make her acquaintance and had been the privileged one to name her. I brushed her and fed her. I talked and sang to her. I was the first person she let lift her leg to clean the bottom of her hooves. She was my horse, and I was her girl.

Ace was an immense stallion that I steered clear of. His prodigious bone structure, muscle mass and flaring nostrils scared the bejeezus out of me, but he was irrefutably an exquisite beast. Seventeen plus hands he was, with an ebony coat that glistened with sweat after an hour of being worked hard in the ring. Deep, black pool eyes seemed to plunge into a deliriously bewitching abyss. The only part of him that was not black was a white triangle on his wide forehead. It resembled an 'A', hence, his name.

A gentle, light golden mare called Curry had a way about her that was easy going and perceptive. She could handle an experienced rider without a bother on her, but even with an inexperienced mount on her back, she would go quiet as a lamb, knowing to take care and step gingerly. She was the horse that many visitors were placed on. Half the time she was called Belle, as in 'Belle of the Ball.'

Mr Queue used to make us all laugh. If he were in a ring, or on a trail with other horses, he would invariably find a way to be last in line. One could coax and plead until the cows came home but invariably he brought up the rear. The ranch had acquired him as an adult horse with this giddy habit, but since it was more comical than irksome, they did little to alter it. His official name was Shortcut, but over time, Mr Queue became a more befitting one.

On my thirteenth birthday, to my great delight and surprise, Julian arrived, bringing Jonathan with him. I was in one of the barns, brushing Nibs, when I heard Julian's voice. My arm stopped mid-stroke and Nibs turned her head round to me, eyes questioning why I had wavered in her grooming.

She snorted and I shushed her, saying, "Nibs, quiet, I am trying to listen."

Then I heard the vocal timbre I knew so well. I threw the brush into the bucket to the side of me and wrapped my arms around my horse's neck.

"Here! He's here! Oh, what a joyful birthday it has turned out to be."

I spun around several times in gleeful abandon and frolicked to the barn door. There, I commenced to compose myself and sauntered out in a lackadaisical style, even though my heart was racing like Ace's when he was worked hard in the corral.

I could tell Jonathan was happy to see me, but he looked rather pale and drawn, as if he had been under the weather for some time. What I did not expect to hear was Yao Jun's voice directly behind me. We had seen each other several times over the years but there had never been a particular fondness between us.

To my surprise, she approached me and hugged me, saying, "Little Genevieve, you're not so little anymore, eh? So good to see you."

I was frankly stunned by this show of affection but was so happy to see Jonathan that I returned a warm smile and pleasant greeting. Mr Nicolas suggested we all go to the house for some refreshment. The adults retreated to the kitchen, while Jonathan and I sat talking in the sun-soaked dining room. We could hear voices in the periphery, but several times the voices would subside to hushed tones. Though I could not make out exactly what was said, I did hear Jonathan's name mentioned several times. Just as I was about to inquire after Jonathan's health, the adults entered the dining room with tea and biscuits.

That night, my mother came to me after I had retired with the news that Jonathan had been quite ill for the past several weeks, with some malady that was yet to be diagnosed. Yao was very concerned that life on the road was becoming far too straining on him, and had approached Mr Nicolas about keeping him on the farm to recuperate for a time.

Mr Nicolas had agreed to have him, under the condition that he worked as a ranch hand when he was able. I swallowed hard, as my mother relayed this news, trying to contain my excitement. Having Jonathan living on the ranch would be a dream come true.

39

*T*he next year flew by, Jonathan's illness was both inexplicable and intermittent. He would be devoid of symptoms for weeks on end, and then, almost overnight, become indisposed. His symptoms were quite variable. Frequently, he would awaken to a severe headache, muscle aches and nausea. Other times his speech would be slurred, and he would appear befuddled, shaking with chills. There were also times when he would break out in a rash or be doubled over with stomach cramps. After a few days, he would wake up tired, but right as rain.

The local doctor, as well as a specialist hired by Mr Nicolas, concurred that a malaria-infected mosquito must have bitten him, since malaria tended to be a condition with re-occurring bouts, and no particular rhythm. Several treatments were administered, including quinine, but there was little that eased the sporadic physical manifestations. Jonathan would be understandably irritable during these times, and it seemed as though I was the one person with whom he would communicate with any modicum of civility. I became his nursemaid during these bouts. I would read to him and bring him his meals, coaxing him to eat just a little bit more.

My parents were concerned that Jonathan was relying too heavily on me, but I did not mind in the least. In hindsight, I think I was enjoying the role of surrogate mother/wife/nurse. It gave me a sense of purpose. My mam and I were to return home to Ireland again, for four months. My heart was rent with despair, as I longed for the black soil of our home but was fretful at leaving Jonathan in his delicate state. On previous trips, I had been distraught with the thought of leaving my father, and though I would indeed miss him sorely, it was to be the absence of Jonathan that would tear at my heart. In the melting pot of life, love is one of the most mysterious ingredients.

Time, as it does, quickly pushed on. Sometimes the voyages to and from Ireland seemed daunting. Much as I loved to place my feet on the soil of my homeland, I was finding it harder and harder to be apart from Jonathan.

On one trip, which included my seventeenth birthday, Mother and I had a wonderful time, including a big celebration for me at the O'Reillys'. And though it was joyous, I was particularly eager to get back to Ellenville, to Jonathan.

This time, when we arrived back to the ranch, Jonathan appeared to be in complete recovery, at long last. He had grown taller and broader, and now favoured the frame of a strapping young man. I too had physically changed. When our eyes met, there arose in me a merging of both fear and excitement. Not dissimilar, I reasoned, to what a river would feel as it reached the ocean.

Julian and Yao returned to visit the ranch on occasion, but Jonathan never wanted to return to circus life. Mr Nicolas liked him well enough as a labourer and was content with him living and working with the other ranch hands. Thus, Jonathan stayed on the ranch. Thus, I was content, too. It came to my attention, however, that my parents, particularly my mother, were finding excuses to happen upon Jonathan and me when we were alone together.

"Just looking for my sketch pad," or "Have you seen my blue shoes, Genevieve?"

This was especially true when we were out in the barns with the horses.

One bright morning my mother entered the barn as I was cleaning muck out of Nibs' mane. Jonathan was in the process of asking me to wander to the river the following day, as he was free from work. She coughed to announce her presence. Jonathan saw her and added, "I have a book I'd like to read to you, Genevieve."

My mam was not thrilled about the prospect of us going to the river alone, but I argued that I was seventeen, soon to be eighteen, and that I could take care of myself. She eventually capitulated, with the proviso that we return by sunset. I had no intention of doing anything other than wandering down by the river, sitting together under one of the elms, and listening to Jonathan's deep voice fill my silent inner void.

The following morning proved to be a rare spring scorcher of a day. I saddled Nibs as Jonathan readied Belle. The sun was high in the sky by the time we rode the five miles to the Twylla River Bridge. Sweat ran in rivulets down our backs. Dismounting, we briskly walked along the river path a ways, until we reached a shaded spot where the water poured itself into a deep secluded pool. There was no need to speak our utter longing when we eyed the sparkling water. The heat of the day was overwhelming, and scant more moments passed before we were seduced into removing our shoes and plunging, fully clothed, into the quenching antidote for our complaint. We floated contentedly on our backs for several minutes, letting the cool water assuage our overheated bodies before emerging onto the bank. My yellow cotton dress clung to my slender frame in a way that made me feel uncomfortably exposed, and I noticed Jonathan observing me. He noticed me observing him and we both blushed. Recovering quickly, he suggested we climb to a nearby outcropping of rocks to dry. I quickly agreed.

Establishing myself in a reclined position on the hot flat surface was as rewarding as the invigorating water had been. I closed my eyes. The contrast of my now chilled body, mingling with the heat of the rock face, and the knowledge that Jonathan was giving me a sideways glance, caused a ripple through my body, that concluded with a pleasurable tingle. Jonathan noisily rummaged through his canvas bag. I opened my eyes and watched him fumble around with fallen contents, until at last he held in his hand a book.

"I know you are a reader, Genevieve. Julian brought me three books by this writer named Arthur Conan Doyle. He writes mysteries about two detectives named Sherlock Holmes and Dr. Watson."

"Yes, I have heard his name. This is what you will be reading then?"

"This first book is called, *A Study in Scarlet.*" Jonathan's voice flowed over and around me like the hot breeze that gently ruffled the leaves. I listened intently for a time, and diligently tried to fight the dreamy haze I fell toward. His voice became distant, muffled, losing its logic. I woke with a start, to Jonathan's face directly above my own. The heat of his breath edged closer to my mouth, and I let his kiss descend upon my lips. I am not sure how long that kiss lasted, but I do know that time ceased to be. The only realities that prevailed in those moments were breath, lips, and my reverberant beating heart.

I avoided my parents that evening as much as was feasible, feeling sure they would see the change in me. After feeding Nibs and eating a light supper, I excused myself to bed, feigning exhaustion from the sun. I lay awake for what seemed like hours, re-visiting the entire day. I could not sleep and eventually rose and walked dreamily to my bedroom window. As I swung open the window, cool air floated upon my face and billowed my nightdress. Casting my mind back to the rocks, I touched my fingers to my mouth and a wild heat rose up my spine.

"It was just a kiss." I whispered to the inky blackness.

Jonathan called on me the next evening, suggesting we sit under the elm at the back of the house to continue our reading. I said yes immediately of course, though I was a wee bit dismayed that he did not suggest a more private spot. We were in full view of the stables and the household. I did not fall asleep on this occasion, nor did a kiss ensue. I did become quite engrossed in the story nonetheless, and before I knew it, two hours had passed.

Reading under the elm tree became a nightly routine that I enjoyed immensely. When Jonathan's voice grew tired, I would proceed to take up the reading, thus we would pass the book back and forth until the light became too difficult to see by. It was not long before we embarked on the second book called *The Sign of the Four*. My parents were placated in the sense that they witnessed the brotherly/sisterly relationship of Jonathan and me. Though we sat rather too far apart for my liking, sparks continued to fly between us. I knew as I looked into Jonathan's eyes there was more to his feelings than platonic inertia.

A few weeks after we concluded *The Sign of Four*, Jonathan asked me to go for a picnic at the river. My parents, feeling confident that there was little to worry about, were much less foreboding this time. I was happy to go, as Julian and Yao were staying with us, and I was a bit circumspect as to the curious nature of Yao's advancing tenderness toward me. She did take me aside and relay her thanks for my care-giving of Jonathan when he had been so ill. She said I was like a family member to her now, as I was, in large part, responsible for his stunning recovery. While she tried to sound sincere, there was something behind her eyes that made me question her remarks.

I was a trifle perturbed when the day turned out to be overcast and chilly, as I had inwardly hoped for another moment of spark after swimming. As we concluded our lunch Jonathan brought out a flask from his pack. He offered it to me.

"Here is something I have been drinking with the boys. It's kind of rugged, but it gets the job done."

I held the flask and sniffed at the clear liquid. "No, I'll pass thanks."

"Suit yourself," he said, as he swigged several large gulps.

"Come Jonathan. Let's just read, shall we?" I was not comfortable with him drinking and was frankly startled by this new behaviour. He shrugged his shoulders and tossed the flask to the side. We began the third book, *The Hound of the Baskervilles*. Jonathan read for a few minutes, and then halted abruptly.

"Would you like me to continue?" I asked.

"Yes please." was all he said.

I rose and went to take the book from his hand. In an instant, he pulled me down to him. He kissed me, which I was not opposed to, but his breath tasted of strong spirits. His hands began to wander, and though it was not displeasing, I was not yet ready for such forward advances. I took his hands in mine in a gesture that insinuated that I wanted him to stop. We resumed kissing but his hands began to wander once again. This time I took hold of his wrists, but he yanked them free and became agitatedly forceful. I pulled away and rose to my feet.

"Genevieve come back here," he pleaded.

"No, I think we should be going."

"But I love you. I thought you loved me too. Come back so I can show you how much I care."

I faltered at his words and almost returned to his arms.

"No, I cannot. You must not push me, Jonathan. Please."

Annoyed, he gathered our assorted paraphernalia, flinging the leather bags over Belle's back.

"Jonathan don't be angry with me. Look at me, Jonathan."

He mounted his horse, mumbling like a petulant child, "Well, let's go if we're going."

The ride home was awkward. I tried opening conversations several times, but Jonathan just grunted one-word answers. I eventually let the silence be my companion. Once at the barn, he hastily un-tacked Belle and stalked away without a word.

When I came in for supper, I was visibly upset, and my father asked me what was wrong. I said I was fine, just tired, but he and my mother persisted in their inquiries. My lack of response only gave them cause to think something unruly had transpired and my father grew red in the face. I reiterated my sense of well-being. My da was not one to show his emotion in belligerent ways, but he rose from the table and slapped his napkin to the floor, stating, "We'll see about that."

He announced he was going to go speak with Jonathan.

"NO!" I heard myself shriek. "Look, he kissed me, that is all. I was not ready for it. Please don't make a fuss. I am fine, really, I promise."

My father sat back down.

"Really Father, I am fine."

My mother calmly said, "No more river trips."

I went to bed that night somewhat baffled. If Jonathan loved me, why would he push himself on me when I obviously did not want him to? If he loved me, why did he act so callously toward me? What was with the drinking? How could I still have feelings for him after the way he had treated me? It occurred to me that perhaps falling in love was more complicated than I had imagined.

Early next morning I heard raised voices coming from the main part of the house. It was barely light, but my curiosity got the better of me. I wrapped myself in my dressing gown and quietly opened my bedroom door, allowing excuses to fill my mind should I be caught snooping. As I passed through the dining room, I realized the voices were those of Yao and Jonathan. They were not in the house at all, but by the koi pond at the front of the house. Yao was furiously moving her hands about and was visibly cross with Jonathan. As I edged closer to the open window, Yao was speaking my name. Then a door suddenly opened behind me, and I jumped.

"What's all the yelling?" It was Mr Nicolas, coming in from the horses.

"I…I don't know. I was thirsty and came out for some water. I believe it is Yao and Jonathan in the front."

Yao and Jonathan undoubtedly heard our voices, as they promptly hushed themselves. I turned to go back to my room and Mr Nicolas said, "I thought you were thirsty."

"Oh yes, I forgot."

"You forgot you were thirsty?"

"Yes, well, you know us young ones. Most forgetful, but thanks for the reminder."

He shook his head, laughed, and I walked into the kitchen for some water.

An hour later I sat at the breakfast table with my mother, father, and Mr Nicolas. I forced myself to eat some porridge and drank my tea, but all the while my stomach was churning with anxiety. The childish part of me wanted to run to my mother's lap for comfort. The maturing part of me felt I should waylay my parent's fears. Deciding on the latter, I chatted lightheartedly about Nibs. Within another few moments, the kitchen door opened, tentatively. Standing in its frame, head bowed and hat in hand was Jonathan.

"I have come to make an apology," he said.

The hat in his hand moved in a circular manner as his fingers turned it round.

"Genevieve, may I speak with you?" I folded my arms across my chest and was about to suggest he come back later, but my mother spoke first.

"Whatever you have to say Jonathan can be said in front of us all."

"Yes, I suppose. I acted in an ungentlemanly manner yesterday, Genevieve. I am sorry. Mr and Mrs Furlong, I assure you that my intentions toward your daughter are good and true. She is … rather … you … are, a wonderful and special person Genevieve."

Though I was still angry, my heart gave way to cascading forgiveness. Perhaps I had led him on by returning his kisses. Perhaps, I thought, escalating intimacy was what was expected when one becomes involved with the opposite sex. I, of course, had nothing to go on, in terms of experience, so I had no way of knowing the rules. Had we been alone, I would have assuredly continued the discussion, but my father answered for me.

"Thank you for the apology, Jonathan. We think it best if you stick to your work and leave Genevieve alone for a time."

I wanted to speak up for Jonathan. I wanted to argue that I was interested in picking things up where we had left off. If nothing else, I wished to continue reading under the elm together. Such are the blinders worn by many a foolish young heart. I was scared to speak though, as my parents thought what had transpired had only been an unwanted kiss. If they thought I had led him on, or even worse, if they thought his hands had gone roaming, and that he had been drinking, they might have kicked him straight off the ranch. I remained silent. Jonathan nodded his head affirmatively and retreated out the door through which he had come.

40

Over the course of the next two weeks, Jonathan and I only saw each other from a distance. Sometimes I would hide behind the trees and watch him work the horses in the ring. He did not let on, if he perchance saw me lurking. I did not care one way or the other. Seeing him at a distance was better than not seeing him at all.

Mr Nicolas asked me to go riding with him one day. He said I was sulking far too much for such a bright young woman and would I like to ride to the far end of the town so he could deliver a few things to another rancher? I hesitated, but he made a sour face, causing me to laugh. I thought the better of my attitude and acquiesced with a nod.

It turned out to be a long but pleasant day. The hitch on the little wagon broke off at midday, after we had piled it high with grain, and we were forced to leave it with the blacksmith to mend. By the time all was said and done, it was near eleven p.m. before we were able to start toward home.

We made it home close to midnight, and I fell into my bed with great contentment. At some point in the night, I woke to what I thought was hail bouncing off my windowpane, but the sound was quite random in nature. I turned on my bedside lamp and walked over to my window. The moon was luminous with a few scattered clouds moving across it.

I was frightened for a moment when a dark figure disappeared behind a tree, but immediately I recognized the silhouette. The wind caught hold of something on the outside window ledge and I opened the window. A piece of paper, tied with string, swung from the handle. I pulled the paper to me and opened it. It was written in Jonathan's hand.

> *Gen,*
> *Please forgive me.*
> *J*

I looked up, but his silhouette was gone.

Every night for a week, Jonathan would fling pebbles at my window. Every night, a note swung from the handle. The content was brief, genial, and complimentary. I knew full well that I should have rejected them, even flung them back at him, but my heart would not succumb to logic, and instead, I swept the notes up into my childish hands. Instead of flinging them back, I wrote my own notes and attached them to the string, for him.

> *J,*
> *If my father catches you, he will kill you! He said as*
> *much when I heard him talking to my mother. 'If he so*
> *much as lays a finger on Genevieve, it will be the last*
> *thing he'll ever do.' This is what he said. I know he is*
> *only being protective but do be careful!*
> *Gen*

Gen,
The heart knows no fear when love is alive. You are my
bright moon and the reason for breathing. I can't live
without you by my side. I have a little treasure box
and am keeping all your notes in it. I read them every
morning as they keep me happy throughout the day.
J

J,
I miss reading with you under the tree.
Gen

Gen,
We are meant to be together. Can't you feel it?
J

J,
You talk so boldly. My father is assuredly suspicious.
He is always checking on me. Checking on you. Woe
betide us if he sees you outside my bedroom window!
Gen

These were the sorts of notes that we sent to each other
on a nightly basis. The eighth night proved to be unlike
the rest. I heard the pebbles, switched on the light, and
opened the window. There was no note. I leaned out the
window, thinking it had fallen to the ground, but there was
nothing. Thinking I had dreamed the tapping, I went to
close the window, but a hand came forward and stopped
me from doing so. It was Jonathan. I am not sure why
his proximity ruffled me, but I let out a squeal, and then
immediately covered my mouth with my own hand.

"What are you doing Jonathan? My parents will have your hide if they catch you."

"I know, but I don't care. Genevieve, I heard Mr Nicolas talking to Yao about sending me back to the circus. I won't go of course. I will leave and travel if I must, but I will not return to her. I do not know how serious Mr Nicolas was but I thought I should let you know; in case I am gone one day soon. I also heard Mr Nicolas say that your father had decided to take you and your mother back to Ireland, permanently."

My heart sank as hard and fast as an anchor flung into the sea. I was unsure of what to do or say.

"Please Genevieve, let me climb in and talk with you. I will behave, I promise."

"I cannot."

"Then meet me. Tomorrow morning. I will sleep in the barn tonight, in the loft. Just give me a few minutes to talk with you."

His entreating blue eyes bore a hole through my better judgment, and I said yes. I returned to my bed and once again raised my fingers to my lips.

A cold wind slapped itself about the place next morning. It seemed as though the colours in the maples had seeped and etched themselves to a brighter shade overnight. I was in a discernibly good mood and lightheartedly chatted over breakfast. When asked what had changed my emotional state, I responded that autumn made me feel bright and gay, and that the horse ride the previous day had lifted my spirits. Since one of my favourite topics of conversation was Nibs, I dove headfirst into singing her praises, and said I would head out to the barn forthwith to give her a thorough grooming.

My father looked askance at me, but then Mr Nicolas said, "Teenagers!" We all laughed, and I exited their company with a sigh of relief.

So as not to give pause for suspicion from my parents should they be checking up on me, I left the barn door ajar and made sure my voice was clearly audible as I passed Nibs' stall on the way to the far end of the barn. I knew Jonathan was in the loft, as the crunching of dry hay was obvious in the otherwise silent space. Jonathan's hand reached for mine as I swung my leg up and over the top rung of the ladder.

"I mustn't stay long Jonathan."

Jonathan's abundant apologies and proclamations of love enveloped my young, inexperienced heart. He was irrefutably sincere, to my mind, and I knew that we were meant to be together forever. He opened his palm and took from it a silver chain with a shiny dangling silver locket.

"I want you to have this as proof of my undying love. Open it, Genevieve."

I opened the locket. A thin gold band lay in its centre.

"It is not much, but it is the only engagement ring I have to offer at the moment."

Engagement ring? Jonathan was asking for my hand in marriage? Tears welled in my eyes.

"My parents would not have it, Jonathan. They think I am far too young, though I am seventeen, and many people marry at this age."

Jonathan shifted his body behind me and tenderly fastened the chain at the base of my neck.

"There now," he whispered, as he slipped his fingers under my hair to release the strands. His touch was practically unbearable, and I knew in that instant that with Jonathan, if I had to, I would beg for my bread. He removed the ring from the locket and slid it over my finger.

"I cannot wear this, Jonathan!"

"No, perhaps not yet. You can wear it when we meet though, so I can pretend we have already wed. I will meet you here whenever you say. Just leave me a note on the window."

I reiterated my concerns about my parents, but Jonathan had a stratagem.

"If we are already married, they will have to accept me. Look, there is to be a party here in a few weeks' time for the staff, their families and well, I don't know who else exactly. People Mr Nicolas knows I guess. Anyway, we could slip away then, with one of the buggies. We can leave a note if you wish, but when we return we shall already be married. There will be nothing for your parents to do but accept me."

For a third time I spoke of my doubts and fears, but Jonathan was commandingly persuasive, and I was a lovesick young woman. He spoke in hushed tones, fingers wrapped around my hair, breath falling intoxicatingly warm upon the back of my neck.

He asked that I look closely at the locket.

"It was my mother's," he said sorrowfully.

"Your Mother's? Yao said she adopted you at birth and that your mother wanted nothing to do with you. She said that your mother had abandoned you."

"That is what I thought for years Genevieve. That is what Yao told me, but that is not the truth."

Jonathan told me he wanted to confess the truth about his past, which he had come by quite by accident.

"This is why I shall never return with her to the circus. I hate that woman. She has robbed me of my family, my history. Genevieve, I think she might have tried to poison me. I became so very sick. Well, you remember what I was like. I think she suspected that I knew the truth and she was afraid I would report her. I truly believe she had it in for me, and only allowed me to stay on the ranch so I might be appeased in some way. She knew I had feelings for you, and I suppose thought I would keep my mouth shut if I were happy. If we are to be married, we need to be truthful in all things, and you must know about my past."

The Mobhrí and my family's secret sprung instantly to mind of course, but I refrained from comment. I simply nodded. Jonathan swung around to face me. Removing a little pin from his jacket lapel, he pricked his own finger and squeezed until he drew blood. Then he gently took hold of my hand.

"This will seal our commitment to each other. Blood mixed with blood."

I was both afraid and excited as he pricked my finger. I winced, but he held my gaze with his own, while our united fingers twisted together.

"Now we are sealed as one, my Genevieve. No secrets. Only truth."

41

Jonathan

A few weeks before I fell ill, we were passing through the southern states. We were doing quite well. Yao was on top of the world and said she had been able to put a fair chunk of savings away. Yao keeps all her cash in the bottom of a large tea canister. Every night she would remove a bag of green tea leaves from the canister and slip coins and bills underneath it. We were doing so well in this particular town, the owners decided to extend our stay by three days.

I could not get over the heat of the place. I know you think it hot here Genevieve, but in certain months of the year the South owns a particular kind of omnipresent heat that is unrelenting. Luckily for me with it comes one of my favourite things, that is mirages, set about by the weather. I frequently wandered the unvarying flat roads for hours on end in pursuit of those heat-reflected images. I just love their shimmering glow. But I digress.

I advised Yao of my plan for the day, which was to hunt the roads for these mirages. I told her I would not return until well after dark. I had, in fact, intended on being absent for hours, but the temperature that day was unabating and I returned to our caravan in the early afternoon, falling into a deep sleep. I heard Yao enter the caravan and begin to putter around the place. My bed was well above the floor, a deep shelf really, so Yao had no idea I was in the caravan at all. I was so tired I did not speak. I fell asleep once again and woke to the sound of a knocking noise.

In a half sleep, I heard Yao answer the caravan door and listened to her surprised pronouncement.

'What are you doing here?'

A man's plodding Southern drawl replied. 'I was just, ya know, passin' by and thought I'd see if ya were still travellin' with this circus. Lucky fer me, you are.'

'Go away.'

'Now that ain't no way to treat a guest.'

'You are no guest. We agreed never to speak again. Now go.'

'I don't think ya want ta send me away Yao. I doubt the owners of this fine establishment would take too kindly ta the likes of you.'

There was silence for a few moments, then Yao muttered something, and I could hear footfall upon the caravan steps.

'What do you want?' Yao asked in a hush, as she closed the door behind her.

'Well, times are hard ya know? I could sure use a little grease for my wheels if ya get my drift.'

I was preparing to roll over to tell the indisputable intruder to get out, but then I heard him say, 'How is that little scrap of yours anyhow…Jonathan, is it? Course, I use the term 'yours' loosely.'

'I paid for him; he is mine. We agreed to a price, you got it.'

I lay in my bed in shock as I heard Yao speak these words. Rather than turn over and interrupt, I lay as still as I could, barely breathing in case I would be noticed.

'Stealin' is a crime Yao. I happen to know where his real mother is at. I could go find her right now and tell her all.'

'You wouldn't.'

'I could take a wander over to her mailbox, I could. I could put a letter in with the other mail just as easily as walkin' through a fresh mown field. The note could say, 'Missus so and so, I knows where yer stolen baby is.' I could say, 'It sure must be hard not knowin' all these years as to where he's at.' I could tell her, 'I know who stole him from his cradle'.'

'You stole him from his cradle.'

'She don't know that.'

'Again, I say, I paid you fairly. You were not suspected in any way.'

'Nope, who in their right mind would suspect a postman of stealin' a baby in the middle of the night?'

'I would take you down with me, Victor Wilborn.'

'Don't think so. I'm an upstandin' citizen. Yer nothin' more than a . . . a circus lady. I saw your scrap leavin' this mornin'. Sure looks like his daddy and he's the spittin' image of his younger brother. Yup, no doubt they're kin all right.'

'What do you want?'

'I could use some cash. Say two hundred dollars.'

'That is everything I have saved.'

'Can't help that. I got debts I gotta take care of.'

'What is to say that you won't take the money like the last time and then come back to hound me again?'

'Nothin' I suppose. Listen, you wanted a child, I scoped out the possibilities. You came up with a deal that I told ya seemed kinda chintzy from my end of the bargain, but I needed the money right away, so I took it.

I also took all the risk. Lucky fer me the little shaver didn't wake up and start bawlin' when I climbed in the winda. I thinks I deserve a bit more and that's all there is. Unless you want me to go to the proper authorities, mind you. Hey, you even got a bonus of the mother's locket an' gold ring that was left on the night table. I coulda kept them for myself but I didn't.'

'You have to leave now. I don't want anyone seeing you here. Meet me at the bridge by the river tonight at eleven. I will bring you what you want.'

Victor Wilborn struck a match. I heard the deep draw from a cigarette, followed by a loud exhalation. This he did a few times, obviously thinking about her proposal.

Then he muttered, deep and slow, "Better show up with it Yao, cause if I have ta come back here, well sir, my match might just miss its mark and land on your floor."

The smoke from his cigarette weaved its way to my bed and I could feel a tickle begin to form.

The door of the caravan was yanked open and as he left, Victor slammed the door so hard the entire caravan shook. At the same moment, I sneezed the smoke from my nostrils. I had to think quickly. I pretended that the slamming door had woken me from a bottomless sleep. I bolted upright on my elbows in the bed and shouted, "Do you have to slam the door when you come in?"

Yao gasped. "Jonathan…What are you doing here! What have you heard?"

I kept my tone as calm as possible, for I was scared for my own life at that point.

"What I heard is you coming in and slamming the door closed. I am not well. Let me go back to sleep."

"What about the man?"

"The man? What man?"

"You heard no man?"

I moaned with displeasure and turned my back to her. "I am going back to sleep. Keep it down, would you?"

Yao did not respond, and I took this as a good sign. I forced myself to creep from the bed an hour later. Yao sat at the back window reading a book.

She had made me soup, saying that she thought it would make me feel better.

I felt I should appease her, so I shuffled sleepily over to the table and sat, slouched, as she poured a bowl of soup from a cast iron pot that sat on our small cook top.

My stomach was entirely empty, seeing as how I hadn't eaten since the early morning. The soup tasted sweet, and it went down easily. I had it in my mind to go in search of Victor Wilborn as soon as possible. If nothing else, I would follow Yao to the bridge, and confront them both.

Yao poured me another bowl of soup and I eagerly consumed it. I lay back down on my bed. Yao yapped on about one of the new acts with the show, but I soon realized that I was, in fact, not feeling very well. Within the hour, I was running chilled to the bone and felt completely drained of all my energy. I don't remember falling asleep, but when I woke many hours later, it was pitch black and I could barely move. What I saw when I managed to open my eyes was Yao, at the water bowl, scrubbing something diligently with her hands. From where I lay, the water looked a brownish red, as did the article of fabric. Was it blood? I fell back into a hallucinatory stupor.

I was too sick to confront Yao. She worked in a friend's caravan for the remaining two nights and then we set off for the next town. Victor Wilborn did not return during that time. By the time we arrived at the next town I was feeling a little stronger. On opening night, Yao went off to work in another caravan, as she felt I needed another night to recuperate.

I was determined to check the tea box. I waited until she had departed the caravan and let an hour pass. Droves of voices circulated around the outside area. I left the caravan dark and felt my way to the tea canister. All of Yao's money was lying underneath the bag of tea, untouched. I nearly fell over with fright as I remembered Yao scrubbing in the early hours of the morning the night she was to meet Victor. Could she be capable of murder? The answer seemed quite apparent.

Then I remembered the locket and ring. I began carefully searching drawers, baskets, and boxes. I pulled the few books we owned down from the shelf to look behind them. Nothing. Then I began replacing the books back on the shelf and observed that one book was extremely light for its size. The title was in Mandarin so it was not a book I would have ever removed for myself. I opened it. The centres of the pages were torn out, creating a hollow space. In that space was a pouch, in that pouch was the locket, and in the locket was a slender gold ring. I held them to my chest for a long time and thought about my real mother. I replaced them that night but took them the day before I came to the ranch. I doubt Yao ever looks at it, at least she has never asked me about it.

Genevieve

Jonathan looked beseechingly at me. His tear-filled eyes, overflowing, dripping as candle wax down his ruddy cheeks.

"You see Genevieve, that is when I became so ill. I am sure now that the food she was serving me had slow acting poison. Remember how I would recover for a time after my bouts, and then fall ill again? It was always after Yao was there that I worsened.

"I must go and find my parents and I must go to the authorities in the south, but Yao must not know of my plans. I have been saving little bits since coming here and may soon have enough for us to travel. There, you have my awful secret. I am a kidnapped child and I am a coward, for I have not confronted Yao, for fear she will kill me."

I wiped the tears from Jonathan's cheeks and neck with the corners of my dress and kissed his forehead.

"You are no coward Jonathan, and no one would think ill of you for being scared of Yao. We will figure out a solution together."

"We will? You do not think I am the most loathsome person you have ever met? You do not mind that my history is so twisted? Could it be that we can share such things so easily?"

I searched his eyes for love and safety, and I was sure I saw both lying boldly exposed to me. Then I did the one thing I should not have done. I told him everything. The power of my family's secret, the history and magic of the Mobhrí and my inheritance therein. I remembered the promise I made to my mother. Only family members and spouses may know the secret. I convinced myself that I was not breaking that promise, as I was about to marry Jonathan.

42

We met in the loft every morning for the next week. Jonathan remained a complete gentleman, never attempting anything more than kissing and snuggling. He declared his love daily and we talked about what our lives would be like together. One night, another tapping on the window produced another note.

> *Gen,*
> *I cannot wait to be your husband; you to be my wife.*
> *Let us pretend we are saying our vows! Let's pretend we*
> *are married. Let's just try it on for size. I shall make a*
> *mock wedding certificate with my vows and signature*
> *and leave it for you tomorrow night. You just write*
> *what I write, and we can put it into my treasure box.*
> *We can show it to our children in years to come. They*
> *will find it a romantic thing their parents did when*
> *they were young.*

J

J,
You are a bold romantic. All right, let's do it.
Gen

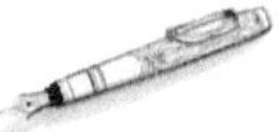

Gen,
Two notes tonight. One to say my love for you knows no
bounds. The other is our mock certificate!
I Jonathan Jun, do take you, Genevieve Norah Furlong,
to be my lawfully wedded wife, from this day forward,
in the presence of these good witnesses.
Jonathan Jun

J,
I like this game of window letters. I added mine under
yours, though our only good witnesses are the owls,
twisting their heads in the trees. Goodnight my dear.
I Genevieve Norah Furlong do take you, Jonathan Jun,
to be my lawfully wedded husband, from this day for-
ward in the presence of these good witnesses.
Genevieve Norah Jun

Dear Gen,
So how is my dear wife this evening?
J

J,
Very well thank you, and you, dear husband?
Gen

When the eve of Mr Nicolas' party finally arrived, I was bouncing with elation. In my mind, it was to be an evening of hope and promise, as I was going to marry the love of my life. It would be a night of new beginnings for Johnathan and me. We would be like two flowers, budding in spring, standing side-by-side, shining brightly.

Instead, it turned into a nightmare beyond reckoning.

The house was a flutter of activity. Neighbours, friends, employees were all strewn about, enjoying the evening. I wore a new green dress with matching over-jacket that my mother had made, and my hair was tied into a knot at the back of my head. Around my neck was the locket Jonathan had given me but due to my mother's insistent high collar the necklace was unseen by anyone. I was surprised to see Julian at the far end of the room and as I went to say hello, Yao appeared. This was most displeasing. I wanted to slap her and make a fool of her in front of the crowd, but thought the better of it, given the plans Jonathan and I had.

Instead of approaching Julian, I went to my mother and put my arms around her.

"I love my new dress mother. I hope you know how much I love you."

"Yes Genevieve, and I love you. Is everything all right?"

"Oh yes, I just haven't told you in a long time."

At that moment, Mr Nicolas called to us, and we were introduced to an associate of his. Then, Jonathan entered the room.

Was I really going through with his plan? I was terrified but seeing him standing in the entryway was enough to send my heart a-jitter and I stopped my mind from second-guessing. We had arranged to meet at the far barns at eleven o'clock, which was two hours away. As I watched him from the far end of the room, two young ranchers approached him. He leaned in toward them to hear what they were saying. A moment later, he was gone.

The next two hours were bottomless. Jonathan did not return, and I flitted about the room like a nervous bird in a barn of cats. My stomach was especially jumpy, as the night before I had quietly gone through our family's legal papers and collected my birth certificate and any legal documents I could find pertaining to me. It had felt a bit like thieving, but since the papers would be returned post haste, I rationalized my actions.

As eleven o'clock approached I boldly walked out the front door and made for the back of the house, where I had stashed a small bag of clothes with the documents. I removed the slender gold ring from the locket and placed it on my wedding finger, continuing then to walk briskly down the dirt path, past the first set of barns. All at once, Jonathan was there, taking my hand and commanding me to run with him. As we passed the second set of barns, one of the older ranch hands exited a side door and we collided with him, scattering his bucket of brushes and cleaning tools to the ground. He shouted his aggravations at us.

"Watch it, you clumsy old oaf!" yelled Jonathan. I turned to look at the man as we kept running. He was bent over, gathering up the strewn items, and eying us with disgust.

"Jonathan, I cannot run so fast in this dress, please slow down."

"But we are almost there now. Just a minute more."

My hair broke free from the clasp that held it in place, sending twisted strands tumbling down my cheek. We ran until we reached the farthest barn. Jonathan swung the smaller side door open wide. I dropped my bag outside while he hustled me inside. Out of breath and sweating,

I eagerly seated myself on a bale of hay. A kerosene lamp burned in one corner.

Jonathan came toward me but stumbled over an empty bucket and landed on the barn floor. Before I could go to him, he was up like a flash, laughing and dusting himself off.

"Really Jonathan, why all the rush?"

As he began to respond I realized that he was three sheets to the wind, slurring his words and weaving his way toward me.

"Why have you been drinking, Jonathan? This was supposed to be our special night."

"Oh just a few drinks with a few friends."

"No, you cannot even walk! This is not how it's supposed to be, and I am not doing this. We must put aside our plans now."

Jonathan sank to his knees and crawled to me on all fours. I was frightened now, remembering our last episode with alcohol.

"You look beautiful, Genevieve. You always look beautiful. My beautiful bride to be."

"I am leaving and going back to the house. Let's talk in the morning."

"NO! We can't talk in the morning. I am not allowed to see you, remember? That is why we are going away tonight."

His eyes flashed to the main barn door. He jumped to it and set the latch.

"I think we can have our nuptials now, don't you think? I mean we are practically married."

I stood, out of breath, adrenaline pumping madly. I searched the room for exit possibilities but saw none. Jonathan stumbled once again. My heart was racing now, hyper-focused on survival. I tried to appeal to his softer nature.

"Think of your mother Jonathan, your real mother that is. She would not like this behaviour. Remember? We are going to find her?"

I was talking about the future but now I knew full well that once I broke free of him, there would be no future for us. What fell from him was a sustained condescending laugh.

I remember so clearly the smell of the stacked hay, the pair of scuffed brown riding boots by the door where Jonathan stood and the sound of his heavy breathing. I tried again to tap into his softer side.

"Listen Jonathan," I said, forcing a smile. "We can figure this out—together, like we always do." I put my hand inside the neck of my dress and removed the locket he had given me. "See? Here is that beautiful gift you gave me on that special day in the barn when we professed our love for each other." My voice quavered. I could hear it but could do nothing about it. I held up my trembling hand, palm facing toward me. "And look! Your mother's wedding ring. Won't it be lovely to show this to her when we find her?"

Jonathan pulled a flask from his back pocket, raised it to his lips and drained the last of whatever was inside.

"You're so gullible, Genevieve. You really believed all that?"

I must have looked shocked and sad, as he laughed mockingly again and shuffled toward me. I backed away until I bumped into a hay bale.

"Well, I am glad you did believe it all. Some of it was true, but you gave us the information we wanted. That little scope of yours will serve Yao and me well."

Jonathan staggered and then rushed toward me, grabbing hold of my over-jacket, and I pushed him away with all my might. He fell with a thud, and I bolted for the door. My hands were shaking uncontrollably, my body vibrating as I attempted to swing the latch to the side. But Jonathan was there again. I tried to scream, but he covered my mouth with his one hand and twisted my arm behind me with the other. Though he was drunk, he was extremely strong. He removed his hand from my mouth and attempted to twist my other arm around my back. I screamed again, and the next thing I knew I was lying on the floor, my head throbbing and bleeding from the fall. He braced my hands with his own, and as I struggled, I was hit with his fist. He told me that if I screamed or struggled again, he would kill me. I believed him.

It was as though a beast had escaped from him. I pleaded for my release, but it was to no avail. I forget the order of events from there. I drifted in and out of a clouded haze. I do remember the sound of ripping cloth. Then I passed out.

The next thing I recall is the sound of my father's screams, followed by a struggle and a cracking noise one might hear when opening a peanut shell. Then voices, arms, night air. Back to oblivion. I woke in my bed, my mother sitting beside me. Confused and disoriented, I tried to sit, only to fall back on my pillow, pain ripping through my body. Strangely, my first thought was *this is what boxers must feel like after several rounds in a ring.*

My mother took my hand and spoke softly. As she spoke, my memory returned and I pulled the blankets up over my face. I was simultaneously afraid and ashamed. I wanted to lie in a tub of hot soapy water, to try and wash away the feeling of vileness that had saturated into my very being. Instead, I asked who had found me and was recounted the proceedings of the evening.

Norah closed the diary, stood, and grabbed a tissue from a box across the room.

Dónal's voice was soft and low. "Aw, Norah my dear. I know this must be beyond upsetting."

Norah blew her nose. "I wish I had known all this. Not that there was much I could've done for Nana, but at least she could have confided any residual emotions about her entry into the world, or her own mother's trauma."

Dónal stood and went to her. "Is this bringing up bad memories for you?"

Norah looked away. "I assume you mean the visiting writer who assaulted me a few years ago. Yes, I suppose my tears reflect that memory, too. I know, I fought him off, but it still angers me when I think about it. I remember fighting, pushing him off me after he grabbed me by my hair, and forced a kiss upon my mouth. Like Jonathan, he was several sheets to the wind, and as he tried to drag me to the couch, I was able to push him off balance. Mostly what comes up is the memory of running home and standing under the soapy scalding water of the shower, the same way Genevieve wanted to soak in a hot tub, to wash away the vileness, that she so aptly describes it as. Of course, this experience was made worse by the organization that had sponsored him. It was as if I must have done something to warrant his advances, which of course, I had not."

It took several minutes for Norah to feel strong enough to continue. When they returned to the couch, Dónal pulled her close, and suggested he take up the reading. Norah agreed, and sat—silently—eyes closed, listening to Dónal's soothing voice.

The rancher, with whom Jonathan and I had collided, found my father at the party and told him he had seen me running with Jonathan to the outside barns. Though Father had been standing alone, Yao was obviously within earshot because both Father and Yao took off toward the outer barns. When they got there the door was locked, but a light shone through the cracks in the door. My father had pounded his fists upon the door, but the only returning sound was that of a grunting animal.

Running around and entering through one of the side doors, he saw Jonathan on top of me. My head was bleeding, one of my eyes was swollen shut and I was quite unconscious.

My father's rage unleashed, he seized Jonathan by the hair, pulled him off me and twisted him around to strike him. Jonathan, however, let go a punch that sent my father flying backward, into a stack of crates that launched him sideways, to land on the barn floor face down. When my father turned to rise, Jonathan was coming at him with a pitchfork and was screaming obscenities about me. My father twisted himself out of the way, causing Jonathan to falter as the spikes hit the dirt.

My father leapt up and swung round to the back of Jonathan, grabbing him by the shirt collar this time. He pulled him back, and subsequently flung him forcefully to the side. Jonathan landed, on his back, on top of farm equipment, and lay, motionless. Yao screamed and ran to Jonathan. My mother had arrived upon the scene to see Yao kneeling over Jonathan and my father scooping me up off the floor.

"You've killed him!" screamed Yao. "You will hang for this."

43

My father had not killed Jonathan but had caused a break in his lower spine, resulting in paralysis from the waist down. This deceiver had sworn to the police that I was, in fact, his lawfully wedded wife. I knew then that Jonathan and Yao had worked together, like the spiders, tucking me securely into their web while conniving to obtain the Mobhrí.

All those years that Jonathan had spent gaining my trust, duping me into falling in love with him, had been a sham. Yao knew our family owned something extraordinarily valuable and the two had decided it should be theirs. They must have been salivating over the possibilities once they understood its potential value. I can only imagine what vile plans they had for it. Their treachery would have succeeded if Jonathan's predilections to alcohol hadn't ruined their plans. Now Yao and Jonathan were out for vengeance and, no doubt, financial gain.

Jonathan had given Yao all the notes we'd sent each other, including the one where I signed my name to wedding vows as Genevieve Norah Jun. Through her network of questionable associates, Yao had managed to procure a legal stamp from an unsavory judge. It was marked with the same date that Jonathan and I had gone out to the river for the second time.

This judge claimed to have married us beside the river, and that he and Yao were witnesses. Jonathan also had notes where I claimed that my father was out to hurt him. Yao swore that she was witness to my father's attempt to murder Jonathan that night in the barn and that it had, in fact, been my father who had tried to skewer Jonathan. Jonathan admitted to drinking too heavily but claimed that I had been in the barn of my own free will; and as his wife, therefore, charges of rape were not valid.

The most condemning evidence against me was the gold ring that was on my finger on the night in question. There was nothing much Mr Nicolas could do for us, though he did try his best to speak on my father's and my behalf. He helped us hire a lawyer and was generally wonderful.

A week later, the overseeing judge had concluded that though my father had been defending me, the outcome had been grievous enough to warrant monetary compensation. Jonathan and Yao would not rescind the assault with a deadly weapon nor the charge of intent to do bodily harm and so my father would also have a minimum of jail time.

The evidence did not prove beyond a shadow of a doubt that we were not married, therefore Jonathan was not charged with rape. In his closing statement, the judge did say that the case might warrant further investigation to prove coercion on Jonathan's part. We believed the judge to be on our side, but the evidence against us had left him no choice in his verdict. None of us ever mentioned the Mobhrí to the judge. If any of us had, we would have been seen as demented, and therefore untrustworthy in our recounting of the events.

We decided, with our lawyer, that we should bring up new charges wherein Jonathan would be held accountable under the 'Act of Seduction' Law, passed in New York in 1848. Unlike a rape charge, the Seduction law charges the perpetrator with emotional manipulation. It had been designed to protect victims who were young and naïve.

These seduction laws were somewhat ambiguous but revolved around proving coercion of an intimate nature.

It was a matter of trying to prove that the male seducer had made false promises and used psychological trickery against the victim. The idea behind the law was to allow both prosecutors and defendants to tell their side of the story, to weigh each party's point of view, and to determine the extent of control each had over their passions. In many trials, victims' testimony revealed that although they had been in love or semi-intimate with the defendant, they did not want nor consent to relations. It had also proved in some trials that even marriages could fall under this law if the victim had been falsely led to union.

I was escorted into the judge's chambers for questioning one month after the assault; the judge required my detailed account of the events. Relaying—reliving—that night took a deep emotional toll on me. The vile nature of the attack had engulfed my soul with an unspoken cloak of self-loathing. I know now that I had nothing to be ashamed of, but at the time I felt psychologically abused, and re-assaulted.

Did you consent to meeting Jonathan in the barn?

Yes.

So, you planned this meeting ahead of time?

Yes, your honour, but I did not plan on being attacked.

Did you try to defend yourself when he allegedly forced himself?

Yes, I screamed and begged him to stop.

Did you scream loud enough for someone to hear you, and why did you stop?

I screamed several times, as loud as I possibly could; but he hit me and threatened to kill me if I made any more noise.

The judge's questions continued in this vein for an hour. All at once, my hands and neck began to sweat, and I felt uncontrollably nauseous. I had to excuse myself twice during the following hour. By the time I emerged from his chambers, I was pale and weak. My mother and Mr Nicolas returned me home and put me straight to bed.

I had to re-appear for questioning for three consecutive days; each day, more exhausting than the last. I felt sick and weak from the emotional toll, and it seemed my poor mother was aging right before my eyes. After listening to all the parties, the new judge deemed our marriage license to be false. This, at least, was one consolation. Jonathan was found guilty of coercion and was sentenced to one year in prison and fined one hundred dollars.

Meanwhile, my father was sentenced to nine months and was responsible to pay Jonathan one hundred dollars a year for six years toward medical expenses. His case would be up for review in three months, to hopefully reduce his sentence.

Due to overcrowded minimum-security prisons, my father was taken to the Eastern New York Correctional Facility. The good thing about this was the prison was in Napanoch, Ulster County, which was the same county as Ellenville. The abysmal aspect was that it was a maximum-security facility. Many inmates were transported from the New York City area, serving sentences of less than one year. We were assured it would be a temporary placement and, given that most inmates had been charged with far more grievous crimes, my father would be given a private cell. Our lawyer informed us that he would work around the clock to decrease and/or eliminate his sentence.

My mother and I became each other's shadow. I began sleeping in her bed as nightmares took over my dream world. We were both worried about my father and having each other as comfort was the one thing that calmed us both. I was still physically indisposed after another week had come and gone but did my best to hide it from everyone. I think I knew the reason for my nausea but was unable or unwilling to admit it. It was not until another three weeks had gone by that my mother found me in the back garden, losing my breakfast.

The doctor was called in and upon examination I was pronounced 'in the family way'. Walls came crashing in with the ramifications of it. That same morning, as my mother and I stared drearily out the kitchen window, word came that my father had been hospitalized. My dilemma instantly took a back burner, as we rushed to his side. He had been beaten and stabbed in the back, near his shoulder.

Da told us that he had received a few threats from acquaintances of Yao and Jonathan in the previous week, by way of notes. The notes were very specific. One said something along the lines of, 'You can't get away with making Jon sit in a chair for the rest of his life. Maybe you need to see how it feels.'

It was while coming out from the shower room that my father was attacked from behind. He was sure there were three of them: two held him, one blindfolded him. They had beaten and stabbed him. He thinks they would have killed him, but for the sound of voices making their way toward them.

One man had grumbled, "Next time you won't survive it."

The wound was not life threatening but serious enough to keep Da in hospital for a few days of observation. The warden was of no help, as my father did not know who was guilty of the crime. The only promise the warden made was that he would try to hasten his relocation.

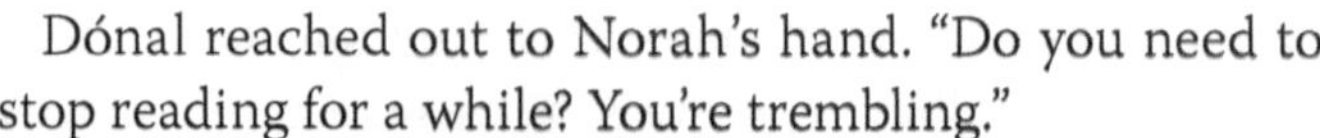

Dónal reached out to Norah's hand. "Do you need to stop reading for a while? You're trembling."

Norah slipped the ribbon over the page and closed the journal, leaning into Dónal.

"I never knew any of this about my Nana. As I already mentioned, I just wish she would have confided in me; not carried all this on her shoulders, alone. I know why she didn't disclose information to my mother, whom I will ring in the morning, as it's right in the middle of her workday now, but I'm just gobsmacked with the intensity of it all."

"Of course you are, my beautiful Norah. I can't even imagine how you must feel. Come, let's walk down the road and catch a bit of air. If you're up for continuing we shall, or we can wait 'til tomorrow. Sound good?"

"Yes, it does sound good. It troubles me that we women still have to endure this kind of behaviour from men. I'm not putting any blame on you Dónal, by any means, truly, but generally men really do not understand what it's like for women to walk out into the dark or be afraid how a date might end."

"You're right. I don't even think about walking at night or walking from a pub to my car. But I'm here for you. You know that."

"Thank you Dónal. I'm so grateful. Learning all this about my family is weight-filled, and I'm just so glad you're here —willing and able to walk through it with me. My days of being a lone wolf really are over."

Dónal took her hand and kissed it. "As are mine my dearest, as are mine ."

The walk did a world of good, and after making a pot of tea, the two returned to the journal, together.

The three of us sat huddled round his bed in the small hospital room whispering our forward plans. My parents had saved a hefty sum of money over the years, and it was decided that my mother should withdraw it all and hand it to me. They mutually agreed that they would go to An Clann Teach. I fervently protested, of course. My father put forth he would rather go to known safety than go back to probable death. My mother agreed, and though I wept an ocean of tears, I could not dispute the logic in his thinking. How was I to live without them? On the other hand, if my father were killed in prison, I would never be able to live with myself. There was no hope of escaping back to Ireland together, as he was in a maximum-security facility.

Mam and I left the hospital and went to the bank. When we arrived back at the ranch, she said she would collect our legal documents and hand them over to me as well. It was only then I remembered that I had deposited all my documents in a side pocket of the little carry bag. I had no idea where that bag was. With all that had transpired, that carry bag was the last thing on my mind. My mother shook her head and raised her finger to her temple. We walked out toward the far barn together, but as we passed the second of the two, I was powerless to continue. My dear mother put her arms around me for a few moments and sent me back to the house.

When she returned, she had the bag in her hand, but it was dripping with water. She had found it outside the side door. In all the chaos, it had gotten to that point and no farther. Everything inside was drenched, including the papers. The documents were mashed together in an impossibly saturated jumble.

"You will have to send for a copy of your birth certificate, Genevieve. I will help you get the process started but you will have to complete it yourself. I am sorry to have to throw so much at you all at once child, but we have no choice."

"Yes mother, I understand. I can manage."

My mother sat up half the night composing a letter to Frank Nicolas, trying to express the gratitude and love she and my father held for him. I was to give it to Mr Nicolas once they were gone. We pulled the stitches out from the hem of her travelling dress and removed the Mobhrí. Instructions were once again given to me in precise and repeated detail, and I spent the rest of the night wrapped in my mother's arms, talking about our lives. She assured me that this was the safest thing for my father, and I agreed. Neither of my parents ever made me feel anything but supported and loved after all the events that had come to pass.

Though I had many options, including giving up my child for adoption, I decided that night that I would keep the child, for though it had been conceived in dire circumstances, I was still its mother, and I could not help but love it. Its innocence was to be my strength. Its company, my comfort . . . and my only family.

44

According to the police report, my father had managed to escape with my mother. There was what they called an all-points bulletin, as well as an intensive local search, but they were never found. How could they have been? They had vanished.

I was questioned of course, but my account was consistent. I had gone to the hospital with my mother to see my father. I was in the room with them for a time and then went out to the nurse's station to make inquiries as to how much longer my father would have to remain hospitalized. I was well aware that the floor nurse was seeing my father at a quarter past the hour to administer pain medication, thus I made sure I was engaged in conversation with one of the other nurses for several minutes before that. The floor nurse had come running out of my father's room, looking anxiously up and down the hall before running to the station desk and sounding an alarm.

If nothing else, it was soothing to know they were both safe. My mother and I mutually decided not to inform Father of my condition until after they had retreated. He would more than likely have refashioned his ideas, and remained, not caring for his own safety.

Moments before I unleashed the vibrating light, my mother turned to me and whispered, "I left a little something at the O'Reilly ranch the last time we were home, Genevieve. I hope you will use it one day. I hope it will bring you the unconditional love that it brought me."

"I will come to you before too long, Mother. I promise I will."

My father heard my words and replied. "You will come when it is time, Genevieve, not before. You must not be foolish in this regard. You must live your life as you see fit. We love you no matter where we all are. We will see you down the road."

Three sets of tears poured in streams down our faces to the dry riverbeds of our hearts.

Mr Nicolas was terribly upset at their disappearance, but I assured him they were safe. He did not question me too heavily on the matter, and I gave him the letter my mother and father had jointly written. There is dizzying detail I could recount about this time, but alas, I fear I have not the strength to write it all.

It was not long before I was in possession of an unmistakable bulge beneath my clothes.

Mr Nicolas took me beneath his wing, which was an unqualified solace. He offered me a place to call home. My plan was to remain on the ranch until my child was old enough to travel, and then to return home to seek a new life. However, disaster struck my life once again when Mr Nicolas fell from his horse one afternoon. We had all thought his horse had spooked, that he had been thrown and knocked unconscious. He had, in fact, had a severe heart attack and had collapsed to the ground. He hung on for five days but passed away on the sixth. He never regained consciousness. I never had a chance to say goodbye.

I felt truly alone. Frank Nicolas had been my strength since the departure of my parents.

His family arrived in droves. At first, I thought it a beautiful thing, a familiar thing, that a clan would rally and come to show respect for their departed relation, but I soon came to realize that the majority were there for possible monetary gain. I wished with all my heart that Julian would be among them but, alas, he was not.

I was happy for Julian. He had met and fallen in love with an audience member named Cora, while on a month-long stint in Ann Arbor, Michigan. The long and the short of it, was that he left the circus to be with her. At the time of Frank's death, the newlyweds were unreachable, and on a three-week honeymoon. Julian would have assuredly been my touchstone; my advocate, but this was not to be.

None of the extended family knew me, of course, and were vexed to have a young, pregnant, and unwed woman in their midst. While they did not ask me to leave directly, it was insinuated in their remarks and facial expressions that my presence was repellent and undesirable.

I, too, was vexed, in fact, at the preponderance of rows over Frank's estate and bank balance. However, I was jubilantly aware that all his fortunes were left to Julian. No amount of family squabbling would alter that fact and I wished at the time to be a fly on the wall, to witness the faces of all the vultures, as Frank's *Last Will & Testament* was read aloud.

I spoke to his younger sister, Betty. She was, in my mind, the softest of them all. I explained how I came to be there, and the arrangement Frank and I had made regarding my staying at the ranch until after the birth of my child. I assured her I had no interest in anything more than that courtesy. Her reply had been a curt one. I could stay until the ranch was sold.

And, I might have stayed until my child was born, as I had nowhere else to go, had it not been for a ghastly encounter with Yao.

Autumn closed in. Green leaves still graced the trees, but the unmistakable autumn hues were slowly seeping through as red and orange flashes in the wind. The temperature was slowly but surely decreasing, and the air had that wonderful, indisputable aroma of seasonal change.

Large charcoal and white puffy clouds, along with increasing wind, were becoming more prevalent by the day. Mind you, I welcomed the change, as autumn has unfailingly been my favourite time of year.

One morning, I accompanied one of the ranch hands into Ellenville to fetch supplies. Seeing that we were well into the colder months, it was easy to conceal my swelling body with layers, but my figure was, as to be expected, noticeably changing and I could no longer wear my old dresses.

Polly's Fashions was a dress shoppe on the main road of town; my mother and I had often browsed through the racks to pass the time with no intention of purchasing anything. Polly Fredrick was both the owner of the shoppe and the town's principal gossip; one of those people who had no compunction about questioning her customers on every aspect of their lives, or the lives of others. She was a slight woman, with a loud demeanor, whose laugh was as false as a counterfeit bill. Polly was not fond of my mother or me, as we did not bite at her verbal bait. My mother's soft-spoken nature would dissolve into a near perfect silence, which flustered Polly to the point of distraction. I was never paid much attention, as I was a mere youngster who would, no doubt, be devoid of substantial gossipy particulars or money.

Roaming up and down the main road, I tried to summon the courage to enter the shoppe. My nervousness stemmed from knowing that if my condition was detected, I would become one of Polly's scandalous and juicy bits of 'gossip'.

On my third pass, I looked directly into the shoppe's window. To my relief, Polly was engaged in a head down hushed conversation with the postmistress, Lucy Towsend. The two oftentimes bent themselves over in this manner, presumably discussing, enhancing, or inventing their own truths about personal details of the town's population. Being the postmistress, Lucy was acquainted with a plethora of potential scandals, including perfume-scented envelopes, recurring overdue payment notices, and at least once, a scandalous book purchase.

A few months prior, while my mother and I were browsing through the shoppe, Lucy had murmured to Polly, "Why, don't you know, a book arrived in a package for Felicity Bower yesterday. The brown paper was torn, and I could see the title." (No doubt she helped the tear along herself.)

She paused for effect, but Polly was on top of the silence.

"What? Tell me what was the book, Lucy!"

Pausing again, Lucy slyly grinned.

"Mind, you didn't hear it from me."

"No, of course not."

Lucy lowered her voice to a hush. "It was entitled, *How to Attract a Man.*"

"No! Felicity?"

"I know, I was astonished. Well, she has been widowed for quite some time. Perhaps she is just bored. Very bored," she retorted coquettishly.

"And to think, she is part of the Ladies' Welcoming Committee. Scandalous!"

On and on they raved and tsked, until mother and I had had enough, and removed ourselves from the shoppe.

I finally entered the shoppe on that third pass. The little doorbell tinkled, but thankfully, the two women declined to inquire who had authored the sound. Maternity garments were at the rear of the shoppe, near the fitting rooms. Hastily, I flung a few dresses over my arm, entered an inadequately sized cubicle, and quietly closed the door.

I removed my heavy coat and hung it on a little peg on the wall. Wiggling out of my old dress was considerably difficult, as it was terribly tight around my middle, and the little room was tight around me. Finally, I was in my undergarments in front of a foggy, slightly cracked, floor-length mirror.

I stood a moment, running my hands around my growing belly, turning this way and that. I had been feeling the child move about in its liquid world for a few weeks, and now stood, marveling at the kicking mound. It was a peaceful moment amid the growing unrest in my life.

All at once, the fitting room door swung wide, almost hitting my belly. A steely and menacing Yao stood before me. The circus must have been on hiatus, and she had thought it a good idea to return, to harass me. I instinctively and immediately pushed the door closed with a bang, forcing Yao backward, and I slid the chipped wooden peg more securely into the hole in the door jamb. As I regained my breath, I chided myself for my initial hesitations outside the shoppe, as my dilly-dallying may have been when she first observed me. I'm sure her intention was just to intimidate me, to remind me of her. But when she saw my rounding belly for that short moment, her motive quickly turned to something darker.

A chilling cackle emanated from Yao. "Too good to be true! Too good. A child. Jonathan to be a father; me, a grandmother. An heir to your high and mighty throne".

All I could think to do was to shakily call back, "You'll never get your hands on my child."

But she moved close to the door and retorted, low and menacingly, "Think what you like, but I have my ways."

What came to mind then was the way in which she had come to possess Jonathan. I knew Yao would resort to lawlessness to also possess Jonathan's offspring. Kidnapping, and even physical harm, to me, was not out of the question. Then she said,

"You're just a mere child yourself, with no parents around to cause trouble. Don't think you can stop me. I *will* find a way to have that child. You can't hide from me. You *will* give me my grandbaby. Sooner than you may think."

Then fading footfall as she walked away, and out of the dress shoppe.

I remained in the tiny space for several minutes, too terrified and breathless to move. All at once, a little knock.

"Hello?" said the voice. "Is everything okay in there?" It was Polly.

"Yes, thank you very much indeed. Be right out."

I squeezed myself back into my clothes and withdrew from the dressing room, trying to remain calm.

Polly was visibly startled to discover it was me in her shoppe. My parents, of course, were already the stars of her tongue-wagging gossip. I guarantee, hours' worth of defamatory speculation, regarding my parents' mysterious disappearance, were concocted and dispersed by this woman and were running rampant around the population like a contagious disease.

I had not had a chance to try on any clothes, but casually remarked that I would purchase the two dresses in my hand.

"Have you tried these on?" asked Polly.

"Yes, of course."

"Are you aware that they are maternity wear?"

"Oh, yes? It is of no matter."

Polly's eyebrows elevated to the ceiling and a small grin ushered from the sides of her mouth.

"You need maternity wear?"

I gulped. "I never said the dresses were for me."

"But whoever else would they be for?"

"I do not see any relevance in the question."

"Either they are for someone at the ranch, or they are for you. Which is it? Surely you can't afford them, can you?"

I eyed her with growing fury. "Are you interested in taking my money or not?"

Polly pulled a sheet of brown paper from under the counter and laid the dresses upon it. As she removed the tags, she wrote the prices on a snowy white ticket. Burning with rage, I wanted to reach across the counter and slap the smug grin off her face. Instead, I picked up a brown wool scarf.

"I'll take this too."

Polly harrumphed.

Several coat clasps were gaily displayed to my right.

"And one of these." I said, as though money were no object.

I left the shoppe with my head held high. In my periphery though, through the shoppe's window, I could see Polly and Lucy pointing at me and jabbering. After a few hundred feet of retreat, I paused and sat on a bench near the town chemist. So, Yao had returned to Ellenville. No doubt to see if I was still at the ranch. She and Jonathan had not given up their wicked quest to appropriate the Mobhrí, or perhaps some of the money that had been awarded to them by the court. No money had ever been exchanged, since my parents were not to be found, and it was not my debt to pay. What awful luck to have my condition found out by Yao, and now, assuredly, thanks to Polly, the entire town.

I feigned illness for the next couple of days, so as not to have to be near Mr Nicolas' family. While preparing to go out to Nibs one evening, June, Frank's eldest sister, came to me with delivered post.

The large envelope, addressed to me, caused my hear to skip a beat. A broad smile brightened my face, as I knew the envelope would contain my legal documents. I would now be free to return home.

June eyed me with curiosity.

"My Irish legal documents," I said cheerily.

June did not respond and turned away, more than likely hoping it would mean my rapid departure.

45

I **left before the** sun rose the following morning without saying farewell to anyone. Nibs gave out to me as I loaded two bulging saddlebags upon her. With nary a soul to be seen, I mounted, with a shudder of unease. Where was my destiny leading me this time? Tears welled in my eyes as the sound of my lone horse's hooves plodded down the dirt drive and onto the main road. The smallness of my years fell over me with a terrible weight. How was I to make a new life on my own? Yet, I was not alone, was I? I had the company of my unborn child. I was now responsible for another's life and was determined to take on any tasks set before me, to see my child born into safety.

My breath became a frosty vapour before my eyes, and I forced myself upright in the saddle. There was no doubt this was going to be a demanding passage of time; one that would require self-discipline, steadfastness and above all, trust in myself. I vowed to set goals, follow them through to fruition, and not allow myself to fall prey to my own uncertainty. I would set short-term, achievable goals, and not grandiose ones. My first was to reach the docks of New York and set sail on the next available ship to Ireland. Once under sail, I would consider my next step, though pray I had no idea what that was to be. After several hours in the saddle, a distant prominent steeple pronounced the promise of nourishment and rest. Within an hour, I made it to a little town called Eastbury.

The surrounding years had seen many changes in the eastern part of the United States. One of the most noticeable changes was the volume of automobiles, owned not only by the elite, but also by many working-class citizens. Roads were continually being built and or expanded. Railroads too, were spreading, fanning out, connecting to other lines, and becoming a sought-after mode of transportation.

Eastbury was a sleepy but quaint township, more a village really. I must have looked a wreck, as when I entered the corner cafe and sat down in the booth nearest to the door, the lone waitress approached me instantaneously with a glass of water and a full pot of hot, black liquid.

"You look like you're in need of immediate coffee," she said sympathetically.

"Tea please, if I may. As well as whatever soup you have on offer. Thank you."

Upon returning with the two steaming nourishments, Helen (notated on her name tag) sat unabashedly across from me. Her languid blue eyes expressed a soft nature as she chatted away about the trials and tribulations of small-town life. Helen was a fetching woman. The profusion of deep facial lines put her well past forty, yet she owned a childlike playfulness that made me feel as though I was across from a woman many years younger.

A man of about sixty entered and sat at the counter.

"Hiya, Helen," he said, as he gave me a long once-over.

"Evenin', William," she answered. "The usual?"

"Don't mind if I do," he chirped.

Helen continued to talk with both of us while cooking over the sizzling grill and eventually inquired as to where I was lodging.

"I am not sure yet. Do you know of a place?"

William spoke. "My wife and I have a house with rooms for let. There's room if you want."

With no options open to me, I replied, "Oh, yes, if you please."

I paid my bill, and William and I walked out of the cafe. When I stepped up to Nibs and took her reins, the man looked at me as though I had three heads.

To make a long story short, Nibs stayed in the back garden of the café, and I slipped into William's Model T.

I had never been in an automobile before and jumped with fright when its wheels began to spin. We did not drive very far before coming to a halt in front of a large three-storey home with a deep front porch. William took my bags, which I had put in the back seat, and we climbed the wide wooden steps. Entering through the front door, I had expected to see light from gas lamps and perhaps the voices of the home's occupants, but all was dead still and dark. William lit a lamp at the door.

"There we are. Now, let me show you to your room."

"I hope we are not disturbing your wife."

"My wife?"

"Yes, you said you and your wife had rooms to let."

"Oh, yes well, we did. That is to say, when she was alive. She passed away a year or so ago."

"And your renters?"

"None at the moment. Just yourself."

I felt uneasy.

He quickly said, "Come along, I'm sure you must be tired and would like to go straight to bed. I'll put you in the room at the top of these stairs. It has a lovely view of the river."

I followed behind him and said good night as quickly as was polite. Upon hearing him climb the next flight up to the third floor, I dragged a trunk and chair to my now closed door and used them as a barricade of sorts.

There was no denying that the view from the bedroom window was lovely, especially with the full moon dripping its light upon the still water, but, too weary to dally, I fell into the bed and did not wake until morning.

The morning was heavily frosted, and I dreaded having to mount Nibs. When I told William of my plans to ride my horse to New York Harbour, he let out a howl.

"At this time of year? Did you look out the window? You'll catch your death. Look, you can stay here if you wish. We can work out an arrangement."

"No, I must go. But thank you."

"What about your horse? Are you taking your horse to Ireland with you?"

The penny dropped. What was I to do with Nibs? My thoughts had been to put miles under my feet. I had not considered what to do with Nibs. My face must have looked miserable.

"She looks like a good horse. I mean well bred."

"The best."

"Tell you what, let's make a deal. You give me your horse, I'll drive you to New York harbour."

I looked at him blankly.

"You can't leave her on the streets of New York, now, can you?"

And so, it was agreed.

William had two commitments that day, so I would spend one more night and we would depart first thing in the morning. I went to bed early and did not secure the door with the trunk and chair. I woke with a start in the middle of the night to William sitting next to me.

"What are you doing in here?" I yelled, pulling the quilt up under my chin.

"Just thought you might enjoy some warm company, is all," William replied. "It's mighty cold, you know."

I could smell spirits and stale cigar smoke on his breath. Memories flooded.

"Get out of my room," I said steadily.

"I'm just being friendly. I'm sure you could use the company. I know I could." William reached out and touched my covered thigh.

I flinched, but then did something surprising, even to me. I threw the covers off my body. My nightdress hugged my middle. The moon's glow illuminated the room and my condition.

"Still interested?" I asked angrily.

William sat stunned, staring at the now kicking mound.

"Not so appealing now, am I, William? Get out."

I did not say goodbye to Nibs. Frankly, I saw no point in extending my pain with it. I was quite numb to the day as it was. I had to be. The drive to the harbour was strained at best. William offered to carry my bags for me when we reached the docks. I glared at him.

He snapped at me. "I did drive you here and gave you a room for two nights. You should be more appreciative!"

"You got my horse, didn't you? That is payment enough, don't you think? I don't owe you anything more, do I?"

I pulled a bill from my coat pocket and threw it on the seat. "For the room."

He flushed with embarrassment. "Look, about what happened. I was drunk is all. You are young and I am lonely."

My eyes flashed once again. "Yes, I am young. You're old enough to be my grandfather for heaven's sake. Furthermore, you should be ashamed of yourself; no doubt your departed wife would be. Perhaps you should find someone your own age, you loathsome maggot of a man."

I heaved a deep breath, turned on my heel, and walked away. A day later, I boarded the SS Marguerite, headed for home.

46

On board the ship I made the decision to go directly to see the O'Reillys. It was the only logical thing I could think of, given my set of circumstances. Surely, after all the years of knowing me, the O'Reilly's would take me in, if only temporarily. Not to mention the fact that my mother had something waiting for me at their place, and I could not wait to make that connection, any connection, with her again.

Mr and Mrs O'Reilly welcomed me with open arms. I had to tell them that both my parents had passed over (though did not clarify how). They took the news hard, especially when I relayed that Frank Nicolas had passed as well. I confirmed that I had been left with child, as it was un-maskable by this time. I did not confirm the circumstances surrounding the conception—and they did not ask. They did request, however, to avoid bringing scandal to their lives, that I tell people that I had been married and that my young husband had passed away. I quickly agreed. Mrs O'Reilly took me to the local midwife who had delivered all the O'Reilly children. All was fine with the baby, but the midwife insisted I eat better to gain a little more weight.

After a few days, as Mrs O'Reilly and I sat with our first afternoon cup of tea, I broached the subject of the package my mother left.

"Yes, of course Genevieve, how forgetful of me. Grace said she did not want to bring it to America or leave it in the cottage. Let me get it for you."

I sat in the plush rose coloured chair in her sitting room, anxiously awaiting her return. After handing me the brown package, she excused herself from the room. The package was quite soft. I choked back tears as I unfolded and lifted out my mother's wedding dress. I held the floor-length cotton and lace dress up to my face, seeking my mother's scent. As I did so, two matching shoes fell to the floor. She had shown me this dress before. The yellow/white pearls that encircled the high collared neckline and trailed down the front of the fabric to the narrow waistline had been my favourite detail. I had long forgotten this dress. I could hear my mother's words clearly as I curled myself over and into the dress.

I left a little something at the O'Reilly ranch the last time we were home, Genevieve. I hope you will use it one day. I hope it will bring you the unconditional love that it brought to me.

My third trimester was easy and rather lovely. Mrs O'Reilly and I became quite close, and though I was unsure as to where my life would eventually lead, I felt a sense of security and familial support. As my middle thickened, I found I could no longer do simple tasks which required bending over. Riding my horses was out of the question thus I had to find contentment with simple grooming, nuzzling their heads and brushing them. Being with Jenny and Luna again was consoling, even though being with them reminded me of Nibs, which broke my heart.

My hips widened as is oft times the case with mid to late pregnancy. It was not uncomfortable exactly, but I could feel the effects of the loosening of my pelvis and surrounding ligaments. I woke one morning and found I was waddling, which is also common, and the truth of it is that I found it rather amusing. As my time grew near, the midwife made more regular visits, generally in the evening, on her way home.

My daughter's entry into the world was as delicate as the breeze off butterfly wings. The midwife had come to perform an evening check and said, "You're as ripe as a newly fallen fig, Genevieve. This wee one is very low now, as low as it can get before delivery. I think tonight's the night, especially given the tightening you say you're experiencing." Cupping her hands around my mid-section, she spoke to the child within. "You can come out of there now, ya little dote."

We both laughed. The midwife decided to spend the night at the house, since in her mind my labour was imminent. I went to bed, lying on my side, with my usual four pillows: one for my head, one anchored at my back and two tucked under my legs and belly for support. I had trouble sleeping, what with trying to find comfortable angles to contort into, which were sometimes decided by a few inches this way or that. Coming toward morning, I heard footsteps outside my room. It was still pitch black, but I could make out the silhouette of the midwife making her way back to the little room next to mine.

"Is everything well?" I inquired.

"Genevieve, yes, all is well. Just a little restless, as I'm sure you must be. Perhaps a bit surprised you didn't call for me in the middle of the night. I think that baby is enjoying its warm environment."

"Come, sit with me awhile, will you?"

"That would be lovely."

The midwife came to my bed and covered her willowy legs with one of my throws. We spoke in hushed tones about trivial things, bright and cheery things, giggling as two young girls might.

After a time, she said, "You should try and get back to sleep. You will need all your strength about you when your time comes. So will I."

She rose and slipped out my bedroom door. No sooner had the door closed, than a warm river surged from me.

"Wait!" I called out.

The look on my face, as the midwife re-opened the door, must have been all telling, and she hastily returned.

"Dear child," she said tenderly, "let us fix your bed with towels."

There was no pain in the contractions.

"They are plenty strong," she pronounced, as she put her hands to my belly. "There is no sharpness at all?"

"No. It is more of a . . . a tickling sensation. You will excuse me, I need to get to the toilet."

"You do?"

"Yes."

"Are you sure?"

"Of course, I am sure."

"Very well."

When I went to rise from the bed however, I found I could not walk. Seeing my floundering, she asked me to lie back down.

"Genevieve, you do not need the toilet. You need to push. The baby's head is emerging."

Within a few short minutes, just as the sun peeked its bright head over the horizon, I held in my arms a wet, squirming child.

"She is beautiful," exclaimed the midwife. "Just a drop of water, like yerself."

She was assuredly that—petite, with big round eyes that looked at me inquisitively, communicating, only seconds after being brought into the world. She lay peacefully across my chest, a mop of dark hair twisting this way and that, glistening.

Shafts of golden light penetrated the window's lacy curtains. As my daughter and I gazed at each other, the light seemed to reach its virtual hands to her, caressing the top of her head, making the thick black strands glow.

"Hello," I whispered. "I am your mother."

A moment later, as if reading my mind, the midwife asked. "Have you decided on a name, Genevieve?"

"Isn't today the first of February?"

"Yes, yes, it is."

I had decided that if I bore a girl, she would have Grace as a second name, Liam as a second name if a boy. Until that point, I had imagined all sorts of first names that might suit a child of mine; none seemed right before this very moment though, and it was one that I had not considered before, but it was a perfect match.

"Her name is Bríghid Grace. Grace, for my mother; Bríghid for the Goddess/Saint Bríghid. Today is the first day of spring in the Celtic pagan calendar, which honours her as the giver of the first signs of spring."

"Ach, sure she's a lovely little lady. May she wear it well."

The next several days were blissful. The midwife came and went and Mrs O'Reilly showered me with soups, fresh breads, roasted chicken, and heaping mounds of mashed potatoes. She lavished Bríghid with ohh's and ahh's and high-pitched cooing noises. One morning she asked if she might take Bríghid for a wander around the gardens, so that I could catch forty winks. I could not seem to sleep and sat instead, writing to my new child.

47

A folded, brittle piece of paper fell from the diary as Norah turned the page.

My dear Bríghid,
I say my, but I use that term with the knowledge that it will last for only a short while. The past week has flown by. How am I to feel when you are three, nine, and twelve? I think that time too will pass in a blink. I do not own you. You will grow into your own self, but for now, my dear child, I will call you mine.
I loved my mother telling me the story of my birth, being born in the straw, as evening fell, and at the same time as our foal. Let me tell you how your name came to be. Your middle name, of course, is that of your nana. Grace. You are named after Bríghid, Goddess and Saint. She is called both. The name means 'fiery arrow'. Bríghid was born at the same moment the sun ascended the horizon. Light beams shone on her forehead and suffused her with golden light. Your birth was a duplicate of this.

*The Goddess Brighid was the keeper of sacred flames
and holy wells. She was a daughter of the high
king Dagda, of the Tuatha dé Danaan. She was a
goddess of all things on high, such as rising flames,
hill forts, highlands, and upland areas. She was
the Goddess of wisdom, poetic eloquence, healing,
and druidic knowledge.*

*Many of her stories and symbolism were reborn later,
in the woman we know as Saint Brighid. Brighid was a
generous, loving woman whose compassion for others
was great and well renowned. She was so generous, in
fact, that she gave numerous gifts to the poor straight
from her parent's house. When she gave away her
father's jewel-encrusted sword to a leper, after having
just refused several marriage proposals, she was sent
to a nunnery.*

*Her influence eventually awarded her an abbey in
Kildare. Brighid chose a site that had been used in
ancient times for the worship of the pagan Goddess
Brighid. The site was also close to Brighid's holy well
where Brighid sacred fires were built. Saint Brigid was
wise in the ways of midwifery. She wrote poetry and
worked untiringly with infants and children in need
of aid. She worked for the advancement of women in
general, ensuring that women were allowed to hold
property in their own names, and that the crime of
rape was unpardonable.*

*The unusual woman had refused to marry, choosing
instead a life where she was under her own authority.
She is an ancient Goddess, as well as a saint. She is the
patron saint of childbirth, a protector of infants, children, and travellers. This is to be the name you carry.
In this country, where the ancient history of the Tuatha
dé Danaan mingles with Christianity, you will carry
a name that is loved by all. One tends to see paintings
and sketches of Brighid and Saint Brighid holding a*

*lamp or candle, illuminating a path for the weary. She
is a light in the dark. You are my light in the dark and
the Mobhrí shall be your shining candle.
I never knew one could love another to the depths
that I love you. I would not flinch at giving my life for
yours. You are my sun, my moon and stars, and though
I know I will make mistakes, know I will make you
cry, I also know that no one will ever love you as I do.
This gives me courage. Our tie cannot be severed, and
I am glad of it. I am your mother. I am honoured to
call you daughter.
Lovingly,
Your mother.*

Norah stopped for a moment, to consider all she had learned about the matriarchal line from which she descends. Unmistakably, it is a long trail of remarkably strong women who confronted life head-on—no matter the danger—and found enough positives to carry on. Was this driven by comfort offered through the power of the Mobhrí? Or simply their own tenacity and desire to claim their space in the world? She wasn't sure, but was clear that she felt inspired by them all.

Dónal suggested a short break. The two walked hand and hand through the garden, reveling in the warm sun and their deepening love, and to talk about their uncommon life. As evening began to roll across the sky, with fresh cups of tea in hand they settled back down to continue reading.

48

Genevieve

I **could hear my** baby crying. I quickly rose and followed the sound, my milk surging, every cell of my being longing to nurture and release the anguished cries.

It amazed me how quickly I recovered from childbirth, gleeful at the speed at which my old clothes fit again, and my old energy flowed. On Bríghid's three-month birthday, I took her for a walk with one of the O'Reilly's sons, who was nine or ten. When we arrived back, the O'Reilly's were waiting on the front steps. I could tell that they were upset from the glaring looks on their faces. They promptly ordered their son to his chores and looked at me sternly.

"Whatever is the matter?" I asked.

"Where are your parents?" Mr O'Reilly demanded.

"I told you."

"Where is your husband?"

"I told you that, too. I have no husband. What has happened?"

"You have deceived us, Genevieve. You have abandoned your loving husband. Lord knows what actually happened to your parents."

My heart sank. What had happened? How could they know such things?

"Please . . . what?"

"Your mother-in-law was here. She said you left your husband in a state of panic; he has been beside himself with worry, Genevieve."

Chapter 48

I was speechless. I could not think of anything to say that would, in any way, make sense.

"This mother-in-law of yours, Yao."

"You mean Yao was here?"

"So, you admit it!" Mr O'Reilly continued to barrage me.

"NO!" I retorted quickly, "She is not any relation of mine. She is a wicked woman, who wishes nothing but ill for my child and me. You must believe me. How did she know where to find me?"

"Your husband thought you might come to us, as you had told him about us back in New York. She also said you have stolen some sort of family heirloom belonging to her. How could you do this? She said too that your husband is an invalid. Could you be this cruel to your own husband?"

"He is NOT my husband."

"She showed us legal documents, Genevieve. You have taken his child away."

"They are false documents!"

"Is this his child?"

I opened my mouth to answer, but all that tumbled out was a whimper.

"Are Grace and Liam dead?"

"They are . . . gone."

"Gone? Gone where?"

"To . . . I cannot explain, but they are well, I can assure you. It is all so very complicated, don't you know?"

Mrs O'Reilly buried her head in her hands and ran inside, unable to look at me. Mr O'Reilly stood his ground, arms crossed over his broad chest, jaw clenched. Seconds passed.

"I don't know who you think you are, coming here, taking advantage, lying, using us. You have caused us much distress, Mrs O'Reilly most of all. You need to go back to your husband, back to New York. I want to know where Grace and Liam are."

"They are just . . . gone." I said weakly. I could not tell them where they were. How could I? I could not explain all that had transpired, or they would have had me locked up with the key thrown away.

"We shall see about that. Yao will return tomorrow. You can go with her or not, I really don't care. But you . . . you will be gone no matter what." Mr O'Reilly turned and walked away.

I was obviously not going to wait for Yao to return. I immediately packed my things and went to the stables, where Mrs O'Reilly was heaving soiled hay from a stall. She looked up from her task. Bríghid fussed in my arms.

I said, "I wish to take my horses."

Mrs O'Reilly came to me. "Genevieve, we cannot help you if you are dishonest. This whole predicament grieves my heart sore. If you don't tell me the truth, we have no choice but to insist you leave. We have our own children to worry about but at the same time, I feel there is more to this story than meets the eye. While I feel certain of this, Mr O'Reilly is having none of it and I must abide his wishes to keep peace within our home. We have known you all your life Genevieve and I also know you are not the kind to deal with people in an unlikable way. For the last time, tell me the truth, child."

But I could not expound on all of life's ordeals; on all that had transpired in my short life. While I did not tell her precisely what had occurred, I did insinuate that Yao's son had assaulted me and had created false documents. Mrs O'Reilly's face grew ashen as she clutched the pitchfork tighter.

In the end, she and I came to an uncomfortable understanding. I would go with my two horses. She would sell me a cart and a travelling trunk. I would write to her after we were settled, after I felt I was safely away from Yao.

Then, and only then, would I give her a deeper explanation, though what that was to be was beyond me at that point.

Mrs O'Reilly helped me pack the trunk with a few blankets, house wares, cloth wraps for Bríghid and some other necessities. This we placed in the back of the cart. She fashioned a carrier for Bríghid from a wooden box, lined and cushioned it with blankets and tied it to the seat next to me. I placed my money and the Mobhrí in a box. This I put into a larger box, with the intention of placing a few wet nappies on the top, as a deterrent for anyone that might come across us and be looking for valuables.

I made Mrs O'Reilly promise to stall Yao from coming after me. She gave me her word.

"Mr O'Reilly will not be pleased," she said, wringing out her hands. I hugged her and said yet another in a long line of wrenched good-byes.

I knew **I had** found a place of new beginnings as soon as I set foot on the tree-lined path that wound its way to a handsome little house and barn. I did not respond to the owner of the house when he called my name. I had been called Genevieve my entire life and being called Caitlín still did not register.

Two days after my departure from the O'Reilly's, I concluded I must change my name; if Yao were to follow me, she would be looking for one Genevieve Norah Furlong. I hadn't yet decided on this new moniker, however. Fate again played its role in my life when one was given to me.

I had entered a little corner shoppe to obtain a few bits and pieces and was sorting through a batch of carrots that had seen better days, when a voice called out. "Caitlín? Caitlín Sinnott?"

A moment later, I felt a light tap my shoulder. "Caitlín?"

I turned. An elderly gentleman with a broad smile stood before me. An embarrassed look crossed his face.

"Sorry. Sorry." he said. "You're the image of Caitlín Sinnott from the back."

"Not a bother." I said.

He was eighty if he was a day. A long black pipe extended from his upturned mouth. As he puffed, a sweet-smelling aroma escaped from the burning embers, rising as grey miniature clouds. The fragrance reminded me of freshly stewed apples with cinnamon. I liked him instantly, based solely on his warm smile and pipe smoke.

Removing his pipe, he winked and said, "All the best now."

It was that simple. The shoppe-keeper passed us by and looked to the old man.

"Dia duit Tom" (Good day Tom).

The old man smiled again. "Dia is muire duit Dermuid, conas tá tú?" (Good day, Dermuid. How are you?).

"Go maith, go maith," (good, well) replied the shoppe keeper. Looking out the window he continued, "Tá an aimsir uafasach." (The weather is terrible).

"Agus bhí sé go hálainn ar maidin." (And it was beautiful this morning.)

The two spoke in Irish as I paid for my thread, nails, candles, bread and carrots. Before leaving the shoppe, I turned to the old man and thanked him.

I am certain Tom did not know what I was thanking him for, but he nodded and smiled just the same. His warmth conjured so many impressions of what home should be: of what his home might be like—of what I desired so painfully for Bríghid and me. Truth be told, I wanted to run back to the old man and plead with him to take us home, even for a little while. Instead, I climbed into my cart and whistled the horses on.

***

Caitlín Norah Sinnott. I would keep my middle name, Norah, Caitlín Norah Sinnott; so it was. My name would remind me always of the old gentleman. It would remind me of the comfort of a home that he compelled me to secure.

The owner of the house called my name again. "Caitlín, do ye like it?"

I answered to my new name for the first time on this very land.

"I am home," is all I said.

The owner, a wiry little man of about fifty, was extremely anxious to sell. His son had moved to Australia and had sent word that he would like his parents to join him. Though he was not happy with selling the property, the money from the sale would allow him and his wife to give their main house to their youngest daughter and still leave ample money to move abroad.

"Sure'n I hate to part with it," he said. "It has been never messed with, as ye can see."

I brightened. "I assure you, I will not mess with it. I will love it."

He eyed me hopefully.

"The thing is," said I, "I have cash for the place if you are interested in selling in that way."

His eyes lit. I could see him calculating many things. "I would give you full price, of course. It could be a quick sale," I added. "All I would ask for is a receipt and my name on the deed."

In a matter of twenty-four hours, I had a deed with the name Caitlín Norah Sinnott neatly penned upon it. He never asked me for formal identification, and I certainly avoided being asked. This deed allowed me to open a bank account.

My parents had left me enough to buy the place outright and to deposit enough money to see me through the mending of the house and the cultivation of the gardens that would prove to be my livelihood for years to come.

PART III

50

Bríghid

My name is Bríghid Grace Sinnott and I do believe my fifth birthday is my first vivid memory. There are flashes of earlier events, but this day is solid and secure in my mind—knee-high purple woolly socks wrapped in brown paper, a yellow cake, and an introduction to the family secret.

The cake my mother made was a visual wonder. Bright yellow icing spiraled its way around the sides and crown. Also on the crown, half-sunken and lying on its side in the very centre, was a red, green, and yellow wooden spinning top. I clearly remember reaching for and raising the smooth little toy, grasping it between my thumb and forefinger and rolling it upon my tongue, relishing the burst of sweetness there.

My mother had tightly knitted the woolly socks. Her addition of two buttons for eyes and a tiny ball of yarn replicating a nose were delightful for a waggish five-year-old. She tried to encourage me to wear the socks on my feet, but I was partial to playing with them as toys. After a mere three hours, she surrendered to my tendencies and commenced to stuff the two cavities with quilting material and sewed the ends closed; thus creating my two favourite dolls, so named Larry and Kitty.

The addition of a red bow to the top of Kitty's head and a green ribbon around the illusory neck of Larry added to my jubilation. We became inseparable, Larry, Kitty, and me. My mother and I spent most of my birthday reading books, colouring, and dying a stark white piece of fabric to a rich golden yellow. I loved the colour yellow. I giggled when my mother re-told how I used to pronounce the word 'lellow'. Its brightness made me feel happy and always put me in a good humour.

In the late afternoon of my fifth birthday, my mother and I sat eating my sumptuous yellow cake and drinking sweetened tea. This was also the evening that my mother showed me the Mobhrí for the first time. The prospect of an eventual reunion with my past relations aroused a keen sense of interest in my psyche; yet I was equally taken with the cake and toys as I was with the Mobhrí. Each held its own magical merit; one did not take precedence over the other.

After returning the Mobhrí to its safe hiding place, my mother ventured out to the shed and returned with an armful of turf. There is nothing to compare with the rewarding, sweet, earthy, aroma of a turf fire, permeating throughout a home.

My mother squatted and added three of the four rect-angular blocks onto the fading coals. I remember asking her to tell me about these rectangular bricks of brown-black goodness. I also asked if she and her mother used to make fires together. For a moment, her spirit darkened as though in emotional pain and I instantly regretting asking the question, but she quickly regained her composure and went on to tell me a little about this life saving fuel.

Brushing the hair out of my eyes with her hand, she said, "Turf has been, and still is, one of the most important things families need to survive. It gives us heat to cook by and warmth for our homes."

I brightened, "Isn't it nice that we have so much of it growing in our shed."

A broad grin flashed upon my mothers face. "No Bríghid. Turf does not grow in our shed. I buy ours from our neighbours, the Doghertys."

"O, I see," said I. "The Doghertys grow it in their shed and we put it in ours."

Again my mother grinned.

"No, my little one. The Doghertys, like many of our neighbours, harvest or dig the turf from the bogland with spades every April and September. It's not an easy task I can tell you."

"Can you and I do it together this year?"

"I think not, Bríghid. First of all, the turf has to be dug up from the earth, and it's very, very heavy as it is about eighty percent water when it is first dug up. Then each chunk is laid out to dry, then flipped over to dry the opposite side, then stacked so it can dry some more and finally carted back to a storing area."

I sat quietly for a few beats and asked, "Bogland . . . were you not talking to Mrs Dogherty about someone finding a body 'in the bog'?"

My mother's eyes widened in surprise. "O, but the wide ears on you, my child. I do remember this conversation but

I didn't think you heard us. But, yes, in truth, a body of a young man was recently found in a bog not far from here."

I pointed to our now lapping flames. "Is part of him in there?"

"Not at all Brìghid. He was removed and buried elsewhere. The young man had probably been wandering at night and fell into a deep bog hole, filled with water. He could have been bog hopping too, which is something some foolish boys do for fun, but it is very dangerous, as some of these bog holes, from recent harvested areas can be rather deep. Let us speak of other, nicer things. I have been thinking that perhaps you may like to attend school next year, Brìghid. Meet some children and become more embraced by this community. What do you think?"

51

Under my mother's watchful eyes, I learned indispensable, practical approaches, as well as tried and true secrets of the plant, vegetable, and herbal world. My mother's favourite birds were the magpies, mine the song thrushes. On bent knees or up on tip toes, we would coax new buds from trees and plants with songs about sunny days being close at hand. (Although we knew full well that we were being optimistic about sun matters, we decided the buds would appreciate the idea that heat would prevail.) It could not be denied that our vegetables were robust and flavourful. I say our vegetables, as my mother always referred to them as ours. It certainly gave me a sense of pride, even though I had little to do with the healthy outcome when I was so young.

I was content. That is, until I began school. I was excited at the thought of school and other children. I recall the look of concern on my mother's face that first morning, but I thought she was merely going to miss my company. It was not until a few weeks later, when she took me out of school to be home-schooled, that I learned her concern and fear of what might occur. It all did.

***

The tinkling of a bell beckoned as we neared the school gate, and a perfectly straight line of children quietly entered the building. I gave my mother a peck on the cheek and promised to behave myself even before the words were out of her mouth. With that peck, I bid my mother goodbye and frolicked my way to the schoolhouse door, which was now closed.

I opened the door with a gleeful smile, to a sourpuss looking nun in a black habit. She looked ancient and tormenting as she glared at me, and many heads turned.

"Turn your heads back around!" she ordered. The children did so.

"Why are you late?" she quacked.

"Am I late?" I asked innocently, still smiling.

The children giggled. The next thing I knew, I was being dragged by the ear to the front of the room. Her wide flowing black dress made a loud swishing noise as she walked, and the long rosary beads hanging from around her neck swung to and fro, the cross hitting me in the face several times.

"Ouch," I exclaimed.

"I'll give you an ouch!" she spat.

She pulled from her drawer three wooden rulers tied together with string. "Where are your shoes?" she inquired loudly.

I said nothing.

"I asked you a question."

Again I said nothing, as I was on the verge of tears. This was not what I had envisioned school to be. She slammed the rulers on her desk and everyone present, save herself, jumped.

Walking to a side table, she scooped up four sheets of blank paper and returned to me. All at once I was in the air. A moment later, I was jarringly lowered to a sitting position on her large, now ominous desk. She fashioned and bound paper shoes together with twine around my feet. The twine was far too tight and the edges of the paper tore at my toes. I was terrified, yes, but also felt a surge of a new intense emotion, one that I now am more than familiar with: defiance.

"Hold out your hands." she ordered.

I did.

"Together! Side by side."

I did.

She picked up the rulers and raised them above her head. They came down upon my outstretched palms. The intense sting was stronger than a handful of late-season nettles.

She said, "That one is for being late."

Again, the rulers descended. "That is for your impertinence."

The rulers rose again, and I fought back the tears. "That is for not wearing shoes to my classroom."

As the rulers ascended for the fourth time, she said, "This one is for that evil pagan mother of yours."

The rulers came down again, but I could not feel the sting. She had called my mother evil. I was unsure of what 'pagan' meant, but assumed it was uncomplimentary. I refused to cry. I refused to lower my head when she pointed to an empty seat midway back. I walked slowly, crunching my way to my first day of school.

The strange thing was, I liked the learning part. The older children were seated on one side of the room, working on more advanced tasks, while we younger children were set to learning sentence structure. I had a hard time understanding it all, but I did my best.

We moved on to science. When Sister Abigail, whose name I learned when the class addressed her soon after my ordeal, drew two amateurish pictures of similar flowers on the chalk board I perked up. She drew the flowers as though they had been cut in half, exposing the internal and external parts. Sister Abigail scoured the room for victims.

"Pádrig Connolly, come up here and stand by that first flower." The legs of Pádrig's chair squeaked loudly across the wooden floorboards as he pushed out from his desk and walked up to the board.

"You…" she said, pointing her bony finger at me, "Little Miss No Shoes. Go stand at the second one."

The children giggled at the name she called me, but she did not hush them. I stood at the board with Pádrig.

"Now," she said sarcastically, "we will review last week's lessons pertaining to the parts and functions of the flower. Pádrig, what part of that flower attracts the bees to it?"

Pádrig looked at the flower as though it was a creature from outer space and shook his head. Then all at once his eyes lit up and he said, "Oh, yes Sister, sure that would be the leaves!"

Sister Abigail rolled her eyes. I slowly raised my hand.

"Well?" she said, obviously expecting an equally inaccurate answer.

"That would be the petals, Sister." I turned and drew an arrow pointing toward them.

"Correct. That was the easy question. Anyone with half a brain should know that."

Pádrig turned crimson.

"Pádrig, would you, by any small chance, know what part of that flower makes the pollen and what that is called?"

Pádrig pointed to the centre of the drawing and weakly ventured a guess. "Here? The…the antler?"

The children laughed heartily. Again, I raised my hand, and she nodded her head begrudgingly. I drew an arrow to one of the eight internal heads she had drawn.

"This is the Anther. The anther makes the pollen. It does sound like antler, though."

Pádrig smiled.

I continued. "This is the stamen; it supports the anther."

Then drawing an arrow to the centre, I added, "this is the stigma, that traps the pollen, and the pistil is what the pollen travels through."

I was going to add that the protective flower bud area is called the sepal but thought better of it.

Instead, I said. "I forget what this is called," pointing to the sepal.

"You can both sit down now." Sister said. "I will take over from here."

Sister Abigail never commented on my knowledge of the flower parts, but I could tell that it annoyed her. No doubt she thought I had learned about such things from my evil pagan mother.

Lunch began on a fairly good foot. I nibbled at my bread and jam, longing to be a part of the circle of girls standing by the building's entrance.

Pádrig came and sat next to me on the narrow stone bench without speaking. His skinny legs swung back and forth under the bench as he devoured his three potato cakes, intermittently licking his fingers to be sure he found every drop of butter left there.

I took his company as a sign of friendship and was about to say something about the flower incident when a group of four boys approached and kicked at his feet.

"Come on, Pádrig, Niall has a ball."

Pádrig had a few bites left and said, "In a minute, I'm still eatin'."

The boys looked toward me and chuckled.

"Pádrig wants to marry you, Pádrig wants to marry you," they sang.

With that, Pádrig jumped to his feet and swung at one of the younger, smaller hecklers. The whole lot of them jumped atop each other in playful fighting and ran away.

I finished my lunch and shyly walked toward the girls. They whispered to each other and skipped off toward the far trees. I stood alone, wondering why the children would not befriend me. Then I looked to my paper covered feet. The paper was beginning to tear in several places, which caused the twine to rub parts of my feet raw.

Sister Abigail rang her bell and all the children filed themselves in an orderly manner along the wall. I followed suit. Once seated, Sister announced that we would be doing our maths and then would be having our music lesson. I cringed, as maths was not something I had understood at all, and though my mother tried to teach me basic concepts, I could not fathom the logic of it. My heart pounded through the lesson for fear Sister Abigail would call on me for an answer, but I was miraculously spared that embarrassment.

I was formulating an internal discussion to have with my mother on never setting foot in the place again when the school door opened, and a cheery-faced nun entered.

"Children," said Sister Abigail, "Sister Gabriel is here, and will now instruct you in music theory."

With that, Sister Abigail swiftly retreated from the building. Sister Gabriel's angelic face smiled brightly, as she looked out upon our young faces. Coming to mine, she lighted.

"Ahh, a new student. And what would your name be then?"

One did not look Sister Abigail directly in the eyes and for a moment I thought I should cast mine to the floor. Sister Gabriel's eyes, however, were as warm and welcoming as a hearth fire on a bitter night.

"Bríghid, Sister. My name is Bríghid. I love singing."

I regretted my forward comment the instant I verbalized it, but it was too late to withdraw it. I had been in school only a few hours and was already fearful and distrusting.

My fears were lifted, however, as Sister Gabriel smiled and said in a friendly, teasing manner, "Grand, grand. We need children who love to sing, don't we?"

The class smiled with her, causing everyone to visibly relax in their seats.

I loved Sister Gabriel. We all did. Why she could not have been our daily teacher was a mystery to us all. We hopped to her every bidding, for she was the kind of person you wanted to please. We longed for her to like us as much as we liked her and, though she was strict, she was by no means harsh in any way. Her approving glances gave us all, even the shyest of the bunch, the impetus to vocally stretch ourselves.

By the end of the hour, she said, "I feel as though I am in a room full of linnets."

Her eyes closed and her hands gracefully glided back and forth. And do you know? I really did feel as though I was a bird among birds, soaring up through the rafters and out to the sky, to join our fellow fledglings in song. My initial determination to be rid of the place was brushed aside during this hour. My new determination was that I could put up with most anything, if it meant I could be close to Sister Gabriel. The remainder of the day did not seem as harsh as the onset, but I am quite sure it was because Sister Gabriel had filled the room with her omnipresent glow. This fact was much to Sister Abigail's chagrin, and no amount of her negativity could erase it from the room.

I had hoped Sister Gabriel was going to be with us every day, but she was to be with us only twice a week, for an hour at a go. My mother was waiting at the gate when the side door opened, and we emerged as bees from a hive. I did not tell her about the trauma I had endured. Instead, I plunged head on in the re-telling of the glorious hour with Sister Gabriel.

"What on earth?" she said, looking at my feet.

"Oh, yes, I must wear shoes, mother."

My mother pulled the twine and paper off my feet and exposed the raw digits. Her eyes began to fume but I brushed off the tiny bits of remaining paper and pushed forward with, "It's grand, mother, let me sing you the song we learned."

I commenced to sing the lullaby with great emotion, and I could tell my rendition dissipated my mother's rightful anger.

Sister Abigail despised me because she despised my mother. The second day of school was as traumatic as the first, as I did not know the prayers the children recited. She paused at my desk and clipped me on the ear.

"I'll box your ears every day until you learn your prayers."

Though I wore shoes to school, it took a week for some of the children to approach me. My days were spent fearing the worst and hoping for the best. Just as I would begin to fall into a deep well of emotional fatigue, Sister Gabriel would appear, shining her glorious light on us all.

The end of the third week was to be my last week of formal school until I was much older. It was a Thursday afternoon; that tedious hour of maths before Sister Gabriel arrived. Sister Abigail had a 'game,' as she called it, which she liked to play. Two students would stand at the chalkboard. She would write an equation of some sort on the board and the students would race to see who could answer it first. The winner could sit down, while the loser had to remain and work on the next problem. This game was disagreeable enough for those who were not proficient with sums, but she added to this discomfort, a rule wherein students had to keep their hand raised to the board at all times. If one lowered their hand, they would get extra maths homework, something no one wished for.

Near the beginning of her game, she called on me. My nervousness caused my palms to sweat as I raised my chalk to her equation. She had written the problem so high on the board that I practically had to stand on tiptoe to reach the looming numbers, but was relieved when the question was one I understood.

To my disappointment, I did not finish first and had to remain, arm held up in the air, as she called on the next student to join me. She wrote the next problem on the board and the next, and the next, all of which I was either unable to answer, or was not fast enough to beat my board partner in answering.

It was not long before my arm began to throb. I used my second arm to support my first. This helped for perhaps a minute but then a painful tingling began, and I tried to lower my arm. Sister Abigail reiterated her rules and informed me that she would not tolerate my cheating, or my insolence.

I began to cry. I had been strong through many days of relentless abuse, but I suppose we all have our thresholds, and I had reached mine. I lowered my arm, saying I could not hold it up any longer. Sister Abigail's face grew flaming red as she strode angrily toward me.

Grabbing the back of my hair, she smacked my head against the chalkboard so hard she broke the skin. Blood trickled down my cheek.

"Sit down you stupid, stupid girl!" she screeched.

Instead of returning to my seat, I ran down the narrow aisle of desks and out into the side yard. I ran until I could run no longer, toward home. I was not sure if I was angrier at Sister Abigail's abuse, or the fact that I was about to miss out on Sister Gabriel's music lesson.

My mother returned from the convent several hours later. She informed me that I was going to continue to be home-schooled by her and would not be returning to the classroom. She was as indignant as I had ever seen her. Many months later, while walking with my mother in town, Sister Gabriel came around the bend. She was pleased to see me and opened her arms to me. She told me that they sorely missed my voice in the group, and I believed her.

When my eyes filled with tears she gently said, "Brighid, not all Sisters are meant to be teachers. Some are forced into the role. This is no excuse for the actions of some, far from it, but just so you know, it has nothing to do with you. You are a bright girl with a bright future."

With that she kissed me on the top of my head and carried on with her day. In hindsight, I suppose that was all she could do for me.

52

*O*nly once do I recall my mother allowing herself to be courted. I was just over nine years old. While not yet cognizant of distractions pertaining to the elusive matters of the heart, I did intuitively sense this man was unlike others that found reasons to drop by our little farm for purchases.

Indeed, many did drop over, devoid of ulterior motives, but some were there, as my mother would say, 'To see if they could acquire more than just my cabbages.' Men found Mother beguiling, but far too independent, and therefore avoided serious approach. This suited her just fine. When some of these men retreated, my mother would grumble for hours under her breath, or perhaps bang the kitchen presses closed with more authority than necessary.

Dara was of a different ilk altogether, she said. He lived two counties away and did not visit regularly. He visited us often enough, though. He sat at our table for tea, and once, while creeping about instead of being in bed, I eyed him stroking the top of my mother's head while they were seated together on our couch.

Dara owned a camera and was learning to develop his own film. He requested a photo shoot of the two of us. He snapped several photos of my mother and me, and then requested a few formal shots. He asked if my mother had any formal wear. The closest thing she had was her mother's wedding dress, which she subsequently changed into.

She looked radiant, breathtaking, and Dara stood, mouth agape, appreciating her frequently hidden elegance. A long cord attached to the back of his camera enabled him to enter a photograph. We all gathered together, with me in the front. When he was ready to trigger the flash, he stepped on the cord. A blast from the flash erupted, and that was that.

After an hour of photo taking, Dara volunteered to go in and make our tea. It was then that my mother decided to take her own photograph. She retrieved the Mobhrí and twisted the device open, just far enough to allow a small stream of light to burst forth. Luna had walked into the frame, and I peeked my head around the corner of the barn at the exact moment Mam stepped on the cord and the camera bulb flashed.

Dara returned a few days later with a large quantity of semi-developed photographs. He had not set the readings accurately on the day of the photo shoot, therefore many of the images were grainy, too light, or conversely, too dark. Only three were clear and true. My mother asked if she might pick one for herself, and Dara agreed. I remember my mother's full smile as she picked up the one that she herself had taken.

One morning I must have caught them at something, since, after calling my mother for a few minutes, the two emerged from the barn. They said they were brushing the horses, but they looked quite flustered and more than a little disheveled. I did not understand it but knew better than to question it.

Many years later, when I questioned Mother about the disappearance of Dara from our lives, she admitted to me that he had been married. She had not known it at the time he was courting her. It was not until a few months had passed that she and a friend had gone out to the city for a day. She had seen him in the distance, walking arm and arm with a woman with two children in tow. I have often felt badly about my mother's unlucky history with regard to men, but she was intolerant of my pity.

"I have you, Bríghid, and this farm. I am content with that."

Soon after my eleventh birthday, the Dogherty household expanded. Their farm lay directly below our property. John's sister, Aoife, became widowed, and consequently moved with her five children from Castlecomer, Kilkenny to the Doghertys' large, childless home. One afternoon I heard the unmistakable sound of children snickering filter through the hedgerow while I sat among the newly burst bluebells at the bottom of our field. Moments later, three hunkered down figures sprang noisily from behind our trees in an unsuccessful attempt to startle me.

Patsy Brennan and I were exactly the same age, down to the very day. Her brothers were Desmond, aged thirteen, Aidan, twelve and twins, Cormac and Shay, aged four.

Being the only girl child was difficult at times, and Patsy was over the moon about making a female friend so quickly. And I, being alone so much of the time, felt equally graced with her friendship. Patsy made other friends at school, but we were best friends, eagerly sharing important discoveries, and confiding in each other about the angst and bafflement of adolescent life.

We girls formed a club with Patsy's two eldest brothers, and christened it, 'The Four Leaf Club'. This was chosen as we thought ourselves rare and lucky, much like a four-leaf clover. We 'Four Leafs' would oftentimes wander the roads and hills, as we all had a predilection for observing and being part of nature in all her seasons.

The Doghertys owned a little piece of land in County Dublin, in a place called Shankill. Many's a time I was invited to accompany the family to their cottage. It was not a large structure and therefore appeared as though it was bursting at the seams with the lot of us, but none of us minded. Patsy and I had to share a single bed, but this adjunct only added to the charm of it all. That cabin saw the lot of us mature as the years pushed on.

Not far from the cottage was one of our favourite stomping grounds, namely Bride's Glen. We spent many summers discovering every nook and cranny of that place. The walk took us along a low stone wall. At one particular spot, we would hop the wall and scamper down a mid-sized hill to a field. Across the far end of the field was an abandoned old shack. The time worn structure possessed the quintessential characteristics of a ghost house, which we loved, thus when in the area, we would sojourn to it. On blustery days, its shelter saved our playing cards from being blown away and kept us dry when caught in the ever-looming cloudbursts of Ireland.

We would invariably race back to the top of that hill, which we dubbed Faery-Clover Hill, (as it was believed finding a four-leaf clover would allow you to contact the faeries). Alas, the lads were always victorious over Patsy and I. Breathless, at the crest, one of us would bemoan, "You two have the distinct advantage of wearing trousers. We'd annihilate the both of you if we weren't constrained to these tight skirts!"

One day, when we knew we would be racing, hence losing, Patsy and I devised a plan to get our own back. In our packs, we stuffed two pairs of trousers, two shirts and two caps belonging to Desmond and Aidan. After the predicted loss, we returned to our blanket. Patsy and I excused ourselves to the shack. Within a few minutes, we bounded out, skirts, blouses, and scarves in hand, wearing the lad's clothes. Desmond and Aidan fell into gales of laughter as we two paraded around, pantomiming our renditions of manliness.

Flinging our feminine constrictions to the blanket, we challenged them to another race. The boys whispered to each other. With that, didn't they spring to their feet, grab our clothes, and take off for the shack themselves; emerging a few minutes later in our clothes, waving the two scarves that we had worn on our heads, swishing and swaying ridiculously. Once again, we all fell to the ground in fits of laughter.

The race commenced, and low and behold, we won! Still catching our breath at the stone wall, Desmond urged us on with a more punishing challenge.

"Here it is, lads and lassies. Back down to the shack, which we must tag, back up again to this wall, then over the wall to the other side of the road, and back down again to the shack. Who's for it?"

All four of us took off at breakneck speed down the hill. Patsy and I were clearly in the lead and slagged the cocky boys over our shoulders mercilessly with playfully deflating insults. Patsy and I touched the shack and ran up the hill once more, Desmond and Aidan not far behind. Once at the stone wall, we swung our legs up and over, falling to the other side in a crouch.

We had not noticed the two old women walking along the road; until we stood up, sweat dripping from underneath woolen caps. We squealed. They cringed. What a sight we must have been: two girls, well past adolescent frivolity, in trousers, boy's shirts, and caps. Patsy and I burst out laughing at the scene. The two women in front of us were, no doubt, praying for our heathen souls. Though we were a sight of maladjusted abnormality, nothing could have prepared them for the pair behind us. Bent on getting over the wall, Desmond and Aidan had taken no notice of our halt and so leapt triumphantly as two lunatics to where we all stood.

Horror swept across the faces of the two ladies, and I was sure they might keel over from heart failure right then and there. To top it all off, the women knew the three from their church.

"What are you like, you little pups!" the one with the thick-rimmed glasses wailed.

The second raised her walking stick and pointed it toward Desmond and Aidan.

"Woe betide the two of you. Wait until your mother hears about this hooligan behaviour. Never in all my days…"

"We'll be getting on then," Patsy said in a polite, breathless tone.

"I'll say you will," said the first woman.

I am not sure if it was because he was adorned in a skirt and had been acting the can with no inhibitions for the previous hour, or, if it was because Desmond was just naturally smart-alecky, but he spoke directly to the ladies.

"Yes, we must be getting on. Good day, ladies."

As that remark poured from his mouth, didn't he pull the sides of the skirt out into a deep curtsy. Well, I can tell you, his actions were too much for the lot of us, and we let loose convulsing laughter, fumbled our way over the stone wall, and ran back down the hill.

We could hear the one with the stick call after us. "You cheeky divils!"

53

*T*ime seemed to fly away from us all. Just after Patsy and I were awarded our leaving certificates from school, Patsy was offered a job in a department store in Dublin city. Her relocation was painful for us both, but I was glad for her. She was a free spirit that needed to fly. We corresponded weekly via the post and kept our friendship cultivated for years. Patsy eventually moved back to our area with her husband and raised her children.

Four months after she took that store clerk position, her brothers and I went to pay her a surprise visit. She was working on the upstairs floor of Elvery's Department Store. Patsy shared a small office with Ealga, a corpulent woman who was an enormous fan of opera. Ealga fancied herself an undiscovered opera Diva and as such spent a good part of her day singing operatic passages from her favourite theatre productions. Ealga was also hard of hearing, which caused her to sing louder than she may have otherwise done. Patsy could not figure how Ealga completed her work while singing arias, but she invariably seemed to be ahead of the stacks of papers that were regularly delivered to her desk.

Patsy lit up with delight when we entered her office and Ealga's voice pushed dramatically forward when she became aware of our presence.

Describing the friendly atmosphere and the overall camaraderie she experienced at Elvery's, Patsy went on to tell us about a new girl, Mary Hickey, who worked in the supply room down the hall. Though Mary had only officially begun her employment that very day, Patsy thought we might all get along famously. Fifteen minutes having come and gone, we arranged to meet after work, and said our good-byes. Patsy turned her back to us.

All at once, Desmond and Aidan grabbed Patsy and held her arms and legs, while I put a gag around her mouth. I tied her legs to the chair and her hands around her back. Patsy squirmed but was unable to wiggle out of her predicament. The three of us shrugged our shoulders as she grumbled at us with inaudible threats through the gag.

Ealga was nearing crescendo and singing at a stentorian volume. She heard not a peep from our side of the room. We removed ourselves with winks and waves. Desmond, our instigator, had yet another brilliant notion. He slipped down the hall and popped his head into Mary Hickey's supply room.

"Pardon me, Mary?"

Mary Hickey's nervous, first-day-of-work face peered out from behind a mountain of supplies. "Yes. Hello?"

"Sorry to bother you, Mary, but Patsy Brennan needs some stationary immediately. It's extremely urgent. Could you manage to bring her a few sheets?" Desmond's enticing blue eyes bore beseechingly into Mary's.

"Of course. Right away!"

Mary rose from her desk and gathered several sheets of paper, but when she looked up, Desmond had disappeared. Poor Mary Hickey—she was about to walk into Patsy's office to find Patsy tied to her chair, no doubt squirming and wiggling. And Ealga, oblivious to Patsy's plight, would no doubt be in full voice, as her internal operatic scene drew to conclusion.

I think back on the many adventurous antics and times we Four Leafs shared and conclude that life was phenomenally stunning. I periodically feel melancholy for those days. I daresay, my heart feels thoroughly pricked by sharp thorns when returning from those memories. Still and all, I would rather feel the thorns than to have never experienced the roses.

Much to Patsy's delight, Desmond and I did eventually concede to our feelings and were wed when I was twenty-one. Patsy never let me forget it was she who had foreseen our union. Desmond moved to our home but continued to work at the Doghertys' farm. He was a good farmer and a loyal employee. My mother and I continued to work on our farm, though it was meager by comparison to the Doghertys'. I loved Desmond desperately, with all my heart, and he returned his love ceaselessly. Our home was a place of love and peace and easy days. I did, however, notice my mother, Caitlín, becoming emotionally distant. Not in a troubling way, merely distracted. When I questioned her, she said she could feel the pull of the Mobhrí. There was no way to describe it, she said. Her biggest fear was how I would feel at the time of her departure.

Some might take pity on me, given the circumstances of my conception. Like my mother, I abhor pity. I carefully selected the passages I have written in this well-worn diary to prove that life, for all of us, is awash with jubilation and sorrows, triumphant s and bewildering valleys.

My mother made her choices. I cannot say I would have made the same ones, but I can say that in the end, I am happy to be here. She taught me, above all else, to accept the consequences of my actions. I am most grateful that my mother was honest with me, revealing the realities of her life. I lost immediate interest in pressing her about my biological beginnings. I lost interest in knowing where and who my father might be. My mother loved me enough for two parents. Our fondness for one another was, and will always be, a crown of beauty; true and unwavering. My personality emerged very much like my mother's: fiery and strong-willed, determined, yet sensitive to nature, with powerful attractions to all things mysterious.

54

*N*orah's phone rang.

"I'll get it," said Dónal. "Hello? …Oh, yes. Hi, April. We were just getting ready…sorry, what? …Yes, I understand."

55

*C*hicken or beef?" asked the flight attendant.
"We're fine, but thanks anyway," answered Dónal. The attendant nodded his head and rolled his trolley on toward the seats behind them.

"Are you right, Norah?"

"I can't believe it Dónal. Tell me again exactly what April said?"

"Not very much, really. Your mother slipped at the top of a long flight of stairs. She was in surgery when April rang. Extensive trauma to the head was all she knew for sure. She was transported from the Vermont hospital to one in upstate New York that specializes in head trauma."

Dónal took a long, slow breath in.

"It will be okay Norah; I know it will. Why don't you take that Ativan and get some rest. This is a long flight, and we'll have a bit of a wait for our next one. April will be waiting for us at the airport."

"Mmmh. Thank you, dearie. My stomach is doing back-flips, and I don't seem to know which end is up. Perhaps forty winks will correct that."

Dónal kissed Norah gently on the mouth giving her a wink, a nod, and a warm smile. "Sleep, my beauty. Take eighty winks, even."

Norah got as comfortable as is humanly possible in a coach airplane seat and was glad she had the forethought to bring her own pillow.

"Breathe," Dónal said tenderly.

Her mind wandered back to the telephone call. Upon hearing the news, Norah had subsequently lost the ability to think rationally. "Wait, no, not now," she'd stammered. "She and I have finally broken through all the shite that's hovered over us like some dark cloud. Years I've been want-ing to address this with her, and we're finally getting to the other side of all that struggle. She can't go now." Dónal took immediate charge, instructing her to clear the dishes, pack a bag, and call her editor. Dónal booked their passages to New York and found a caretaker for Luain.

At the last minute, without thinking too much about it, Norah packed the Mobhrí in her carry-on. As they were about to board, Norah second-guessed her actions. Dónal had not known Norah had packed the thing and was frankly agitated that she had. He knew it was an unrea-sonable emotion, but he did not want to leave Norah, not even for a minute during this very trying time. If they were not allowed on board with the Mobhrí, he would have to return home and take a later flight; leaving Norah to travel alone and distressed.

Chapter 55

The peculiar thing is it did not even register on the x-ray machine. The two watched the x-ray screen as the carry-on bags passed through the conveyor belt. Many colourful outlines of bags, bottles, etc., were easily recognizable, but there was no hint of the Mobhrí's mass.

Norah leaned into Dónal. "It's fine. It's passed."

He nodded and sighed with relief.

The drive to the hospital felt incessantly long. They exited the elevator on the fifth floor, reported to the bustling nurses' station, and were shown to a waiting area. Doctor Abbott was paged over the PA system. A few moments later, a tall, quite attractive, 40-something man, with a trim salt-and-pepper beard—wearing the proverbial white coat—approached.

"Would you be Norah, Úla's daughter?"

"Yes."

Even though he had a heavy New York accent, Norah was relieved to know her mother's doctor had an Irish last name. He sat next to her and Dónal and took Norah's hand in his. She did not pull away.

"Your mother is out of surgery."

She searched his face for answers. He quickly added, "She has not regained consciousness as yet."

"When will she?"

"That is hard to say. She has had a very nasty blow to her skull. We have done what we can for now."

"Done what you can?"

"Yes, these cases can go in several directions. She might wake up in the morning."

"Or?"

"The truth of the matter is that we do not know if there has been any permanent damage. Things are a bit swollen at the moment, internally as well as externally. Only time will give us the answers. Her vital signs are good though, and that is very positive news."

"Can we see her?"

"Follow me. She is in intensive care for now."

Entering the room was surreal. Norah's vibrant, resilient mother lay motionless. Large white bandages encircled her head. Her eye sockets were black, and her face swollen beyond recognition. Had her name not been clearly displayed on the chart on the end of the bed, Norah would have sworn they'd been taken to the wrong room.

Doctor Abbott described the monitors, medications and antibiotics being pumped into Úla and why they were necessary, but Norah was in no fit state to comprehend it all.

Seeing her glazed expression, the doctor finally said, "Norah, of course, you are welcome to stay by your mother's side all night if you wish, but honestly, I would recommend that you both go and try to get a little sleep. She certainly won't be waking tonight, and you will need your strength tomorrow." Dónal placed his hand gently upon Norah's shoulder in agreement.

They spent the night at a hotel not far from the hospital. It was a strange night, to say the least, but they were cheered the next morning when they had a call saying Úla had opened her eyes.

Úla was unable to communicate verbally. Norah gently held one of her hands. Úla's squeeze was weak, but it was there. She closed her eyes and drifted back to sleep. This pattern continued throughout that day, and Norah stayed, often breathless, running scenarios in her head about how losing Úla now would shatter her. They'd come so far, finding one another again and forging a new, profound connection.

As the days passed, Úla seemed to rally, and was able to chat a little. By the end of the week, she was much stronger and on the tenth day she suggested that Dónal and Norah go off and have a day or two exploring. After much discussion, it was agreed that they would indeed take two days together.

56

Dónal rummaged through the rack of booklets and tourist information guides in the lobby of their hotel room.

"I don't know, Norah. There are so many options. I'd love to get out of the city though. Why don't you make a decision? Surprise me."

Norah picked up a brochure that had attracted her when they first entered the office called *Hiking Trails of the Adirondack Mountains*. It boasted peaks of over five thousand feet, with lakes, streams, trails, and beauty beyond compare.

She selected a trail that would bring them to a viewing plateau. The writeup said it was for intermediate hikers.

"Let's give it a go," agreed Dónal.

The hike began in a grove of lush trees, with consistent signs clearly marking the trail. This they liked. It was more strenuous than they'd anticipated, though, and Norah quickly noticed negative mental thoughts creeping in. Dónal too, was struggling, and they laughed at how out of shape they both felt.

After two hours and several two-minute breaks, they reached the promised plateau and inhaled the crisp air.

"This seems like a good place for lunch."

"If it means we can stop, I will eat while balancing on my head," Dónal quipped.

Their lunch consumed, the contented pair lay on their backs, legs touching, hands laced together, as the sun shone down upon them. Quiet drifting came effortlessly to them both. The resonance of gentle snoring emanated from Dónal's reclined body. Was he snoring, wondered Norah, or was it stomach grumbling? She opened her eyes and rose up on one elbow. All was quiet. Norah lay back down, watching the mingling clouds make their way across the sky. Perhaps it was distant thunder she had heard. Perhaps they should make their way back down the trail.

The next rumble caused Norah to shoot upwards to a sitting position.

"Holy mother…Dónal," she whispered, "Dónal!"

Dónal started awake at the urgent sound of her voice.

"Look to your left, very slowly."

It was standing on its two hind legs, under the trees perhaps thirty metres away, sniffing the air, and grunting.

"He smells our food," whispered Dónal.

"And us." Norah replied.

The black bear looked massive from where they lay. The two whispered and spoke of options. Slowly but steadily, they began to retreat to the trees at their backs. The bear ambled its way to the food. When it reached the pile of leftovers, it rose again to its hind legs, sniffed the air, and released a steady roar. Norah and Dónal felt semi-protected under the darkness of the trees, but knew they were in no way safe or out of harm's way.

The bear ripped the food bags apart and launched into eating whatever scraps had been left behind. Then he picked up Norah's backpack and in one easy swipe, tore the front completely off causing the contents to scatter at his feet.

"Norah, we need to move."

Norah needed no prompting.

They turned their backs to the bear and began moving through the forest. It was not long before they noticed a rustling in the undergrowth beside them. What met their gaze were two cubs, rolling on the ground in play. It was as though someone pressed the pause button on a film. All four eyed each other cautiously. Dónal gently tugged at the sleeve of Norah's jacket, and they moved on. They had barely taken a dozen steps when the cubs let loose two baby cub yowls.

"Shite, Norah, move."

Move they did, as fast as possible, without breaking into a run. The bear had not been a male, as they had both assumed, but a female. A mother bear, who had no doubt left her cubs under the protection of the trees. The cubs had obviously not behaved themselves and stayed put but had skirted around the wood to where Norah and Dónal had retreated.

Panic grew inside them both. Normal forest noises caused them to move faster, forward, away. Time altered.

"I think we're safe enough now, Dónal."

Dónal assessed the situation. Clouds covered the sun, and they were surrounded in every direction by massive pine, spruce, and broad-leafed trees. After several seconds of disquieting silence, Norah ventured to pose the question they both had in their minds.

"Which way do you think?"

"Your guess is as good as mine. Let's see, if we move back in the direction from which we came, I'm nervous we'll come across the bears."

"If we move forward, we've no way of knowing where we'll end up. I think we should assume the bears are long gone and retrace our steps? It's been at least forty-five minutes since we left them, don't you think?"

"We can try it. Yes, that seems like the logical thing to do." Dónal's eyes widened. "Whoa, look at that pine, Norah; split straight down the middle as though someone sliced it with an axe. Lightning can be very precise."

"Thank you Dónal, I needed to hear that right now."

"Sorry. Let's go."

They spoke little, stopping every so often; trying to decide which way would lead back to the plateau. There was no trail and they had not thought to make markers as they retreated. Intermediate hikers they were not.

"Does anything look familiar Dónal?"

Dónal looked worried. "Not particularly. You?"

"Not a thing. That is to say, everything looks the same."

They continued tromping, until Dónal stopped and held up his hand. Norah halted. Dónal lowered his hand, heaving an elongated sigh.

"What is it? Do you hear the bears?"

Dónal turned to Norah and wrapped his arms around her.

"Dónal, what?"

He pointed.

"Oh no! No, it can't be," she cried dejectedly.

It was true though; not six metres ahead of them lay the stricken tree that Dónal had commented on. They had made a complete circle and had ended up exactly where they had started.

"What time is it?" asked Dónal.

Norah was not sure why Dónal had the habit of asking the time, when he himself owned and wore a watch. Mildly exasperated, she squinted and looked at her watch.

"Four o'clock. Jaysus Dónal, what are we to do? Wait! The phone!"

Norah unzipped her coat pocket and pulled out her phone. She also had the car keys, which they were both relieved about.

"We'll get help." Norah said cheerily.

Turning the phone on however, proved futile . . . no bars.

"What's the bloody point of a mobile phone in an emergency if it isn't going to work?"

"Norah," said Dónal softly.

"This is ridiculous. Out of range. Maybe you can shove me up a tree and I can see if there is better reception."

"Norah."

"Really Dónal, give me a boost up this one with low branches."

"Norah, you don't like heights. It's a good idea though. Give it to me and I'll try. But Norah?"

"What?"

"If it doesn't work, if there's no reception, we must re-consider our evening."

"What do you mean? Surely you don't think we're going to stay here, do you?"

He looked at her compassionately.

"Oh no, we'll walk all night if we have to."

Dónal climbed a tree but was unable to ascend very high. Norah forced him to come down after only a few seconds, panicking that he might fall and be hurt. There were still no bars. They were lost. Dónal stood before Norah, speaking calmly but assertively.

"Norah. We now have two options. We can continue walking in search of a trail, or any signs of life for that matter, or re-focus our efforts and build a makeshift sleeping hut."

The horrified look on Norah's face prompted Dónal to continue without a beat. "If we keep walking, making a shelter will prove extremely difficult, not only because it's getting dark, but can you feel the cold and damp about to swoop?"

After a few moments of marinating on the reality of their situation, she offered a slight alternative. "Could we compromise? Can we walk on for say another half hour? If there are no signs of trails or people after that, we can decide to stop and well . . . ,"

Dónal agreed to the plan and the two continued on through the forest.

As the half-hour loomed down upon them, Dónal cheerily injected, "I've read books about guys being lost. I was heavily into survival books at one time. *Miracle in the Andes* kind of books, where climbers or plane crash survivors, or what have you, had to survive for days in the snow or on the ocean."

"Anything useful come to mind?"

"I've been pondering that. I can't say I remember particulars, but I feel like we can build something that will get us through."

"Good God."

"Norah, we need to stop. The light is fading and believe me, I am no expert on building a house of sticks."

"So, what do we do now?"

"Well, I know how a sleeping bag works. It's the 'dead air' theory."

"I don't like the sound of that already, Dónal. Isn't there an 'alive and well' theory?"

They laughed.

"Excellent, Norah, you're right; in that we need to keep our spirits as high as we can. The dead air in the insulation of a sleeping bag is unable to move, so no cold air can move through it. Obviously, the more insulation, the more dead air space."

Norah sighed. "I wrote a story once about a boy who liked to sleep under the autumn leaves, because he found it warm and cozy. That is until a wind blew them off him."

"That's right, it's the same basic principle. Let's keep it low to the ground—it will be less likely to collapse that way."

They worked together, gathering branches, sticks, debris, fern leaves; anything they could find that could serve as hut makings, or soft bedding. They stuffed the largest and sturdiest of the green tree branches into the foot of a tree that had a deep gouge in its base. Then, bending the branch away from the tree, they created an arc. This would serve as their security roof for their low-lying arc, which was reinforced by more overlapping branches. It began to take shape. Dónal crawled in to check the interior size. It needed to be as cramped as possible to make use of the warmth of their bodies, yet large enough for two people to lie side by side. Norah began stuffing the inside with leaves, ferns, and debris to soften the ground.

"We will need plenty of that Norah. Our weight will crush it all quickly enough and we need to cover ourselves with it too." The hut was close to completion as darkness engulfed the sky.

Dónal entered first. As Norah followed suit, she said, "I feel like I am being put back into the womb," and she squirmed her way down to the far end.

"Now we can cover ourselves with fern leaves and, no doubt, creepy crawlies."

They spent the night curled up together under the semi-illusion of safety. Norah woke several times, thinking she could hear the heavy breathing of night creatures, but much to her relief, each fright turned out to be nothing more than the steady breathing of her sleeping companion. She lay awake, re-thinking the evening and shook her head in astonishment at what a day of rest had transformed into.

They woke in the morning to disappointing drizzle and fog. Norah spoke optimistically. "I wasn't as cold as I thought I'd be."

"Neither was I. We make a good survival team."

"Let's get moving. My intuition tells me, that way," Norah said, pointing to the right.

"What I wouldn't give for eggs and rashers."

"Don't forget the tea."

By noon, they were famished and exceedingly thirsty.

A new set of fears crept in: they needed food and water. Dónal's head was throbbing, and Norah's stomach churned with hunger and nausea. The only thing that kept either of them going was adrenaline. Neither desired a second night in the woods.

"I must stop for a few tics, Dónal. My blisters are naggin' at me." Norah lay on the ground, not caring about the little bugs crawling along her hands.

After resting for a few minutes, Dónal said, "Norah, listen. Do you hear that?"

She listened. "Hear what?"

"I think…yes, I think I hear water. A stream?"

Norah jumped to her feet. Dónal looked hopeful.

"Wait here, I will explore and come back if it's water."

"No! I'm not staying anywhere on my own, Dónal."

They listened intently and moved slowly toward the distant sound, moving this way and that until it was distinct and steady. As the trickling sound became pronounced and clearly audible, the two yelped with joy. Pushing through heavy underbrush, they came to an embankment. A beautiful flowing stream sang to them from below and they slid down the embankment on their rear ends to meet its melody. Cupping their hands, they drank the sweet, quenching snow cap nectar until their hands were frozen.

Streams run downhill. That was their mantra for the following few hours. It was slow going; they had to be sure the stream was never far from sight or from earshot. It was close to four o'clock before they came to a trail that crossed the stream. A little signpost read Meadow Trail.

"Sounds friendly enough, Dónal, I think we should take it. It's the first sign of a trail we have seen since yesterday and it's heading downhill. What do you think?"

"I agree, let's get a last large drink and go for it."

They had barely walked fifteen minutes, when they saw a man sitting in the rear of his truck, fixing mono-filament to a fishing rod. His hair was long and black, pulled back into a ponytail. He patiently listened as Norah and Dónal relayed their plight. Charlie looked at the scrunched brochure that Dónal had in his pocket and said he could take them to the trailhead.

As they climbed into the front seat of his truck and he turned over the engine, Charlie said, "Sandwiches in that bag if you want. Coffee in the flask." Charlie was friendly but not overly talkative. Norah commented on the size of the trees and Charlie said that the lands were under a Land Protection Act and could never be destroyed, sold, or used for timber, and that was why there was so much old growth. Dónal was particularly impressed at that forethought.

"Our brochure says the name Adirondack is a Mohawk name. Are you Mohawk?"

"No. I am Algonquian. The Mohawks did name it, though. They named it 'Ratirontaks', which means 'they eat trees.' It was a derogatory term for us Algonquian's. When food was scarce, we were known to eat buds and tree bark. Adirondack is merely an anglicized version of Ratirontaks."

"Oh." Norah said, a little embarrassed.

Norah and Dónal arrived back at the hospital that evening to find that Úla was undergoing additional tests. They waited in her room for her return.

"Norah, I think we shouldn't bother telling Úla about our adventure, do you agree?"

The door swung wide and Úla was wheeled in.

"Yes, I absolutely agree," answered Norah.

Úla's face appeared drawn and ashen, but she assured Norah it was just the strain of being moved and having just had blood taken. Feeling confident about her condition, Norah and Dónal retreated to their hotel. The neutral-toned voice of a hospital nurse woke them at half-past twelve.

"Your mother has taken a turn. We think you should get here as soon as you can. She is presently in surgery."

The waiting area was empty, save for the occasional comings and goings of the night shift workers. At half-past three, Doctor Abbott approached. Norah and Dónal stood to greet him.

"An infection developed in the brain. I have done what I can, but I am afraid the news is not good. Would you like to sit down Norah?"

"No. How bad is not good?"

"Norah, if your mother survives the night, it will be a miracle. I do not mean to be harsh, but I don't think she has much time. There is little brain activity, and she will most likely slip into a coma soon. Then…"

"There must be something medicine can do to help her. She is too young to ..."

Dónal put his arm around Norah's shoulder. Dr. Abbott shook his head.

"I am so sorry to have to tell you she has about a one in a hundred chance of surviving this night. I am sorry Norah, but you must try to prepare yourself for her passing. Would you like me to give you something to calm your nerves?"

"No. Just leave us alone with her for the night."

Dr. Abbott's eyes questioned Norah's curt statement.

"What I mean is, I don't want to be disturbed by anyone. If it is indeed my mother's time to go, we wish to be alone with her."

"Yes, I understand." Dr. Abbott said as he walked them down to Úla's private room.

"There is a call button right here at her bedside should you need to contact a nurse. And, Norah . . . ,"

"Yes?"

"I truly am sorry."

"Thank you."

Úla's breathing was unsteady, shallow, and quite raspy. Norah looked intently at Dónal, who was seated on the other side of the bed. He met her gaze, and then closed his eyes, bowing his head slightly.

"Norah, no. I know what you are thinking."

"Why ever not? She's going to die Dónal. If I can send her while she's still alive, perhaps they can heal her. I brought it with me. It's right here in my bag."

Dónal endeavored to find a rationale for disagreeing with Norah, but what he found instead was fundamental logic.

"What would you tell the Doctor and staff?"

"I'd have to cross that bridge when I came to it."

"Okay, Norah. Let's do it. And just to say, I'm sorry I got a bit hot under the collar at the airport. I am glad you brought it now."

"Help me sit her in the chair, Dónal, please."

Shrugging, Dónal rose from his own seat.

"I think I remember how this is supposed to go."

57

Úla sat slumped in a chair by the end of the bed. Norah removed the Mobhrí from her oversized bag and did as the instructions bade. Taking a deep breath, she held the Mobhrí to her chest and repeated the words: '*Goddess Danú An Clann Teach*', and turned the inside ring two turns to the right.

Silvery threads shone out of one end and Norah pointed the light toward her mother. Úla fell forward. It was pure, unadulterated instinct. Norah sprang to her mother, encircling her around the middle to prevent the fall. The realization of her irreversible actions became clear as the two women were enveloped in translucent shimmering light. Norah's final image, before being swept into the silvery arc with her mother, was the look of astonishment and grief unfurling across Dónal's face, as he stood, helpless, under the florescent glow of the hospital room's overhead fixture.

An Clann Teach

The swirling in Norah's stomach was similar to the sensation one encounters when driving over a hump on a road at high speed: a rolling swell of upward motion, not unpleasant, but surprising. There was no change in their positions. Norah was still in a crouch, holding Úla's crumpled body inside her arms. They were moving through space. Gone were the floor, ceiling, and walls. They were simply two bodies, wrapped in a silvery vibrating cocoon, moving at unimaginable speed. Then, the cocoon burst into billions of tiny dispersing starry particles. Warm wind unfolded their bodies into a recumbent position, with Norah still holding tight to her mother. They were stretched out inside a convexity of shimmering colour. Norah knew they were moving toward one thing and away from another, yet she was curiously unafraid.

A sense of well-being came over Norah as her body sank deeper into the comforting rainbow. Then, the reverberations of voices, singing so angelically, so harmoniously, it gave rise to a tributary of tears, drenching her cheeks. The melody penetrated her soul so deeply, almost unbearably. She could not resist allowing its magnificence to wash over her; and to possibly heal her still unconscious mother. All at once, they were back inside a silvery cocoon.

Norah woke with a start to pitch-blackness.

"Dónal?" Silence.

Louder now, "Dónal!"

Light footsteps. A candle flame. A figure approaching. An undeniable scent—lavender.

"Nana?"

"Yes, my Norah," said Bríghid as she sat on the bed.

"Nana!"

Norah flew into her arms, tears flowing from both women. "Where am…where is…oh God…Dónal…I left him… mother…mother…where is my mother? Nana help me!"

Fear and anxiety set into Norah's entire being and she began to quake. Her breath rose and fell in tight short gulps. Bríghid removed a dropper from a round dark bottle, administering five droplets of sweet tasting liquid into Norah's mouth.

"Breathe deeply, Norah. Just breathe a moment."

Norah's heart rate slowed. The lavender scent penetrated her entire system, and opened pathways to memories, reducing the overwhelming sense of dread that had consumed her only minutes before.

"I have as many questions for you Norah, as you have for me. First, please tell me what happened to my daughter."

Norah gave an abridgment.

"I see. Come, I will bring you to your mother."

Norah's legs quivered as she and her nana left her little room and made their way down a candle-lit hallway to an arched door. Upon entering, they saw Úla, reclined and bundled with blankets in the centre of a wide, low-lying bed. A profusion of sweet-scented candles illuminated the room, catching the formidable golden eyes of a massive wolfhound, curled in front of a blazing hearth fire in the corner. The hound sprung up defiantly, protectively; but upon seeing Bríghid, he lay back down, assuaged by the recognition of the company.

"Good dog, Tadhg," murmured Bríghid. Walking to the bed, she said, "She is resting peacefully, Norah."

"She is not...? Gone?"

"No. She is sleeping. I was, to put it mildly, most startled by your arrival. Now that you have told me what brought you here, I will tell you what transpired on this side."

"What is her head wrapped in Nana?"

"I will come to that. Come sit by the fire with me and let me have a proper look at you child."

"Did I hear you call this dog Tadhg? As in Donncha's dog?"

"Yes, the very one."

"This is surreal."

"One gets used to it all. I suppose one can get used to anything. I knew you had found the Mobhrí, Norah. You see, once it comes into possession by a new minder, it emits a low-pitched sound that can be heard by the previous minder. It is a way for those here to know that it has pledged itself, if you will, to someone new. I heard such a sound not so very long ago and knew you had indeed found the green box and the diary, and the second diary with the treasure.

"If the minder opens the doorway from that world to this, the Mobhrí emits a high-pitched sound. I must tell you that I was shocked and confused to hear its high-pitched calling and I was not sure what to expect when I went to the arrival site. Whenever someone new comes, the Clann guards go to the site as well. There is always an underlying fear that the Mobhrí might fall into the wrong hands; therefore, we always take precautions. Only twice has the Mobhrí ever emitted its unusual croaking call, mind you. Both times it happened when it left Ireland's shores. Once when it left with Grace, Liam, and Genevieve and once not long ago. Now I understand the reason."

"Yes, right before I fell asleep on the plane over to the States, it began to make the very sound Grace talked about in the diary. I went at once to the toilet and did as Genevieve had done. I talked softly and assured those in An Clann Teach that all was well and that it was with its rightful minder. No light or men appeared as they did with Genevieve though. The croaking noise just ceased as abruptly as it had begun. Norah took a breath, "Where is the Mobhrí now, Nana?"

"I have it in our shelter, along with many other artifacts brought here throughout time."

"And where are the people?"

"Most are at 'cruinniú na clann' (a meeting of the clan). You must understand that time does not move along here in the same way as it does with you. Many things are, in fact, contrasting. Even the seasons are divergent. We have seasons, yes, but it is the elders who meet and decide when they will change. They are unlike seasons that you are used to, but that is getting too complicated just now. Suffice it to say that most everyone has gone to the gathering to hear what the elders have decided on whether it is time to move into our spring.

"I am the last minder of the Mobhrí. I must therefore remain close to home base. Once the next family member arrives, then the last minder may begin to explore outside the large homestead perimeter. Clann guards rotate their working cycle. There are always thirteen in the immediate area, though more can be summoned if need be. There is always a healer on site as well. She and I work together of late. Lilly is many years my junior, yet I have been her apprentice. She should be returning shortly, and we shall check on Úla together."

"So much to take in."

"Yes. It is overwhelming enough for those who come with a desire to be here. For you, who arrived unintentionally, well, it must be exceedingly taxing."

"Dónal. Poor Dónal. What must he think? I feel wretched. What of my mother? Can she be saved?"

"Once someone on your side has died, it is impossible to revive them. There have been times when people have arrived near death; some have survived, some have not. Úla was on the border when you brought her. Lilly has taken great care in deciding what to administer for…"

Tadhg growled, once again scrutinizing the arched door-way in a powerful gaze.

"Here she is now."

To say that Lilly *entered* the room would be an inaccurate and clinical description. She was very young, perhaps only twenty, but radiated an old-soul serenity. On either side of her sunny face, two fine, thick, sable-coloured plaits descended to below her waist, tied at the bottom with narrow yellow cloth. Lilly glided fluidly toward the two women, piercing each of their auras with her electric green eyes; her long scarlet skirt gently brushing the ground.

"Beannacht leat Bríghid (Blessings on you, Bríghid)," she said, curtsying. Her vocal timbre was akin to soft rain, trickling down a flower stalk.

Lilly and Norah were introduced, and the three women approached the bed where Úla lay.

As though her nana was reading her mind, Bríghid leaned in close to Norah and softly said, "Do not let her appearance fool you, my dear. You are now in the presence of one of the most powerful healers either of our worlds have ever known."

Lilly looked toward Norah. "I am sorry for your troubles. We are doing all we can toward the recovery of your mother."

"Thank you," Norah replied reticently.

"Let us show you what we have issued thus far, while we change the dressings." Lilly possessed such light-footedness and grace, it made one feel they were witnessing a dance performance, not a healing session. "We have mashed yarrow in this fine cloth and placed it under Úla's nose. Yarrow can be used to stop bleeding from cuts and wounds. When placed by or in the nostrils, it drains the head of blood, causing relief from swelling. This cloth over Úla's eyes is soaked in Juniper to relieve soreness there."

Lilly removed the cloth and dunked it in a full basin by the bed, wrung it out and replaced it over Úla's eyes. Lilly gently raised Úla's head, while Bríghid unwound the cloth that they had wrapped around it.

"Ribwort, crushed to a pulp with hemlock and chamomile water, then seeped in cotton and applied to the head to aid in healing the wounds."

Bríghid spooned two teaspoons of amber liquid into Úla's mouth. "Milk of poppy mixed with valerian to keep her rested while healing."

Lilly sprinkled the area around Úla with violet water and added tiny pillows stuffed with lavender flowers along her body.

Listening to her heart and feeling her pulse, she said, "Strong pulse and heart. Much better than the last time we checked. These are good signs, Norah."

After weighty deliberation regarding the circumstances of Norah and Úla's arrival, Bríghid and Lilly agreed that it warranted the interruption of the meeting, and the summoning of Searlait.

"Nana, I never knew the beginnings of your life. You would never share them with me, nor would my mother. Did she even know? Your mother, Genevieve . . . Caitlín; what a woman. The things you have both been through . . ."

Bríghid righted the slightly askew cloth over her daughters eyes and looked to her granddaughter. "The truth of it is that I didn't confide many intimate details of my life with your mother. I took her recurrent silences on many topics as final underscores. For a woman so keenly curious about the world, she has never, as you know, shown much interest in the topics I hold dear. In order for me to expound on my life, she would have had to accept all that went before so . . . ,"

Brighid let a few moments of silence pass and then added, "As for you, well, I knew you would one day find the diaries but I felt it best not to burden you with the intensity of things that could not be altered. Not that I didn't think of telling you many times, but that would have opened up a very large can of worms with your mother."

The two women looked to the reclined Úla and Norah said, "I get it, Nana. No other explanation needed. Though, I dare say, when she wakes, and I believe she will, her opinions may shift."

The women smiled at each other and chuckled.

"Norah, there is a balance in all things. Do not feel sorry for my mother and certainly do not feel sorry for me. Genevieve, whom she is known as here, is off at the gathering as we speak, with Grace and Liam.

"Nana? Can I return to Dónal and my life?"

"I do not have an answer to that, Norah. I am hoping that Searlait will help guide us on that matter. The Mobhrí has never been here before. It was designed for the passage of people from your world to this."

"I suddenly feel quite tired. It's as if the universe has conspired to burden me with all its weight."

"Let us take you back to your room for a rest. When you wake, you will feel refreshed and by then Searlait will have returned."

"Who is Searlait?"

"She is the daughter of Éiru, to whom the Mobhrí was originally given in the ancient time. She is obviously an elder, but is also the one who is called upon for emergencies that might be out of the ordinary. I dare say this is one of those times."

58

*F*alling—**she was falling** through space, arms and legs flailing. From above, she could see Dónal, his arms outstretched, trying to reach her, calling to her, but she could not hear him. She too was calling, "Dónal, help me Dónal, I am falling away from you!"

Norah woke, once again to blackness. A dream; she hoped it had all been a dream. She would open her eyes and Dónal would be next to her in their bed, and her mother would be well and in Vermont. Slowly, so slowly, Norah stretched her leg outward, searching for the familiar. Her leg travelled along the cool bedding, meeting no obstacle, no heat. She was alone.

Norah walked out her door and down the dark corridor to the arched entrance of her mother's bedroom. Tadhg lifted his head in sleepy frustration, but soon lowered it again, now recognizing Norah.

The glow of one candle on the bedside table exhibited enough light for Norah to catch a glimpse of her mother's hand movement.

"Mother!" Norah moved quickly to the bedside and sat carefully next to her mother, removing the covering from her eyes and nose.

"Norah? God Norah, where am I?"

"You are with me."

"And glad of it. I thought I was delirious, or even dead. My head feels…large. I can barely open my eyes. There is a mixture of sweet and pungent odors. What was under my nose and over my eyes? I was afraid to move them, afraid to call out. I'm very confused."

Norah described the events that had taken place as sensitively as she could, but Úla was showing signs of distress. Norah was on the verge of searching for her nana or Lilly, but both appeared at the door forthwith. Úla could scarcely believe the truth of it all.

"Úla," said Lilly, "I am going to give you another sleeping potion. Your pulse is elevating, and you must sleep again. We will be here when you wake."

"I'll lie next to you," said Norah.

"Yes, that would be a comforting thing."

Úla fell back into a deep sleep, with her daughter nestled closely, lovingly, beside her.

*Y*es, yes, things are looking much better this hour, Úla. Your eyes are open at least, and the swelling in your head has been greatly reduced. Searlait has been informed of all that has occurred. She will be here as soon as she can. I will return with her," Lilly said with a calming smile.

Three generations sat on the wide bed together. There was nothing to say; there was everything to say.

Searlait arrived but was unsure what the chances were of returning us safely to our former lives.

"It has never been done before. I cannot say what the outcome might be, Norah."

"I'm ready to take that chance. If I don't, the repercussions for both Dónal and me are unimaginable. I'm not ready to be here. This isn't my home. I'm not afraid, but I wish to get on with it before I change my mind."

"I'll go with you Norah," said Úla. "It's not my time to be here either. I haven't been called here by the Mobhrí's powers, though I dare say I am grateful to have been given another chance at life because of it."

It was impossible for Norah to hide her joy. "Oh, Mam . . . I'd never have suggested you return with me if you wished to remain here, but . . . I'm so happy you're willing to join me—into the unknown. I'd be devastated to lose you now, after how far we have come."

Smiling broadly, Úla replied, "I couldn't agree more, my Norah. Couldn't agree more."

Norah caught sight of the puddles in her nana's eyes. This reconciliation was affecting Bríghid deeply, too, she and Norah, being kindred. Witnessing the reshaping relationship of her two progeny gave Bríghid solace. Úla's unexpected arrival at—and acceptance of—An Clann Teach bridged a gap of knowledge that allowed her and Bríghid to baste their own relationship back together. The love between the three of them was luminous.

Giving herself a wee shake and placing her hand over her own heart, Bríghid added, "We have no way of knowing if this will work. We all believe that the Mobhrí must only be opened periodically, as none of us know how long its power may last. When you get to . . . where you are going . . . open the Mobhrí so we can see each other. I shall go directly to the arrival area and wait. If this works, there are both unfathomable possibilities as well as numerous complications. Let us not dwell on that at present, though. Go with all our blessings."

Searlait suggested it be done immediately.

Lilly spoke up presently. "There are no guarantees that you will be safe. If you do return safely, Norah, there are no guarantees that you will retain your pregnancy."

Úla and Bríghid stared at Norah's bewildered face.

"Pregnancy? I'm not pregnant . . . Am I?"

Lilly smiled. "Perhaps only by a few weeks, but I do believe I am correct. A daughter, if I am reading you correctly."

Stepping into the rippling argent light was no doubt the most intense leap of faith either of the women had ever taken. One thing was certain, wherever they were going, they would be going there together. With the Mobhrí securely sewn into Norah's cardigan, mother and daughter stood in a tight embrace and looked lovingly to Bríghid.

Tears welled in the eyes of all three women, as Bríghid held up her hand in farewell, saying, "See you down the road . . . ."

60

A sense of familiarity washed over Norah as she and her mother were, once again, amidst shafts of pulsating light. Úla was trembling—she had been unconscious the first time. Norah hugged her tightly. Mostly, Norah recognized the sensations and visuals. Voices rising in song, moving through space, an embracing cocoon, a warm wind unfolding their bodies. But wait. On the way toward An Clann Teach, their bodies were stretched out, on their backs. This time they were belly down.

It's of no matter I'm sure, thought Norah.

"Is this really happening?" whispered Úla.

Norah was surprised they could converse. She had assumed, for no particular reason, that they could not.

"Just hold tight to me," instructed Norah, as she pulled her mother toward her. "This is just as I remember it. Have no fear." But, fear *was* beginning to bubble within Norah, as they seemed to be accelerating. Perhaps it was her imagination, perhaps she was not remembering correctly. Within moments of reassuring her mother, Norah knew something was perilously wrong. Their velocity was causing lightheadedness; the air was thickening, the wind was building, and the light began racing around them.

Wanting to set her mother's mind at ease, Norah lightheartedly commented, "Maybe there was a less tumultuous way to get you on board the belief train about An Clann Teach . . . "

Úla laughed, half-heartedly.

The warm wind pushed harder against their feet, so much so, that the two were almost torn apart, fingers barely touching.

"Norah!" cried her mother. "We've got to stay connected!"

With all the strength they could muster, the two succeeded in entwining their fingers. Norah fumbled with her belt, almost dropped it, but caught it just before it plummeted to nothingness. She wrapped it around their wrists; Norah using her right hand, Úla her left to secure it, so the two were fastened together.

In the distance, through the now milky haze, something massive came into view. "What is that? Can you tell what that is, Norah?"

"No, I didn't see that on the way to An Clann Teach. But we're heading straight toward it, and fast."

The mother and daughter instinctively chased the same solution, and simultaneously back-pedaled their legs, as though moving into a vertical position would slow them down. It worked to a certain degree, but they were still rapidly approaching.

"We're going to hit it, Norah!"

There was seemingly no top, no bottom, to the slightly orange, block-like mass. Some sections spread horizontally; amorphous tree limbs, with ample, open spaces. Other parts looked more dense, deeper orange, and somewhat sharp.

The closer they got to it, the more fearsome it was. The barrier, however, while menacing did not compare to the endless space on the other side of it. That empyrean beyond was a tangled spider web of glowing threads, with a surreal, pulsing energy; a yawning cavern, erupting with crimson dye, and it terrified the women completely.

"Norah! Grab on to this . . . thing . . . if you can. I don't know about you, but I do not want to slide into that red horror beyond!"

The wall was upon them now. Norah reached out with her right hand as the air current blew them in-between two sections. She grabbed hold, and her mother followed suit. Still tied at the wrist, the women hung on as best they could, but the wind was picking up again causing Úla to lose her hold, so now only three hands were in play in their security.

Norah held tight. Úla twisted and turned, straining to get her left hand back up, but the wind was simply too mighty for her to gain connection. Norah and Úla both wailed with frustration and panic as Norah lost her hold, sweeping the two away from the wall, immediately pushing them into the deep, dark red expanse.

61

Norah felt the full weight of failure.

She and her mother would undoubtedly die now, as it was she who had lost hold of the wall.

62

A low, anguished moan rose from Dónal as he leapt toward the chair where Norah and Úla had just disappeared. Hyperventilating, grief-stricken, he slunk to the floor, blaming himself for not making sure Norah had been well away from Úla, the chair, and the Mobhrí's light.

The two women were simply gone.

Norah had the Mobhrí, so there was not even the chance of him following her. The light was gone, as Norah had purposefully set it to shine just long enough to get Úla off to An Clann Teach. Dónal's distress mounted. He paced the room, unsure what to do, until he could contain his sorrow no longer, and collapsed onto the bed in body-wracking sobs.

Deep in his heart, he knew that Norah had simply reacted to the moment. Despite their clear differences, Úla was still her mother and the intrinsic values of that relationship had been paramount in her call to action.

Chapter 63

What was he to do now? Hope Norah will return somehow? Call the doctor? And tell him what?

With no plan in mind, Dónal got up and peered out the door. A nurse, pushing a trolley of medications, was making her way down the corridor, one room at a time. She was only three doors away.

Then two.

As the trolley neared Úla's door, Dónal slipped out to meet the nurse; his arms crossed. The concerned face of the nurse met his and she asked, "How's . . ." The nurse looked at her chart. "Úla doing? Not good, by the looks of you."

Dónal lied. "There's nothing to be done at this point. I've left mother and daughter to say their goodbyes. Norah is praying by her side. Please don't disturb them just now, I beg you."

The nurse reached out her hand and gently touched Dónal's folded arm. "It's okay. I'll come back in a little while to check on things."

At least that was a bit of relief. It had bought him a little time—for now. But a little time . . . for what?

Every so often, Dónal heard footsteps, and his heart raced. He'd break for the door, trying to think of excuses for why no entry would be permitted. Luckily, no one knocked or entered.

The only thing he could do was wait. Wait and hope.

63

Norah's ears were buzzing, her head ached and the voice she heard was distant, muffled. It took a few moments for her to gain the strength to open her eyes.

Úla was caressing her forehead. "Norah? Norah, can you hear me? Oh, thank God, I thought you might be dead."

Norah came to a shaky sitting position atop soft grass and looked to the familiar garden. "We're home? How can that be? Where's Dónal? Dónal!" shouted Norah.

Úla laid a hand on Norah's knee, trying to calm her daughter's panic, and looked around Norah's front garden. "I don't know Norah, but something's not right. Look." Úla pointed to the climbing rose bushes that Dónal had planted just before she'd left for Vermont. "They were only about half a metre tall when he planted them, right?"

Swallowing hard, Norah nodded. "They look to be about two full metres tall now. That's not even possible. Unless . . . unless."

Úla turned to the house. "When did you get a new front door, Norah?"

"We haven't. Not yet anyway. And look! The tree house. It's all fixed up and there's a swing."

There was no getting around the fact that the red web had propelled them into the future. Once gaining their strength, the two walked to the house, to see if Dónal might be there. When they each reached out to touch the front door, their hands disappeared into it.

The two women turned to the sound of tires crunching up the unpaved drive. Relief washed over Norah, as it was surely Dónal returning home. However, an unfamiliar car stopped well before the entry gate, and the pair watched as a man, dressed completely in black, carrying a cloth bag, slinked along the perimeter. He obviously didn't see or hear them.

"Who the feck is that?" said Norah. "What's he up to? I've never seen him before in my life."

Chapter 64

The women followed the man to the barn and watched as the stranger went to the far wall, and began tapping his knuckles along it.

"What's he after?" asked Úla, hoping her intuition was wrong.

All at once, the stranger stopped and removed what looked like a carving tool from his back pocket. Before long, he had pried away a chunk of wood, revealing a cavity. From that space, the man removed the unmistakable Mobhrí box, slipped it into his bag, and made a hasty exit.

64

Norah and Úla stood, unseen, on the grounds of the house, and spoke at length about their options. For all intents and purposes, it appeared they were ghosts. They had to get back to their present day. But how? They had to at least try, now that there was a future thief absconding with their invaluable heirloom.

Úla spoke in an upbeat manner, coming to an encouraging realization. "There is good news though, Norah. The Mobhrí was in the barn. You and I are in possession of it now, which means it does make it back here, somehow. That should give us hope."

"Seems you have shifted your thinking about all things ethereal, Mother, yes?"

Úla wrapped her arms around her daughter. "Can't say I'm enjoying this, but I'm glad to be with you and grateful to have seen my mother again. I now feel exhilarated that you and I are part of this clan and, most importantly, to know that it is mystery and power that engulf us, and not madness!"

"But, now what?" Norah asked. "We can't stay stuck in the future as ghosts."

Úla nodded. "I think we may have to open the Mobhrí and see if anyone answers. Perhaps they'll know what to do, or at least have a suggestion. We did promise to contact them when we reached our destination safely. This isn't exactly where we planned to be, but we do at least seem to be safe."

Mother and daughter were relieved that both Bríghid and Searlait were waiting for them. As before, they could not guarantee their safety since this was new to everyone, but suggested that they re-enter the light, return to An Clann Teach and start over, making some unproven adjustments to the mechanisms of the Mobhrí. This being agreed upon, Norah and Úla walked to the back of the house where they were confident of privacy and opened the Mobhrí for a duration of one minute.

The two stepped into the light, hands entwined, assuming they would be returned to An Clann Teach, to reassess and try again.

Moments later, to their own and Dónal's astonishment, they found themselves right back in the hospital room.

65

Norah awakened to the sound of lashing rain falling heavily upon their slanted roof. Dónal stood gazing out the bedroom window at the lush, soaking greenness, his back to her.

"Good morning, my dearie," said Norah amidst a sleepy yawn and stretch.

Dónal crawled back into bed and kissed her forehead. Placing his hand on Norah's protruding belly, he whispered, "Won't be long now."

"I dreamt about Nana again last night. I so wish she were here for this event. She and the clan were so elated when we finally made it home all in one piece, as were we."

Dónal added, "Indeed. And, I must say, isn't it amazing that we were able to send flower seeds without incident?"

Norah cocked her head to one side. "There's just so much open to us now that travel seems like a real possibility. And, sure, all has worked in our favour, but we are all still very concerned about the man Ma and I saw stealing the Mobhrí. None of us are sure if our safe return will alter that occurrence or if that is indeed an eventuality. At least those in An Clann Teach can prepare themselves for this possibility now. What were you thinking about while peering out into the wet?"

Dónal chuckled. "I was just recalling the look on Doctor Abbott's face when he came into your mother's room to find Úla sitting up in the bed, smiling. I thought he might topple over."

Norah heaved a deep sigh. "This life of ours is certainly not what anyone could call ordinary. What time did my mother say she was coming over?"

"Ten. I will put the kettle on while you waddle yourself dressed."

66

Three Days Later

Norah **opened the** diary and flipped to the back pages. The last paragraph read:

There is one more diary in the tack room of the barn. Remove the mirror in the far corner and you will find a cubby behind the three panels of wood. It is a far different sort of diary than this, but one that we all believe should keep you entertained on a day when you want to be removed from your own reality. We say to you now, 'Come, let us dip you into a fresh cascading waterfall of escapades.'

Norah cradled her tiny daughter in the crook of her left arm, and wrote in the diary . . .

*Niamh Ríonach, my daughter, my light, my heart:
Your first name means, 'luster, brilliance', and we
promise you, you are that to us. You're our brilliant
star, whose luster shines before us. Ríonach means
'regal, like a queen'. To be perfectly honest, your
father pleaded for this name, as he loves to call you
his 'wee queen bee'. No doubt he will have you down
the field with his hives before you can walk. At any
rate, this was far too lovely a notion to deny, thus
your second name.
As I hold you, I cannot imagine being separated from
you, though I know that one day this shall come to
pass. One day, I will feel the tug of the Mobhrí and our
distant family. But not for a long time yet, my dear and
darling one, my heart.
These pages, which you will one day read, will teach
you the history of our Clan as it has been passed down
for generations. The secrets within are a sacred gift
from our Irish mothers, written out of love… out of
family… out of the Emerald Diaries.*

…to be continued…

INSPIRATION

While this is a work of fiction, there are some parts resourced from history. Mythologically speaking, there was an early race of people called the Tuatha dé Danaan who were gifted four treasures. There is a pre-historic monument (also referred to as an Ancient Temple) in County Meath, called Newgrange. I felt this was a perfect touchstone for creating the thread that runs through this book—that being a fifth treasure, conjured by me and gifted to this significant race of people.

The realities of immigrant ships and the landing at Ellis Island is also based in fact. I inserted my characters and their experiences from within my research of the realities of crossing the Atlantic on a steam ship and landing in New York harbour in those times.

The Choctaw Nation lived in the area that is now known as Mississippi. As the United States expanded throughout the nineteenth century so too did the desire of Europeans to acquire cotton. Choctaw land was prime real estate for this expansion, thus about thirteen thousand Choctaw were forced to relocate (walk) to Oklahoma. This mass 'migration' is known to this day as *The Trail of Tears*. The Choctaw, like the Irish, knew what dire consequences occurred when being occupied by foreign governance. The Choctaw Nation raised money to help the Irish population during 'The Great Starvation' (Famine). Since then, there has been a special bond between the Irish and the Choctaw Nation. I so appreciate the permission given to me by Blue Panther—Keeper of Stories, of the Manataka Council—to use one of their stories, *When Parents ask their Children to be Noisy*. The names and scenes in The Emerald Diaries regarding this compassionate gesture are created by me, the author.

The section of this book where Úla goes to her friend working in Elvery's Department Store in Dublin City, and the scene where the 'four leafs' switch clothes and run into the two women, are both based on true stories of my mother's life. I have changed the details to match the characters, but the basic story-line is from my mother, who loved the re-telling of both.

The 'professional' joke is one told to me by my brother Ronan, I just changed the animals involved to protect the innocent.

ACKNOWLEDGEMENTS

Love to my husband, Paul, for his profound and continued support and encouragement.

Boundless thanks to Kera McHugh, who took the original version of this book and did her usual deep-dive analysis, pushing me (in a great editor way) to re-create this final version, now tidied to a shiny finish, including the fresh cover design. I want to scream her name from the rooftops as an exceptional editor, but selfishly, I secretly want to keep her all to myself. She is that good.

A very big thank you to my brother Michael, who was the final proofreader of this book. He relayed many key insights and points for which I will be forever grateful.

Will Millar, loyal comrade, thank you for the thought-filled foreword.

Fiona Van Housen, for her lovely frontispiece drawing, 'A gift of words.'

And, as always, you, for purchasing this book, thereby supporting the arts.

THE CLAN

Tuatha dé Danaan
(multiple generations)
Old Woman of the Road
Róisín
Fiona
Odhrán
(died in childbirth)
Siobhán Murphy
(aka Teresa Smith)
Séamus
(lost at sea)
(forced apart before they could marry)
Donncha
(aka Ronan)
Orlaith
Liam Furlong
Grace
Jonathan
(rape)
Caitlín Norah Sinnott
(aka Genevieve)
Bríghid
Desmond
Úla
Phillip
Norah
Dónal
Niamh Ríonach
Legend
Mobhrí Minder
Female
Male

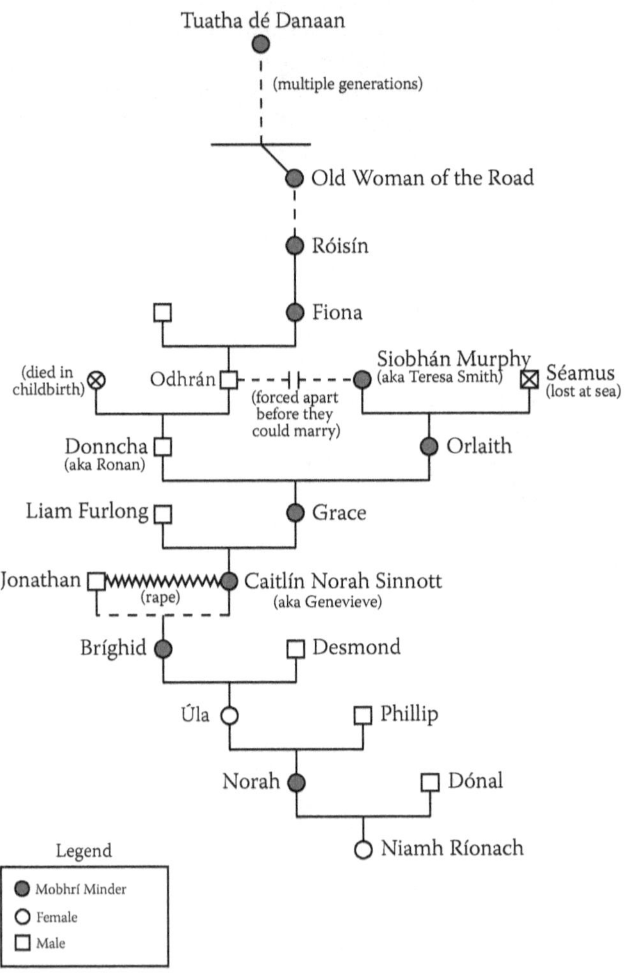

ABOUT THE AUTHOR

Mary Murphy is a touchstone to the ancient land of Ireland. Her authenticity garners pride in the Irish-born, takes first-generation immigrants home again, gifts those with Irish roots a taste of inheritance, and ushers those who wish they were a wee bit Irish into an ephemeral union.

Murphy's extensive experience as a songwriter first spurred her into taking the plunge into the marvellous and sometimes murky depths of book writing in 2009. Is it any wonder that she writes with such diversity? Mary's insatiable curiosity for life has presented sixteen (and counting) varied pen-to-the-page releases and musical accomplishments. Mary has been a touring musical artist for many years and created a sometimes comical lecture entitled "The Alchemy of Words – A Journey in the Psyche of an Irish Writer.'

Novelist, short story writer, poet, children's writer, singer, whistle player and performer, this small but mighty woman fervently embraces her multi-faceted creative fire.

ALSO BY MARY MURPHY

Adult releases

Speaking Of: A houseful of eclectic works of fiction (Sept 2022) Available at all online and independent booksellers, as well as all major ebook platforms.

Stay tuned for audio books of *Speaking Of* and *The Emerald Diaries.*

Children's Releases

All releases include audio of book and extras.

Sweet Peas and Bees: Life at the Flower Farm, Book One (2023, collaboration with illustrator, Fiona Van Housen) Available at all online and independent booksellers.

Away with the Fairies series (with illustrator, Fiona Van Housen)

Book Three: The Adventures of Nash the Dash (2020)

Book Two: Away with the Fairies (2015)

Book One: Away with the Fairies (2012)

CD's by Mary Murphy

Lucy's Fling (2020)

Honey from Heather (2013)

Three Hand Reel (2008, includes songs from this book!)

A Painted Moon (2007)

Dancing Barefoot (2003, collaboration with Paul Keim)

Always a Flame (2002, TaXim Records, Celtic crossover)

Thirty Waves Out (2001)

Yearnings (1996, out of stock)

Rising of the Road (1992, out of stock)

Mary Murphy and the Troon Sisters (1991, collaboration with Rebecca Troon, out of stock)

Brewing on the Book Stove

Speaking Of, Volume Two

Book of Poetry

Life at the Flower Farm: Book Two

The Emerald Diaries, Book Two

Brewing on the Music Stove

Such Fine Days

www.ingramcontent.com/pod-product-compliance
Lightning Source LLC
Chambersburg PA
CBHW032148190726
48290CB00005BB/1464